AROUND THE WORLD
IN EIGHTY DAYS
&
FIVE WEEKS IN A BALLOON

Around the World in Eighty Days

&

Five Weeks in a Balloon

———————— ◆ ————————

Jules Verne

Introduction and Notes by
PROFESSOR ROGER CARDINAL
University of Kent at Canterbury

WORDSWORTH CLASSICS

In loving memory of
MICHAEL TRAYLER
the founder of Wordsworth Editions

12

Readers who are interested in other titles from
Wordsworth Editions are invited to visit our website at
www.wordsworth-editions.com

For our latest list and a full mail-order service, contact
Bibliophile Books, 5 Thomas Road, London E14 7BN
TEL: +44 (0)20 7515 9222 FAX: +44 (0)20 7538 4115
E-MAIL: orders@bibliophilebooks.com

This edition published 1994 by Wordsworth Editions Limited
8B East Street, Ware, Hertfordshire SG12 9HJ
Introduction and Notes added 2002

ISBN 978-1-85326-090-2

Text © Wordsworth Editions Limited 1994
Introduction and Notes © Roger Cardinal 2002

Wordsworth® is a registered trademark of
Wordsworth Editions Limited

All rights reserved. This publication may not be
reproduced, stored in a retrieval system or
transmitted, in any form or by any means, electronic,
mechanical, photocopying, recording or otherwise,
without the prior permission of the publishers.

Typeset in Great Britain by Antony Gray
Printed and bound by Clays Ltd, St Ives plc

GENERAL INTRODUCTION

Wordsworth Classics are inexpensive editions designed to appeal to the general reader and students. We commissioned teachers and specialists to write wide ranging, jargon-free introductions and to provide notes that would assist the understanding of our readers rather than interpret the stories for them. In the same spirit, because the pleasures of reading are inseparable from the surprises, secrets and revelations that all narratives contain, we strongly advise you to enjoy this book before turning to the Introduction.

General Adviser
KEITH CARABINE
Rutherford College
University of Kent at Canterbury

INTRODUCTION

Jules Verne (1828–1905) possessed that rare storyteller's gift of being able to present the far-fetched and the downright unbelievable in such a way as effortlessly to inspire his reader's allegiance and trust. His publisher once congratulated him on his unerring 'sense of the perpendicular'. This volume contains two of his best-loved yarns, chosen from among the sixty-four titles of *Les Voyages extraordinaires*, Verne's pioneering contribution to the canon of modern Science Fiction.

*   *   *

Born in Nantes in 1828, Verne was the first child of a successful lawyer who fondly imagined his son would follow in his footsteps. Nantes was a maritime port on the River Loire in Brittany, and Jules and his brother Paul learned to sail as children. At the age of eleven, Jules tried to enlist as a cabin-boy on a ship to the Indies, but was caught and punished by his father. Having subsequently applied himself to legal studies in his home-town, he moved to Paris, where he began to nourish a distinctly literary ambition. He befriended Alexandre Dumas *père* (1802–70), the celebrated author of the adventure novels *The Count of Monte Cristo* (1844–5) and *The Three Musketeers* (1844), as well as the playwright Alexandre Dumas *fils* (1824–95). When he graduated in 1849, Jules Verne promptly informed his family that he was dropping law in favour of literature: although he was obliged to take a stockbroker's job in the Stock Exchange to make ends meet, his principal activity would now be the writing of short stories, plays and libretti for operettas. Verne spent most of his spare time in the Bibliothèque Nationale on Rue Richelieu, where he followed an autodidact's discipline, accumulating piles of notes on a vast range of scientific topics, most especially those relating to the latest advances and discoveries.

In 1857 Verne married and set up home close to the National Library and the Stock Exchange. He undertook a number of journeys, among them a trip to Scotland in 1859 and to Denmark in 1861. At about this time he became a close friend of Félix Tournachon, otherwise known as Nadar, who was not only the leading portrait-photographer of the age but also a passionate aeronaut. Verne had found the subject for his first novel, for his fictional *Victoria* is unmistakably based on Nadar's real-life balloon, *Le Géant*, said to have been as high as Notre-Dame.

In 1862, at the age of thirty-four, Verne submitted the draft of *Five Weeks in a Balloon* to the publisher Jules Hetzel, whose list comprised several titles for children and who edited an educational magazine for the young. Hetzel was delighted with Verne's approach and at once offered him a long-term contract: the arrangement, involving a commitment to produce two books a year, was to last for the rest of the author's life and established his financial security. Verne could now afford to purchase a fishing-boat, on which he made various excursions into the Atlantic. In 1867, he ventured across the ocean with his brother aboard the *Great Eastern*, the huge iron-hulled liner designed by the great engineer Isambard Kingdom Brunel; his return ticket allowed him only enough time to visit New York City and to make a brief foray by rail into Canada by way of the Niagara Falls. A political moderate, Verne was horrified by the events of the Siege of Paris and the Commune of 1870–1; though he would surely have been delighted to hear of the service which Nadar organised to carry letters by balloon to the outside world, and of his friend's daring aerial sorties as a military observer. As for Verne himself, he made his one and only trip in a balloon at Amiens in September 1873.

By the mid-1870s, the success of *Around the World in Eighty Days* had established Verne as a household name. He proceeded to acquire a luxury house in Amiens as well as an elegant yacht. His career continued to flourish, as a regular output of adventure novels complemented his regular cruises in the Mediterranean, the North Sea and the Baltic. In 1886, a bizarre attack by a deranged nephew who shot him in the foot was followed by the shock of his publisher's death. Verne's health soon began to deteriorate, and although he kept up his writing, he lapsed more and more into a melancholy solipsism. He died in Amiens in 1905, a couple of years after hearing the news of the Wright Brothers' first motor-driven airplane flight.

It has to be acknowledged that Verne's books were largely conceived as money-spinners targeting a wide popular audience. The Hetzel firm had a reputation as the publisher of serious writers like Balzac, Hugo and Proudhon, yet the ornate book-covers and copious woodcut illustrations devised by the likes of Édouard Rioui (1833–1906) or Léon Benett (1839–1917) undeniably proclaim that the *Voyages extraordinaires* are, first and foremost, works of spectacle and entertainment. At the same time, these books disclose a strong educational bias: they are full of erudite passages about geography, history, engineering and physics, and seem generally symptomatic of an autodidact's passion for encyclopedias and archives. Verne's insistent provision of scientific detail reflects the contemporary fascination with the novelties of exploration and technology during what may be seen as the golden age of the popularisation of the sciences.

No doubt Verne's greatest strength as a narrator is his ability to extrapolate the giddiest twists and turns of adventure from a solid fund of technical data: as the contemporary critic and poet Théophile Gautier observed, 'here the chimerical is propelled and guided by a mind of mathematical cast'. More often than not the fictions transgress all plausibility – for, in the course of the *Extraordinary Voyages*, the reader is propelled to the moon as well as to the centre of the earth – and yet Verne always made sure there were enough technological and scientific references in the text to add, as it were, ballast to the buoyant fantasy, thereby allaying the fears of anyone who might feel the ground of commonsense slipping away. It is true that there are occasions, as in *Five Weeks in a Balloon*, when the author's pedantic technical specifications seem calculated to prevent his heroes from ever taking off!

*   *   *

As Verne's first contribution to the genre of veridical fantasy, *Five Weeks in a Balloon* (1863) creaks more than a little as it seeks to blend the resources of scholarship with the stock formulae of the adventure tale. The choice of ballooning as the means of locomotion for his first fictional journey tacitly registers a debt not only to his friend Nadar, but also to a long-dead literary hero, Edgar Allan Poe (1809–49). In 1844, Poe had published the tale 'The Balloon-Hoax' as a single news-sheet, causing an uproar when its New York readers swallowed every word of its tongue-in-cheek report of a balloon crossing the Atlantic in just three days. Previously, Poe's tale 'The Unparalleled Adventures of One Hans Pfaall' (1835) had documented an excursion to the moon: though unlikely to fool any but the most naïve reader, its text is sufficiently larded with spoof calculations and quasi-scientific corroborations as to establish a special pact between narrator and reader. In this respect, Science Fiction had identified one of its prime strategies in the earnest elaboration of cogent and enticing lies.

Thus Verne's first novel is offered as a sober document tied to apparent fact. Its early pages lay out the premisses of the plot, which hinges on the construction of a unique and highly versatile hydrogen balloon, masterminded by a certain Dr Samuel Fergusson. Having laid out a network of references to such unimpeachable sources as the proceedings of the Royal Geographical Society in London, the novelist engages in more and more flabbergasting flights of fancy while linking Fergusson's aerial crossing of the African continent to a history of the many earlier journeys made overland by a whole catalogue of explorers. At one point he even offers a roll-call of these heroes, citing no less than a hundred and thirty surnames, of whom all appear to be authentic bar the last, Dr Samuel Fergusson (p. 169). Since he is designated as a hero from the outset, Fergusson's leadership of his expedition is uncontested and beyond reproach. He manifests an imperturbable confidence, reacting rationally and without panic to all eventualities and insisting that nothing can possibly go wrong – though it is manifestly the case that a lot of things *do* go wrong. Two companions, the boisterous Scotsman Dick Kennedy and the improbably versatile manservant Joe (the proto-type of Passepartout in *Around the World*) complete the intrepid team.

It is consistent with the reader's expectations that Fergusson should succeed in his vow to cross the continent, and that he and his compan-ions should survive the collapse of the balloon after its five-week adventure. Yet they *only just* manage to do so, and herein lies the key to the reader's pleasure. This tale of derring-do thrives upon the reader's awareness that Verne has set out the serial vicissitudes of the *Victoria* and its passengers in such a way as to qualify each triumph with a sense of anxiety. *Only just* is hardly the most positive way to round off an enterprise initiated with such a fanfare: yet the fact that the balloon manages to limp across jungle, desert and mountain range, completing its trajectory against horrendous odds while realising the scientific ambition of making sense of the murky map of Africa, offers the reader a strangely potent satisfaction. (Many readers, I suspect, assume that the coast-to-coast itinerary is indeed fulfilled, although it remains an anomaly that, having sent the *Victoria* aloft at Zanzibar, Verne should have terminated its flight at a point rather a long way upstream on the Senegal River: it is as though he sensed that a crash on the Atlantic shore itself would have stretched credibility too far.)

As a novelist, Verne was inept at sociological or psychological portrayal; he was far more interested in gadgets and maps, and was content to invoke fashionable stereotypes for his characters. The acrobatic Joe speaks scarcely a line which reveals any level of mental dexterity; while Dick Kennedy epitomises the British sportsman whose speciality is bagging game for dinner and whose hobby is taking indiscriminate potshots at wild animals or natives. (Here Verne reflects, almost unawares, a type of colonialist irresponsibility which would nowadays be deemed highly culpable.) It falls to Dr Fergusson to exhibit intellectual profundity and to embody a certain type of the cerebral adventurer which Verne would develop in several later novels, notably in the implacable Captain Nemo of *Twenty Thousand Leagues under the Sea* (1869) and the unflappable Phileas Fogg of *Around the World in Eighty Days*.

*   *   *

Around the World in Eighty Days (1873) narrates a hair-raising journey carried out as a wager by the Victorian gentleman Phileas Fogg, who succeeds – but again *only just*! – in circling the globe within eighty days. (Verne had appropriated his precise timeline from a speculative article of 1870 in *Le Magasin pittoresque*.) With his usual encyclopedic verve, the author seems intent on the exhaustive coverage of every possible mode of conveyance, boasting at the end of his yarn that the journey has involved 'liners, railways, carriages, yachts, trading vessels, sledges, elephants' (p. 161). (We may be amused to note that Fogg does without balloons, submarines and rockets, presumably because Verne needed to keep them fresh for other occasions.)

Typical of Verne's pseudo-realism is his scrupulous marshalling of topographical detail, from the mention of Fogg's exact postal address in the opening line to the successive citing of real places on an itinerary which traverses each continent in the northern hemisphere. *Five Weeks* comprises a full African gazetteer, but the mention of names like the Usagara Mountains or the Agadez-Murzuk road is unlikely to mean much to the European reader, whether of the nineteenth or the twenty-first century. *Around the World*, on the other hand, follows up the names of far-flung destinations with a detailed description, and generally sustains an air of omniscience, as if its author had himself stopped off at each and every station on Fogg's route, and had had personal experience of the unreliable rail links through India, the commercial life of Hong Kong or the electoral processes in San Francisco. Naturally we must suppose that Verne was lifting his material from secondary sources, such as guidebooks and history books, as well as calibrating the stages of Fogg's advance against a large-scale atlas (as no doubt he had done with *Five Weeks*). In truth, our author's actual travel experience hardly extended beyond Europe. Never once did he set foot farther east than Italy, nor did he ever see the Pacific Ocean; his acquaintance with Africa was confined to the ports of Morocco and Algeria, while his North American sojourn lasted no more than a week. I imagine that a diligent scanning of the detail of Fogg's itinerary would disclose several gaffes or omissions. However, it would seem pointless to seize upon any deviations from fact, given that the unwritten pact between writer and reader authorises the former to stretch the truth more than a little. The irony about the success of *Around the World* is that its reader is actually engaging in *hypothetical* journeying, an armchair traveller piloted by the seasoned veteran of the Bibliothèque Nationale.

Yet the masterstroke of *Around the World* is surely its invention of a comic partnership between two utterly contrasted characters, the Englishman Phileas Fogg and the Frenchman Jean Passepartout. Here Verne draws unabashedly upon a long-established typology of supposed national characteristics dating back at least to the Napoleonic Wars, whereby the phlegmatic austerity of the English clashes against the ebullient excitability of the French. Verne's originality lies in his adaptation of these stereotypes to the specific context of a journey to foreign parts, whereupon the oxymoronic duo begins to create a different kind of impact, articulating two different approaches to travel abroad.

In an intriguing theoretical study of travel writing, *The Ethics of Travel* (1996), the literary scholar Syed Manzurul Islam puts forward a suggestive distinction between the modes of *sedentary* and *nomadic* travelling. 'Sedentary' travellers, he argues, are not necessarily inactive, but they concentrate so much upon reaching a pre-established destination that they entirely ignore the ground covered. Islam comments that 'they might travel in the fastest possible vehicle and cover a thousand miles yet they remain where they are, because they are on a rigid line which keeps them grounded in the enclosure of their home'. Such journeying amounts to a mere swapping of abstract locales rather than a conscious advance across a textured terrain. Conversely, 'nomadic' travellers follow a 'supple' rather than a 'rigid' line, experiencing movement as a continuous shifting, a vivid and bumpy ride across boundaries and cultures which brings about what Islam calls 'the openness of the encounter with the other and the process of becoming'.

Without necessarily claiming that each given individual must slot into one or other of these notional categories, Islam's travel schema allows us to posit a pair of mutually defining extremes. One sort of traveller may be so eager to arrive as to be blind to the landscape he is crossing – rather like the apocryphal Englishman mentioned by Verne (p. 168) who takes a coach all the way around Lake Geneva while keeping his back to the water. By extension, he is likely to cling to his prejudices and shun contact with the unfamiliar culture he has entered. Such is the sedentary traveller, a mere location-swapper whose cultural baggage insulates him from external influence: he never troubles to learn a foreign language and insists on dressing in his habitual garb. The nomadic traveller, on the other hand, relishes the nameless spaces *in between* major cities and especially the delays and detours which give rise to those unforeseen encounters, challenges and negotiations which are indeed the essential raw material of travel literature.

I would further suggest that Islam's two types correspond to a perception of the historical shift from the era of Romantic travel to that of late Victorian travel, synonymous with the rise of *tourism*. As late as the mid-nineteenth century, it was still possible to welcome delays and diversions as opportunities to make personal discoveries. But developments in rail and steamship travel, especially after mid-century, drew even the world's remotest corners within reach, and, with the advent of the popular guidebook and its lists of 'must see' landmarks, group visits to prescribed locations became more and more the norm. Furthermore, the democratization of access to distant spots was accompanied by stereotyped conceptions of such places and the notion that travel should be smooth and easy rather than awkward and risky. To the Victorian, the Murray and Baedeker guidebooks were a guarantee that nothing unto-ward could befall the person venturing outside their normal habitat: such guides advised on where to spend the night and how to cope with foreign cooking, generally seeking to stave off every accident and emergency. That, in 1872, the fictional Fogg can tuck *Bradshaw's Guide* under his arm on the assumption that it will 'provide him with all the information required for his journey' (p. 16) is a clear index of the new touristic mind-set. Given that Verne himself seems to consider the world as mapped and measured in its entirety, then, as the critic Roland Barthes observes, that world 'even in its most distant part, is like an object in his hand'. To circle the globe means simply to adhere to a fixed track punctuated by named locations, in a repetition of the known rather than an exposure to the unforeseen. In this perspective, the early detail of the stages and timing of Fogg's itinerary, cited from the *Morning Chronicle* at the Reform Club, establishes a sense of smooth progression which corresponds to the touristic ideal of 'nothing going wrong' – a prospect of travel so predictable that homecoming becomes its sole highpoint. Admittedly, things *do* go wrong for Fogg, just as they do for Fergusson: yet if in either case the hero tolerates interruptions, it is not because these are occasions for discovery but because they allow him to assert his ascendency. Today's politically alert reader might want to take this further and read into such attitudes a revealing parallel with the colonialist and imperialist approaches to remote territories and peoples which were characteristic of Verne's own age: but this might be to place too heavy an emphasis on the Vernian entertainment.

To maximise their comic impact, Verne presses his caricatures to the limit. Phileas Fogg is presented as utterly enigmatic or 'sphinx-like' (p. 3). Hence, no doubt, his surname, indicative of some inherent mystery (although the allusion to *fog* may also be a Parisian quip about the typical London weather). From the outset, Verne refuses to countenance any social or professional connection which might contextualise his hero, even supplying a long list of professional societies to which Fogg does *not* belong. Outside his membership of the Reform Club, Fogg has no social existence. Into this emptiness, Verne proceeds to pour at least some characteristics, constructing a species of identity for his hero, albeit one which amounts to little more than a series of variants on the image of the mechanical man. Fogg is as cool as the iced beverages he sips at his club; he insists on standards of punctuality and regularity which are utterly inhumane, as witness the way he sacks his first servant because the poor fellow brings him shaving-water two degrees colder than usual (p. 5). Once having laid down the parameters of Fogg's London routines, Verne has only to transfer these to the context of a journey round the world: whereupon Fogg emerges as the sedentary traveller *par excellence*, oblivious to everything except the rigid schedule he has adopted. Verne makes Fogg's monomania comically obvious when he retires to his cabin upon arriving at Suez: 'The thought of going ashore to see the town never occurred to him, for he was one of those Englishmen who, when travelling, leave their servants to do their sight-seeing for them' (p. 25).

The dour Englishman's blinkered commitment would hardly be a basis for an adventure story were it not for the verve and adaptability exhibited by his French manservant, Passepartout, whose function is to provide comic relief through his talent for getting into scrapes and out again. The man's successive misdemeanours and narrow escapes are counterbalanced by occasional strokes of luck and some striking acts of bravery, such as his rescue of the bride from the burning pyre (p. 53–4). Passepartout may be deemed 'nomadic', in so far as he genuinely exposes himself to non-European cultures and even participates in foreign rituals; he has no trouble disguising himself as a local, and even manages to infiltrate a troupe of Japanese acrobats (p. 99). As a nomadic traveller, Passepartout 'passes everywhere', ever curious as to the specificity of the exotic locale. He remains open to the demands and opportunities of circumstance, and is only stubbornly 'sedentary' in a single respect: he won't adjust his watch to local time.

In point of fact, Verne's authorial management of contrasted travel modes is more subtle than I have made out, for Fogg does gradually shed some of his rigidity and become more human and vulnerable. After all, he falls in love with Aouda and goes out of his way to rescue Passepartout from the Sioux raiders; so that, despite his English decorum (compounded by Verne's disinclination to delve into the affections), one infers that there is warm blood running through his veins. Moreover, Fogg is a *gambler*, and the reckless way he spends his fortune in order to win a capricious bet reveals a sensibility rather less consistent and regulated than that of a dispassionate robot.

As a species of quest narrative, Fogg's globetrotting odyssey might bear some analysis as an allegory which highlights an epic attempt to challenge the constraints of our mortal condition and to triumph over earthly circumstance. We might also consider Fogg's airily accepted deadline as just another variant on the topos of the *absurd challenge* which permeates British popular culture: the crossing of the Antarctic, the climbing of Everest, the four-minute mile, the solo circumnavigation of the globe – all such feats signal an enduring fascination with 'first time' achievements, along with speed records and demonstrations of outstanding physical and moral daring. Fogg remains a hero for our contemporary culture in his bold and, in truth, rather crazy adherence to an arbitrary set of rules. His scrupulous 'playing of the game' leads him to financial penury, with only a loving bride and a uniquely loyal servant as compensation. Is Fogg really so admirable in his perverse consistency? I suspect that we admire him – like Captain Ahab or the Count of Monte Cristo – for his very madness, even his criminality – for even if he is exonerated from the suspicion of having sequestered money from the Bank of England, he does break several laws on his travels, including kidnapping a sea-captain and commandeering his vessel. In effect, as readers and as quasi-accomplices, we are encouraged to set store by the positive qualities which underlie his eccentricity: so that we see Fogg's

uncanny effort in terms of an uplifting morality, overlooking its foolish-
ness in the name of a higher ethos.

Indeed, what both Phileas Fogg and Dr Fergusson represent may be
something which runs a little deeper than the surface narrative of risks
and surprises. It's not that Fergusson's balloon traverses Africa, it's that
it does so in just five weeks; while Fogg's madcap race is squeezed into a
time-span of dazzling exactitude. Within the Vernian universe, *time* can
never be a light-hearted matter – despite the fact that *Around the World*
exploits that droll paradox whereby one gains an extra day by travelling
eastwards. A good many readers find it hard to grasp the point of this
twist, although Verne does have his facts right about what happens if you
journey in the opposite direction to the sun. My point is that, behind this
bit of leg-pulling, there lies a potentially profound message about the
folly of seeking to possess time and space as if they were discrete objects.
In his writings, the twentieth-century French philosopher Henri
Bergson (1859–1941) draws a fundamental distinction between, on the
one hand, chronological or clock time and, on the other, the true sense
of temporal flow which he terms *la durée*, or duration. Clock time is what
dictates the tempo of the tourist and the sedentary traveller. It is time cut
into regular bits, and corresponds to a fickle clutching at segments of
experience. It must, argues Bergson, be far preferable to avoid fragmen-
tation and instead to seek to coincide with the temporal flow through
acts of intuition: by immersing oneself in duration, one embraces flux,
the natural pacing of life as it unfolds and heralds what he calls
'becoming'. For Bergson, such wholehearted commitment is indeed a
condition of human freedom.

This way of considering time might shed some light on our reading
experience. It might be said that the reader who shadows the Vernian
hero in his abrupt switches from place to place submits to the textual
journey as a set of isolated chapters and episodes, a staccato procession of
moments ticked off against clock-face and calendar. Yet to the extent
that, every so often, the reader loses track of time and is carried away on
some giddy aerial race against Arab horsemen or some wild dash on the
back of an elephant (but surely elephants don't gallop as fast as that?),
then there may arise a sense of participation in the imagined journey, of
somehow coinciding with its intensity, its impetus, its vivid becoming.
What I am suggesting is that the responsive reader can sometimes slip
into a dimension of excitement so thrilling as to supersede awareness of
clichés and bare-faced fabrications. In such moments, the text palpitates,
so to speak, transporting us out of ourselves, seducing us into an ecstatic
abandonment of our rigidity, our pedantry. Of course, everyone knows
that adventure yarns are really meant for kids; Science Fiction is infantile

fantasy; world travel is a doddle. Yet in his far-fetched enactments of triumphant travelling, Verne may be offering something more acute than we suppose – perhaps the outline of an intuition concerning human time: the time we each have left, the implied urgency of our mortal span. Fergusson and Fogg do both come home, and expect to get on with their ensuing lives; yet in both cases the single extraordinary voyage seems to stand as a condensation of an entire existence. Dare I suggest there is an implicit allusion in both novels to the ultimate metaphor of the journey of life?

*   *   *

Both these fraught escapades enjoyed immense popularity in their author's own lifetime. A year after the publication of *Around the World*, Verne co-produced a stage version which remained for half a century in the repertoire of the Châtelet Theatre in Paris. Ever alert to spin-offs, Jules Hetzel even marketed a family board-game with dice and a world-map. Like so many of Verne's works, both novels were subsequently filmed. Michael Todd's version of *Around the World* appeared in 1956, starring David Niven as Fogg and the Mexican comic Cantinflas as his manservant; it offered cameo appearances by over forty celebrities and won five Oscars. (It may be noted that Todd's screenplay departs from the strict original by conflating our two narratives and depicting Fogg in a balloon, as though to regularise a popular mistake.) Today, the name Phileas Fogg has been copyrighted by a manufacturer of packeted snacks, thus guaranteeing that it remains 'on everyone's lips', while the yarn continues to inspire globetrotting fictions, not to mention real-life journeys and travel books based on the precepts of the unlikely wager and the race against the clock, among them the round-the-world yachting competition for the Jules Verne Trophy and the 1989 BBC television travelogue based on Michael Palin's emulation of Fogg's feat. (Palin made it back to London in good time, only to be frustrated when the Reform Club declined to allow him and his camera team into its precincts to celebrate with a glass of champagne!) Finally, the fluency of today's Internet – that armchair utopia of ubiquity and encyclopedic knowledge – guarantees instantaneous access to a spectacular archive of well over a hundred thousand Jules Verne websites of every imaginable kind. In short, whether it be a matter of careering above the tropics in a balloon or sailing breakneck across the oceans, Verne's fantasias of urgency have gained an enduring place amid the archetypal narratives of our culture.

ROGER CARDINAL
University of Kent at Canterbury

BIBLIOGRAPHY

Allott, Kenneth, *Jules Verne*, Cresset Press, London 1940

Allotte de la Fuye, Marguerite, *Jules Verne*, Staples Press, London 1954

Barthes, Roland, 'The *Nautilus* and the Drunken Boat', in *Mythologies*, Paladin, London 1973

Beaver, Harold (ed.), *The Science Fiction of Edgar Allan Poe*, Penguin Books, Harmondsworth 1976

Bergson, Henri, *Essai sur les données immédiates de la conscience*, Félix Alcan, Paris 1908

Bessière, Jean (ed.), *Modernités de Jules Verne*, Presses universitaires de France, Paris 1988

Butcher, William, *Jules Verne's Journey to the Centre of the Self: Space and Time in the 'Voyages extraordinaires'*, St Martin's Press, New York and London 1990

Butor, Michel, 'Le Point suprême et l'âge d'or à travers quelques oeuvres de Jules Verne', in *Répertoire*, Minuit, Paris 1960

Buzard, James, *The Beaten Track: European Tourism, Literature, and the Ways to Culture, 1800–1918*, Clarendon Press, Oxford 1993

Cardinal, Roger, 'Romantic Travel', in *Rewriting the Self: Histories from the Renaissance to the Present*, edited by Roy Porter, Routledge, London and New York 1997

Compère, Daniel, *Jules Verne écrivain*, Droz, Geneva 1991

Compère, Daniel, *Jules Verne: parcours d'une oeuvre*, Encrage, Amiens 1996

Costello, Peter, *Jules Verne: Inventor of Science Fiction*, London 1978

DeKiss, Jean-Paul, *Jules Verne: Le Rêve du progrès*, 'Découvertes', Gallimard, Paris 1991

Deys, Volker; Har'El, Zvi; & Margot, Jean-Michel, *The Complete Jules Verne Bibliography*, htttp://jv.gilead.org.il/biblio/

Diesbach, Ghislain de, *Le Tour de Jules Verne en quatre-vingts livres*, Julliard, Paris 1969

Dumas, Olivier, *Jules Verne*, La Manufacture, Lyon 1988

Escaich, René, *Voyage au monde de Jules Verne*, Éditions Plantin, Paris 1955

Evans, Arthur B., *Jules Verne Rediscovered: Didacticism and the Scientific Novel*, Greenwood Press, Westport CT and London 1988

Evans, Arthur B., 'The Illustrators of Jules Verne's *Voyages extraordinaires*', in *Science-Fiction Studies*, Vol. XXV, No 2, July 1998, pp. 241–70

Haining, Peter (ed.), *The Jules Verne Companion*, Souvenir Press, London 1978

Islam, Syed Manzurul, *The Ethics of Travel: From Marco Polo to Kafka*, Manchester University Press, Manchester and New York 1996

Jules-Verne, Jean, *Jules Verne: A Biography*, Macdonald and Jane's, London 1976

Leed, Eric J., *The Mind of the Traveler: From Gilgamesh to Global Tourism*, Basic Books, New York 1991

Lottman, Herbert, *Jules Verne: An Exploratory Biography*, St Martin's Press, London 1997

Lynch, Lawrence, *Jules Verne*, Twayne, New York 1992

Marcucci, Edmondo, *Les Illustrations des 'Voyages extraordinaires' de Jules Verne. Dessinateurs et graveurs*, Société Jules Verne, Bordeaux 1956

Martin, Andrew, *The Mask of the Prophet: The Extraordinary Fictions of Jules Verne*, Clarendon Press, Oxford 1993

Moré, Marcel, *Nouvelles explorations de Jules Verne: musique, misogamie, machine*, Gallimard, Paris 1963

Nicholls, Peter (ed.), *The Encyclopedia of Science Fiction: An Illustrated A to Z*, Granada, London, Toronto, Sydney, and New York 1981

Nouvelles Recherches sur Jules Verne et le voyage, Minard, Paris 1978

Palin, Michael, *Around the World in 80 Days with Michael Palin*, BBC Books, London 1989

Renzi, Thomas C., *Jules Verne on Film: A Filmography of the Cinematic Adaptations of his Works, 1902 through 1997*, McFarland, London 1998

Serres, Michel, *Jouvences sur Jules Verne*, Minuit, Paris 1974

Smyth, Edmund J. (ed.), *Jules Verne: Narratives of Modernity*, Liverpool University Press, Liverpool 2000

Soriano, Marc, *Jules Verne*, Julliard, Paris 1978

Unwin, Timothy, *Jules Verne: Le Tour du monde en quatre-vingts jours*, University of Glasgow French & German Publications, Glasgow 1992

Versins, Pierre, *Encyclopédie de l'utopie, des voyages extraordinaires et de la science-fiction*, L'Age d'homme, Lausanne 1972

Vierne, Simone, *Jules Verne*, Balland, Paris 1986

Vierne, Simone, *Jules Verne, mythe et modernité*, Presses universitaires de France, Paris 1989

Waltz, G. H., *Jules Verne: The Biography of an Imagination*, New York 1943

CONTENTS

AROUND THE WORLD IN EIGHTY DAYS

FIVE WEEKS IN A BALLOON

AROUND THE WORLD IN
EIGHTY DAYS

CHAPTER I

In which Phileas Fogg and Passepartout accept each other as master and man

IN THE YEAR 1872, No. 7 Savile Row, Burlington Gardens, the house in which Sheridan[1] died in 1816, was occupied by Phileas Fogg, Esq. Of the members of the Reform Club in London few, if any, were more peculiar or more specially noticed than Phileas Fogg, although he seemed to make a point of doing nothing that could draw attention.

So one of the greatest orators who honour England had for a successor this man, Phileas Fogg, a sphinx-like person, of whom nothing was known except that he was a thorough gentleman and one of the handsomest men in English high society.

He was said to be like Byron[2] – his head, at least, was supposed to be like Byron's, for his feet were faultless – a Byron with moustache and whiskers, a phlegmatic Byron, who would have lived a thousand years without getting any older.

English Phileas Fogg certainly was, though perhaps not a Londoner. No one had ever seen him at the Stock Exchange or the Bank, or at any of the offices in the City.

No ship owned by Phileas Fogg had ever been berthed in the basins or docks of London. He was not to be found on any board of directors. His name had never been heard among the barristers of the Temple, Lincoln's Inn or Gray's Inn. He was never known to plead in the Court of Chancery or of Queen's Bench, in the Court of Exchequer or in an Ecclesiastical Court. He was neither manufacturer nor merchant, tradesman nor farmer. The Royal Society of Great Britain, the London Society, the Workmen's Society, the Russell Society, the Western Literary Society, the Law Society, the Society of United Arts and Sciences, which is under the patronage of Her Gracious Majesty – he belonged to none of these. In a word, he was not a member of a single one of the many associations that swarm in the English capital, from the Armonica Society to the Entomological Society, founded chiefly for the object of destroying noxious insects.

Phileas Fogg was a member of the Reform Club,[3] he was nothing else.

That such a mysterious person should have been numbered among this honourable company might cause astonishment; let me say, then, that he was admitted on the recommendation of Messrs Baring Brothers,[4] on whom he was at liberty to draw to an extent unlimited. From this fact he derived a certain standing, as his cheques were regularly cashed at sight out of the balance of his current account, always in credit.

Phileas Fogg was undeniably a wealthy man, but how he had made his fortune was more than the best-informed could say, and Mr Fogg was the last person to whom it would have been wise to apply for information on the subject. At all events, while in no way extravagant, he was not mean, for wherever a sum of money was wanted to make up the amount required for some noble, useful or generous object, he gave it quietly and even anonymously. Well, nothing could be more uncommunicative than this gentleman. He spoke as little as possible, and this silence made him appear all the more mysterious. And yet he lived quite openly, but there was ever such a mathematical regularity about everything he did, that imagination was disappointed and went beyond the facts. Had he travelled? Probably, for nobody had a more intimate knowledge of the map of the world. There was not a spot, however remote, with which he did not appear to be specially acquainted. Sometimes, in a few words succinct and clear, he would correct the statements innumerable current in the Club about those travellers who had been lost or had gone astray; he would point out what had in all probability happened, and his words often turned out to have been as though inspired by a gift of second-sight, so completely justified were they always in the event.

The man must have travelled everywhere – mentally, if in no other way.

One thing was certain, however: Phileas Fogg had not left London for years. Those who had the honour of knowing him a little better than the rest asserted that no one could say he had ever seen him elsewhere than at the Club, or on his way to the Club, whither he went straight from his house day after day.

His one pastime consisted in reading the papers and playing whist. At this silent game, so congenial to his nature, he often won, but the money he won never went into his purse; it represented an important sum in the budget of his charity. Moreover, be it noted that Mr Fogg obviously played for the sake of playing, not of winning. For him the game was a fight, a struggle against a difficulty, but a struggle free from motion, change of place or fatigue. This just suited his temperament. As far as anyone knew, Phileas Fogg had neither wife nor child, which may happen to the most respectable people; he had no relations, no friends, which verily is more exceptional.

Phileas Fogg lived by himself in his house in Savile Row, which nobody ever entered.

Of his home life never a word.

One servant ministered to all his wants. He lunched and dined at the Club at absolutely regular hours, in the same room, at the same table; he never treated his fellow-members, never invited a stranger. He never availed himself of those comfortable bedrooms that the Reform Club places at the disposal of its members, but went home at midnight punctually, just to go to bed. Out of twenty-four hours he spent ten at home, either sleeping or attending to his toilet. If he took walking exercise, he invariably did so with measured step on the inlaid floor of the front hall, or in the circular gallery under a dome of blue glass supported by twenty Ionic pillars of red porphyry. Whether he dined or lunched, it was the Club's kitchens, the Club's larder, pantry, fish-stores, and dairy that supplied his table with their savoury provisions; it was the Club's waiters, solemn-faced men in dress-coats, with molleton under the soles of their shoes, who served his food on special china, upon admirable Saxony napery; it was out of the Club's matchless glasses that he drank his sherry, his port, or his claret flavoured with cinnamon and capillaire; and it was the ice of the Club, imported at great expense from the American lakes, that kept his beverages in a satisfactory state of coolness.

If such a mode of life denotes eccentricity, there is no denying that eccentricity has points. Though not palatial, the house in Savile Row was commendable for extreme comfort. And the habits of its tenant being what they were, the service was very light; but Phileas Fogg required quite exceptional punctuality and regularity of his one servant.

That very day, the second of October, Phileas Fogg had dismissed James Foster, because the fellow had committed the offence of bringing him shaving-water at eighty-four Fahrenheit instead of eighty-six, and he was expecting the new servant, who was to report himself between eleven and half-past.

Phileas Fogg, sitting in his armchair, squarely and bolt upright, with head erect, his feet close together like those of a soldier on parade, his hands resting on his knees, was watching the progress of the hand of the clock, a complicated piece of mechanism, which marked the hours, the minutes, the seconds, the days of the month with their names, and the year. On the stroke of half-past eleven Mr Fogg, as was his wont day after day, would be leaving home to go to the Reform Club.

At this moment there was a knock at the door of the morning-room in which Mr Phileas Fogg was sitting. James Foster, the dismissed servant, appeared and said:

'The new servant.'

A man some thirty years of age presented himself and bowed.

'You are a Frenchman, and your name is John?' queried Phileas Fogg.

'Jean, if you please, sir,' replied the newcomer, 'Jean Passepartout.[5] The surname has stuck to me, justified as it was by my natural gumption for getting out of scrapes. I believe I am an honest fellow, sir, but, to tell you the truth, I have done more things than one to earn a living. Street singing, vaulting like Léotard,[6] tight-rope walking like Blondin;[7] I did all this and then, to make better use of my attainments, I became a teacher of gymnastics, and last I was a sergeant of firemen in Paris. My service record actually contains mention of noteworthy fires. But it is now five years since I left France and became a valet in England, having a mind to see how I should like family life. Now, being out of a place, and hearing that Mr Phileas Fogg was the most particular and most sedentary gentleman in the United Kingdom, I have come to you, sir, in the hope of living here in peace and quietness, and forgetting the very name of Passepartout.'

'Passepartout suits me very well,' replied the gentleman; 'you have been recommended to me. Your references are good. You know my terms?'

'Yes, sir.'

'That is all right. What time do you make it?'

'Twenty-two minutes past eleven,' answered Passepartout, pulling out a huge silver watch from the depths of his pocket.

'You are slow,' said Mr Fogg.

'Pardon me, sir, but that's impossible.'

'You are four minutes slow. It is of no consequence; I wish to point out the error, nothing more. Well then, from this moment, eleven-twenty-nine a.m., Wednesday, October 2nd, 1872, you are in my service.'

Thereupon Phileas Fogg got up, took his hat with his left hand, put it on his head with the action of an automaton, and disappeared without saying another word.

Passepartout heard the street-door shut once; it was his new master going out; then he heard it shut a second time; that was his predecessor, James Foster, likewise making his exit.

Passepartout remained alone in the house in Savile Row.

CHAPTER II

*In which Passepartout is convinced that he has at last found his
ideal*

'MY WORD,' said Passepartout to himself, a little dazed at first, 'I have
known at Madame Tussaud's folks with just as much life in them as my
new master!'

It should be said that Madame Tussaud's 'folks' are wax figures, very
popular with sight-seers in London, and in which speech alone is
lacking. Passepartout had just had a very hurried glimpse of Phileas
Fogg, but he had quickly, yet carefully, looked over his new master.

His age might have been forty, his countenance was noble and
handsome, his figure tall, and none the worse for a slight tendency to
stoutness, his hair and whiskers were fair, his forehead was smooth and
bore no signs of wrinkles at the temples; the face had little colour, the
teeth were splendid. He appeared to possess in the highest degree what
physiognomists call 'rest in action,' a virtue shared by all who are more
efficient than noisy. Even-tempered, phlegmatic, with a clear and
steady eye, he was the perfect type of those cool Englishmen who are
fairly numerous in the United Kingdom, and whose somewhat aca-
demic pose has been wonderfully portrayed by the brush of Angelica
Kaufmann.[8] When you considered the various functions of this man's
existence, you conceived the idea of a being well balanced and
accurately harmonised throughout, as perfect as a chronometer by
Leroy or Earnshaw.

The fact is Phileas Fogg was the personification of accuracy. This
was clearly shown by the 'expression of his feet and hands,' for in man,
as well as in animals, the limbs themselves are organs that express the
passions.

Phileas Fogg was one of those mathematically precise people who,
never hurried and always ready, waste no step or movement. He always
went by the shortest way, so never took a stride more than was needed.
He never gave the ceiling an unnecessary glance, and never indulged in
a superfluous gesture. No one ever saw him moved or put out. Though
no man ever hurried so little, he was always in time.

Howbeit, one can understand why he lived alone, and, so to speak,
outside all social intercourse. He knew that there is always in social life

a certain amount of friction to be taken into account, and, as friction is a cause of delay, he avoided all human contact.

As for Jean, surnamed Passepartout, he was a real Parisian of Paris; for five years he had been living in England, acting as valet in London, and in vain looking for a master he could like. He was none of your swaggering comedy flunkeys, with a look of airy assurance and callous indifference – impudent rascals at best. Not a bit of it. Passepartout was a good fellow with a pleasant face, lips rather prominent, ever ready to taste and to kiss; he was a gentle, obliging creature, with one of those honest round heads that you like to see on the shoulders of a friend. His eyes were blue, his complexion warm, his face was chubby enough to allow him to see his cheek-bones. His chest was broad, his frame big and muscular, and he was endowed with Herculean strength which had been admirably developed by the exercises of his youth. His hair, which was brown, was somewhat ruffled. If the sculptors of antiquity knew eighteen ways of dressing Minerva's locks, Passepartout knew but one for the disposal of his: three strokes of a large toothcomb, and the operation was over.

Whether or not the man's open-hearted, impulsive nature would harmonise with Phileas Fogg's, the most elementary prudence forbids us to say. Would Passepartout prove to be the thoroughly precise and punctual servant his master required? Experience alone could show. His youth, as we know, had been largely spent in wandering about, and he was now anxious to settle down. Having heard much good of English regularity of life and the proverbial reserve of English gentlemen, he came to try his luck in England. Hitherto, however, fate had been unkind. He had not been able to take root anywhere. He had been in ten places. In every one his employers were crotchety, capricious, fond of adventures or travelling, which no longer appealed to Passepartout. His last master, young Lord Longsferry, M.P., after spending his nights at the Haymarket Oyster Rooms, only too often returned home on the shoulders of the police. Passepartout, who more than anything wanted to be able to respect his master, ventured on a few words of humble remonstrance, which were not well received, so he left. He, thereupon, heard that Phileas Fogg, Esq., was looking out for a servant, and found out what he could about this gentleman. A man whose manner of life was so regular, who never slept out, never travelled, who was never away from home, even for a day, must be just what he wanted. He called and was accepted as we have seen.

Well, half-past eleven had struck, and Passepartout was alone in the house in Savile Row. He forthwith began to inspect this house. He went over it from cellar to attic. It was a clean house, orderly, austere, puritanical, well arranged for service; he liked it. It gave him the impression of a handsome snail-shell, but a shell lighted and heated by gas, for all the requirements of light and warmth were supplied through the agency of carburetted hydrogen. Passepartout had no difficulty in finding, on the third floor, the room intended for him. He liked it. Electric bells and speaking-tubes enabled him to communicate with the rooms on the first and second floors. On the mantelpiece stood an electric clock synchronising with the clock in Phileas Fogg's bedroom; the two time-keepers beat the same second at the very same instant. 'This is all right; this will suit me down to the ground,' said Passepartout to himself. He likewise noticed in his room a card of instructions stuck over the clock. This was the daily-service routine.

From eight o'clock in the morning, the regulation time at which Phileas Fogg got up, till half-past eleven, the hour at which he went out to lunch at the Reform Club, it specified every item of service: the tea and toast at twenty-three minutes past eight, the shaving-water at thirty-seven minutes past nine, the hair-dressing at twenty minutes to ten, etc. Then from half-past twelve in the morning to twelve at night, when the methodical gentleman went to bed, everything was noted down and settled in advance. To think over this programme and impress its various details on his mind was sheer delight to Passepartout. The gentleman's wardrobe was very well supplied and chosen with excellent judgement. Every pair of trousers, coat or waistcoat, bore a number; this number was reproduced on a register, which stated when the garments were put in or taken out, and showed the date at which they were to be worn in turn, according to the time of the year. Like regulations obtained for the boots and shoes.

This house in Savile Row, which must have been the temple of disorder in the days of the illustrious but dissipated Sheridan, was furnished with a comfort that told of ample means. There was no library, no books, which would have been of no use to Mr Fogg, as the Reform Club placed two libraries at his disposal, one for general literature, the other for law and politics. In his bedroom stood an average-sized safe, which was so constructed as to defy fire and theft alike. There were no weapons in the house, not a single utensil of the hunter or warrior. Everything pointed to the most pacific habits.

After a detailed examination of the house, Passepartout rubbed his hands, his broad face beamed, and he joyfully said over and over again: 'This will suit me! It's the very thing I wanted! We shall get on famously together, Mr Fogg and I! A man of stay-at-home and regular habits! A real machine! Well, I'm not sorry to serve a machine!'

CHAPTER III

*In which a conversation takes place which may prove costly
for Phileas Fogg*

PHILEAS FOGG LEFT his house in Savile Row at half-past eleven and,
when he had put down his right foot five hundred and seventy-five
times before his left foot, and his left foot five hundred and seventy-six
times before his right foot, he arrived at the Reform Club, a huge
edifice, standing in Pall Mall, that cost quite a hundred and twenty
thousand pounds to build.

Phileas Fogg went straight into the dining-room, whose nine
windows looked out on a beautiful garden with trees already touched
with the gilding of autumn. He sat down at the accustomed table,
where his place was ready for him. His lunch consisted of a side-dish,
boiled fish with tip-top Reading sauce, underdone roast beef flavoured
with mushroom ketchup, rhubarb and gooseberry tart, and a piece of
Cheshire cheese, washed down with a few cups of that excellent tea
specially procured for the Reform Club's buttery.

At forty-seven minutes past twelve, he got up and made his way to
the big drawing-room, a magnificent room adorned with paintings in
splendid frames. There a servant handed him the uncut *Times*, which
Phileas Fogg unfolded and cut with much care and a dexterity that
denoted great familiarity with this difficult operation. The reading of
this paper occupied Phileas Fogg till forty-five minutes past three, and
that of the *Standard*, which followed, lasted till dinner. This meal was
accomplished in the same conditions as lunch, with the addition of
Royal British sauce.

At twenty minutes to six, he returned to the big drawing-room and
gave his whole attention to the *Morning Chronicle*. Half an hour later,
several members of the Reform Club came in and drew near to the
hearth on which burnt a coal fire. They were Mr Phileas Fogg's
habitual partners at whist, passionately fond of the game like himself:
the engineer Andrew Stuart, the bankers John Sullivan and Samuel
Fallentin, the brewer Thomas Flanagan, and Gauthier Ralph, one of
the governors of the Bank of England.

They were wealthy and respected persons even in this Club, which
numbers amongst its members the princes of industry and finance.

'How now, Ralph,' said Thomas Flanagan, 'what about this theft business?' 'Well,' replied Andrew Stuart, 'the Bank will lose the money.' 'I think not,' said Gauthier Ralph. 'I hope we shall lay hands on the thief. Police-inspectors, very smart fellows, have been sent to America and the Continent, to all the principal ports, and the gentleman will have a job to escape them.' 'Have they his description, then?' asked Andrew Stuart. 'In the first place, the man is not a thief,' replied Gauthier Ralph seriously. 'Not a thief, what? the fellow who purloined fifty-five thousand pounds in banknotes!' 'No,' answered Gauthier Ralph. 'What then, is he a manufacturer?' said John Sullivan.

'The *Morning Chronicle* says he's a gentleman.' The man who gave this reply was none other than Phileas Fogg, whose head was at that moment emerging from the sea of paper about him.

So saying, Phileas Fogg bowed to his fellow-members, who returned his salutation.

The case in question, which was being keenly discussed in all the newspapers of the United Kingdom, had happened three days before, on the 29th of September. A bundle of banknotes, amounting to the enormous sum of fifty-five thousand pounds, had been taken from the table of the chief cashier of the Bank of England.

When someone expressed astonishment that such a theft could have been carried out so easily, the sub-manager, Gauthier Ralph, replied simply that at that very moment the cashier was busy entering the receipt of three shillings and sixpence, and that a man could not attend to everything.

But there is one thing to be said which makes the matter more explicable: that admirable establishment, the Bank of England, appears to have the utmost regard for the dignity of the public. There are no guards, no old soldiers, no gratings! The gold, silver and banknotes are freely exposed and, so to speak, at the mercy of anyone. It would not do to cast the slur of suspicion on the respectability of the man in the street, no matter who he may be. One of the best observers of English customs relates the following incident.

He happened one day to be in one of the rooms of the Bank and, feeling curious to see more closely an ingot of gold weighing seven or eight pounds, which lay on the cashier's table, he took it up, examined it, passed it on to his neighbour, who handed it to someone else, so that this ingot travelled from hand to hand to the very end of a dark passage, and it was half an hour before it returned to its former place, and the cashier never even looked up.

But, on September 29, things did not happen quite in this manner. The bundle of banknotes did not return, and when the magnificent clock, installed over the drawing-office, struck five, the closing hour, the Bank of England was reduced to passing fifty-five thousand pounds to the account of profit and loss.

When the theft had been duly verified, picked detectives were sent to the principal ports, to Liverpool, Glasgow, Havre, Suez, Brindisi, New York, etc., and, in case of success, there was a promise of a reward of two thousand pounds and five per cent. of the sum recovered.

Until the inquiry, which had been opened immediately, should furnish them with information, these police-officers were to watch closely all arriving or departing travellers.

Now, as was stated in the *Morning Chronicle*, there was reason to suppose that the man who had committed the theft was not a member of any English gang. On that day of September 29, a well-dressed gentleman of polished manners and refined appearance had been observed walking about the pay-room, where the theft had taken place. As a result of the inquiry, a fairly precise description of this gentleman was obtained and this description at once dispatched to all the detectives of the United Kingdom and the Continent. In consequence a few sensible people, one of whom was Gauthier Ralph, felt justified in hoping that the culprit would not escape. The event, as you can imagine, was the daily talk of London and the whole country. People argued excitedly for or against the probabilities of the Metropolitan Police being successful. A debate of the same question among the members of the Reform Club will, therefore, cause no astonishment, all the more that one of them was a sub-manager of the Bank.

The Honourable Gauthier Ralph refused to believe that this search would fail, as he considered that the proffered reward must make the detectives exceptionally keen and acute. But his colleague, Andrew Stuart, was far from sharing this confidence. The discussion continued even after they had sat down at a card-table, Stuart opposite Flanagan, and Fallentin opposite Phileas Fogg. When play started conversation ceased, but it was renewed between the rubbers, and became more and more heated.

'I maintain,' said Andrew Stuart, 'that the chances are in favour of the thief, who is sure to be no fool.' 'Nonsense!' replied Ralph, 'there is not a country left in which he can take refuge.' 'What an idea!' 'Where do you want him to go?' 'I can't say,' replied Andrew Stuart, 'but, after all, the world is large enough.' 'It was so . . . ' said Phileas Fogg in an undertone. Then, placing the cards before Thomas Flanagan, he added, 'Will you cut?'

The discussion was interrupted during the rubber. But Andrew Stuart soon took it up again, saying: 'What do you mean by *was*? Has the world got smaller, eh?' 'Of course it has,' rejoined Gauthier Ralph; 'I agree with Mr Fogg. The world has got smaller, since one can travel over it ten times more rapidly than a hundred years ago. And that is just the thing that will hasten the pursuit of the thief.' 'And will likewise facilitate his escape!' 'It is your turn to play, Mr Stuart,' said Phileas Fogg. But the incredulous Stuart was not convinced. 'You must confess,' he said, addressing Ralph, when the rubber was finished, 'that you have hit upon a funny way of showing that the world has got smaller. So, because one can now go round it in three months . . .'

'In as few as eighty days,' said Phileas Fogg.

'Yes, indeed,' added John Sullivan, 'in eighty days, now that the section of the Great Indian Peninsula Railway between Rothal and Allahabad has been opened; and this is how the *Morning Chronicle* tabulates the journey:

From London to Suez via Mont-Cenis and Brindisi, by rail and boat	7 days
From Suez to Bombay, by boat	13 „
From Bombay to Calcutta, by rail	3 „
From Calcutta to Hong-Kong (China), by boat	13 „
From Hong-Kong to Yokohama (Japan), by boat	6 „
From Yokohama to San Francisco, by boat	22 „
From San Francisco to New York, by rail	7 „
From New York to London, by boat and rail	9 „
Total	80 days.'

'Yes, eighty days!' exclaimed Andrew Stuart, who inadvertently trumped a winning card; 'but that is making no allowance for rough weather, head winds, wrecks, etc.'

'Allowing for everything,' replied Phileas Fogg, who went on playing, for by now they were talking regardless of the game.

'What! Even if the Hindus or Indians removed the rails!' cried Andrew Stuart; 'if they stopped the trains, plundered the luggage-vans, and scalped the travellers!'

'Allowing for everything,' replied Phileas Fogg, and added, laying his cards on the table: 'Two winning trumps.'

Andrew Stuart, whose turn it was to shuffle, picked up the cards and said:

'In theory you are right, Mr Fogg, but practically . . . ' 'Practically too, Mr Stuart.' 'I should like to see you do it.' 'That lies with you. Let us go together.' 'Heaven forbid!' cried Stuart, 'but I would readily wager four thousand pounds that such a journey, made in such conditions, is impossible.' 'Nay, rather, quite possible,' replied Mr

Fogg. 'Well, then, go and do it!' 'Around the world in eighty days?' 'Yes.' 'All right.' 'When?' 'This minute. Only I warn you that I shall do it at your expense.' 'This is madness!' exclaimed Andrew Stuart, who was getting annoyed at his partner's pertinacity. 'Look here, better play on.' 'Shuffle again, then,' said Phileas Fogg, 'it's a misdeal.' Andrew Stuart took up the cards with a shaky hand, then suddenly he put them down again and said:

'Well, Mr Fogg, I will bet four thousand pounds! . . . ' 'My dear Stuart,' said Fallentin, 'calm yourself. This is not serious.'

'When I make a bet,' replied Andrew Stuart, 'I always mean what I say.' 'Very well,' said Mr Fogg, turning to his fellow-members; 'I have twenty thousand pounds on deposit at Baring's Bank. I am quite prepared to venture this sum . . . ' 'Twenty thousand pounds!' exclaimed John Sullivan, 'twenty thousand pounds that you might lose through a single unforeseen delay!' 'There is no such thing as the unforeseen,' was Phileas Fogg's simple reply. 'But, Mr Fogg, this space of eighty days is calculated as a minimum of time!'

'A minimum, if properly used, is sufficient for anything.' 'But, if you are not to exceed it, you will have to jump mathematically from trains to boats and from boats to trains!' 'I shall jump mathematically.' 'You are joking!' 'A true Englishman never jokes, when it is a question of a thing so serious as a wager,' replied Phileas Fogg. 'I will bet twenty thousand pounds with anyone that I shall make the tour of the world in eighty days or less, that is in nineteen hundred and twenty hours or one hundred and fifteen thousand two hundred minutes. Do you accept?'

Messrs Stuart, Fallentin, Sullivan, Flanagan and Ralph consulted together and signified their acceptance.

'Very well,' said Mr Fogg. 'The Dover train leaves at eight-forty-five. I shall take it.' 'This very evening?' asked Stuart. 'This very evening,' replied Phileas Fogg. 'Therefore,' he added, consulting a pocket-calendar, 'since today is Wednesday, the 2nd of October, I shall have to be back in London, in this very drawing-room of the Reform Club, on Saturday, the 21st of December, at eight-forty-five in the evening, in default of which the twenty thousand pounds deposited in my name at Baring's will be yours *de facto* and *de jure*, gentlemen. Here is a cheque for the amount.'

A statement of the wager was written down and signed there and then by the six persons interested. Phileas Fogg remained quite cool. He had not made the bet to win, and had only staked these twenty thousand pounds, the half of his fortune, because he foresaw he might have to spend the other half in order to achieve this difficult, not to say impracticable project. His adversaries, for their part, appeared uncomfortable, not on account of the amount of the stake, but because they felt that the conditions of the wager made it one-sided and unfair.

At that moment seven o'clock was striking. Mr Fogg was asked if he would like to stop playing, that he might prepare for his departure. 'I am always ready!' answered the impassive gentleman, and, having dealt, he said, 'Diamonds are trumps; you begin, Mr Stuart.'

CHAPTER IV

In which Phileas Fogg astounds his servant Passepartout

At twenty-five minutes past seven, Phileas Fogg, who had won some twenty guineas at whist, took leave of his respected associates and left the Reform Club. At fifty minutes past seven he opened his front door and entered his house.

Passepartout, who had made a minute study of his programme, was somewhat surprised on seeing Mr Fogg commit such an act of irregularity, by turning up at this unwonted hour. According to the memorandum, this inmate of Savile Row was not to come in before twelve at night exactly.

Phileas Fogg went straight to his bedroom, and then shouted, 'Passepartout.'

Passepartout made no reply. The call could not be meant for him. It was not the right time. 'Passepartout,' repeated Mr Fogg, in the same tone of voice. Passepartout made his appearance. 'I have called you twice,' said Mr Fogg. 'But it is not twelve o'clock,' replied Passepartout, watch in hand.

'I know it is not,' said Phileas Fogg, 'and I am not finding fault. We shall start for Dover and Calais in ten minutes.'

A faint grin peered on the Frenchman's round face. He could not have heard aright.

'Are you going away, sir?' he asked.

'Yes,' answered Phileas Fogg. 'We are going to travel round the world.'

Passepartout, with wide-staring eyes, hanging arms and limp body, then showed all the symptoms of astonishment bordering on stupor.

'Around the world,' he murmured. 'In eighty days,' replied Mr Fogg. 'So we must not lose a moment.'

'But the trunks?' said Passepartout, unconsciously swaying his head from side to side.

'No trunks. Just a travelling-bag. Put in two woollen shirts and three pairs of stockings, and the same for yourself. We shall buy what we require on the way. You will bring down my raincoat and travelling-rug. See that you have strong boots, though we shall do very little walking. Go ahead.'

Passepartout wished to say something in reply, but he simply could not. He went out of Mr Fogg's bedroom, went up to his own, collapsed on a chair and made use of a rather vulgar expression of his native land: 'Well, here's a go, and I thought I was going to have a quiet time.'

Then, mechanically, he made the required preparations for departure. Around the world in eighty days. Was his master a madman? No . . . it must be a joke? They were going to Dover, right; to Calais, right again. After all, the good fellow could not feel any great objection to this, as he had not trodden the soil of his native country for five years. It was just possible they might go as far as Paris, and there was no denying that it would give him pleasure to see the great capital again. But there could be no manner of doubt that a gentleman who was so economical of his footsteps would not go beyond Paris. – And yet the fact remained that this stay-at-home gentleman was now going away.

At eight o'clock, Passepartout had got ready the humble bag which contained his wardrobe and his master's; then, still very perturbed, he left his room, carefully closing the door, and went back to his master. Mr Fogg was ready. He had under his arm Bradshaw's *Continental Railway, Steam Transit and General Guide*,[9] which was to provide him with all the information required for his journey. He took the bag from Passepartout's hands, opened it and slipped into it a large bundle of those beautiful banknotes which are current in all countries.

'You have forgotten nothing?' he asked.

'Nothing, sir.'

'Where are my raincoat and travelling-rug?' 'Here they are.' 'All right, take this bag.' Mr Fogg handed the bag to Passepartout. 'And take great care of it,' he added. 'It contains twenty thousand pounds.' Passepartout nearly dropped the bag, as though the twenty thousand pounds had been in gold and a considerable weight.

Master and man then came downstairs, and the street-door was double-locked. There was a cab-stand at the end of Savile Row, where Phileas Fogg and his servant jumped into a cab which conveyed them at a good pace to Charing Cross Station, the terminus of one of the branch lines of the South-Eastern Railway. At eight-twenty the cab stopped in front of the station railing and Passepartout jumped out. His master followed and paid the cab-driver.

At this moment, a poor beggar-woman, standing barefooted in the mud, wearing a crazy bonnet, from which drooped a miserable feather, and with a ragged shawl over her tatters, came up to Mr Fogg, holding a child by the hand, and begged of him. Mr Fogg took from his pocket the twenty guineas which he had just won at whist, and presented the beggar-woman with them, saying: 'Take this, my good woman, I am pleased to have met you.' Then he passed on. Passepartout felt his eyes grow moist. He began to love his master.

Mr Fogg and he at once went on to the main platform, and Passepartout was told to get two first-class tickets for Paris.

Turning round, Mr Fogg saw his five fellow-members of the Reform Club.

'Gentlemen,' he said, 'I am off; I am taking a passport with me, so that the various *visas* it will bear may enable you to check my itinerary when I return.' 'Oh, Mr Fogg, that is not necessary,' was Gauthier Ralph's polite reply. 'We will trust your word as a gentleman.' 'Better as it is,' said Mr Fogg. 'You remember the date when you are due here?' observed Andrew Stuart. 'In eighty days,' replied Mr Fogg, 'on Saturday, December 21st, 1872, at forty-five minutes past eight in the evening. Goodbye till we meet again, gentlemen.'

At eight-forty, Phileas Fogg and his servant took their seats in the same compartment. At eight-forty-five, a loud whistle was heard and the train started.

The night was dark and it was drizzling. Phileas Fogg settled down comfortably in his corner and remained silent. Passepartout, still bewildered, mechanically hugged the bag with the banknotes. But, before the train had passed Sydenham, he uttered a real cry of despair. 'What's the matter?' asked Mr Fogg. 'In my hurry and flurry . . . I forgot . . . ' 'What?' 'To put out the gas in my room!' 'Well, my boy,' replied Mr Fogg coldly, 'it will burn at your expense.'

CHAPTER V

In which a new kind of scrip makes its appearance on 'Change[10]

DOUBTLESS, AS HE LEFT London, Phileas Fogg had no idea of the sensation his departure was about to produce. The report of the wager was first circulated among the members of the Reform Club, where it caused immense excitement. This excitement then passed from the Club to the papers through the reporters, and the papers communicated it to London and the whole of the United Kingdom. This 'question of a journey around the world' was commented, discussed, analysed, as keenly and passionately as if it had been a case of a new Alabama Claim. Some sided with Phileas Fogg, others, who were soon in a great majority, declared against him. Whatever it might be in theory and on paper, this journey around the world, to be made in this minimum of time, with the means of communication then available, was not only impossible but mad.

The Times, the *Standard*, the *Evening Star*, the *Morning Chronicle*, and twenty other papers with a large circulation declared against Mr Fogg. The *Daily Telegraph* alone gave him a measure of support. The names of lunatic and madman were freely bestowed on Phileas Fogg, and his friends of the Reform Club were blamed for having taken this bet, which pointed to a decline in the mental faculties of the man who proposed it.

Highly impassioned but logical articles were published on the question. Everyone knows how keenly interested the English are in anything connected with geography. So every reader, no matter to what class he belonged, greedily pored over the columns devoted to the Phileas Fogg case.

In the early days, a few bold spirits, the women principally, backed him, especially after the *Illustrated London News* had published a likeness of him from a photograph left among the records of the Reform Club. There were men who ventured to say: 'Well, after all, why not? Things more extraordinary have been done.' Those who spoke thus were mostly readers of the *Daily Telegraph*. But it was soon felt that even this paper was growing lukewarm.

In fact, a long article appeared on October 7 in the Report of the Royal Geographical Society. The question was treated from every point of view, and the folly of the enterprise clearly demonstrated. According to this article, the traveller had everything against him – obstacles both human and natural. The success of the project presupposed a miraculous fitting-in of the departure and arrival of means of transport; this neither existed nor could exist. In Europe, where distances are comparatively moderate, one can just depend on the punctual arrival of trains; but with trains taking three days to cross India, and seven to cross the United States, could one possibly base the solution of such a problem on their punctuality? And then there were engine troubles, derailments, collisions, bad weather, snowdrifts; Phileas Fogg had everything to contend with. In winter, when travelling by boat, he would be at the mercy of storms and fogs. It was not such a rare occurrence for the fastest of ocean liners to be two or three days late. Now one single day's delay was enough to snap the chain of communications irretrievably. Should Phileas Fogg miss a boat, if only by a few hours, he would be compelled to wait for the next, and that one failure would fatally compromise his venture.

This article made a great sensation. It was reproduced in almost every paper, and Phileas Fogg shares went down badly. During the first days after the gentleman's departure, important transactions were started on the chances of his enterprise. Everybody knows the sort of people who go in for betting in England; they are a cleverer and better class than gamblers.

An Englishman is by nature inclined to bet; so not only did the members of the Reform Club wager considerable sums for or against Phileas Fogg, but the great majority of the public joined in.

Phileas Fogg was registered in a sort of stud-book, like a race-horse. He was also converted into stock, which was at once quoted on 'Change.[10] 'Phileas Fogg' was asked for and offered at par or at a premium, and enormous business was done. But five days after his departure, after the publication of the article in the Royal Geographical Society's Report, offers of shares began to pour in. Phileas Fogg scrip declined. It was offered in bundles. At first people accepted five to one, then ten, and then not less than twenty, fifty, a hundred. One single supporter remained faithful to him: an old paralytic, Lord Albemarle. The noble lord, confined to his armchair, would have given his whole fortune to be able to travel around the world, in ten years even; and he bet four thousand pounds on Phileas Fogg. Whenever one showed him both the folly and the uselessness of the project, he simply replied: 'If the thing can be done, it is well that an Englishman should be the first to do it.'

This was the state of things, and the number of Phileas Fogg's backers was getting smaller and smaller; everyone was turning against him, not without reason; people would not take a bet on him at less than a hundred and fifty or two hundred to one; and seven days after his departure something absolutely unexpected happened, which put an end to all speculation on his success.

During that day, at nine o'clock in the evening, the Chief of the Metropolitan Police received a telegram which ran thus:

'Suez.

'Rowan, Chief of Police, Scotland Yard, London.

'Am shadowing bank thief, Phileas Fogg. Send without delay warrant for arrest Bombay.

Detective Fix.'

The effect of this telegram was immediate. The honourable gentleman vanished and was replaced by the bank thief.

His photograph, left at the Reform Club with those of all the other members, was examined, and reproduced feature for feature the man whose description had been obtained at the inquiry. The mysterious peculiarities of Phileas Fogg's mode of life were then recalled; his lonely existence, his sudden departure; and it appeared evident that the fellow had invented a journey around the world and propped it up by an insane wager to the sole end of putting the English detectives off the scent.

CHAPTER VI

In which Detective Fix shows very justifiable impatience

THE TELEGRAM CONCERNING Mr Phileas Fogg was dispatched in the following circumstances. On Wednesday, October 9, the P. & O. liner *Mongolia* was expected at eleven a.m. at Suez. She was a screw-propelled steel boat with spar-deck, of two thousand eight hundred tons burden, and five hundred horse-power. The *Mongolia* plied regularly between Brindisi and Bombay through the Suez Canal. She was one of the fastest boats of the company, and had always beaten the regulation speed of ten miles an hour between Brindisi and Suez, and nine miles and fifty-three-hundredths between Suez and Bombay.

Awaiting the arrival of the *Mongolia* were two men, walking about the quay amid the crowd of natives and foreigners who flock to this town, which was but lately a mere village, and is now assured of considerable importance in the future by M. de Lesseps's[11] great work. Of these two men, one was the British consul, resident at Suez, who, in spite of the unfavourable prognostications of the British Government and sinister predictions of the engineer, Stephenson, daily saw English ships pass through the canal, thus shortening by half the old route from England to India via the Cape of Good Hope. The other was a thin little man, fairly intelligent-looking and wiry, who kept on knitting his eyebrows with remarkable persistency. Through his long eyelashes shone a pair of very bright eyes, which he could make dull at will. At this particular moment he was showing certain signs of impatience, walking to and fro, and unable to stand still. This man's name was Fix. He was one of the English detectives who were sent to the different ports after the theft committed at the Bank of England. Fix was to keep the sharpest look-out on all travellers going through Suez, and should one of them seem suspicious, he was to shadow him until he received a warrant for his arrest. And two days before, Fix had received the description of the supposed culprit from the Chief of the Metropolitan Police. It was that of the well-dressed, gentlemanly person who had been noticed in the pay-room of the Bank.

The detective, obviously much attracted by the substantial reward held out in case of success, was therefore awaiting the arrival of the *Mongolia* with an impatience that needs no further explanation.

'I think you said she could not be long, sir?' asked Fix for the tenth time. 'No, Mr Fix, she won't be long,' replied the consul. 'She was signalled yesterday off Port Said, and the length of the canal, some ninety miles, does not count for such a fast boat. Let me tell you once more that the *Mongolia* has never failed to earn the bounty of twenty-five pounds granted by the Government for every twenty-four hours' gain over scheduled time.' 'This boat comes direct from Brindisi, does she not?' asked Fix.

'Yes, from Brindisi, where she took the Indian mail; she left Brindisi on Saturday at five p.m., so you can wait patiently; she cannot be long now. But I really fail to see how you will spot your man from the description you have received, even if he is on board the *Mongolia*.'

'Sir,' said Fix in reply, 'with these fellows it is more a case of scenting them out. It is *flair* that is required, and *flair* is a special sense in which ear, eye and nose all play a part. I have arrested more than one gentleman of the sort in my life, and, if only my thief is on board, I promise you he won't give me the slip.' 'I hope so, Mr Fix, for the robbery is a big one.' 'A glorious one,' replied the detective, with growing excitement, 'fifty-five thousand pounds! Such windfalls don't often come our way. Robbers are getting quite contemptible. The Jack

Sheppards[12] of today have no grit: they will go and get hanged for a few shillings.'

'Mr Fix,' rejoined the consul, 'I cannot hear you without heartily wishing you all success; but I say it again, with the means at your disposal, I fear you will find it no easy task. Do you realise that, according to the description you have received, the thief looks exactly like an honest man?' 'Sir,' answered the detective dogmatically, 'high-class thieves always look like honest people. You quite see that people with rascally faces have but one course open to them: they must keep straight, or they would be arrested. It is your honest-looking rogues that it is our special business to see through. This, I own, is a tough job. It ceases to be humdrum routine; it is art.'

Friend Fix had obviously a fair amount of conceit in his composition.

Meanwhile the wharf was gradually showing more signs of anima-tion. There was a growing crowd of sailor-men of divers nationalities, of traders, brokers and porters. The arrival of the boat was evidently not far off. The weather was fair, but the air cold, the wind being easterly. A few minarets stood out above the town in the pale light of the sun. Towards the south a pier over two thousand yards in length stretched like an arm along the Suez roadstead. On the surface of the Red Sea rocked several fishing boats and coasting craft, some of which still preserve the graceful mould of the ancient galley. As he moved about this motley crowd, Fix, through professional habit, gave each of the passers-by a quick but searching glance. It was then half-past ten.

'Heaven knows when this boat will get here!' he cried, when he heard the port clock strike. 'She can't be far off,' replied the consul. 'How long will she put in for at Suez?' asked Fix. 'Four hours, just long enough to coal. From Suez to Aden, at the other end of the Red Sea, it is thirteen hundred and ten miles, so they have to take in a supply of fuel.'

'And does she go direct from Suez to Bombay?' asked Fix. 'Yes, direct, without breaking bulk.' 'Well, then,' continued Fix, 'if the culprit has taken this route and this boat, he must intend to land at Suez, so as to get to the Dutch or French colonies in Asia by some other route. He cannot but know that he would not be safe in India, which is British territory.' 'Unless,' replied the consul, 'the man is a particularly cunning customer. As you know, an English criminal is always harder to find in London than he would be abroad.'

Having made this observation, which gave the detective considerable matter for reflection, the consul returned to his office close by. The police-officer, a prey to nervous impatience, remained alone with this somewhat strange feeling that the thief must be on board the *Mongolia*.

And, as a matter of fact, if the rascal had left England, intending to make for the New World, he would naturally choose the route through India, which was less watched and more difficult to watch than that of the Atlantic.

Fix was soon roused from his thoughts by the shrill signal announcing the arrival of the boat. The whole mob of porters and fellahs made a rush for the wharf, and the resulting scramble was somewhat alarming for the limbs and garments of the passengers. Some ten boats or so put out from the shore to go and meet the *Mongolia*.

Soon her huge hull was seen gliding along between the banks of the canal, and eleven o'clock struck as she cast anchor in the road, and her waste steam roared out of her escape-pipes. She had a considerable number of passengers on board, some of whom remained on the spardeck, gazing at the picturesque panorama of the town; while the majority were landed by means of the boats which had come alongside the steamer. Fix scrutinised with the utmost care every one of the passengers as he stepped ashore.

Thereupon one of them, vigorously forcing his way through the fellahs who assailed him with their offers of service, came up to him and asked with the utmost politeness if he could tell him where to find the British consulate. At the same time the traveller held out a passport for which, apparently, he wished to procure the British official's *visa*. Fix, instinctively, took the passport and glanced rapidly through the description it contained. An involuntary sign of emotion nearly escaped him. The paper shook in his hand. The description in the passport was identical with that which he had received from Scotland Yard.

'This passport is not yours, is it?' he asked. 'No,' replied the passenger, 'it is my master's.' 'Where is your master?' 'He has remained on board.' 'He will have to go to the consulate in person,' rejoined the detective, 'in order to prove his identity.' 'Oh, is that necessary?' 'Absolutely necessary.' 'Where is this office?' 'There, at the corner of the square,' replied Fix, pointing to a house two hundred yards away. 'All right then, I will fetch my master, but he won't be best pleased to have the bother of coming.'

Having said this, the passenger bowed and returned to the liner.

CHAPTER VII

Which once more shows the futility of passports for police purposes

THE DETECTIVE MADE his way briskly down the quay to the consulate, where his urgent request to be admitted to the consul's presence was granted.

'Sir,' said he, going straight to the point, 'I have strong reasons for presuming that the man I am after is a passenger on board the *Mongolia.*' He then related the incident of the passport.

'Well, Mr Fix,' replied the consul, 'I should rather like to see the rascal's face. But I dare say he won't show himself in my office, if he is the sort of man you think him. A thief does not care to leave traces of his itinerary behind him; moreover, passports are no longer obligatory.'

'Sir,' replied the detective, 'if he is the clever fellow I take him for, he will come.'

'To have his passport *visaed?*' 'Yes, passports have but one use; to be a nuisance to honest people and assist the flight of rogues. I can assure you this passport will be in order, but I hope you will not *visa* it.' 'Why not?' answered the consul. 'If the passport is all right, I have no right to refuse my *visa.*' 'Still, sir, I am bound to keep the man here until I get a warrant from London.' 'Ah, that is your business, Mr Fix; but I cannot . . .'

The consul's sentence was not finished; there was a knock at the door and the office-boy introduced two strangers, one of whom was no other than the servant who had spoken to the detective on the quay. With him was his master, who produced his passport, and, in a few words, requested the favour of the consul's *visa.* The latter took the passport and read it attentively, while Fix observed or rather greedily eyed the stranger from a corner of the room.

'You are Mr Phileas Fogg?' queried the consul, when he had finished reading the passport. 'Yes.' 'And this man is your servant?' 'Yes. A Frenchman called Passepartout.' 'Do you come from London?' 'Yes.' 'And you are going to . . . ?' 'Bombay.' 'Very good, sir. You know that a *visa* is a formality of no value, and that travellers are no longer required to show passports?' 'I am aware of this, sir,' replied Phileas Fogg, 'but I want to prove by your *visa* that I passed through Suez.'

'All right, sir.'

The consul then signed and dated the passport, and stamped it with his official seal.

Mr Fogg paid the required fee, bowed stiffly, and went out, followed by his servant.

'Well?' said the detective. 'Well,' said the consul, 'he looks a perfectly honest man.' 'May be,' replied Fix, 'but that is not the point. In your opinion, is this phlegmatic gentleman in every feature the exact picture of the thief whose description I hold?' 'I agree, but, as you know, all descriptions . . . ' 'I am going to make quite sure,' broke in Fix. 'The servant, I should say, is less inscrutable than the master. He is a Frenchman, too, so won't be able to keep his mouth shut. Goodbye for the present, consul.'

Meanwhile Mr Fogg, after leaving the consulate, made his way to the quay, gave some orders to his servant, took a boat and returned to the *Mongolia*. He then went to his cabin and took up his note-book, in which were jotted down the following memoranda:

'Left London, Wednesday, October 2nd, 8.45 p.m.

'Arrived Paris, Thursday, October 3rd, 7.20 a.m.

'Left Paris, Thursday, 8.40 a.m

'Arrived Turin, by Mont-Cenis, Friday, October 4th, 6.35 a.m.

'Left Turin, Friday, 7.20 a.m.

'Arrived Brindisi, Saturday, October 5th, 4 p.m.

'Sailed on the *Mongolia*, Saturday, 5 p.m.

'Arrived Suez, Wednesday, October 9th, 11 a.m.

'Total hours spent, 158 or days, 6.'

Mr Fogg wrote down these dates in an itinerary divided into columns, showing, as from the 2nd of October to the 21st of December, the month, the day of the month, the scheduled and actual time of arrival at each principal place – Paris, Brindisi, Suez, Bombay, Calcutta, Singapore, Hong-Kong, Yokohama, San Francisco, New York, Liverpool, London – and enabling him to keep a record of his gain or loss on arrival at each stage of the journey. This methodical time-table contained every necessary information, so that Mr Fogg always knew whether he was gaining or losing time.

On this Wednesday, October 9, he noted down his arrival at Suez, by which, as it was in accordance with the scheduled time, he neither gained nor lost. Then he ordered lunch in his cabin. The thought of going ashore to see the town never occurred to him, for he was one of those Englishmen who, when travelling, leave their servants to do their sight-seeing for them.

CHAPTER VIII

In which Passepartout talks rather more freely, perhaps, than is advisable

FIX SOON CAUGHT UP Passepartout on the quay; he was strolling and looking about him, feeling under no obligation to deny himself the pleasure of seeing things just because his master took no interest in them.

'Well, my friend,' said Fix, going up to him, 'is your passport *visaed?*' 'Oh, it's you, is it, sir?' replied the Frenchman. 'Yes, everything is in order, thank you.' 'You are having a look round?' 'Yes, but we are travelling at such a pace that I seem to be going about in a dream. So this is Suez?' 'Yes.' 'In Egypt?' 'Yes, in Egypt, certainly.' 'And in Africa?' 'Of course.'

'In Africa!' repeated Passepartout. 'It's beyond me! Just think, sir, I looked upon Paris as the end of our journey, and absolutely all the time I had to renew acquaintance with the great capital was from twenty minutes past seven to forty minutes past eight in the morning, between the Northern and Lyons stations, through the windows of a cab and in pelting rain! I wanted to see Père Lachaise[13] again and the circus in the Champs-Élysées.'

'Are you in such a desperate hurry, then?' asked the detective. 'I am not, but my master is. By the way, I must buy some socks and shirts. We came away without any trunks, with just a carpet-bag.' 'I will take you to a bazaar where you will find anything you want.' 'Really, sir, this is most kind of you.'

And they walked off together, Passepartout talking away all the time.

'There is one thing I must not do,' he said; 'that is, miss the boat.' 'There is plenty of time,' answered Fix, 'it is only twelve o'clock.' Passepartout took out his big watch. 'Twelve o'clock!' he exclaimed. 'Never! it is eight minutes to ten!' 'Your watch is slow,' replied Fix. 'My watch! A family watch which has been handed down from my great-grandfather! It doesn't vary five minutes in twelve months. It's a perfect chronometer.' 'I see what's the matter,' replied Fix. 'Your time is London time, which you have kept, and which is about two hours behind that of Suez. You must be careful to set your watch by the midday hour of each country.' 'I meddle with my watch! Never!' cried

Passepartout. 'If you don't, it will never agree with the sun.' 'So much the worse for the sun, sir! The sun will be at fault, then, not my watch.' And the honest fellow replaced his watch in his pocket with a gesture of defiant pride.

A few moments later Fix was saying to him: 'So you left London in a great hurry?' 'I should say we did! Last Wednesday, Mr Fogg came home from his club at eight o'clock – a thing he never does – and three-quarters of an hour later we were off.' 'But where is your master going?' 'Right ahead all the time; he is going round the world.' 'Round the world?' cried Fix. 'Yes, in eighty days! He says it's for a bet. But, between us, I don't believe a word of it. The thing would be too absurd. There must be some other reason.'

'Your Mr Fogg is an odd sort of fellow, I see.' 'It seems so.' 'I suppose he is a wealthy man?' 'Oh, yes. He is taking with him a large sum of money in brand-new banknotes. And he spends freely on the way. Why, he has promised a handsome reward to the engineer of the *Mongolia* if we get to Bombay well in advance of time.'

'You have known your master for some time, I suppose?' 'No, I have not,' answered Passepartout; 'I entered his service on the very day of our departure.'

One can easily imagine what effect these replies were bound to produce on the detective's highly-excited mind.

The hurried departure from London a short time after the robbery, the large amount of money taken with him by Fogg, his anxiety to get to distant countries as fast as possible, this cover of a wild wager, all inevitably confirmed Fix in his theory. He continued to make the Frenchman talk and was soon convinced that his master was really a stranger to him, living to himself in London, where he was reputed to be rich, though no one knew whence this wealth came, and that he was a mysterious, inscrutable fellow and so on. At the same time, Fix acquired the certainty that Phileas Fogg would not escape at Suez, but was really going on to Bombay.

'Is Bombay a long way off?' asked Passepartout. 'It is some way off,' answered the detective. 'You will have to put in another ten days on the sea.' 'And where do you place Bombay?' 'In India.' 'In Asia?' 'Of course.'

'The deuce! – I must tell you, I have a great worry on my mind, my burner.'

'What burner?' 'My gas-burner. I forgot to turn it off, and the gas is burning at my expense. Now I reckon this costs me two shillings every twenty-four hours, exactly sixpence more than I earn; and you can see that if the journey lasts any time . . .'

Whether Fix understood what Passepartout said about his gas trouble is very doubtful, as, by this time, he was not listening; he was making up his mind.

They now came to the bazaar, where he left the Frenchman to make his purchases, telling him to be sure not to miss the boat; he then hurried back to find the consul.

Feeling perfectly sure that he was right, Fix was now quite cool. 'Sir,' he said to the consul, 'it is an absolute certainty! I've got him. He wants to be taken for an eccentric bloke who has set his heart on going round the world in eighty days.' 'A cunning fellow, eh?' replied the consul. 'He expects to get back to London, after putting all the police agents of both continents off his track.' 'We shall see about that,' replied Fix. 'Are you not making a mistake?' the consul asked once more. 'I am making no mistake.' 'In that case, why did this thief insist on proving by means of a *visa* that he had been to Suez?'

'That I cannot say,' replied the detective, 'but listen to this.' And in a few words he made known to the consul the telling points of his conversation with Fogg's servant.

'Yes,' said the consul, 'to all appearances the man is guilty. What do you propose to do?'

'Send a telegram to London for the immediate dispatch of a warrant of arrest to Bombay, take a berth on the *Mongolia*, shadow my thief to India, and there, on British soil, speak to him politely, my warrant in one hand, and the other on his shoulder.'

Having uttered these words with cool decision, the detective took leave of the consul and went to the telegraph-office, whence he sent to the head of the Metropolitan Police the sensational message with which the reader is acquainted.

A quarter of an hour later, Fix stepped on board the *Mongolia*, holding a travelling-bag in his hand; he had no other luggage, but plenty of money; and ere long the powerful steamship was running at full speed over the waters of the Red Sea.

CHAPTER IX

In which the Red Sea and the Indian Ocean prove favourable to the designs of Phileas Fogg

BETWEEN SUEZ AND ADEN the distance is exactly thirteen hundred and ten miles, and by the conditions of the company the boats are allowed one hundred and thirty-eight hours to cross it. The *Mongolia*, stoked as she was with exceptional zeal, was making such a quick passage that she would be in advance of her time.

The greater part of the passengers taken on board at Brindisi were bound for India.

Some were going to Bombay, others to Calcutta, via Bombay, for, now that a railway runs from one side to the other of the Indian Peninsula, it is no longer necessary to sail round past Ceylon.

Among these passengers of the *Mongolia* were a number of Civil Service men and officers of all grades; some of the latter were in the regular British forces, others commanded the native sepoy troops. They were all well paid, though now under the British Government, which has assumed the rights and liabilities of the East India Company: second-lieutenants get £280 a-year, brigadiers £2400, and generals £4000. And the pay of Civil Servants is higher still.

Besides these men in Government employ, there were a certain number of young Englishmen well supplied with funds, on their way to found business establishments in distant parts. So the food on board the *Mongolia* was good and plentiful. The purser, the company's trusted servant, as important as the captain, did things lavishly. At breakfast, at two o'clock lunch, at half-past five dinner, at eight o'clock supper, the tables were loaded with dishes of fresh meat and entremets supplied from the boat's larder.

There were a few lady passengers. They changed their dresses twice daily; and there was music, and dancing even, when the sea allowed it.

But the Red Sea is liable to sudden and violent changes and very often rough, like all those long, narrow gulfs. When the wind blew from the Asiatic or the Arabian coast, the *Mongolia*, like a long screw-propelled spindle, being caught athwart, rolled horribly. At such times the ladies vanished; pianos were silent; songs and dances ceased at the same instant. Yet, despite squall and swell, the steamer, impelled by its powerful engines, lost no time as she forged ahead to the Straits of Bab-el-Mandeb.

You wonder what Phileas Fogg was doing all this time. You probably think he was anxious and worrying over weather conditions that might impede the ship's progress, and the raging seas that might affect the engines; in short, over all possible damage that might compel the *Mongolia* to put into some port, thereby endangering the success of his journey.

But there was nothing of the sort, or at any rate, if he thought of these possibilities, he showed not the least sign of it.

He was ever the same impassive gentleman, the imperturbable member of the Reform Club, upon whom no incident or accident could come as a surprise. He appeared to be just as little affected as the ship's chronometers. He was seldom seen on deck, and seemed to feel but little curiosity to observe that Red Sea, so full of memories, the scene of the first historic happenings of mankind. He felt no interest in the curious towns scattered on its shores, and whose picturesque outlines occasionally stood out on the skyline. He did not even give a thought to the perils of this Arabic gulf of which the old historians, Strabo, Arrian, Arthemidorus and Edrisi,[14] always spoke with dread, and upon which, in the days of old, navigators never ventured without first commending their voyage to the protection of the gods with propitiatory sacrifices.

How was the whimsical fellow spending his time within the *Mongolia*'s precincts? In the first place, as neither rolling nor pitching could put such a marvellously well-constituted machine out of order, he fed heartily four times a day; then he played whist, for he had found partners as infatuated with the game as himself: a collector of taxes on his way to his station at Goa, a clergyman, the Reverend Decimus Smith, returning to Bombay; and a brigadier-general of the English Army, who was rejoining his brigade at Benares. These three passengers were just as passionately fond of whist as Mr Fogg, and they played on for hours as silently absorbed as himself.

As for Passepartout, he was quite immune from sea-sickness; he had a cabin forward and, like his master, took his meals with scrupulous regularity. He was getting reconciled to the voyage in such conditions, and even began to enjoy it. He was well fed, had good quarters, saw new scenes, and, moreover, felt pretty confident this foolery would end at Bombay.

On October 10, the day after they left Suez, Passepartout was rather pleased to see on deck the obliging person to whom he had applied for information on landing in Egypt.

'If I am not mistaken,' he said, accosting him with his most genial smile, 'you are the gentleman who so kindly piloted me about in Suez?' 'Yes, of course,' replied the detective, 'I know you all right! You are the servant of that odd English fellow.' 'Quite right, Mr . . . ?'

'Fix; my name is Fix.' 'Mr Fix,' replied Passepartout, 'I am delighted to find you on board. Where are you going?' 'To Bombay, like yourself.' 'Is this your first trip to India?' 'No,' replied Fix. 'I have been there several times; I am in the service of the Peninsular and Oriental Company.' 'Then you know the country?' 'Yes, pretty well,' answered Fix, who was anxious not to commit himself.

'I suppose India is a curious sort of place?'

'Very; mosques, minarets, temples, fakirs, pagodas, tigers, snakes, Hindu dancing-girls! But it is to be hoped you will have time to see the country.' 'I hope so, Mr Fix. You see, no sane man can be expected to spend his life hopping from a steamer into a train, and from a train into a steamer again, just to go round the world in eighty days; there's no sense in it. All these antics will come to an end at Bombay, you may be sure.'

'And is Mr Fogg quite well?' asked Fix, in the most natural tone. 'Very well indeed, Mr Fix, and so am I. A ravenous ogre couldn't eat more than I do! It's the sea-air.' 'I never see your master on deck.' 'Never; he never wants to see anything.' 'You know, Mr Passepartout, this supposed tour in eighty days might be a blind concealing some secret mission – a diplomatic mission, possibly.' 'Honour bright, Mr Fix, I have not the least notion, I confess, and the fact is, I wouldn't give half-a-crown to know.'

This was the first of many similar conversations between Passepartout and Fix, as the detective was anxious to be on the best of terms with Fogg's servant. It might prove useful on occasion. Thus it was that he frequently treated him to a few glasses of whisky or pale ale, which the good fellow accepted unhesitatingly, even returning the compliment, so as not to lag in politeness, and thinking Fix a right-down good fellow.

Meanwhile the liner was making rapid progress. On the 13th, Mocha was sighted, peering out of its girdle of ruined walls, over which a few date-palms stood out in their greenery. In the distance, amid the mountains stretched wide fields of coffee trees. When he gazed upon this far-famed place, Passepartout was delighted; he even thought that its circular walls and a dismantled fort with the outline of a handle, gave it the look of an enormous coffee-cup.[15]

During the following night, the *Mongolia* crossed the Straits of Babel-Mandeb, Arabic for 'gate of tears,' and on the morrow (14th), she put in at Steamer Point, north-west of Aden roadstead, in order to take in a fresh supply of coal.

This fuelling of steamers at such distances from the centres of production is a very serious matter. For the Peninsular Company alone it means an expense of eight hundred thousand pounds a-year. For coal depôts had to be established in several ports, and the coal comes to four pounds a ton. The *Mongolia* had another sixteen hundred and fifty miles to run before reaching Bombay, and it would take her four hours to fill her coal-bunkers at Steamer Point. But this delay could not have the slightest effect on Phileas Fogg's programme, for he had taken it into account. Moreover, the *Mongolia* arrived at Aden on the evening of the 14th, and she was not due before the morning of the 15th, a gain of fifteen hours.

Mr Fogg and his servant went ashore, as Mr Fogg wished to have his passport *visaed*. Fix followed him without being noticed. As soon as the passport was in order, Phileas Fogg returned on board and continued his interrupted game of whist.

Passepartout went his way, and, as was his wont, sauntered about among the Somalis, Banyans, Parsees, Jews, Arabs, and Europeans who make up Aden's population of twenty-five thousand inhabitants. He admired the fortifications which make this town the Gibraltar of the Indian Ocean, and magnificent cisterns on which the English engineers were still at work, two thousand years after the engineers of King Solomon.

'Very curious, very curious,' said Passepartout to himself, returning on board. 'I can see that a man who wants to see something new loses nothing by travelling.'

At six o'clock in the evening the *Mongolia* was churning up the waters of the roadstead, and was soon running at full speed over the Indian Ocean. She was allowed a hundred and sixty-eight hours between Aden and Bombay. And the sea proved favourable, as the wind blew steadily from the north-west. She was able to put on all sail, which added considerably to her steam-power. Thus steadied, the ship had less roll on. The ladies, in fresh toilets, came up on deck, and singing and dancing went on again. The passage was quite pleasant, and Passepartout was delighted with the genial companion whom chance had put in his way.

On Sunday, October 20, about noon, the Indian coast was sighted, and two hours later the pilot came on board. On the horizon, a background of hills, showing up against the sky, made a fitting frame for the picture; and soon the rows of palms which spread their foliage over the town came clearly into view. The *Mongolia* made her way into this roadstead, formed by the islands of Salsette, Colaba, Elephanta and Butcher, and at half-past four she was brought alongside the quays of Bombay.

Phileas Fogg was at that moment finishing the thirty-third rubber of the day; and he and his partner, by a bold move, took all thirteen tricks, and ended a fine passage with a splendid slam.

The *Mongolia* was not due at Bombay before the 22nd. She arrived on the 20th. This constituted a gain of two days since Phileas Fogg's departure from London, and, methodically, he noted it down in his itinerary, in the column of gains.

CHAPTER X

In which Passepartout is only too fortunate in getting off with the loss of his shoes

EVERYBODY KNOWS THAT India, that great reversed triangle, with its base in the north and apex in the south, has an area of one million four hundred thousand square miles, over which is unequally distributed a population of one hundred and eighty millions of inhabitants.

The British Government exercises effective power over a certain portion of this huge country; there is a governor-general at Calcutta, a governor at Madras, another at Bombay and in Bengal, and a lieuten-ant-governor at Agra.

But British India, properly so-called, has an area of not more than seven hundred thousand square miles, with a population of from a hundred to a hundred and ten millions. No further proof is needed to show that there is still a considerable part of the country over which the Queen's Government has no authority. In fact, in the dominions of certain fierce and dreaded rajahs of the interior Hindu independence is still complete.

The first English settlement was founded in 1756, on the site now occupied by the city of Madras. From that time till the year of the great Mutiny of the sepoys the famous East India Company was all-powerful. It gradually annexed the various provinces obtained from the rajahs in return for annuities, of which little or nothing was paid them. It appointed its governor-general and all its servants, civil or military; but the East India Company is no more, and the British possessions in India are under the immediate control of the Crown. Thus it is that the general appearance, the manners and ethnographic divisions of the peninsula show day by day a tendency to change.

Formerly travellers in India used all the old means of locomotion; they went on foot, on horseback, in carts, wheel-barrows, palanquins, on men's backs, in coaches, and so on. But now fast steamboats ply on the Indus and the Ganges, and one can cross the peninsula from Bombay to Calcutta by rail in the short space of three days; and the main line is joined by numerous branch lines all along the route.

This railway does not cross India in a straight line. The distance between Bombay and Calcutta as the crow flies is not more than one thousand to eleven hundred miles; trains of average speed would not take three days to cross it; but the distance is increased by a third, at least, by going round as far as Allahabad in the north.

Roughly the great Indian Peninsular Railway runs in the following way. Leaving the island of Bombay, it goes through Salsette, crosses over to the continent opposite Tannah, clears the range of the Western Ghauts, then runs in a north-east direction as far as Burhanpur, dashes through the almost independent territory of Bundelkhand, goes up to Allahabad, bends its course eastward, meets the Ganges at Benares, then leaves it at no great distance, and striking down again south-eastward through Burdwan and the French town of Chandernagore, has its terminus at Calcutta.

The passengers of the *Mongolia* landed at half-past four, and the train would leave Bombay for Calcutta at eight exactly.

So Mr Fogg, after saying goodbye to his whist partners, left the liner, sent his servant to make a few purchases, giving him strict injunctions to be at the station before eight, and with that regular step of his, that marked the seconds like the pendulum of an astronomic clock, made his way to the passport office.

The town hall, the magnificent library, the forts and docks, the cotton market, the bazaars, the mosques and synagogues, the Armenian churches, the splendid pagoda on Malabar Hill, with its two polygonal towers, to all these marvels of Bombay he gave not a thought. The masterpieces of Elephanta, the mysterious hypogea hidden away south-east of the harbour, those admirable remains of Buddhist architecture, the grottoes of Salsette Island, could all be treated with like indifference.

Phileas Fogg saw absolutely nothing.

On leaving the passport office, he quietly betook himself to the station and ordered dinner. Among the dishes there was a certain stew of 'native rabbit,' which the host thought fit to recommend to him in words of especial praise.

Phileas Fogg took some of this stew and tasted it with scrupulous care; but, in spite of the highly-spiced sauce, he found it abominable. He rang for the host, and, looking him in the face, he said to him, 'Is this rabbit, sir?' 'Yes, my lord,' the rascal replied without wincing, 'jungle rabbit.'

'Do you mean to say this rabbit didn't mew when it was killed?'

'Mew, my lord! a rabbit mew! I swear to you. . .'

'Sir host,' returned Mr Fogg, frigidly, 'do not swear, and remember this: in India, cats were once held to be sacred animals. Those were happy days.'

'For the cat, my lord?'

'And possibly for travellers too!'

Having said this much, Mr Fogg quietly went on with his dinner.

Like Mr Fogg, and very soon after, Fix left the *Mongolia*, and hurried to the head-quarters of the Bombay police, where he made himself known as a detective. He then explained the nature of the business which had been entrusted to him, his position with respect to the supposed culprit, and inquired whether a warrant had been received from London. The answer was in the negative. Of course, the warrant having been dispatched after Fogg's departure, could not have arrived by then.

Fix was sorely put out. He tried to induce the chief of the Bombay police to give him a warrant for Fogg's arrest. This the chief of police would not do, as the case concerned the London police, which alone was empowered by law to issue a warrant. Such rigid principle and strict observance of legality are quite in accordance with English life, which will not tolerate arbitrary action where individual liberty is concerned. Fix did not insist; he realised that he must resign himself to wait for the warrant, but determined not to lose sight of the inscrutable rascal for a moment while he stayed in Bombay. Like Passepartout, Fix felt convinced that Fogg would stay there some time, and meanwhile the warrant would arrive.

Nevertheless, after receiving his master's last orders on landing, Passepartout understood perfectly well that what had happened at Suez and Paris would happen at Bombay: that this was not the end of their journey, which would be pursued at least as far as Calcutta, possibly farther. And he began to wonder whether this wager of Mr Fogg's was not absolutely serious after all, and whether he who yearned for a life of repose was not really being compelled by fate to move round the world in eighty days.

Having purchased a few shirts and socks, he was strolling in the streets of Bombay, which were exceptionally crowded with the lower orders. In the midst of Europeans of all nationalities, there were

Persians with pointed caps, Bunhyas with round turbans, Sindes with square bonnets, Armenians in flowing robes, Parsees with black mitres. It just happened that the Parsees or Guebres were observing a festival. These direct descendants of the followers of Zoroaster are the most industrious, most highly civilised, most intelligent and most austere of the Hindus, and at the present day the wealthiest native merchants of Bombay are Parsees. They were celebrating a sort of religious carnival, with processions, and entertainments at which dancing-girls clothed in pink gauze, embossed with gold and silver, danced to the sound of viols and the clang of tambourines with marvellous grace, and perfect decency withal.

Needless to say, Passepartout watched these ceremonies with wide-staring eyes and gaping mouth; he was so bent on losing nothing of it all, that his whole demeanour and expression portrayed the greenest booby one can imagine.

Unhappily for himself and for his master, whose venture he ran the risk of wrecking, his curiosity carried him to improper lengths.

When he had seen something of this Parsee carnival, Passepartout, on his way to the station, passed in front of the beautiful pagoda on Malabar Hill, and an unlucky thought moved him to see its interior. Now there are certain Indian pagodas which Christians are absolutely forbidden to enter, and into which even the faithful may not go without first leaving their shoes outside. Both these facts were quite unknown to Passepartout.

It should be mentioned in this connection that the British Government, from sound policy, not only respects the native religions, but enforces respect for the most trivial of native religious observances, and punishes severely anyone who offends against them.

Having entered the Malabar pagoda in all innocence, and like any simple tourist, Passepartout was gazing in admiration upon the dazzling tinsel of Brahmin ornamentation, when all of a sudden he was knocked down on the sacred flagging. Three furious-looking priests flung themselves upon him, wrenched off his shoes and socks, and proceeded to belabour him, uttering savage yells the while. The Frenchman, powerful and agile, was on his feet in a moment; with one blow of his fist he knocked down one of his adversaries, and with a kick he sent another sprawling, the long robes by which they were hampered making this the easier; then rushing out of the pagoda as fast as his legs would carry him, he soon left a long way behind him the third Hindu, who had hastened to give chase, hounding on the crowd as he went.

At five minutes to eight, a few minutes only before the departure of the train, Passepartout reached the station, hatless and barefooted, and without the parcel containing his purchases, which had been lost in the scuffle.

Fix had followed Fogg to the station, and was there on the platform. He now perceived that the rogue was leaving Bombay, and at once made up his mind to accompany him as far as Calcutta, or farther, if necessary. Passepartout did not see Fix, who stood in a dark recess, but when he gave his master a hurried account of his adventures, Fix overheard him.

'I trust you will not do this sort of thing again,' was all Phileas Fogg said in reply, as he took his seat in the train.

The poor fellow, barefooted and utterly dejected, followed his master without saying a word.

Fix was on the point of stepping into another carriage, when a sudden idea made him there and then change his mind and stay.

'I don't go,' he said to himself. 'This is an offence committed on Indian soil. I've got him.'

At that moment the engine whistled loud, and the train vanished in the darkness of the night.

CHAPTER XI

In which Phileas Fogg buys a mount at a fabulous price

THE TRAIN STARTED at the scheduled time. There was a fair number of passengers, among whom were a few officers, some Indian Civil Servants, and opium and indigo merchants, whose presence was required by their business in the eastern part of the peninsula.

Passepartout was travelling in the same compartment as his master, and a third passenger faced them, seated in one of the opposite corners. This was Sir Francis Cromarty, one of the men who had played whist with Mr Fogg during the passage from Suez to Bombay, now on his way back to his men in cantonments near Benares.

Sir Francis Cromarty, a tall, fair man of some fifty years of age, had greatly distinguished himself in the last sepoy revolt.

He had gone to India in his youth, and had lived there ever since, with the exception of a few brief visits to his native country; so India was practically as much his home as if he had been a Hindu. Being a man of considerable learning, he would readily have supplied Phileas

Fogg with information concerning the customs, history and organisa-
tion of India, if Phileas Fogg had been the sort of man to ask. But
Phileas Fogg had no desire for information. He was not travelling, he
was merely describing a circumference. He was a solid body moving
through an orbit around the terrestrial globe, in obedience to the laws
of rational mechanics. At this particular moment he was mentally
reckoning up the hours spent since his departure from London, and,
had not all useless manifestation been quite alien to his nature, he
would have rubbed his hands for satisfaction.

The oddity of his fellow-traveller had not escaped Sir Francis
Cromarty, although his sole opportunity for observing him had been
during the game and between two rubbers. Well might he ask himself,
then, whether a human heart actually beat under this cold exterior, and
whether Phileas Fogg had a soul alive to the beauties of Nature and to
moral aspirations. He was not sure. Of all the queer human specimens
the brigadier-general had ever come across, none could be compared
to this product of the exact sciences.

In talking to Sir Francis Cromarty, Phileas Fogg had made no secret
of his projected tour around the world, and of the conditions of the
enterprise. To the brigadier this wager seemed nothing but a silly
whim, which could serve no useful purpose, and was therefore lacking
in that *transire benefaciendo*[16] which should guide every sensible man's
judgement. Should this strange gentleman go on as he was doing, he
would obviously pass through life without having done any good to
himself or anybody else. An hour after leaving Bombay, the train had
passed over the viaducts, crossed Salsette Island, and was speeding on
its way over the continent. At Callyan it left on the right the branch
line which descends through Kandallah and Poona towards south-
eastern India, and came to Pauwell station. There it entered the far-
spreading mountain system of the Western Ghauts, whose base is of
trap rock and basalt, and whose highest peaks are densely wooded.
From time to time, Sir Francis Cromarty and Phileas Fogg exchanged
a few words, and now, renewing the conversation which constantly
flagged, the brigadier said, 'A few years ago, Mr Fogg, you would have
been so delayed here that your journey would probably not have ended
at the appointed time.'

'Why, Sir Francis?' 'Because the railway did not go beyond the foot
of these mountains, which had to be crossed in palanquins or on the
backs of ponies to Kandallah station on the other side.' 'Such a delay
would not have upset my plans in the least,' replied Mr Fogg. 'I have
carefully anticipated the possibility of certain obstacles.'

'All the same, Mr Fogg,' returned the brigadier-general, 'you are in danger of having very serious unpleasantness to face in connection with this fellow's adventure.'

Passepartout, his feet wrapped up in his travelling-rug, was sound asleep and never dreamt that he was the subject of conversation. 'The British Government is extremely severe, and rightly so, on this kind of offence,' resumed Sir Francis. 'It makes a very special point of compelling respect for the religious customs of the Hindus, and if your servant had been caught . . . ' 'Well, Sir Francis,' replied Mr Fogg, 'if he had been caught, he would have been condemned and punished, and then would have returned to Europe without more ado. I fail to see in what way this matter could have delayed his master.' Here the conversation dropped again.

During the night the train crossed the Ghauts, passed through Nassik, and on the morrow, October 21, it ran at high speed through the comparatively flat country of the Khandeish. The land was well cultivated and dotted with villages, above which the minarets of the pagodas stood out like the church steeples of Europe. This fertile region was watered by a number of small streams, most of them direct or indirect tributaries of the Godavari.

Passepartout, now awake, was looking out, and could not believe he was crossing the land of the Hindus in a train of the great Peninsular Railway. The thing seemed fantastic. And yet it was a fact! The engine, driven by an Englishman and fuelled with English coal, belched out its smoke over the plantations of cotton, coffee, nutmeg, clove and pepper, while the steam wound its spirals round clumps of palm trees, among which were seen picturesque bungalows, here and there a sort of derelict monastery, called *vihari*, and marvellous temples decked in all the inexhaustible wealth of ornamentation of Indian architecture. Then, stretching out of sight, lay a vast expanse of jungle, the home of abounding snakes and tigers, terrified by the snorting screech of the engine; and after this the forests cleft by the line, and still frequented by elephants, that gazed with wistful eye as the train rushed past in its dishevelled flurry.

In the course of that morning, beyond Malligam station, the travellers crossed the fatal country so often stained with blood by the votaries of the goddess Kali. At no great distance rose Ellora with its beautiful pagodas, and far-famed Aurungabad, fierce Aurungzeb's capital, now no more than the chief town of one of the provinces detached from the Nizam's dominions. It was over this region that Feringhea, chief of the Thugs, king of the Stranglers, exerted his despotic power. These assassins bound together as members of an association that defied all detection, strangled victims of all ages in honour of the goddess of Death, without ever shedding blood, and there was a time when one could not have dug up a single spot on this soil without finding a corpse. The British Government has certainly found means to effect a considerable reduction in the number of these murders, but the dread association still exists and is still at work.

At half-past twelve the train stopped at Burhanpur, and Passepartout was able to buy a pair of Indian slippers ornamented with false pearls, for which he gave an exorbitant price, and which he proceeded to put on with unconcealed vanity. After a hasty lunch, our travellers started for Assurghur, running for a short time along the bank of the Tapti, a small river that empties itself into the Gulf of Cambray, near Surat.

Passepartout's state of mind at this juncture claims our attention. Up to the moment when he reached Bombay, he believed, not without some show of reason, that Bombay would be the end of it all. But now that he was being whisked along at full speed by rail across India, a sudden change came over him. He was the old Passepartout once more, full of the spirit of adventure and the wild imaginings of his youth. He began to take his master's project seriously, the bet became a reality, with this journey around the world within the strictly limited time as a logical consequence. He there and then began to worry over possible delays and such accidents as might happen on the way. He became, so to say, a party to this wager, and was much perturbed at the thought of the possible consequences of his unpardonable foolery of the day before. And, being much less unemotional than Mr Fogg, he was much more anxious. He kept counting the passing days, cursed the train whenever it stopped, and accused it of crawling, mentally blaming his master for not having promised the engine-driver a tip. The good fellow did not know that, while this was possible on the boat, it could not be done on the railway, where the rate of going is fixed by regulations. Toward evening they entered the defiles of the Sutpur Mountains, which separate Khaidish territory from Bundelkhand.

On the morrow, October 22, in reply to a question from Sir Francis Cromarty, Passepartout looked at his watch and said it was three o'clock in the morning. And, as this precious watch was still set by the Greenwich meridian, now some seventy-seven degrees west of them, it was, and was likely to be, four hours slow. Sir Francis corrected Passepartout's time, repeating what Fix had already told him. He tried to make him see that the watch should be set by each new meridian, and that, as he was constantly advancing eastward, that is to say meeting the sun, the days were shorter by as many times four minutes as there were degrees travelled through. The brigadier-general's explan-ation, whether understood or not, was completely thrown away on Passepartout, who obstinately refused to put his watch on. The stubborn fellow, obsessed by this perfectly harmless mania, kept it ever at London time.

At eight o'clock in the morning, the train stopped fifteen miles beyond Rothal, in the middle of an extensive glade, on the border of which were a few bungalows and workmen's huts. The guard in charge of the train passed along the carriages shouting, 'All change! All change!'

Phileas Fogg looked at Sir Francis Cromarty, who seemed amazed at this halt in the heart of a forest of tamarinds and khajours. Passepartout, equally surprised, jumped down on the line and came back almost at once shouting, 'Sir, that's the end of the railway!'

'Whatever do you mean?' asked Sir Francis Cromarty. 'I mean that the train does not go any farther!' The brigadier-general got out at once, and Phileas Fogg got out too, but in a leisurely way. Both questioned the guard. 'Where are we?' asked Sir Francis. 'At Kholby hamlet,' answered the guard. 'Do we stop here?' 'Of course; the railway isn't finished.' 'Not finished; what!' 'There is a section of some fifty miles to be laid from here to Allahabad, where the line begins again.'

'But the papers announced the opening of the line right through!'

'Well, sir, the papers made a mistake.'

'But you issue tickets from Bombay to Calcutta!' said Sir Francis Cromarty, who was getting angry.

'Certainly,' replied the guard, 'but the passengers are aware that they will have to find means of transport from Kholby to Allahabad.'

Sir Francis was furious; and Passepartout would have felled the guard with pleasure, though the guard had nothing to do with it. He dared not look at his master.

'Sir Francis,' said Mr Fogg quietly, 'if you are agreeable, we will set about procuring the means of getting to Allahabad.'

'This sort of delay, Mr Fogg, will fatally affect your interests.'

'No, Sir Francis; it was foreseen.'

'Do you mean to say that you knew that the line . . . ?' 'Not at all, but I knew that some obstacle or other would crop up on my way. Now there is no particular damage done. I have two days to the good, which I must sacrifice. There is a boat leaving Calcutta for Hong-Kong at noon on the 25th, today is the 22nd; we shall get to Calcutta in time.' This reply was made with such perfect assurance that there was nothing more to be said.

It was only too true that there was no railway or sign of one beyond this place. The papers are like certain watches that have a craze for being fast. They had prematurely announced the completion of the railway. The majority of the travellers knew of this break in the line; on getting out of the train, they at once proceeded to secure every kind of conveyance to be found in the little town; four-wheeled palki-garis, carts drawn by zebus, a sort of humped oxen, travelling-cars that looked like pagodas on wheels, palanquins, ponies, all these and other vehicles were pressed into service. The result was that Mr Fogg and Sir Francis Cromarty, after looking everywhere, came back having found nothing.

'I shall walk,' said Phileas Fogg.

Passepartout, coming up at this moment, heard him, and made an expressive grimace, as he looked down at his gorgeous but flimsy slippers. Very fortunately he too had been trying to find something, and, speaking with some diffidence, he said, 'Sir, I think I have found a conveyance.' 'What is it?' 'An elephant! An elephant belonging to an Indian who lives but a hundred yards from here.' 'Let us go and see the elephant,' replied Mr Fogg.

Five minutes later, Phileas Fogg, Sir Francis Cromarty and Passepartout reached a hut adjoining a paddock with a very high paling. The hut contained an Indian, and the paddock an elephant. At their request, the Indian took Mr Fogg and his two companions into the paddock. There they found an animal, that was only half-domesticated, and that its owner had reared, not as a beast of burden, but as a beast of combat. With that object in view, he had begun to alter the naturally gentle disposition of the elephant so as to bring him gradually to that intense state of fury which the Hindus term *mulsh*. This he did by feeding him for three months on sugar and butter. The treatment may appear unlikely to produce such a result, but it is none the less used with success by trainers. Most fortunately for Mr Fogg, this elephant had only just commenced the diet, and *mulsh* had not broken out as yet.

Like all animals of the same kind, Kiouni – its name was Kiouni – could travel rapidly for a long time at a stretch, so, in default of every other sort of mount, Phileas Fogg determined to make use of him.

But elephants are not so plentiful as they were in India, and are therefore far from cheap. There is a very great demand for the males, which alone are suitable for circus contests. Moreover, as elephants rarely reproduce their species in the state of domesticity, the only means of supply is hunting.

Their owners, therefore, take the utmost care of them. When Mr Fogg asked the Indian if he was willing to let him have his beast on hire, the Indian refused flatly. Fogg persisted and offered the excessive sum of ten pounds an hour for the use of the beast. This was refused. Twenty pounds, forty pounds, nothing doing. Passepartout gave a jump at each advance. But the Indian was not to be tempted.

Yet the offer was handsome; for, supposing the elephant took fifteen hours to get to Allahabad, it would mean six hundred pounds for the owner. Phileas Fogg, absolutely unperturbed, then offered to purchase the beast, and straightway suggested a thousand pounds. The crafty native, possibly scenting a magnificent bargain, said he did not want to sell.

Sir Francis took Mr Fogg aside and advised him to think before proceeding with the matter. Phileas Fogg replied that he was not in the habit of acting without thinking; that, after all, the bet was a matter of twenty thousand pounds; that he could not do without the elephant, and that he must have it, even if he had to pay twenty times what it was worth.

Mr Fogg returned to the Indian, whose small eyes, aglow with greed, could not conceal the fact that with him it was only a question of how much he could get. Phileas Fogg offered first twelve hundred pounds, then fifteen hundred, then eighteen hundred, and finally two thousand. Passepartout, usually so red, was pale with emotion.

At two thousand pounds the Indian gave in.

'By my slippers!' exclaimed Passepartout. 'What price elephant-steak after this?'

The transaction once concluded, all they had to do was to find a guide, which proved to be a matter of less difficulty. A bright-looking young Parsee[17] offered his services, which Mr Fogg accepted, promising him high remuneration, thereby stimulating his intelligence to greater exertion.

The elephant was brought out and equipped without delay. The Parsee, who was an expert mahout, covered the animal's back with a sort of saddle-cloth and fixed on either side a couple of rather uncomfortable litters. Phileas Fogg paid the Indian with banknotes drawn from the depths of the famous travelling-bag, an operation so painful to Passepartout that it seemed they were being extracted from his own bowels. Mr Fogg thereupon offered to carry Sir Francis Cromarty to Allahabad station, and the offer was accepted. One more traveller would not overtire the gigantic beast.

Provisions were procured at Kholby and, Sir Francis and Phileas Fogg having taken their seats in the howdahs, Passepartout placed himself astride between his master and the brigadier, and the Parsee perched himself on the elephant's neck. At nine o'clock they left the small town and made their way by the shortest cut into the thick forest of fan-palms.

CHAPTER XII

In which Phileas Fogg and his companions venture across the
forests of India, and the events that ensue

IN ORDER TO SHORTEN the journey, the guide left on his right the
railway line still in the making. Being constantly obliged to avoid the
capricious ramifications of the Vindhia Mountains, the line did not
pursue a direct course, which it was Phileas Fogg's interest to take, as it
would be the shortest. The Parsee, to whom the roads and paths of the
locality were quite familiar, declared there would be a gain of twenty
miles in striking across the forest, and they took his word for it. Phileas
Fogg and Sir Francis Cromarty, up to their necks in the howdahs, were
much shaken by the elephant's sharp trotting, for the mahout was
driving fast. But they suffered with the most perfect British unconcern,
talking little and hardly able to see each other.

Passepartout stuck on the animal's back and, receiving directly the
full force of every jolt, was all the time trying to remember his master's
recommendation and to keep his tongue from getting between his
teeth, as in that position it would have been bitten in two. The worthy
fellow, at one time flung on to the elephant's neck, at another on to his
rump, was vaulting about like a clown on a spring-board. But he joked
and laughed as he tossed about, and, from time to time, took a lump of
sugar out of his bag, and the intelligent Kiouni received it at the end of
his trunk, without a moment's interruption of his regular trot.

After two hours the guide stopped the elephant and gave him two
hours' rest. The animal first quenched his thirst at a pond hard by, and
then proceeded to devour the branches and shrubs about him. Sir
Francis Cromarty was only too pleased with this halt. He was dead-
tired. Mr Fogg looked as fresh and fit as if he had just jumped out of
bed.

'He must be made of iron,' said the brigadier-general, looking at him
admiringly. 'Of wrought-iron,' replied Passepartout, as he set about
preparing a hasty breakfast.

At noon the Parsee gave the signal for departure. The country soon
began to look very wild. The great forests gave place to copses of
tamarinds and dwarf palms, after which came wide-spreading, arid
plains, bristling with wretched shrubs and dotted with great boulders of

syenite. The whole of this part of upper Bundelkhand, but little visited by travellers, is inhabited by a fanatical people hardened in the most terrible practices of the Hindu religion. The English have been unable to establish their rule efficiently over this region, subject as it is to the influence of the rajahs, whom it would have been no easy matter to reach in their inaccessible fastnesses in the Vindhia Mountains.

More than once troops of fierce-looking Indians were descried making wrathful gestures as they watched the great quadruped speeding by. But the Parsee avoided them as much as possible, for he thought it unsafe to meet them. They saw few animals in the course of that day; here and there a monkey or two, that scampered away making endless contortions and grimaces, to Passepartout's great delight.

Among many disturbing thoughts one in particular kept worrying him. He wondered what Mr Fogg would do with the elephant when they reached Allahabad. Would he take him with him? That was impossible. The cost of conveyance added to the purchase-price would make the beast quite ruinous. Would he sell him or set him free? It was only right that the estimable animal should be treated with proper consideration. Passepartout wondered what on earth he should do if Mr Fogg by any chance were to make him a present of the beast. He was much perturbed by this possibility.

The main range of the Vindhias was crossed at eight o'clock in the evening, and the travellers made a halt in a dilapidated bungalow at the foot of the northern slope. They had ridden about twenty-five miles that day, and they had another twenty-five before them to get to Allahabad. The night was cold, so the Parsee made a fire of dry branches, which was much appreciated. The provisions bought at Kholby supplied the supper, and the travellers ate like the dog-tired men they were. The conversation, begun in a few disjointed sentences, soon ended in loud snoring. The guide kept watch close to Kiouni, who went to sleep standing, leaning against the trunk of a thick tree. The night passed without any noteworthy incident. At times the silence was broken by the snarling of cheetahs and panthers, and the sharp tittering of monkeys. But, beyond noise, the carnivorous animals made no hostile demonstration against the occupants of the bungalow. Sir Francis Cromarty slept heavily, like a gallant soldier exhausted with fatigue. Passepartout had a somewhat restless night, dreaming that he was still tossing on the elephant's back. Mr Fogg slept as peacefully as if he had been in his own quiet home in Savile Row.

The journey was resumed at six in the morning, and the guide hoped to reach Allahabad station that very evening. So Mr Fogg would lose only a part of the forty-eight hours he had saved since the beginning of his venture.

Descending the last slopes of the Vindhias, Kiouni got into his stride, and about noon they arrived near the small town of Kallinger, on the Cani, a feeder of the Ganges. The guide passed at some distance from the town, as he was always careful to avoid inhabited places, feeling safer in those lonely plains which announce the first depressions of the basin of the great river. Allahabad was now only twelve miles away to the north-east. They stopped under a clump of banana trees, and greatly enjoyed the fruit, wholesome as bread, and 'luscious as cream,' as is the saying among travellers.

At two o'clock the guide entered a dense forest, across which he would have to travel for several miles. He preferred to remain under cover of the woods.

So far, at all events, there had been no unpleasant encounter, and it looked as if the journey would be successfully accomplished, when the elephant, showing signs of uneasiness, stopped dead.

It was then four o'clock. 'What is the matter?' asked Sir Francis Cromarty, looking out of his howdah. 'I don't know, sir,' replied the Parsee, listening attentively to a confused murmur that came along under the thick branches.

A few moments later the murmur became more distinct. It was now like a still very distant concert of human voices and brass instruments.

Passepartout was all eyes and ears.

Phileas Fogg uttered not a word, but waited patiently.

The Parsee jumped down, tied the elephant to a tree and disappeared in the thickest part of the wood. He returned a few minutes later, saying, 'It is a procession of Brahmins coming this way. We must avoid being seen, if possible.'

The guide untied the elephant and led him into a thicket telling the travellers to be sure not to dismount, and holding himself in readiness to mount quickly, should flight become necessary. But he was confident that the procession of the faithful would pass on without seeing him, as he was completely hidden by the dense foliage.

The discordant sound of voices and instruments drew nearer. Monotonous chants mingled with the beating of drums and clanging of cymbals. The head of the procession soon made its appearance under the trees, some fifty yards away from the position occupied by Mr Fogg and his companions; and they could easily distinguish through the branches the strange performers of this religious ceremony.

First came the priests, wearing mitres and clothed in flowing embroidered robes.

They were surrounded by men, women and children singing a kind of dirge, interrupted at regular intervals by the tom-toms and cymbals. Behind them stood a hideous statue on a car with wide wheels, the spokes and felly of which represented serpents coiled about each other. This car was drawn by four richly-caparisoned zebus. The statue had four arms, the body coloured a dark red, haggard eyes, tangled hair, a lolling tongue and lips tinted with henna and betel. Its neck was circled by a collar of death's heads, its flanks by a belt of cut hands. It stood upright on a prostrate giant without a head.

Sir Francis Cromarty, who recognised the statue, whispered, 'It is the goddess Kali, the goddess of love and death.'

'Of death, possibly, but of love, never!' said Passepartout. 'Horrible hag!'

The Parsee signed to him to be silent.

Around the statue a group of old fakirs, striped with ochre and covered with cross-wise cuts, from which their blood trickled drop by drop, were bestirring themselves with wild capers and frantic contortions. These stupid fanatics, at the great Hindu ceremonies, will still throw themselves under the wheels of the car of Juggernaut.

Next came a few Brahmins, in all the splendour of their oriental vestments, leading a woman who could scarcely stand. She was a young woman, with a skin as white as a European's. Her head, neck and shoulders, her ears, arms, hands and toes were weighed down with jewels, necklaces, bracelets, ear-rings and rings; and a tunic spangled with gold, and veiled with light muslin, showed the outline of her figure.

In violent contrast to the spectacle presented by this young woman were some guards who followed her, armed with naked sabres hanging from their waists, and long damascened pistols, and carrying a corpse on a palanquin.

This was the body of an old man, clothed in his gorgeous rajah's raiment. As in his lifetime, he wore a turban embroidered with pearls, a robe of silk and gold tissue, a sash of cashmere studded with diamonds, and the splendid weapons of an Indian prince.

Then came musicians and a rearguard of fanatics, whose yells at times drowned the deafening din of the instruments, and who closed the procession.

As Sir Francis Cromarty observed all this ceremony, his face bore a singularly sad expression, and, turning to the guide, he said, 'A suttee.' The Parsee nodded and raised a finger to his lips. The long procession slowly passed away under the trees, and soon its rear ranks disappeared in the depths of the forest.

Little by little the singing died down; yet a few cries were heard in the distance, then at last all this commotion gave place to profound stillness. As soon as the procession had disappeared, Phileas Fogg, who had heard the word uttered by Sir Francis Cromarty, asked what a 'suttee' was.

'A suttee, Mr Fogg,' answered the brigadier-general, 'is a human sacrifice, but a voluntary sacrifice. The woman you have just seen will be burnt tomorrow at early dawn.' 'Oh, the villains!' cried Passepartout, unable to restrain his indignation.

'What about that corpse?' asked Mr Fogg.

'It is the body of the prince, her husband, an independent rajah of Bundelkhand,' said the guide. 'What!' continued Phileas Fogg, in a perfectly calm tone of voice. 'Do these barbarous customs still prevail in India? Have not the English been able to put an end to them?' 'These sacrifices are no longer performed in the greater part of India,' replied Sir Francis, 'but we have no control over these wild regions, over this territory of Bundelkhand in particular. The whole district on the northern slope of the Vindhias is the scene of incessant murder and plundering.'

'Poor wretched woman!' muttered Passepartout, 'to be burnt alive!' 'Yes, burnt alive,' rejoined the brigadier; 'and you cannot imagine what she would have to suffer at the hands of her relatives, if she were not burnt. They would shave off her hair, and feed her on a scanty dole of rice; she would be spurned as an unclean creature, and be left to die in some corner like a mangy dog. So it is frequently the prospect of such a frightful existence, rather than love or religious fanaticism, that drives these poor wretches to self-immolation. Still it occasionally happens that this sacrifice is really voluntary, and it requires the forcible intervention of the Government to prevent it. For instance, a few years ago I was living in Bombay, when a young widow came and requested the governor's permission to be burnt with her husband's body. As you may imagine, the governor refused. Thereupon the widow left the town, took refuge with an independent rajah, and there gave effect to her resolution of self-sacrifice.'

As Sir Francis recorded this incident, the guide shook his head from time to time, and when the brigadier had finished, he said, 'The sacrifice that will take place tomorrow at sunrise is not a voluntary one.' 'How do you know?' 'Everybody in Bundelkhand knows the story,' answered the guide. 'The wretched woman appeared to be offering no resistance,' observed Sir Francis. 'That was because she had been intoxicated with the fumes of hemp and opium.' 'But where are they taking her?' 'To the pagoda of Pillagi, two miles from here. She will pass the night there, awaiting the hour of sacrifice.' 'And the sacrifice will take place when?' 'Tomorrow, at earliest dawn.'

So saying, the guide led the elephant out of the thick cover and scrambled up to his neck. But just as he was about to urge the animal forward by means of a peculiar whistle, Mr Fogg stopped him, and speaking to Sir Francis Cromarty, he said, 'What if we rescued this woman?' 'Rescued this woman, Mr Fogg!' cried the brigadier. 'I have still twelve hours to the good. I can devote them to this.' 'By Jove! You are a man of heart, then!' exclaimed Sir Francis. 'Occasionally,' replied Phileas Fogg quietly, 'when I have time.'

CHAPTER XIII

In which Passepartout proves once more that fortune favours the bold

THE PROJECT was a bold one, bristling with difficulties, perhaps impracticable. Mr Fogg was going to jeopardise his life or at the least his liberty, and consequently the success of his plans, but he did not hesitate; and he found a resolute ally in Sir Francis Cromarty. Passepartout was ready for anything, and entirely at the disposal of his master, whose idea excited him to enthusiasm.

He felt there was a warm heart and generous soul under that icy exterior, and began to love Phileas Fogg dearly.

What, now, would be the guide's decision? Would he not be inclined to side with the Hindus? If they could not secure his assistance, they must at any rate make sure of his neutrality. Sir Francis Cromarty frankly asked him what he would do. 'Officer,' replied the guide, 'I am a Parsee, and this woman is a Parsee. I am yours to command.' 'Good,' said Mr Fogg. 'But I must tell you,' resumed the Parsee, 'that we are not only running the risk of losing our lives, but of suffering horrible tortures, if we are caught, so judge for yourselves.' 'That's settled,' replied Mr Fogg. 'I think we must wait until it is dark, before setting to work.' 'I think so, too,' said the guide. The good Indian then proceeded to give them a few particulars concerning the victim. She was a celebrated beauty of the Parsee race, the daughter of a wealthy Bombay merchant. She had received a thoroughly English education in that city, and from her manners and attainments she would be taken for a European. Her name was Aouda. Being left an orphan, she was married against her will to this old rajah of Bundelkhand. Three months after, she became a widow and, knowing the fate that was in store for her, she escaped, but was at once recaptured, and doomed by the rajah's relatives, who were interested in her death, to this sacrifice from which apparently there was no escape.

This narrative only confirmed Mr Fogg and his companions in their generous resolution.

It was decided that the guide should direct the elephant towards the pagoda of Pillagi and get as near to it as possible.

Half an hour later, they halted under cover of a copse, five hundred yards from the pagoda, which was just visible, while the howls of the fanatics were distinctly heard.

The means of reaching the victim were then discussed. The guide was acquainted with the pagoda of Pillagi, in which he asserted the young woman was held captive. Would it be possible to get in by one of the doors, when the whole crowd was plunged in a drunken sleep, or would it be necessary to make a hole in one of the walls? The answer to this question could only be given at the time of action and on the spot. But one thing left no manner of doubt in their minds: it was that the abduction must be carried out that very night, and not after daybreak, when the victim was taken out to die. At that moment no human intervention could save her.

Mr Fogg and his companions waited for the night. As soon as it was dark, about six o'clock, they decided to make a reconnaissance around the pagoda. The last cries of the fakirs were just coming to an end. According to custom, the Indians must be heavily intoxicated with 'bang,' liquid opium mixed with infusion of hemp. It might, therefore, be possible to slip in between them and reach the temple.

Followed by Mr Fogg, Sir Francis and Passepartout, the guide made his way noiselessly through the forest. After crawling ten minutes under the branches, they came to the bank of a small stream, where, by the light of resin burning at the end of iron torches, they saw a pile of wood. This was the pyre, made of costly sandal, and already soaked in perfumed oil. On the top lay the embalmed body of the rajah, which was to be burnt, together with his widow. The pagoda, whose minarets were dimly seen rising above the tops of the trees, stood a hundred yards away from the pyre.

'Come,' whispered the guide. And with the utmost caution he silently slipped through the tall grass, followed by his companions.

Nothing now broke the stillness of night save the soughing of the wind in the foliage.

Ere long the guide stopped on the edge of a glade. The open space was lit up by a few torches, the ground covered with groups of men sleeping the heavy sleep of drunkenness. It looked like a field of battle strewn with the dead. Men, women and children lay huddled together. Here and there, there was still an occasional rattle from the throat of a drunkard or two.

In the background, encompassed by the forest, loomed the temple of Pillagi. But, to the guide's great disappointment, the guards of the rajahs, lighted by smoky torches, were keeping watch at the doors, and walking to and fro with drawn swords. It was reasonable to suppose that the priests, too, were watching inside.

The Parsee went no farther. Having recognised the impossibility of getting into the temple by force, he made his companions retrace their steps.

Phileas Fogg and Sir Francis Cromarty likewise saw that it was useless to attempt anything in this direction. They stopped and discussed the situation in whispers.

'Let us wait a while,' said the brigadier; 'it is only eight o'clock; it is possible these guards may also be overcome by sleep.' 'Yes, it is possible,' answered the Parsee. So Phileas Fogg and his companions lay down at the foot of a tree and waited. Time seemed to stand still. The guide left them now and again to see what was happening on the edge of the wood, but the guards were watching as before by the glimmer of the torches, and a dim light trickled through the windows of the pagoda. They waited thus till midnight, and there was no change; the guards still kept watch outside; to depend on their drowsiness was evidently hopeless. They had probably been spared intoxication from 'bang.' It therefore became necessary to adopt another plan and to gain access to the pagoda by making a hole in the wall.

The next thing to ascertain was whether the priests were watching by their victim as keenly as the soldiers at the door of the temple.

After a last consultation, the guide said he was ready to start, and was followed by Mr Fogg, Sir Francis and Passepartout. They made a rather long detour so as to get round to the back of the pagoda, and reached the foot of the walls by about half-past twelve, without having met anyone. No watch was kept on this side, but then there were absolutely no doors nor windows.

The night was dark. The moon in its last quarter scarcely left the horizon, which was shrouded with heavy clouds, and the height of the trees made the darkness deeper still. To have reached the walls was not enough, however; Phileas Fogg and his companions must manage to make an opening in them; and for this operation they had absolutely nothing but their pocket-knives. Fortunately the walls of the temple were built of bricks and wood, which could be pierced with little difficulty. Once the first brick was removed, the others would come out easily. They set to work as noiselessly as possible. The Parsee on one side and Passepartout on the other exerted themselves to loosen the bricks, so as to contrive an opening two feet wide. They were making good progress, when a cry rang out within the temple, to which almost at once other cries made answer from without. Passepartout and the guide stopped. Were they detected? Was that the alarm being given? The most elementary prudence bade them retire. So the four of them sought cover again in the wood, ready to get to work once more, should the alarm, real or otherwise, pass away. But guards now made their appearance at the back of the pagoda, and took up such a position as to make all approach impossible.

Here was a fatal obstacle. The disappointment of these four men, thus interrupted in their work of rescue, would be hard to describe; for, now that it was impossible to reach the victim, how could they hope to save her?

Sir Francis Cromarty was desperately angry, Passepartout was beside himself, and the guide had some difficulty in keeping him quiet. Fogg, cool as ever, waited on apparently unmoved.

'I suppose all we can do now is to go?' suggested the brigadier in an undertone. 'Yes, go we must, there is nothing else to be done,' answered the guide. 'Wait a bit,' said Fogg, 'I need not be at Allahabad before tomorrow, any time before midday.' 'But what can you hope for?' replied Sir Francis. 'It will be daylight a few hours hence and – ' 'The opportunity which is now slipping from us may occur again at the last moment.'

The brigadier wished he could have read Phileas Fogg's eyes. What had this cool Englishman at the back of his mind? Did he purpose to make a rush at the very moment when the young woman was about to die, and to snatch her openly from her executioners? This would be an act of utter folly, and he could not admit that the man was mad enough for that. Nevertheless Sir Francis consented to see the end of the terrible drama. But the guide did not leave his companions in their present place of concealment; he led them back to the front of the glade, whence, screened by a clump of trees, they surveyed the groups of sleeping humanity.

Meanwhile Passepartout, who had perched himself on the lowest branches of a tree, was revolving an idea which had first crossed his mind like a flash, and had now taken firm hold of it.

He had first said to himself that this idea was sheer madness, and now he kept muttering, 'Why not, after all? It's a chance – possibly the only chance; and with such a besotted crowd!' Passepartout, leaving his plan thus undefined, was soon slipping, with the litheness of a serpent, along the low branches, the ends of which were bent towards the ground.

The hours passed and lighter shades heralded the approach of dawn, though it was still very dark. The moment had come. The slumbering crowd rose as if from the sleep of death. The various groups began to bestir themselves. Tom-toms resounded; songs and cries broke out anew. The hour was at hand when the unfortunate woman must die. The doors of the pagoda burst open, and a brighter light escaped from the interior. Mr Fogg and Sir Francis Cromarty now caught sight of the victim in the vivid glare, as she was being taken out by two priests. It even seemed to them that the wretched woman, obeying the final prompting of the instinct of self-preservation, had shaken off the torpor of intoxication and was endeavouring to escape from her tormentors. Sir Francis Cromarty's heart gave a great throb, and, impulsively gripping Phileas Fogg's hand, he felt that it held an open knife. At this moment the crowd began to move. The young woman, who had fallen back into the state of torpor induced by the fumes of hemp, passed through the fakirs, who accompanied her with their religious bawling.

Phileas Fogg and his companions, mixing with the last ranks of the crowd, followed. In two minutes they reached the bank of the river, and stopped less than fifty paces from the pyre, on which lay the rajah's body. In the semi-obscurity they perceived the victim perfectly inert, lying beside her husband's corpse.

Then a torch was applied, and the wood, soaked with oil, blazed up at once. It was then that Sir Francis Cromarty and the guide held back Phileas Fogg, who, in a moment of generous frenzy, was in the act of dashing towards the pyre. But Phileas Fogg had already thrust them aside, when a sudden change came over the scene.

There was a cry of terror, and the whole multitude fell prostrate, stricken with dismay.

The old rajah, then, was not dead, for here he was rising suddenly like a phantom, taking up the young woman in his arms and coming down from the pyre enveloped in whirling clouds which gave him a spectral appearance!

The fakirs, guards and priests, seized with panic, lay there with their faces to the ground, not daring to lift their eyes and look upon such a miracle.

The insensible victim was carried along in the strong arms that held her, and for which she seemed a light burden.

Mr Fogg and Sir Francis were erect at the same place, the Parsee had bowed his head, and, doubtless Passepartout was no less dumbfounded.

The resuscitated man moved in this manner as far as Mr Fogg and Sir Francis, and there gave the abrupt order, 'Let us be off!'

It was none other than Passepartout, who had made his way to the pyre in the midst of the thick smoke, and, taking advantage of the darkness, which was still opaque, had snatched the young woman from the jaws of death! It was Passepartout who, playing his part with lucky audacity, was able to go right through the crowd during the ensuing panic!

A moment later all four had disappeared in the woods, and the elephant was taking them away at a speedy trot.

But the shouts and hubbub, and a bullet that made a hole in Phileas Fogg's hat, told them that their stratagem was discovered. On the blazing pyre the old rajah's body was now plainly visible, and the priests, recovering from their terror, and perceiving that an abduction had just been effected, rushed headlong into the forest, with the guards close behind them. A volley was fired at the captors, but in a few moments their rapid flight took them beyond the reach of bullets and arrows.

CHAPTER XIV

In which Phileas Fogg travels down the whole length of the beautiful Ganges without as much as thinking of seeing it

THE BOLD ABDUCTION had been quite successful.

An hour later Passepartout was still chuckling over it, and Sir Francis Cromarty exchanged a vigorous handshake with the worthy fellow. His master simply said, 'Well done,' which, from such a man, was high praise. To this Passepartout replied that the whole credit of the affair was his master's. A 'quaint' idea had struck him, and that was all he had had to do with it. It made him laugh to think that for a short time he, Passepartout, the ex-gymnast, ex-sergeant of firemen, had been parted by death from a charming woman, and then become an embalmed old rajah!

As for the young Indian, she knew nothing of what had taken place. She was wrapped up in the travelling-rugs and reposing in one of the howdahs.

Meanwhile the elephant, directed with unerring skill by the Parsee, was making rapid progress through the forest, though it was still dark; and an hour after leaving the pagoda of Pillagi, he was travelling at great speed across an immense plain. They halted at seven o'clock, and, as the young woman was still in a state of complete prostration, the guide made her drink a little brandy and water; but she was to remain in the grip of this stupor for some time longer. Sir Francis Cromarty, who knew the effects of intoxication produced by inhaling hemp fumes, had no anxiety on her account. But, while he felt quite sure the young Indian would come round, he showed far less confidence with respect to her future. He told Phileas Fogg plainly that, should Aouda remain in India, she would inevitably fall again into the hands of her executioners. These fanatics were to be found throughout the peninsula, and surely, in spite of the English police, they would manage to recapture their victim, were it in Madras, Bombay or Calcutta. And in support of his assertion, Sir Francis mentioned a similar case of recent occurrence. In his opinion the young woman would not be really safe until she had left India.

Phileas Fogg replied that he would keep this in mind and see what could be done. About ten o'clock the guide was at Allahabad; the interrupted line started there again, and trains ran from Allahabad to Calcutta in less than twenty-four hours. Phileas Fogg would therefore arrive in time to take a boat due to leave Calcutta on the next day, October 25, at noon, for Hong-Kong.

The young woman was taken to a room at the station, and Passepartout was entrusted with the task of purchasing for her various requisites of a lady's toilet – a dress, a shawl, some furs, etc., in fact anything necessary that he could find. His master gave him unlimited credit for the purpose. Passepartout set out at once on his errand, exploring the streets of Allahabad, the 'city of God.' It is one of the most venerated in India, as it stands at the junction of the two sacred rivers, the Ganges and the Jumna, whose waters attract pilgrims from every part of the peninsula. It need scarcely be mentioned that, according to the legend of the Ramayana,[18] the Ganges rises in heaven, and comes down to earth through Brahma's bounty.

While making his purchases, Passepartout saw a good deal of the city, once protected by a very fine fort, which is now a state prison. Allahabad, formerly an industrial and trading centre, has now neither commerce nor industry. Expecting to find a Regent Street with a Farmer and Co. close by, Passepartout looked about for a linen-draper, and saw none. He was at last able to get what he wanted at the second-hand shop of a tough old Jew, who sold him a dress of Scotch material, a large cloak, and a magnificent otter-skin pelisse, for which he readily gave seventy-five pounds. He then returned to the station, immensely pleased with himself.

Aouda was gradually recovering as the effect of the narcotics to which the priests of Pillagi had subjected her wore off, and her beautiful eyes were regaining all their Indian softness.

When the poet king, Usaf Uddaul, celebrates the charms of the Queen of Ahmehnagara, he says:

> Her glossy hair evenly parted, encircles the harmonious lines of her soft white cheeks, radiant in their smooth freshness. Her brows, black as ebony, have the shape and potency of the bow of Kama, the god of Love; and beneath her long silken lashes, in the dark pupils of her large clear eyes, swim the purest reflections of celestial light, as in the sacred lakes of Himalaya. Her teeth, small, even and white, sparkle between her smiling lips like dewdrops in the half-closed heart of a pomegranate flower. Her lovely little ears, of symmetric mould, her rosy hands, her small feet, rounded and dainty as lotus-buds, glitter with the brilliance of the finest pearls of Ceylon, the most splendid diamonds of Golconda. Her slim, supple waist, that one hand can circle, sets off the graceful bend of her rounded back and the rich beauty of her bust, where flowering youth displays the most perfect of its treasures; beneath the silken folds of her tunic, she seems to have been modelled in pure silver by the hand divine of Vicvacarma, the eternal statuary.

Without using all this poetic imagery, one may say that Aouda, the widow of the Bundelkhand rajah, was a charming woman in the full European acceptation of the word, and this is enough. She expressed herself in purest English, and the guide had not exaggerated when he affirmed that the young Parsee had been transformed by the manner of her upbringing.

The train was now about to leave Allahabad, and the Parsee guide was paid the sum agreed upon. Mr Fogg did not give a farthing more, which rather surprised Passepartout, who knew what his master owed to the man's devoted service. The Parsee had, in fact, willingly run the risk of losing his life in the Pillagi business, and, should the Hindus hear of this later, he would find it difficult to escape their vengeance.

The next thing was to dispose of Kiouni. What was to be done with an elephant bought at such a price? But Phileas Fogg had already settled the question. 'Parsee,' he said to the guide, 'you have been useful and devoted. I have paid you for your service, but not for your devotion. Would you like the elephant? If so, it is yours.'

The guide's eyes glowed.

'Your honour is giving me a fortune!' he exclaimed. 'Accept my offer,' replied Mr Fogg; 'I shall still be your debtor.'

'Splendid!' cried Passepartout. 'Take him, friend! Kiouni is a right-down good and plucky animal!' He then went up to Kiouni and offered him a few pieces of sugar, saying, 'Here you are, Kiouni; here you are.' The elephant gave a grunt or two of satisfaction, and, seizing Passepartout around the waist with his trunk, lifted him as high as his head. Passepartout, not in the least frightened, gave the animal a friendly pat, and was gently replaced on the ground, and then honest Kiouni's trunk-grip was returned by a hearty hand-grip from the worthy fellow.

A few minutes later, Phileas Fogg, Sir Francis Cromarty and Passepartout, having taken their seats in a comfortable carriage, in which Aouda occupied the best place, were running at full-speed on their way to Benares. The distance between the latter town and Allahabad is at most eighty miles, and the run took two hours.

During the journey the young Indian became herself completely. The effects of the stupefying fumes of the 'bang' had passed away.

What was her amazement on finding herself in this railway carriage, dressed in European garments, and in the company of travellers who were absolute strangers!

Their very first care was to restore her completely, and to this end, among many attentions, they made her drink a few drops of spirit. The brigadier then proceeded to inform her of what had happened to her. He dwelt on the devotion of Phileas Fogg, who had not hesitated to stake his life in order to save hers, and on the happy termination of the adventure, due to Passepartout's bold conception.

Mr Fogg let him speak without uttering one word, while Passepartout, immensely shy, said more than once, 'Not worth mentioning.'

Aouda thanked her deliverers effusively, more by her tears than by her words. Her glorious eyes were even better interpreters of her gratitude than her lips. Then, as her thoughts travelled back to the scenes of the suttee, and she looked once more on this land of India, where she had still so many dangers to face, she shuddered with terror.

Phileas Fogg, who perceived what was passing in her mind, tried to reassure her, and offered, in his coldest manner, to take her to Hong-Kong, where she could stay until the affair had blown over.

The offer was gratefully accepted. It so happened that Aouda had a relation living at Hong-Kong, a Parsee like herself, and one of the leading merchants in that city, which is quite English, though situated off the coast of China.

The train pulled up at Benares at half-past twelve. The Brahminical legends assert that this city stands on the site of ancient Casi, which, like Mahomet's tomb, was once suspended in space between the zenith and the nadir. But in these more realistic days, Benares, called the Athens of India by orientalists, rested quite prosaically on the ground, and Passepartout had a hurried view of its brick houses and wattling huts, giving the place a perfectly desolate aspect, absolutely without local colour.

Sir Francis Cromarty was not going beyond Benares; the troops he was rejoining were encamped a few miles away to the north of the town. He therefore bade Phileas Fogg farewell, wishing him all possible success, and expressing the hope that he might come again, in a less original but more profitable way. Mr Fogg lightly pressed his fingers in return. Aouda took leave of Sir Francis with much more emotion, saying she could never forget all she owed him. As for Passepartout, he was honoured with a hearty shake of the hand, which affected him so much that he asked himself where and when he could give his life for the brigadier. Then Sir Francis Cromarty left them.

After Benares, the railway followed the valley of the Ganges for a time. In sufficiently clear weather the travellers could see through the windows of their carriage the varied landscape of Behar; mountains clothed in verdure, fields of barley, maize and wheat, streams and pools teeming with greenish alligators, well-kept villages, and forests still green. A few elephants and some zebus, with their great humps, came down to bathe in the waters of the sacred river, and parties of Indians, men and women, piously performed their holy ablutions in spite of the advanced season and chilly temperature. These devotees, bitter foes of Buddhism, are fervent followers of the Brahminical religion, with its three godheads, Vishnu, the sun god, Shiva, the divine impersonation of the natural forces, and Brahma, the supreme lord of priests and lawgivers. What must Brahma, Shiva and Vishnu have thought of this anglicised India, when some steamboat scurried screeching by, churning the sacred waters of the Ganges, scaring away the gulls that flitted about on its surface, the turtles teeming on its shores, and the faithful lying all along its banks!

The panorama passed before them like a flash, and its details were often hidden by a cloud of white mist. They had but a fleeting glimpse of the fort of Chunar, twenty miles south-east of Benares, an ancient stronghold of the rajahs of Behar; of Ghazipur and its important rose-water factories; Lord Cornwallis's tomb standing on the left bank of the Ganges; the fortified town of Buxar; Patna, a large manufacturing and commercial centre, the principal seat of the opium trade in India; Monghyr, a more than European town, being as English as Manchester or Birmingham, famous for its iron foundries, and its factories of edge-tools and side-arms, and whose high chimneys besmirched Brahma's sky with murky smoke – brutal assault upon the land of dreams.

Night came, and the train passed on at full-speed in the midst of the roaring of tigers and bears and the howling of wolves, that scampered off before the engine; and nothing more was seen of the marvels of Bengal – Golconda, the ruins of Gour, Murshidabad, once a capital, Burdwan, Hugli, Chandernagore, that bit of French soil on Indian territory where the sight of his country's flag would have gladdened Passepartout's heart –   night hid them all. Calcutta was reached at seven o'clock in the morning, and the boat about to sail for Hong-Kong would not weigh anchor before twelve. Phileas Fogg had five hours to spare. According to his time-table he was to arrive at the Indian capital on the 25th of October, twenty-three days after leaving London, and he had arrived on the appointed day. He was therefore neither behind nor before his time. Unfortunately the two days he had gained between London and Bombay had been lost, as we have seen, in the journey across the Indian peninsula, but we may reasonably suppose that Phileas Fogg did not regret them.

CHAPTER XV

In which the bag containing the banknotes is again lightened by a few thousand pounds

WHEN THE TRAIN stopped, Passepartout was the first to get down; then came Mr Fogg, who helped his fair young companion out of the carriage.

Phileas Fogg intended to go straight to the Hong-Kong boat, in order to see Aouda comfortably settled for the voyage. He was anxious to be with her until she left a country so full of danger for her.

Just as he was leaving the station, a policeman walked up to him and said, 'Mr Phileas Fogg?' 'That is my name.' 'Is this man your servant?' asked the policeman, pointing to Passepartout. 'Yes.' 'Be good enough to follow me, both of you.'

Mr Fogg showed not the slightest sign of surprise. This man was a representative of the law, and the law is sacred to all Englishmen.

Passepartout, being a Frenchman, tried to argue, but the policeman tapped him with his stick, and Phileas Fogg motioned to him to obey.

'May this young lady come with us?' asked Mr Fogg. 'She may,' replied the policeman.

Mr Fogg, Aouda and Passepartout were taken to a *palki-gari*, a sort of four-wheeled carriage for four people, drawn by two horses, and they were driven away. The *palki-gari* took about twenty minutes, and no one spoke on the way. They first passed through the 'black town,' with its narrow streets, between rows of hovels in which swarmed a squalid, ragged cosmopolitan population; then through the European town, with its cheery brick houses, and shady coco-nut trees, and its forest of masts. Although it was early morning, smart-looking men on horseback and splendid equipages were already passing to and fro.

The *palki-gari* stopped before an unpretentious-looking house, which was obviously not a private residence. The policeman requested his prisoners to descend – I say prisoners because they really might be considered as such – and conducted them into a room with barred windows, where he said to them, 'You will appear before Judge Obadiah at half-past eight.' He then withdrew and shut the door.

'So we are trapped!' exclaimed Passepartout, limply sitting down on a chair.

'Sir,' said Aouda to Mr Fogg with ill-concealed emotion, 'you must leave me to my fate! It is on my account that you are being prosecuted; it is because you saved me.'

To this Phileas Fogg simply replied that the thing was not possible, that it was not admissible that he could be prosecuted for that suttee business, as the plaintiffs would never dare to come forward. There was a mistake somewhere. He added that, in any case, he would not abandon her, but would take her to Hong-Kong.

'But the boat leaves at twelve!' observed Passepartout. 'We shall be on board before twelve,' was all his imperturbable master replied, but it was said with such positive assurance, that Passepartout could not help saying to himself:

'Why, of course, we shall be on board before twelve!' But he felt anything but comfortable about it.

At half-past eight the door opened, and the policeman ushered the prisoners into the adjoining room. This was the court, and the part reserved for the public was occupied by a fairly numerous gathering of Europeans and natives.

Mr Fogg, Aouda and Passepartout sat down on a bench opposite the seats reserved for the magistrate and the clerk of the court.

A moment after, Judge Obadiah, a stout, rotund-looking man, entered, followed by the clerk. He took down a wig hanging on a nail and put it on hurriedly.

'The first case,' said he; then, raising his hand to his head, he exclaimed, 'Hallo! This is not my wig!' 'No, my lord, it is mine,' answered the clerk.

'My dear Mr Oysterpuf, pray tell me how a judge is to pass a just sentence in a clerk's wig!'

They then exchanged wigs. During these preliminaries, Passepartout was fuming with impatience, for the hand of the big clock in the court-room seemed to be travelling around the dial at a terrible pace.

'The first case,' repeated Judge Obadiah. 'Phileas Fogg?' called out the clerk.

'Here,' answered Mr Fogg. 'Passepartout?' 'Here!' replied Passepartout. 'All right,' said the judge. 'Prisoners at the bar, the police have been looking for you on every train from Bombay for the last two days.' 'But what is the charge against us?' cried Passepartout, getting out of patience. 'This you will now be told,' replied the judge. 'I am an Englishman, sir,' said Mr Fogg, 'and am entitled to . . . ' 'Have you been ill-used?' interrupted the judge. 'Not in the least.'

'Well, then, bring in the plaintiffs.'

At the judge's order, a door swung open, and three priests were shown in by an usher.

'That is it, of course,' muttered Passepartout; 'there are the scoundrels who wished to burn our young lady!'

The priests remained standing before the judge, and the clerk read in a loud voice a charge of sacrilege against Phileas Fogg and his servant, who were accused of having violated a place consecrated by the Brahmin religion.

'You have heard the accusation?' the judge asked Phileas Fogg. 'Yes, sir,' replied Mr Fogg, consulting his watch, 'and confess' 'Ah! You confess?' 'I confess, and I am waiting for these three priests to confess in their turn what they intended to do in the pagoda of Pillagi.'

The priests looked at each other, apparently unable to understand anything of the defendant's statement. 'Certainly!' cried Passepartout indignantly; 'at the pagoda of Pillagi, in front of which they were about to burn their victim!'

The priests were again astounded, and the judge asked in amazement, 'What victim? Burn whom? In the heart of Bombay?' 'Bombay?' exclaimed Passepartout. 'Yes, Bombay. This has nothing to do with the pagoda of Pillagi, but with the pagoda of Malabar Hill.'

'And as a proof,' added the clerk, 'here are the desecrator's shoes.' And he deposited a pair of shoes on his desk. 'My shoes!' exclaimed Passepartout, who, in his intense surprises could not keep back this impulsive cry.

The confusion which had taken place in the minds of master and man is obvious. They had clean forgotten this incident of the Bombay pagoda, for which they were now arraigned before the Calcutta magistrate.

Detective Fix, fully grasping all the advantage he could derive from that unfortunate affair, had postponed his departure by twelve hours, and had taken upon himself to advise the priests of Malabar Hill. He held out to them the prospect of heavy damages, knowing full well that the English Government treated this sort of offence with great severity. The next step he took was to send them off by the next train in pursuit of the culprit. But as a result of the time spent in rescuing the young widow, Fix and the Hindus arrived in Calcutta before Phileas Fogg and his servant, whom the magistrates, instructed by telegram, were to arrest as they stepped out of the train. One may imagine Fix's disappointment on hearing that Phileas Fogg had not yet reached the capital. He naturally inferred that the thief he was tracking had stopped at one of the stations of the Peninsular Railway and taken refuge in the Northern Provinces. For twenty-four hours Fix looked out for him at the station, a prey to the most harassing anxiety. Imagine his exultation when, that very morning, he saw him get down from the train, howbeit in the company of a young woman whose presence he could not understand. He at once directed a policeman to take him into custody, and thus it was that Mr Fogg, Passepartout and the widow of the Bundelkhand rajah were brought before Judge Obadiah.

Had not Passepartout's attention been so engrossed by his case, he would have noticed the detective in a corner of the court, watching the proceedings with an interest which was quite intelligible, for he was in the same position at Calcutta as he had been at Bombay and Suez: he was still without the warrant. Judge Obadiah took note of the confession that had escaped Passepartout, who would have given all he had in the world to recall his rash utterance.

'The facts are admitted?' asked the judge. 'They are admitted,' replied Mr Fogg coldly. 'Inasmuch,' continued the judge, 'as English law makes a point of giving equal and strict protection to all the religions of the peoples of India, and as the offence is admitted by the man Passepartout, convicted of having desecrated with sacrilegious foot the floor of the Malabar Hill pagoda at Bombay, during the 20th of October, I condemn the said Passepartout to go to prison for fifteen days and to pay a fine of three hundred pounds.' 'Three hundred pounds!' cried Passepartout, to whom the fine alone was a matter of concern. 'Silence!' yelped the usher.

'And,' added Judge Obadiah, 'inasmuch as it is not substantially established that there was no connivance between the servant and his master, and as, in any case, the master must be held responsible for the doings of a paid servant, I condemn the said Phileas Fogg to eight days' imprisonment and a fine of one hundred and fifty pounds. Clerk, call up the next case.'

Passepartout was stunned by this sentence, which spelt ruin for his master. It meant the loss of a wager for twenty thousand pounds, and all because, like a silly fool, he had walked into that cursed pagoda.

Phileas Fogg, just as cool as if the judgement had nothing to do with him, had not even frowned. But, just as the clerk was calling up another case, he stood up and said, 'I am prepared to give bail.' 'That is your right,' replied the judge. Fix felt a cold shiver down his back, but regained his composure when he heard the judge declare, 'As Phileas Fogg and his servant are strangers, each of them will have to find bail for the enormous sum of one thousand pounds.'

Should Mr Fogg fail to serve his sentence, it would cost him two thousand pounds. 'Here is the money,' said Phileas Fogg; and from the bag in Passepartout's keeping he took out a bundle of banknotes, which he placed on the clerk's desk.

'This money will be returned to you when you leave prison,' said the judge. 'In the meantime you are liberated on bail.'

'Come along,' said Phileas Fogg to his servant.

'The least they can do is to return the shoes!' cried Passepartout angrily; whereupon the shoes were given back to him.

'A precious sum they have cost!' he muttered. 'More than a thousand pounds each! And they are not even comfortable!'

Passepartout, thoroughly disgusted with things, followed Mr Fogg, who offered his arm to Aouda. Fix still hoped that the thief would never make up his mind to forfeit the sum of two thousand pounds, and that he would serve his sentence of eight days' imprisonment. He therefore hurried out after Fogg.

Mr Fogg at once took a carriage for himself and his two companions, and they drove off. Fix thereupon ran behind the carriage, which soon stopped on one of the quays. Half a mile away, in the roadstead, the *Rangoon* lay at anchor, with the blue peter at the mast-head. Eleven o'clock was striking; Mr Fogg was an hour in advance of time.

Fix saw him get down from the carriage and put out in a small boat with Aouda and his servant. The detective stamped his foot with rage. 'The scoundrel is off once more!' he cried. 'Two thousand pounds gone! None more wasteful than a thief! I'll shadow him to the end of the world, if I must, but at this rate there will be nothing left of the stolen money.'

The detective had some ground for this conclusion, for, what with travelling expenses, bribes, elephant buying, bails and fines, Phileas Fogg had already frittered away more than five thousand pounds since leaving London, and the percentage on the sum recovered, assigned as a reward for the detectives, was constantly growing less.

CHAPTER XVI

In which Fix appears to know nothing of what is said to him

THE *Rangoon*, one of the P. & O. liners plying in the Chinese and Japanese seas, was an iron screw-propelled boat, of seventeen hundred and seventy tons gross, and nominally of four hundred horse-power. She was as fast as the *Mongolia* but not so well appointed. So Aouda was not so comfortable as Phileas Fogg would have liked. But the passage was one of only three thousand five hundred miles, a matter of eleven or twelve days, and the young woman made a point of being easily pleased.

During the first days of the voyage, Aouda became better acquainted with Phileas Fogg, and lost no opportunity of showing him her intense gratitude; but all her protestations, apparently at least, left the phlegmatic gentleman perfectly cold; he listened, but neither by voice nor manner did he betray the slightest emotion. He took care that Aouda should have every possible comfort, and regularly came at certain hours to talk with her, or rather to hear her talk. While doing all that the strictest politeness could require, he behaved to her with just the graciousness and spontaneity that an automaton might have shown, whose movements had been contrived for the purpose.

Aouda was rather puzzled by this attitude, but Passepartout enlightened her to some extent on his master's eccentric character. He told her of the wager which was hurrying him round the world. This made Aouda smile, but, after all, she owed Phileas Fogg her life, and he could only gain in her estimation by being seen through the medium of her gratitude. The guide's narrative of her touching history was confirmed by Aouda herself. It was quite true that she belonged to the Parsee race, which holds the first rank among the natives. Many Parsee merchants have made great fortunes in India in the cotton trade. One of them, Sir James Jejeebhoy, received a title from the English Government, and Aouda was related to this wealthy person, who lived in Bombay. As a matter of fact, it was a cousin of his, Jejeeh by name, whom she hoped to join at Hong-Kong. Whether he would give her the protection and assistance she needed, she could not say. Mr Fogg assured her that there was no cause for anxiety, and that everything would be arranged mathematically, which was the very word he used. How far Aouda understood this horrible adverb it is hard to say, but her great eyes looked into Mr Fogg's, her great eyes, 'clear as the sacred lakes of Himalaya,' yet the unconscionable Fogg, reserved as ever, did not seem disposed to throw himself into the lake.

The first part of the voyage was accomplished in excellent conditions. The weather was mild, and throughout a long stretch of the immense bay the liner was favoured by wind and sea.

The *Rangoon* soon came in sight of Great Andaman, the principal island of the group, made conspicuous to navigators from a very great distance by its picturesque mountain, the Saddle-Peak, rising to a height of two thousand four hundred feet.

The ship passed fairly close inshore, but the savage aborigines of the island, rightly placed at the lowest grade of humanity, but wrongly termed cannibals, were not to be seen.

The panorama presented by these islands was superb. The foreground was a mass of forests of fan-palms, areca, bamboo, nutmeg, teak, gigantic mimosa and arborescent ferns, and behind this maze of greenery the mountains rose in graceful outlines against the sky. Along the coast swarmed in their thousands the precious swallows, whose edible nests are esteemed a great delicacy in the Celestial Empire. But all this varied landscape of the Andaman Islands was soon out of sight, and the *Rangoon* passed on rapidly towards the Straits of Malacca, through which she would enter the China seas.

And now, what was Detective Fix doing all this while, unfortunately faced as he was with the prospect of a compulsory voyage around the world? Leaving instructions at Calcutta that the warrant, should it arrive, was to be dispatched to him at Hong-Kong, he had managed to embark on the *Rangoon* without being seen by Passepartout, and he hoped to conceal his presence till the ship reached her destination. For it would be no easy matter to account for his being on board without arousing Passepartout's suspicions, as Passepartout could not but think he was still in Bombay. Nevertheless the force of circumstances induced him quite logically to change his mind and to renew his acquaintance with the worthy fellow; and it happened in this wise.

The one spot in the whole world on which all the detective's hopes and wishes were centred was Hong-Kong; for the boat's stay at Singapore would be too short to allow him to take effective steps there. The arrest must therefore be made at Hong-Kong, or the thief would escape him irretrievably.

Hong-Kong was English soil, but it was the last English soil they would touch. Beyond that, China, Japan, America, all held out to the man Fogg a practically safe retreat.

Should Fix at last find at Hong-Kong the warrant of arrest, which must have been sent after him post-haste, he would arrest Fogg and give him into the custody of the local police. It was quite simple. But beyond Hong-Kong, a mere warrant of arrest would not be sufficient; an extradition order would be necessary. That would mean endless delays and difficulties of all sorts, of which the rogue would take advantage to get away for good.

If his plans failed at Hong-Kong, it would be very difficult, if not quite impossible, to resume operations with any chance of success.

During the long hours which he spent in his cabin, Fix kept repeating to himself, 'One of two things – either the warrant will be at Hong-Kong, in which case I shall arrest my man; or it will not be there, and then I must at all cost find means to delay his departure. I failed at Bombay, I failed at Calcutta; if I fail at Hong-Kong, it is all up with my reputation. I must succeed, cost what it will. But, should it prove necessary, how on earth am I to delay the cursed fellow's departure!'

Should everything else come to naught Fix had quite made up his mind to tell Passepartout everything and show him the true character of his master. Passepartout, who without a doubt was no accomplice, when enlightened by this disclosure would most probably join hands with the detective, if only from fear of being himself implicated in Fogg's offence. But, after all, this was a risky expedient, not to be tried until everything else had failed, for one word from Passepartout to his master would be enough to ruin everything. The detective was in the midst of these sorely perplexing reflections, when the presence of Aouda on the *Rangoon* in Phileas Fogg's company opened up a vista of new possibilities.

Who was this woman? By what concurrence of circumstances had she become Fogg's companion? They had obviously met somewhere between Bombay and Calcutta; but where? Was this meeting of Phileas Fogg with the fair young traveller the result of chance, or was Fogg's journey across India undertaken with the express object of joining this charming damsel? For charming she was; Fix had noticed the fact in the court-room at Calcutta.

Naturally the detective was intensely interested and puzzled. The possibility of a criminal elopement occurred to him. The possibility soon became a probability, and then a fixed idea, and he realised the great advantage he could derive from this state of affairs. Whether the young woman was married or not, it was a case of elopement, and, at Hong-Kong, it would be possible to create such difficulties for the culprit that no amount of money would set him free.

But he must act before the *Rangoon* reached Hong-Kong. The fellow had an abominable habit of jumping out of one boat into another, and might be a long way off before the matter was in hand. Fix must therefore warn the English authorities and signal the coming of the *Rangoon* before Fogg could get ashore. This was easy, since the ship stopped at Singapore, which is in telegraphic communication with the Chinese coast. However, before acting, and in order to work with greater certainty, Fix decided to question Passepartout. He knew it was easy enough to make him talk, and he made up his mind to remain concealed no longer, as there was no time to be lost. It was now the 30th of October, and the *Rangoon* was due at Singapore on the morrow.

So Fix, leaving his cabin, went on deck with the intention of going up to Passepartout and being the first to show very great surprise. Passepartout was walking about on the forepart of the ship, when the detective rushed at him with the exclamation: 'What! you here on the *Rangoon*!' 'You on board, Mr Fix!' replied Passepartout, in amazement, as he recognised his fellow-passenger of the *Mongolia*. 'This beats me. I left you at Bombay, and here you are on the way to Hong-Kong! Are you, too, going round the world?'

'Oh, no,' replied Fix, 'I intend to stop at Hong-Kong – a few days at any rate.' 'I see,' said Passepartout, who seemed surprised for a moment. 'But how is it I have not seen you once on board since we left Calcutta?' 'Well, the fact is I have been a little queer, a bit sea-sick – I have been lying down in my berth – the Bay of Bengal does not suit me so well as the Indian Ocean. Is your master all right?' 'Perfectly well, and absolutely up to time; not a day late. By the way, Mr Fix, you didn't know that we had a young lady with us.' 'A young lady?' replied the detective, appearing to be completely at a loss to understand what was said to him.

Passepartout soon told him all about himself. He gave him an account of the incident of the Bombay pagoda, of the purchase of the elephant for two thousand pounds, the suttee affair, the carrying off of Aouda, the sentence of the Calcutta court and their liberation on bail. Fix, who knew the latter part of these happenings, pretended to be completely ignorant of them all, and Passepartout went on talking about his adventures, carried away by the delight of finding a listener who appeared to be so interested in him.

'But,' asked Fix, 'what is the upshot of this going to be? Does your master intend to take this young woman to Europe?' 'Oh, no, Mr Fix, not at all! We are simply going to hand her over to the care of a relative of hers, a rich merchant of Hong-Kong.' 'No go!' said the detective to himself, concealing his disappointment. 'Will you accept a glass of gin, Mr Passepartout?' 'With pleasure, Mr Fix. We will drink in honour of our meeting on board the *Rangoon* – we could scarcely do less.'

CHAPTER XVII

Concerning a variety of things between Singapore and Hong-Kong

PASSEPARTOUT AND FIX met frequently after this, but the detective was extremely reserved, and made no attempt to make his companion talk. On one or two occasions only did he catch a glimpse of Mr Fogg, who rarely left the saloon, where he either kept Aouda company or took a hand at whist, in accordance with his unvarying habit.

Passepartout now began very seriously to reflect on the strange chance which had once more placed Fix on the same route as his master; he was surprised at the singular coincidence, and no wonder. Here was this very pleasant and certainly most obliging gentleman, first coming across them at Suez, then embarking on the *Mongolia*, landing at Bombay, with the avowed intention of staying there, and now cropping up again on board the *Rangoon*, on the way to Hong-Kong; in fact, dogging Mr Fogg's footsteps. What was this fellow Fix after?

The matter deserved consideration, and Passepartout did some hard thinking, with the result that he was ready to wager his Turkish slippers, which he had very carefully preserved, that Fix would leave Hong-Kong when they did, and probably on the same boat.

Had Passepartout racked his brain for a century, he would never have guessed the nature of the detective's errand. He never could have imagined that Phileas Fogg was being shadowed around the earth as a thief.

But as it is in human nature to find an explanation for everything, Passepartout, by what seemed to him a flash of intuition, discovered a highly probable reason for Fix's abiding presence. Fix, he concluded, must be an agent sent by Mr Fogg's fellow-members of the Reform Club with orders to follow him closely and ascertain that he really travelled round the world along the route agreed upon.

'That's it! That's it!' repeated the good fellow to himself, very proud of his shrewdness. 'He's a spy sent by these gentlemen to track us! Not a very nice proceeding! To think of their having such an upright and honourable man as Mr Fogg watched by a spy! Ah, gentlemen of the Reform Club, you shall pay dearly for this!'

Delighted with his discovery, Passepartout decided, none the less, to say nothing about it to his master, lest he should be justly offended at this distrust on the part of his adversaries. But he resolved to chaff Fix, whenever he had the opportunity, with obscure allusions, yet without committing himself.

In the afternoon of Wednesday, the 30th of October, the *Rangoon* entered the Straits of Malacca, between the peninsula of that name and Sumatra. Most picturesque islets with very steep mountains hid the main island from view.

At four o'clock in the morning on the next day, the *Rangoon*, twelve hours in advance of her scheduled time, called at Singapore in order to take in a new supply of coal.

Phileas Fogg made a note of the gain, and this time went ashore to accompany Aouda, who expressed the desire to walk for some hours on land. Fix, to whom Fogg's every action appeared suspicious, followed him, taking care he himself should not be seen, while Passepartout, secretly much amused at Fix's slyness, went to make the usual purchases.

The island of Singapore is neither large nor imposing in appearance. There are no mountains, and therefore no sharp outlines. But despite its flatness, it is not lacking in charm. You might call it a park intersected with handsome roads. Mr Fogg and Aouda took a pretty carriage drawn by two of those smart horses imported from New Holland, and were driven through dense groves of palm trees with brilliant foliage, and clove trees on which the very bud of the half-open flower forms the cloves. Bushes of the pepper plant replaced the thorny hedges of European fields; sago-palms, great ferns with their magnificent branches lent variety to the gorgeous beauty of this tropical land; nutmeg trees with glistening leaves filled the air with their all-permeating scent. Troops of nimble, grinning apes peopled the woods, and possibly tigers were not rare in the jungle.

The fact that these terrible beasts of prey have not been utterly exterminated in such a comparatively small island may cause surprise, but their numbers are recruited from Malacca, whence they swim across the intervening strait.

After a two hours' drive in the country, Mr Fogg, who noticed very little of what he saw, brought back his companion to the town, a mass of squat, heavy-looking houses, surrounded by charming gardens luxuriant with the most luscious fruits of the earth, such as the pineapple and mangosteen.

At ten o'clock they re-embarked, unaware that they had been followed all the time by the detective, who likewise had gone to the expense of taking a carriage. They found Passepartout waiting for them on deck. The good fellow had bought several dozen mangosteens, a fruit of the size of an average apple, dark brown outside and bright red inside, and whose white flesh, as it melts in the mouth, gives your real epicure a delicious sensation like none other. He was only too pleased to offer them to Aouda, who was most gracious in her acceptance.

At eleven o'clock the *Rangoon*, having finished coaling, weighed anchor, and a few hours later her passengers lost sight of the high mountains of Malacca, with their forests where lurk the finest tigers in the world.

Some three hundred miles of sea separate Singapore from the island of Hong-Kong, a small English possession off the Chinese coast. It was important for Phileas Fogg that the voyage should not take more than six days, as he would then be in time to catch the boat due to leave Hong-Kong on November 6 for Yokohama, one of the chief ports of Japan.

The *Rangoon* was now heavily loaded, having taken on board a large number of passengers at Singapore, Hindus, Ceylonese, Chinese, Malays and Portuguese, who were mostly second-class travellers. The weather, which had been fine up till then, changed with the last quarter of the moon. The sea became rough, and the wind rose at times to half a gale, but very fortunately blew from the south-east, and was favourable to the ship's progress. When it was not too squally, the captain put up canvas. The *Rangoon*, rigged like a brig, often sailed under her two top-sails and fore-sail, and the double action of steam and wind gave her the greater speed. In this way, on a choppy and at times very trying sea, she forged ahead along the coasts of Annam and Cochin China.[19]

The majority of the passengers were ill, but the *Rangoon* was more to blame than the sea. For the ships of the Peninsular and Oriental Company which ply in the China seas have a serious structural defect. The ratio between their draught when loaded and their depth was wrongly calculated, with the result that their power of resistance to the sea is small. Their watertight bulkheads are not large enough, so they are 'drowned,' as the sailors say; if they ship a few heavy seas, their behaviour is seriously affected. These vessels are therefore very inferior, though not necessarily as regards their motor and evaporating apparatus, to the types of the French Messageries, such as the *Impératrice* and the *Cambodge*. Whereas these vessels, according to the engineers' calculations, can ship a weight of water equal to their own, the boats of the P. & O. Company, the *Golconda*, the *Corea* and the *Rangoon*, would not ship the sixth of their own weight without sinking.

So in foul weather great precautions were necessary, and, at times, the captain had to lay the ship to, under easy steam. This meant a loss of time, by which Phileas Fogg seemed to be completely unaffected, but which aggravated Passepartout beyond measure. He blamed the captain, the engineer and the Company, and consigned to the devil all those who make it their business to convey travellers. It is just possible, too, that his impatience was provoked in no small measure by the thought of that gas-burner which was still on at his expense in the house in Savile Row.

'You seem to be in a great hurry to get to Hong-Kong,' Fix said to him one day. 'Yes, I am,' replied Passepartout. 'You think Mr Fogg is anxious to catch the boat for Yokohama?' 'Frightfully anxious.' 'You do believe in this mysterious journey around the world, then?' 'Absolutely. Don't you, Mr Fix?' 'No, I don't.' 'You sly dog!' replied Passepartout with a wink. This expression made the detective think. The epithet worried him, though he could not say why. Had the Frenchman found him out? He was puzzled. But no one knew he was a detective; how could Passepartout have discovered that? Yet he could hardly have made use of such words unless he had something at the back of his head.

Passepartout ventured even further on another occasion; he simply could not help himself, his tongue ran away with him. 'Now, then, Mr Fix,' he said to his companion in a quizzing tone, 'shall we have the misfortune to leave you behind in Hong-Kong, when we get there?' 'Well,' answered Fix, rather uncomfortable, 'I can't say. It's just possible that . . . ' 'Ah,' broke in Passepartout, 'I should be so pleased if you would go on with us! Come, surely an agent of the Peninsular and Oriental Company cannot stop on the way, Bombay was your destination, and here you are now almost in China. America is not far away, and it is only a step from America to Europe.'

Fix, watching the other man's face intently, and seeing nothing but the most friendly benevolence there, thought it best to laugh with him. But Passepartout, feeling in the humour for banter, asked him whether his present job was a paying one.

'Yes, and no,' replied Fix, without wincing. 'There is good and bad business in it. But you must understand that I don't travel at my own expense.' 'Oh, you need not tell me that!' exclaimed Passepartout, laughing more heartily than ever.

This was the end of their conversation, and Fix returned to his cabin and began to think. He was evidently found out. In one way or another, the Frenchman had discovered that he was a detective. But had he told his master? What part was he playing in all this? Was he an accomplice or not? Had they wind of his object, in which case the game was up? The detective spent some hours in a state of great perplexity, sometimes thinking that all was lost; then hoping that Fogg knew nothing, and then again unable to decide what line of action to pursue.

Nevertheless, after a time he recovered his coolness of mind, and determined to deal frankly with Passepartout. Should he not be in a position to arrest Fogg at Hong-Kong, and should Fogg be taking steps to leave this English soil, the last they would touch, then he would tell Passepartout everything. One of two things: either the servant was the accomplice of his master, who in that case was aware of the measures taken against him, which made success very doubtful and reserve useless, or the servant had nothing to do with the theft, and it would then be his interest to leave the thief in the lurch.

Such was the respective positions of these two men, while above them Phileas Fogg soared in the majesty of his indifference. He was moving rationally around the world, regardless of the lesser planets that gravitated around him. And yet there was, not far away, what astronomers call a disturbing star, which ought to have produced certain tremors in the gentleman's heart. But it was not so; Aouda's charm failed to act, to Passepartout's great surprise; if any perturbations did exist, they would have been more difficult to calculate than those of Uranus which led to the discovery of Neptune.

This was a daily wonder to Passepartout, who read in Aouda's eyes such heartfelt gratitude to his master.

Very reluctantly he came to the conclusion that Phileas Fogg's heart was just capable of heroic conduct, but quite incapable of love.

As to the worries which the chances of the journey might have caused him, there was not a trace of any; whereas Passepartout lived in a state of perpetual alarm. One day, as he was leaning on the breast-rail of the engine-room, watching the powerful engine, he saw it race away from time to time, when, owing to a heavy pitch of the vessel, the screw was spinning round wildly in the air, and the steam rushing out through the valves; this made the good fellow very angry.

'Those valves are not sufficiently weighted!' he cried. 'We are not getting on at all! It's just like the English! If this were an American ship, we might blow up, but we should be going faster!'

CHAPTER XVIII

In which Phileas Fogg, Passepartout and Fix attend to their business, each on his own account

DURING THE LATTER DAYS of the voyage, the weather was rather rough. The wind, which had settled in the north-west, delayed the ship's progress, and made her roll heavily, owing to her want of stability. The passengers suffered a good deal from the long nauseating waves which the wind churned up from the open sea.

On the 3rd and 4th of November they encountered almost a gale, which lashed the sea with fury, and compelled the captain to lay to for half a day, while the ship was kept on her course with only ten revolutions of her screw, and in such manner as to receive the waves aslant. All sail had been taken in, but even the rigging was a great strain, as it laboured, whistling in the squalls.

The ship's pace was, of course, considerably slowed, and it was reasonably estimated that she would reach Hong-Kong twenty hours behind time, and even more if the storm continued.

Phileas Fogg contemplated this raging sea, that seemed to be battling against him personally, with his usual serenity. His brow was not clouded for one moment, although a delay of twenty hours might be the cause of failure by making him miss the boat at Yokohama. But the man had no nerves; he was neither impatient nor annoyed. It really seemed as though this storm formed part of his programme and had been foreseen. When Aouda discussed this set-back with him, she found him calm as ever.

For Fix the matter had a very different aspect. The storm delighted him. His satisfaction would have been boundless, if the *Rangoon* had been forced to turn and run before the hurricane. All these delays fitted in with his schemes, for they would compel this man Fogg to remain a few days in Hong-Kong. At last the heavens themselves were taking a hand on his side with their gusts and squalls. True he was a little sea-sick, but what did that matter! While his body writhed in the grip of nausea, he heeded it not, for his spirit exulted with exceeding great joy.

One can easily imagine with what ill-concealed wrath Passepartout went through this trying time. Earth and sea had hitherto seemed to be at his master's service; steamers and trains at his beck and call; wind and steam had joined forces in furthering his voyage. But now it looked as though the hour of disappointments had struck. Passepartout was as truly racked as if the twenty thousand pounds of the wager were to come from his own pocket. He was exasperated by the storm, infuriated by the squall, and ready to scourge the rebellious sea. Poor fellow! Fix took care not to let him see how delighted he was; and he was wise, for had Passepartout had an inkling of his secret satisfaction, Fix would have had a rough time of it. Throughout the storm Passepartout stayed on deck; it would have been quite impossible for him to remain below. He climbed up the masts and lent a helping hand everywhere with the clever agility of a monkey, to the astonishment of the crew. The captain, officers and sailors were worried by him with endless questions, and could not help laughing at seeing a man in such a flurry. He insisted on knowing how long the gale would last, whereupon he was told to go and consult the barometer, which still showed no sign of rising. He shook the barometer, but with no result, for neither shaking nor the curses which he heaped upon the irresponsible instrument had the least effect.

At long last, however, the hurricane abated, and during the 4th of November the sea became less rough; the wind shifted through two points of the compass to the south, and was once more favourable. Passepartout brightened up with the weather. The top-sails and lower sails were set, and the *Rangoon* proceeded once more at her highest speed. It was, however, impossible to make good all the time that had been lost. That could not be helped, and land was not signalled before the 6th, at five o'clock in the morning. According to Phileas Fogg's time-table the liner was to arrive on the 5th. He would therefore be twenty-four hours late, and would necessarily miss the connection with Yokohama.

At six o'clock the pilot stepped on board the *Rangoon* and went up on the bridge in order to steer the ship through the fair-way into Hong-Kong harbour.

Passepartout was dying to ask him if the Yokohama boat had sailed, but he dared not, preferring to keep a little hope to the last minute. He had confided his anxiety to Fix, who, sly fox that he was, tried to comfort him by telling him that if the worst came to the worst, Mr Fogg would take the next boat, but this, of course, only made Passepartout furious.

Mr Fogg, feeling none of Passepartout's restraining apprehensions, consulted his *Bradshaw*, and asked the said pilot, in his quiet way, whether he knew when there would be a boat for Yokohama.

'At high tide tomorrow morning,' replied the pilot. 'Is that so?' said Mr Fogg, without showing the slightest surprise.

Passepartout, who heard this, would have been happy to embrace the pilot, whilst Fix would have gladly wrung his neck.

'What is the name of the ship?' asked Mr Fogg. 'The *Carnatic*,' replied the pilot. 'Was she not due to sail yesterday?' 'Yes, sir, but one of her boilers had to undergo repairs; so her departure was put off till tomorrow.' 'Thank you,' answered Mr Fogg, who then returned to the saloon, descending with that automatic step of his.

As for Passepartout, he gripped the pilot's hand, gave it a hearty squeeze and said: 'Pilot, you are a brick!'

Doubtless the pilot never knew why his answers were rewarded with this effusive demonstration. On hearing a whistle, he went up again on the bridge, and guided the steamer through the flotilla of junks, tankas, fishing-boats, and ships of every kind which crowded Hong-Kong harbour. At one o'clock the *Rangoon* was berthed, and the passengers were landing.

It cannot be denied that chance had been singularly kind to Phileas Fogg on this occasion. But for this necessary repair to her boilers, the *Carnatic* would have left on the 5th of November, and the passengers for Japan would have had to wait eight days for the sailing of the next boat. True, Mr Fogg was twenty-four hours late, but this loss of time could not affect adversely the remainder of the journey, for the steamer plying between Yokohama and San Francisco ran in direct connection with the Hong-Kong boat, and could not sail before her arrival. Of course, they would leave Yokohama twenty-four hours late, but the voyage through the Pacific lasts twenty-two days, and in that time it would be easy to make good these twenty-four hours. So Phileas Fogg, thirty-five days after leaving London, was twenty-four hours behind his time-table.

As the *Carnatic* would not leave Hong-Kong before five o'clock next morning, Mr Fogg had sixteen hours to attend to his business in that town: that is to say, to arrange for Aouda's future. On landing, he offered her his arm and took her to a palanquin.

On his inquiring for some hotel, the men mentioned the Club Hotel, and the palanquin moved on, followed by Passepartout, and twenty minutes after they reached their destination. A room was engaged for the young woman, and Phileas Fogg, having seen that she had all she wanted, told her he was going to try and find the relative in whose care he was to leave her, and directed Passepartout to remain at the hotel until he returned, that she should not be left there alone.

Mr Fogg then drove off to the Stock Exchange, feeling sure that a person who ranked among the richest merchants of the town must be well known there.

Mr Fogg applied to a broker for the information he desired, and was told by this broker, who knew the merchant Jejeeh, that he had left China two years before. Having made his fortune, he had gone to Europe to live; to Holland, it was thought, which was natural, as he had had a great deal to do with that country in the course of his commercial career.

Phileas Fogg returned to the Club Hotel, and at once asked if he could see Aouda. Going straight to the point, he informed her that her relative was no longer in Hong-Kong, but was probably living in Holland.

Aouda at first said nothing; then, passing her hand over her forehead, she remained thinking a while, whereupon in her gentle voice she said, 'What am I to do, Mr Fogg?' 'It is very simple,' he replied. 'Return with us to Europe.' 'But I cannot abuse your . . . ' 'You abuse nothing, and your presence does not interfere in the least with my plan. Passepartout?'

'Sir.' 'Go and engage three cabins on the *Carnatic*.'

Passepartout hurried out on his errand, delighted that he was not to lose the company of the young woman who always treated him with great kindness.

CHAPTER XIX

In which Passepartout takes too keen an interest in his master, and the consequence

HONG-KONG is a small island which was secured to England by the Treaty of Nanking, after the war of 1842. In a few years the colonising genius of Great Britain created upon it the important seaport town of Victoria. The island is situated at the mouth of the Canton River, not more than sixty miles from the Portuguese city of Macao, on the opposite shore. In the commercial struggle between the two settlements, Hong-Kong necessarily defeated her rival, and now the greater part of the Chinese transit trade is carried on through the English town. With docks, hospitals, wharves, warehouses, a Gothic cathedral, a Government house, macadamised streets, Hong-Kong looks exactly like a busy town in Kent or Surrey transported through the globe to this Chinese locality, almost at the Antipodes.

Passepartout, his hands in his pockets, made his way towards

Victoria Port, gazing at the palanquins, the hand-chairs with sails, still in favour in the Celestial Empire, and the crowds of Chinese, Japanese and Europeans that thronged the streets. It was all very much like Bombay, Calcutta or Singapore over again. There is thus, so to speak, a trail of English towns all round the world.

Passepartout, arriving at Victoria Port, at the mouth of Canton River, found a swarming mass of ships of every nation – English, French, American, Dutch, some of them men-of-war, Japanese or Chinese boats, junks, sampans, tankas, and even flower-boats, dotting the water like so many floating flower-beds. As he strolled, Passepartout observed a certain number of natives dressed in yellow, all very old. On going into a barber's shop to get shaved in the Chinese fashion, he was told by the local Figaro, who spoke English fairly well, that these old people were octogenarians at least, and that in consequence they were entitled to wear yellow, the imperial colour. This struck Passepartout as very funny, though he did not quite know why. After his shave, he proceeded to find the quay whence the *Carnatic* would sail, and saw Fix walking to and fro. He was not surprised at finding the detective there, but noticed that his face showed signs of intense disappointment.

'Good!' said Passepartout to himself. 'Things are not going well for the gentlemen of the Reform Club.' He went up to Fix with his sunny smile, appearing not to notice his companion's chagrin.

It was not without good reason that the detective was cursing the infernal bad luck that dogged his steps. Still no warrant! It was evident that the warrant was being dispatched after him, and that it would not get to him unless he could remain a few days in this town. Now Hong-Kong was the last English territory on the route, and this man Fogg would escape him for good and all, if he failed to find some device for keeping him here.

'Well, Mr Fix, have you made up your mind to come with us as far as America?' asked Passepartout. 'Yes,' replied Fix through clenched teeth. 'Come, come!' cried Passepartout, breaking into a loud guffaw. 'Didn't I know that you could not leave us? Come and book your passage; come along.' Thereupon they went together to the Company's office and engaged cabins for four persons.

The clerk informed them that the *Carnatic*'s repairs were finished, and that the ship would consequently sail that very evening at eight o'clock, and not next morning, as had been announced.

'All the better!' replied Passepartout. 'This will fit in excellently with my master's plans. I will go at once and let him know.'

At this moment Fix decided on an extreme measure, and determined to tell Passepartout everything, as it was perhaps the only means at his command for keeping back Phileas Fogg a few days at Hong-Kong.

When they left the office, Fix offered his companion a drink. Passepartout, having plenty of time, accepted the invitation. There was a pleasant-looking tavern on the quay, and they went in and found themselves in a large, well-decorated room, at the far end of which was a camp-bed, covered with cushions, and on this bed lay a certain number of persons asleep. Some thirty customers were seated at small tables made of plaited rushes. A few were draining mugs of English beer or porter; others jugs of spirits, gin or brandy. Most of them were also smoking long red-clay pipes stuffed with small pellets of opium mingled with attar of roses. From time to time one of the smokers, overcome by the fumes, would slip under the table, and the waiters, taking him by the head and feet, carried him away and deposited him on the camp-bed beside a fellow-sleeper. About twenty of these inebriates were thus laid out on the bed, side by side, in the last stage of stupefied intoxication.

Fix and Passepartout perceived that the place they were in was a smoking-house, a haunt of those besotted, emaciated, idiot wretches to whom England, in her commercialism, sells every year ten million four hundred thousand pounds' worth of that fatal drug called opium. A mournful revenue this, raised from one of the most deadly vices of humanity!

The Chinese Government has in vain tried to put a stop to the evil by stringent laws. The use of opium was at first strictly confined to the wealthy, but it gradually reached the lower classes, and the havoc it worked could not be arrested. Opium is smoked everywhere and on all occasions in the Middle Kingdom. Men and women are addicted to this deplorable craze, and once accustomed to inhale these fumes, they cannot leave off the habit without experiencing horrible spasms of the stomach. A great smoker can smoke as many as eight pipes a day, but he dies in five years.

It was one of these dens, of which there are any number even in Hong-Kong, that Fix and Passepartout entered to get something to drink. Passepartout had no money, but he readily accepted his companion's friendly offer, intending to return the compliment on some future occasion.

Two bottles of port were ordered, to which the Frenchman did ample justice, whilst Fix, drinking more cautiously, observed him with the closest attention. They chatted about one thing and another, and in particular about Fix's splendid idea of booking a berth on the *Carnatic*. Talking of the ship reminded Passepartout of her sailing some hours before the time announced, so, the bottles being empty, he got up to go and inform his master.

Fix detained him. 'One moment,' he said. 'Why do you wish me to stay, Mr Fix?' 'I want to talk to you about a serious matter.' 'A serious matter!' exclaimed Passepartout, drinking a few drops of wine left at the bottom of his glass. 'Well, we can talk about that tomorrow. I have no time today.' 'Stay,' replied Fix, 'this concerns your master.' On hearing this, Passepartout looked at Fix attentively, and the expression on his face struck him as being so strange that he sat down again and said, 'Well, what is this that you have to say to me?' Fix laid his hand impressively on his companion's arm, and, lowering his voice, said, 'You have found me out?' 'Of course I have!' said Passepartout, smiling. 'Then I am going to tell you everything – ' 'Now that I know everything, my friend! No, I cannot call it very clever. However, go ahead. But let me tell you at once that those gentlemen have gone to very useless expense.' 'Useless!' said Fix. 'That's all very well! You evidently don't know how large the sum is.' 'Yes, I do,' replied Passepartout. 'Twenty thousand pounds.' 'Fifty-five thousand!' returned Fix, pressing the Frenchman's hand. 'What!' cried Passepartout, 'do you mean to say Mr Fogg dared! – Fifty-five thousand pounds! – Well, then, that's all the more reason for not losing a moment,' he added, getting up once more. 'Fifty-five thousand pounds!' resumed Fix, making Passepartout sit down again, and ordering a bottle of brandy, 'and if I am successful, I shall get two thousand pounds. I will give you five hundred, if you will help me.' 'Help you?' cried Passepartout, whose eyes were almost out of their sockets. 'Yes, help me keep this man Fogg here in Hong-Kong for a few days.'

'Eh, what!' cried Passepartout; 'it is not enough for them to send a man on my master's track and suspect his honour; now they want to put obstacles in his way! I blush for these gentlemen!' 'Whatever do you mean?' asked Fix. 'What I mean is that this is nothing but a shabby trick. They might just as well plunder Mr Fogg and pick his pockets!' 'Well, that is just what we hope to do sooner or later.'

'Then it's a case of foul play!' cried Passepartout, getting more and more excited under the effect of the brandy which Fix kept on pouring out to him, and which he drank without noticing what he was doing. 'It's regular foul play! And gentlemen, too! Colleagues!' Fix was getting more and more bewildered. 'Colleagues!' exclaimed Passepartout. 'Members of the Reform Club! Let me tell you, Mr Fix, that my master is an honest man, and that when he makes a bet, he means to win it honourably.'

'But who on earth do you think I am?' asked Fix, looking at him intently. 'You're an agent of the Reform Club, of course. And your business is to check my master's journey. This is so humiliating a proceeding that I have taken great care not to tell Mr Fogg what you were up to, although I found you out some time ago.' 'Doesn't he know?' asked Fix eagerly. 'He knows nothing,' replied Passepartout, once more draining his glass.

The detective passed his hand across his forehead, thinking what he should say next, and wondering what to do. Passepartout's mistake seemed quite genuine, but made his plan all the more difficult of execution. The fellow obviously spoke in perfect good faith, and was not his master's accomplice, as Fix might have feared.

'Well, then,' he said to himself, 'since he is not his accomplice, he will help me.'

Once again the detective decided on a line of action, having no time to wait, as at any cost he must arrest Fogg at Hong-Kong. 'Listen,' said Fix sharply. 'Hear me out attentively. I am not what you imagine; that is, I am no agent of the members of the Reform Club – '

'Pooh!' broke in Passepartout, looking at him with an air of mockery.

'I am a police-inspector, sent out on special duty by Scotland Yard – ' 'You a police-inspector?' 'Yes, I am,' resumed Fix; 'and I will prove it. Here is my warrant.' Thereupon the official took a paper from his pocket-book and showed his companion a warrant signed by the head of the London Police. Passepartout, absolutely dumbfounded, gazed at Fix, unable to utter a word. 'Fogg's wager,' continued Fix, 'is nothing but a blind, which has taken you all in, you and his fellow-members of the Reform Club. He found it useful to secure your unconscious complicity.' 'But why?' exclaimed Passepartout.

'Listen. On the 29th of last September, a theft of fifty-five thousand pounds was committed at the Bank of England by a person whose description was fortunately obtained. Now this description is in every feature a true one of the man Fogg.'

'What nonsense!' cried Passepartout, striking the table with a bang of his powerful fist. 'My master is the most honourable man in the world!'

'What do you know about it?' answered Fix. 'How can you know the man? You entered his service the very day of his departure, and he left in a hurry, on a senseless pretext, without luggage, and taking with him a huge sum in banknotes. And yet you make bold to maintain he is an honest man!' 'Yes, yes,' repeated the poor fellow mechanically.

'Do you want to be arrested as his accomplice?' Passepartout buried his distorted countenance in his hands. He dared not look the detective in the face. Phileas Fogg a thief! The saviour of Aouda, a man so eminently generous and brave, a thief! And yet how black things looked against him! Passepartout strove to reject the suspicions which were stealing into his mind. He refused to believe his master guilty.

'Well, what do you want of me?' he said, controlling his feelings by a supreme effort.

'This is the point,' replied Fix. 'I have tracked Fogg as far as here, but I have not yet received the warrant of arrest for which I applied in London. You must therefore help me to keep him back here in Hong-Kong.' 'You want me to – !' 'And I will share with you the reward of two thousand pounds to be given by the Bank of England.' 'Never!' replied Passepartout, who tried to rise, but fell back, feeling that both his reason and his strength were leaving him.

'Mr Fix,' he stammered, 'even though everything you have told me were true, though my master were the thief you are looking for, which I deny, I have been, and am still in his service. I have never seen him anything but good and generous. I betray him! Never! No, not for all the gold in the world. They don't eat that sort of bread where I come from.' 'You refuse?' 'I refuse.' 'Then take it that I have said nothing, and let us drink on it.' 'All right, let us drink!'

Passepartout felt he was getting more and more intoxicated. Fix, seeing that, come what might, he must separate him from his master, decided to incapacitate him completely. There were a few pipes filled with opium on the table. Fix slipped one of these into Passepartout's hand. He seized it, raised it to his lips, lit it, drew a few puffs out of it, and collapsed, stupefied by the narcotic.

'At last!' said Fix, seeing Passepartout down and out. 'That man Fogg will not be informed in time of the hour of sailing of the *Carnatic*; and, if he does get away, he will at all events go without that cursed Frenchman.'

He then paid the bill and left the tavern.

CHAPTER XX

In which Fix comes into contact with Phileas Fogg

WHILE THIS WAS taking place at the opium-den, Mr Fogg, little suspecting the danger that threatened him, was walking leisurely with Aouda in the streets of the English quarter. Aouda having accepted his offer to take her to Europe, a great many things, made necessary by such a long voyage, had to be thought of. An Englishman like Mr Fogg might possibly travel round the world with a carpet-bag, but a lady could not undertake such a journey in the same way. Clothing and other objects needed for prolonged travel had to be procured. Mr Fogg accomplished his task with characteristic composure, and whenever the young widow offered apologies or objections, feeling embarrassed by so much kindness, he invariably replied: 'It will conduce to the success of my journey; it is all part of my programme.'

Having made their purchases, they returned to the hotel and dined at a sumptuous table d'hôte; after which Aouda, feeling rather tired, shook hands with her impassive deliverer, as is the English custom, and retired to her room. Mr Fogg spent the whole evening immersed in the reading of *The Times* and *Illustrated London News*.

If anything could have surprised him, it would have been the failure of his servant to appear at bedtime. But, as he knew the boat would not leave for Yokohama until the next morning, the matter caused him no anxiety. Next morning Passepartout did not answer his master's bell, and Mr Fogg was told that his servant had not returned to the hotel. What he thought of it, no one could have told, for all he did was to take his travelling-bag, send word to Aouda, and order a palanquin.

It was then eight o'clock; at half-past nine it would be high tide, and the *Carnatic* would then be able to leave port. The palanquin having arrived, Mr Fogg and Aouda got into this comfortable conveyance, and their luggage followed them in a wheelbarrow. Half an hour later the travellers descended on the quay, and Mr Fogg was told that the *Carnatic* had sailed the day before. He had expected to find the liner and his servant, and now he was forced to face the loss of both. But his face showed not the slightest sign of disappointment, and as Aouda looked at him anxiously, all he said was, 'It is a mere incident, madam; nothing more.' At this moment a man who had been observing him attentively came up to him. It was Fix, who bowed, saying, 'Were you not, sir, like myself a passenger on the *Rangoon*, which arrived yesterday?' 'Yes, I was, sir,' replied Mr Fogg coldly, 'but I have not the honour – ' 'Excuse me, but I expected to find your servant here.' 'Do you know where he is, sir?' asked Aouda eagerly. 'What!' replied Fix, feigning surprise, 'is he not with you?' 'No,' answered Aouda. 'We have not seen him since yesterday. I wonder if he sailed on the *Carnatic* without us?' 'Without you, madam?' replied the detective. 'But, excuse my question, was it your intention, then, to go by this boat?' 'Yes, sir.' 'It was mine too, and I am extremely disappointed. Her repairs being completed, the *Carnatic* left Hong-Kong twelve hours sooner than she was expected to do, and without notice, and now we shall have to wait a week for the next boat.'

As he uttered the words, 'a week,' Fix felt his heart leap with joy. A week! Fogg kept back a week in Hong-Kong! This would give him time to receive the warrant. At last luck was showing itself favourable to the representative of the law.

One can imagine what a stunning blow he received when he heard Phileas Fogg say in his cool, quiet tone of voice: 'But it seems to me there are other ships besides the *Carnatic* in Hong-Kong harbour.' And Mr Fogg, offering his arm to Aouda, made his way to the docks in search of a ship about to sail.

Fix followed in a state of amazement; it looked as though he were tied to this man by a thread.

Chance, however, quite seemed to have deserted the man it had hitherto served so well. For three hours Phileas Fogg thoroughly searched the docks, having decided to charter a ship, if necessary, to convey him to Yokohama. But all the vessels he saw were either loading or unloading, and consequently could not make ready for sea. Fix began to hope again.

Nevertheless Mr Fogg, not in the least disconcerted, was about to continue his search, even at Macao, when he was accosted by a sailor on the outer harbour.

'Is your honour looking for a boat?' asked the sailor, uncovering. 'Have you a boat ready to sail?' asked Mr Fogg. 'Yes, your honour, a pilot-boat, No. 43 – the best one of the lot.' 'Is she a fast boat?' 'Her speed is from eight to nine knots an hour, near as can be. Would you like to see her?' 'Yes.' 'You'll be pleased with her, sir. You want to go for a trip?' 'No, for a voyage.' 'A voyage?' 'Will you undertake to carry me to Yokohama?'

On hearing this proposal the sailor stood with his arms limp at his sides and his eyes wide open. 'Your honour is joking?' he said.

'No. I have missed the *Carnatic*, and I must be at Yokohama on the 14th at latest, to take the boat for San Francisco.' 'I am sorry,' replied the sailor, 'but the thing is impossible.' 'I am prepared to give you a hundred pounds a day, and a bonus of two hundred pounds, if I get there in time.'

'Are you in earnest?' asked the pilot. 'Very much in earnest,' answered Mr Fogg. The pilot stood aside, looking at the sea; he was evidently pulled one way by the desire to earn a huge sum of money, and another by the fear of venturing so far away. Fix was on the rack. Mr Fogg, turning to Aouda, said to her, 'You are not afraid, madam?' 'Not with you, Mr Fogg,' she replied.

The pilot now came forward, fidgeting with his hat. 'Well, pilot?'

said Mr Fogg. 'Well, your honour,' he replied, 'I cannot endanger my men, myself and you, by undertaking such a long voyage on a boat of scarcely twenty tons, and at this time of the year. Besides, we should not get there in time, for it is sixteen hundred and fifty miles to Yokohama.' 'Not more than sixteen hundred,' said Mr Fogg. 'That makes no difference.' Fix breathed freely. 'But,' continued the pilot, 'we might possibly manage it another way.' Fix choked. 'What way?' asked Phileas Fogg. 'By going to Nagasaki, in the extreme south of Japan, a distance of eleven hundred miles, or even to Shanghai, which is eight hundred miles from this port. The latter voyage would not take us far from the Chinese coast, which would be a great advantage, all the more that the currents run northward.' 'Pilot,' answered Phileas Fogg, 'it is at Yokohama that I must take the American mail-boat, not at Shanghai or Nagasaki.'

'Why not?' replied the pilot. 'The San Francisco boat does not start at Yokohama. Yokohama and Nagasaki are ports of call, but the port of departure is Shanghai.' 'Are you sure of that?' 'Quite sure.' 'When does the boat leave Shanghai?' 'On the 11th, at seven o'clock in the evening. This gives us four days to do it in. Four days make ninety-six hours, so that with an average speed of eight knots an hour, if we are in luck, if the wind remains in the south-east, and if the sea is calm, we can cover the eight hundred miles between here and Shanghai.' 'When can you start?' 'In an hour. I just want time enough to buy provisions and get under sail.' 'Done! You are the skipper of the boat?' 'Yes, I am John Bunsby, master of the *Tankadere*.' 'Would you like some earnest-money?' 'If it is not inconvenient to your honour.' 'Take these two hundred pounds on account.' Then Phileas Fogg turned round and said to Fix, 'Sir, if you care to avail yourself of – ' 'I was just going to ask this favour of you,' replied Fix resolutely. 'All right; we shall be on board in half an hour.' 'But what about your poor servant?' said Aouda, who was excessively worried by Passepartout's disappearance. 'I shall do all I possibly can for him,' answered Phileas Fogg. Fix, nervous, restless and fuming, went to the pilot-boat, and Mr Fogg and Aouda made their way to the Hong-Kong Police Station, where Mr Fogg gave Passepartout's description and left sufficient money to take him back to France. Similar steps were taken at the French consulate, and, after going to the hotel to fetch their luggage, they returned in the palanquin to the outer harbour. At three o'clock punctually, pilot-boat No. 43, with her crew on board and her provisions stowed away, was ready to set sail.

The *Tankadere* was a beautiful little schooner of twenty tons, long in the beam, with fine bows and graceful lines. She looked like a racing yacht. Her shining brass and galvanised ironwork, her deck white as ivory, all pointed to the care and skill with which her master, John Bunsby, kept her seaworthy and smart. Her two masts leaned backward a little; she carried spanker, foresail, fore-staysail, jibs, and could put up canvas to run before the wind. She was obviously a very fast sailer, and, as a matter of fact, she had won several prizes in pilot-boat races. The crew of the *Tankadere* was composed of the skipper, John Bunsby, and four men, fearless seamen, who in all weathers ventured out in search of ships in need of them, and were perfectly familiar with the Chinese seas. John Bunsby, a man of forty-five or so, sturdy, sunburnt, keen-eyed, with a strong face, thoroughly steady and devoted to his business, would have inspired confidence in the most timid.

Phileas Fogg and Aouda went on board, whither Fix had preceded them.

Aft the hood led down the hatchway to a square cabin, the sides of which bulged out so as to form cots above a circular divan. In the middle stood a table lighted by a swinging-lamp. There was not much room, but everything was neat.

'I am sorry I have nothing better to offer you,' said Mr Fogg to Fix, whose only answer was a bow. The detective felt something like humiliation at benefiting thus by Fogg's kindness. 'Certainly,' he thought, 'the man is a polite rascal, but a rascal none the less.'

The sails were hoisted at ten minutes past three, and the English flag fluttered at the schooner's gaff. As the passengers sat on deck, Mr Fogg and Aouda looked once more at the quay, in the hope of seeing Passepartout turn up. Fix was by no means free from anxiety, for chance might have brought to this very spot the unfortunate fellow whom he had treated so abominably, and in that case an explanation and indignant reproaches would have followed, which must have proved anything but advantageous for the detective. But the Frenchman was not to be seen; doubtless he was still in the grip of the stupefying narcotic.

Skipper John Bunsby having at last gained the open sea, the *Tankadere* took the wind under her spanker, foresail and jibs, and leaped forward over the waves.

CHAPTER XXI

In which the master of the Tankadere *runs great danger of losing a bonus of two hundred pounds*

THIS VOYAGE of eight hundred miles, on a craft of twenty tons, was a dangerous venture, especially at that time of the year. The Chinese seas are generally rough and liable to sudden squalls of terrible violence, particularly during the equinox; and it was still early November. It would undoubtedly have been to the pilot's advantage to take his passengers to Yokohama, since he was paid so much per day. But he would have been very rash in attempting such a long voyage in these conditions; it was bold enough, not to say foolhardy, to sail up the coast as far as Shanghai. But John Bunsby had full confidence in his *Tankadere*, which rose to the wave like a gull, and he was perhaps justified.

During the last hours of the day, the *Tankadere* made her way through the capricious channels of Hong-Kong, and, whether under full sail or close-hauled, or with wind astern, she behaved admirably.

'Pilot,' said Phileas Fogg, just as the schooner was coming out into the open sea, 'I need not urge upon you the necessity for making all possible speed.' 'Your honour can leave that to me,' replied John Bunsby. 'We are carrying all the canvas the wind will let us. Our jibs, far from helping, would only make her labour and reduce her pace.' 'This is your job, not mine, pilot, and I trust you.'

Phileas Fogg, with body erect and legs well apart and firmly planted like a sailor, watched the heavy sea without faltering. The young woman, seated aft, was not unmoved, as she gazed on that ocean, already darkened in the twilight, whose fearsome perils she was facing on a frail vessel. Above her head stretched the white sails, hurrying her through space like huge wings, for the schooner seemed to be lifted by the wind and actually flying.

Night came. The moon was entering her first quarter, and her feeble light would soon flicker out altogether behind the misty horizon. Clouds were driving up from the east, and had already overcast a part of the heavens. The pilot had hung out his lights, a very necessary precaution in these seas crowded with ships making port. Collisions were of frequent occurrence and, at the speed she was going, the schooner would have been shattered by the slightest shock.

Fix, in the fore part of the ship, was buried in thought. Knowing Fogg's uncommunicative disposition, he remained apart; all the more that he disliked talking to this man whose assistance he had accepted. The future, too, claimed his attention. It seemed a certainty that Fogg would not stop at Yokohama, but would at once take the boat for San Francisco, so as to get to America, where the vast extent of the country would ensure for him both impunity and security. Phileas Fogg's plan, he thought, was simplicity itself. Instead of sailing from England to the United States, like an ordinary malefactor, the fellow had taken a very roundabout way, travelling through three-quarters of the globe, in order to reach the American continent the more surely, where, having thrown the police off his track, he would enjoy in peace the thousands of pounds stolen from the bank. But once they landed in the United States, what was he, Fix, going to do? Should he let the man go? No; a hundred times no! He would hold on to him until he obtained an extradition order. It was his duty, and he would fulfil it to the end. At all events there was now one thing in his favour. Passepartout was no longer with his master. After Fix's confidential revelations, it was more than ever necessary that they never should come together again.

Phileas Fogg also was thinking about Passepartout, and his very strange disappearance. Looking at the matter in every way, he came to the conclusion that it was not impossible that, through some misunderstanding, the poor fellow had at the last moment embarked on the *Carnatic*. This was also Aouda's opinion. She felt keenly the loss of this honest servant to whom she owed so much. There was, then, just a possibility that they might find him at Yokohama, and it would be easy to ascertain whether he had arrived there on board the *Carnatic*. About ten o'clock it began to blow. It might have been wise to take in a reef, but the pilot, after scanning the sky with great care, left the ship rigged as she was. As a matter of fact, the *Tankadere* carried canvas admirably, for she drew a great deal of water, and everything was in readiness to take in sail, in case of a sudden squall.

At midnight Phileas Fogg and Aouda went below. Fix was there already, lying on one of the cots. The pilot and his men remained all night on deck. On the next day, November 8, at sunrise, the schooner had sailed more than a hundred miles. The log, repeatedly consulted, showed an average speed of between eight and nine miles. With every sail taking the wind fully, the *Tankadere* was making the best speed of which she was capable. Should the wind hold as it was, the chances were in her favour.

During the whole of that day the *Tankadere* kept fairly close to land, where the currents helped her. The coast was not more than five miles distant on her port quarter. Its irregular outline was occasionally visible when the mist cleared. As the wind blew from the land, the sea was not so heavy, which was fortunate for the schooner, for small vessels labour a great deal in the swell, which breaks their speed, or, as sailors say, 'takes the life out of them.' The breeze abated a little and set in from the south-east. The pilot put up the jibs, but two hours after they had to be taken down again, for the wind freshened anew.

Mr Fogg and Aouda, happily proof against sea-sickness, ate the ship's preserves and biscuit with a good appetite. Fix was invited to join them, and could not refuse, as he knew that food was as necessary for the human stomach as ballast for the ship's hold, but it galled him. To travel at this man's expense and live on his provisions struck him as being rather unfair; still, eat he must, and eat he did, though it was only a snack. When the meal was over, he thought it his duty to take Fogg apart, and said, 'Sir,' – the word blistered his lips; it was all he could do not to collar this 'gentleman.' 'Sir, it was very kind of you to offer me a passage, but, although I am not in a position to spend as freely as you do, I must insist on paying my share – ' 'Don't mention it, sir,' replied Mr Fogg. 'Indeed, I absolutely must – ' 'No, sir,' repeated Fogg in a tone which admitted of no reply. 'This is only one item in my general outlay.' Fix felt as if he would choke; he bowed and went to lie down at full length on the fore-deck. He never spoke another word for the rest of that day.

Meanwhile they were going fast, and John Bunsby was in high hope. He told Mr Fogg more than once that they would get to Shanghai in time, to which Mr Fogg merely answered that he depended upon it. Moreover the whole crew of the little schooner worked with a will; the worthy fellows being greatly stimulated by the attractive reward to be gained. There was not a sheet but was properly taut, not a sail but was vigorously set. The man at the helm could not have been blamed for a single yaw. The seamanship would not have been more strictly correct in a race of the Royal Yacht Club regatta.

In the evening the log showed a run of two hundred and twenty miles since leaving Hong-Kong, and Phileas Fogg might hope that, on reaching Yokohama, he would have no loss of time to record in his diary, and in that case the first serious mishap he had experienced since his departure from London would probably not interfere at all with his success.

Before dawn next morning the *Tankadere* was sailing right into the straits of Fo-Kien, which separate the large island of Formosa from the Chinese coast, and she crossed the Tropic of Cancer. The sea was very trying in the straits, which are full of eddies formed by the counter-currents. The schooner laboured greatly amid the chopping waves, which broke her progress, and it became very difficult to stand on deck.

At daybreak the wind began to blow harder, and the sky showed signs of a coming gale. The barometer, too, announced an early change of weather by its daily vagaries, the mercury rising and falling fitfully. And the sea in the south-east was seen to rise in long surges, ominous of storm. The evening before, the sun had gone down in a red mist, in an ocean sparkling with phosphorescent light.

The pilot, having long scanned the threatening appearance of the heavens, muttered something between his teeth. At a certain moment, happening to be near Mr Fogg, he said to him in a low voice: 'May I tell your honour frankly what is in my mind?' 'Of course,' replied Phileas Fogg. 'Well, we are in for a squall.' 'Will it come from the north or the south?' asked Mr Fogg quietly. 'From the south. Look, there's a typhoon on the way.' 'It's all right; if it's a typhoon from the south, it will blow us in the right direction,' answered Mr Fogg. 'If that is the way you look at it, I have nothing more to say,' replied the pilot.

John Bunsby's forebodings proved only too well-grounded. At a less advanced season of the year the typhoon – to use a celebrated meteorologist's words – would have passed away like a luminous cascade of electric flames, but at a time of winter equinox it was to be feared that it would break out with great fury.

The pilot took his precautions in advance. All sails were furled and the yards lowered on deck. The poles were struck and the boom taken in. The hatches were securely battened down, so that not a drop of water could get into the hull. A single triangular sail, a storm-jib of strong canvas, was hoisted as a fore-stay-sail, so as to keep the schooner's stern to the wind. Then they waited.

John Bunsby strongly urged his passengers to go below; but to be confined in a small space almost without air, and tossed about by the surge, was anything but pleasant. Mr Fogg and Aouda, and even Fix, refused to leave the deck.

The raging storm of rain and wind fell upon them about eight o'clock. Though she had but one little bit of sail, the *Tankadere* was lifted like a feather by this wind, which defies accurate description when it blows its worst. To compare its velocity to four times the speed of a locomotive going on full steam would be short of the truth. During the whole of that day the vessel scudded northward, carried along by the monstrous waves, fortunately not lagging behind them in speed.

Twenty times she was on the point of being overwhelmed by the mountainous seas that rose behind her, but a skilful shift of the helm by the pilot prevented the catastrophe. The passengers were at times smothered in spray, but bore it stoically. Fix cursed, without a doubt, but Aouda, her eyes never leaving her companion, whose coolness filled her with admiration, showed herself worthy of him, and, unafraid, faced the tempest at his side. As for Phileas Fogg, the typhoon might have been a detail in his programme.

Up till now the *Tankadere* had held her course to the north, but towards evening the wind, as was to be feared, veered threequarters and blew from the north-west. The schooner, now broadside on to the waves, was horribly shaken. The sea struck her with a violence simply appalling for anyone who does not know how solidly all the parts of a ship are knit together. At nightfall the gale increased in fury. Seeing that the hurricane grew worse as the darkness grew more dense, John Bunsby became seriously alarmed; and, thinking it might be time to put into some port, he consulted his men, after which he approached Mr Fogg, and said, 'I think, your honour, we should do well to make for one of the ports on the coast.' 'I think so too,' replied Mr Fogg. 'Ah!' said the pilot. 'Now which shall it be?' 'There is but one for me,' answered Mr Fogg quietly. 'And which is that?' 'Shanghai.' For some moments the pilot failed to understand the meaning, the purposeful tenacity of the answer. Then he exclaimed, 'Well, yes, your honour is right. Shanghai it will be!' So the *Tankadere* was steadfastly kept on her northward course. It was a perfectly terrible night; that the small craft did not capsize was a miracle. She was twice swept by the seas, and everything would have been washed overboard had the gripes failed. Aouda was thoroughly exhausted, but not one complaint escaped her lips. Repeatedly Mr Fogg had to rush to her help against the violence of the waves.

Day reappeared. The storm was still raging with extreme fury, but the wind now returned to the south-east. This was a favourable change, and the *Tankadere* once more forged ahead on this vile sea whose waves now clashed with those that sprang from the new direction of the wind. Caught in the trough of these conflicting surges, any boat less stoutly built would have been crushed out of existence.

From time to time one caught glimpses of the coast through rifts in the mist, but there was not a ship in sight. The *Tankadere* alone kept at sea.

At noon there were some signs that the wind was abating, and, as the sun went down on the horizon, the lull became more marked. The storm had been too violent to last very long. The passengers, who were now dead-beat, could take a little food and rest a while. The night was comparatively quiet. The pilot made some use of his sails, and the schooner made considerable progress. On the next day, the 11th, at daybreak, after examining the coastline, John Bunsby was able to declare that Shanghai was not a hundred miles off. A hundred miles, and this was the last day they had to cover the distance. Mr Fogg had to reach Shanghai that very evening, otherwise he would miss the boat to Yokohama. But for the storm, which had caused a loss of several hours, he would at this moment have been within thirty miles of Shanghai port.

The breeze was slackening perceptibly; unfortunately the sea was slackening too. All sails were set; jibs, stay-sails, flying-jib, every bit of canvas was out, and the sea foamed under the boat's stem. By twelve o'clock the *Tankadere* was not more than forty-five miles away from her destination. Six hours remained in which to make the port before the departure of the Yokohama boat.

All on board were in a state of painful suspense. Everybody, no doubt with the exception of Phileas Fogg, felt his heart throb with impatience. Everybody wanted to get to port in time at any cost. It was absolutely necessary that the little schooner should keep up an average speed of nine miles an hour, and the wind went on dropping! It was a fitful breeze, blowing from land in capricious gusts, which left the sea quite smooth as soon as they had passed. Still, the *Tankadere* was so light, her upper sails of fine material caught every flurry so well that John Bunsby, with a helpful current behind him, found himself at six o'clock no more than ten miles from the mouth of Shanghai River; the town is at least twelve miles farther up.

At seven o'clock they were still three miles from Shanghai. The pilot let fall an angry oath as he saw the bonus of two hundred pounds slipping from his grasp. He looked at Mr Fogg. Mr Fogg was quite unmoved, though at this moment his whole fortune was at stake.

At this moment, too, a long, black, spindle-shaped object, crowned with a plume-like tuft of smoke, appeared on a level with the water. It was the American liner leaving at the appointed time.

'Curse it!' cried John Bunsby, thrusting away the helm with a jerk of despair.

'Signal her,' said Phileas Fogg quietly.

A small brass cannon lay on the foredeck of the *Tankadere*, for the purpose of making signals in foggy weather. This gun was loaded to the muzzle, but, just as the pilot was about to apply a red-hot coal to the touch-hole, Mr Fogg said to him, 'Put your flag at half-mast.' The flag was lowered at half-mast, which was a signal of distress. It was reasonable to hope that the American ship, on seeing it, would alter her course for a moment so as to stand by the pilot-boat.

'Fire!' said Mr Fogg. And the report of the small brass cannon burst upon the air.

CHAPTER XXII

In which Passepartout sees that, even at the Antipodes, it is wise to have some money in one's pocket

THE *Carnatic*, having left Hong-Kong on November 7, at half-past six in the evening, directed her course at full speed towards Japan. She carried a full cargo, and her full complement of passengers. Two quarter-deck cabins were unoccupied, those which had been engaged by Phileas Fogg.

Next morning the men in the bow of the ship were somewhat surprised to see a passenger, who looked half-dazed, whose step was shaky and hair ruffled, come out of the second-class hatchway and totter as far as some spars, on which he sat down.

The passenger was no other than Passepartout. What had happened was this.

A few moments after Fix left the opium-den, two attendants lifted Passepartout, fast asleep, and carried him to the bed reserved for smokers. But three hours later, pursued even in his nightmares by a fixed idea, Passepartout woke up and struggled against the stupefying action of the narcotic. The thought of duty unfulfilled shook off his torpor. He left the drunkards' bed and, stumbling, supporting himself against the walls, falling and getting up again, but ever irresistibly impelled by a sort of instinct, he came out of the den, shouting as in a dream, 'The *Carnatic*! the *Carnatic*!' The liner lay close by with steam up, ready to start. Passepartout had only a few yards to go. He rushed on to the gangway, went as far as the foredeck and there fell down insensible, at the very moment when the *Carnatic* was casting off. Sailors are used to scenes of this kind, so two or three carried the poor fellow down into a second-class cabin, and, when he awoke next morning, he was a hundred and fifty miles from China.

Thus it was that on that morning Passepartout found himself on the deck of the *Carnatic*, and came up to open his lungs to the fresh sea-breeze. The air sobered him. He began to collect his thoughts, which he found anything but easy work. At last he recalled the happenings of the day before, Fix's revelations, the opium-den, etc.

'Certainly,' said he to himself, 'I was made abominably drunk! What is Mr Fogg going to say? Anyhow I did not miss the boat, which is the main thing.' Then he thought of Fix: 'As for that fellow, I hope and believe we are rid of him, and that he did not dare follow us on the *Carnatic* after his proposal to me. A police-inspector, a detective on the track of my master, accused of robbing the Bank of England! What utter nonsense! Mr Fogg is no more a thief than I am a murderer.' Ought he to tell his master? Was it advisable to inform him of the part Fix was playing in this matter? Would it not be better to wait until Mr Fogg reached London, and then let him know that an agent of the Metropolitan Police had been shadowing him around the world? How they would laugh over it! Yes, that was the best course; no doubt of it. At all events, it was worth considering. But the first thing to do was to go to Mr Fogg, and obtain his pardon for the outrageous conduct of which he had been guilty.

The sea was rough and the boat rolled heavily, so the good fellow, getting on his feet, managed to reach the after-deck, not without difficulty, as his legs were still very unsteady. He saw nobody on deck who was like his master or Aouda. 'That's all right,' he said, 'Aouda has not got up yet, and Mr Fogg has probably found a partner and is playing whist as usual.' Thus soliloquising, he went down to the saloon. Mr Fogg was not there. The only thing to be done was to ask the purser which was Mr Fogg's cabin. The purser told him he didn't know of any passenger of that name. 'I beg your pardon,' continued Passepartout insistently, 'the man I mean is a tall gentleman, who is very reserved and talks very little, and has a young lady with him.'

'We have no young lady on board,' replied the purser. 'But here is the list of the passengers. See for yourself.'

Passepartout read the list through. His master's name was not there. He was staggered; then an idea flashed through his mind. 'I am not mistaken, I am on the *Carnatic* all right, am I not?' 'Yes,' answered the purser. 'Bound for Yokohama?' 'Certainly.' Passepartout had feared for one moment that he had got into the wrong boat. But, if it was true he was on the *Carnatic*, it was equally true his master was not. Passepartout collapsed in an armchair; it was a crushing blow. Then, all of a sudden, the whole thing dawned on him. He remembered that the hour of sailing of the *Carnatic* had been advanced, that he was to have informed his master of the fact, and that he had failed to do so. It was his fault, then, that Mr Fogg and Aouda had missed the boat.

Yes, it was his fault, but it was still more the fault of the traitor who, in order to separate him from his master and keep the latter in Hong-Kong, had tempted him to drink to intoxication! He now quite understood the detective's trickery. By this time Mr Fogg was ruined to a certainty, for his bet was lost; he was arrested, possibly in prison!

At this thought Passepartout tore his hair. Ah! if ever Fix should fall into his hands, what a settling of scores there would be! After a time Passepartout shook off his overwhelming depression and became calm enough to consider his position, which was anything but pleasant. Here was he, a Frenchman, on the way to Japan. He was bound to get there; how should he get back? His pocket was empty. He hadn't a shilling, not a penny! But his passage had been paid for in advance, so that he had five or six days in which to make up his mind. His consumption of food and drink during this passage would beggar all description. He ate for his master, for Aouda and for himself. He ate as if Japan, the land on which he would soon set foot, were a howling wilderness, where no food whatever could be found.

On the 13th the *Carnatic* entered the port of Yokohama on the morning tide. Yokohama is an important port of call in the Pacific. All boats carrying mails or passengers between North America, China, Japan and the Malaysian Islands, put in there. It is situated in the Bay of Yeddo, at a short distance from that huge city, the second capital of the Japanese Empire, once the residence of the Tycoon, in the days when the civil emperor existed, and a rival of Meako, the great city which is the seat of the Mikado, the spiritual emperor, descended from the gods.

The *Carnatic* took up her moorings in Yokohama harbour alongside the quay, near the custom-house, in the midst of a multitude of ships of all nations.

Passepartout set foot on this curious land of the Sons of the Sun without feeling the least excitement. Having nothing better to do than let chance take him where it would, he started to walk haphazard about the streets. He found himself at first in a perfectly European town, of which the houses with low fronts were adorned with verandas, under which ran graceful peristyles. This part of Yokohama covered, with its streets, squares, docks and warehouses, the whole space between the 'promontory of the Treaty' and the river. Here, as at Hong-Kong and Calcutta, swarmed a medley of all races, Americans, English, Chinamen, Dutchmen, merchants prepared to sell and buy anything. The Frenchman, in the midst of this crowd, felt as completely stranded as if he had been dropped among the Hottentots.

There was certainly one way in which Passepartout could get assistance: he could go to the French or English consul at Yokohama.

But he was loath to tell his story, so intimately connected with his master's. Before having recourse to this extreme measure, he resolved to exhaust all other possible means of facing his desperate position.

Having wandered about the European quarter without meeting with the slightest luck, he made his way into the native part of the city, determined, if necessary, to push on to Yeddo.

The Japanese quarter of Yokohama is called Benlen, from the name of a sea goddess worshipped on the neighbouring islands. There Passepartout saw beautiful avenues of fir and cedar trees, sacred gates of strange architecture, bridges hidden under bamboos and reeds, temples sheltering in the widespread gloom of secular cedars, convents within whose walls the priests of Buddhism and the sectaries of Confucius led a negative existence, unending streets in which one might have gathered a regular harvest of pink-complexioned and red-cheeked children, little people who looked as if they had been cut out of some native screen, and who were disporting themselves in the midst of short-legged poodles and yellowish tailless cats, with lazy, wheedling ways.

The streets were alive with people going to and fro, processions of bonzes beating their monotonous tom-toms, yakoonins, custom-house and police officers in pointed hats encrusted with lacquer, and carrying two swords hanging from their belts, soldiers clothed in blue cotton stuff with white stripes, and armed with percussion guns, men-at-arms of the Mikado, cased in their silken doublets, hauberks and coats of mail, and numbers of other military men of all ranks; for in Japan the soldier's profession is as highly respected as it is despised in China. Then Passepartout saw mendicant friars, long-robed pilgrims, ordinary civilians, with smooth, ebony-black hair, big heads, long busts, thin legs, of short stature, whose complexion varied from dark copper tints to dull white, but was never yellow like the Chinaman's; for the two races have essentially different characteristics. Among the carriages, palanquins and barrows fitted with sails, the 'norimons' with sides of lacquer, the soft luxurious 'cangos,' regular litters made of bamboo, a few women were seen making their way through the traffic, with small steps of their small feet, shod in canvas shoes, straw sandals or clogs of ornamented wood. They were not good-looking, these flat-chested women with childish eyes, and teeth blackened to suit the prevailing fashion, but they wore gracefully their national garment, the 'kimono,' a sort of dressing-down fastened across with a broad silk sash tied in an enormous knot behind, which up-to-date Parisian ladies seem to have borrowed from the women of Japan.

Passepartout strolled about for some hours in the midst of this motley multitude, sometimes looking at the quaint, gorgeous shops, the bazaars with their crowded display of the Japanese jeweller's tinsel, the eating-houses, decked with streamers and banners, which he was not in a position to enter, and those teahouses in which the fragrant hot water is drunk by the cupful with 'saki,' a liquor obtained from fermented rice, and those comfortable smoking-houses where a very fine tobacco is smoked – not opium, the use of which is almost unknown in Japan.

Presently Passepartout found himself in the country, in the midst of immense paddy-fields. There, not on shrubs but on trees, the full-blown blossoms of dazzling camelias were putting forth their last colours and perfumes, and, within bamboo enclosures, cherry trees, plum trees, and apple trees, which the natives grow rather for their blossom than for their fruit, and which forbidding scarecrows and loud whirligigs protect from the beaks of sparrows, pigeons, ravens, and other voracious birds. Every majestic cedar had a large eagle, every weeping willow spread its foliage over some heron, gloomily perched on one leg; and on all sides were crows, ducks, hawks, wild geese, and numbers of cranes, on which the Japanese confer nobility, and which in their eyes symbolise long life and happiness.

As he wandered about, Passepartout noticed a few violets in the grass. 'Good!' said he, 'there's my supper.' He smelt them and found them quite odourless. 'No luck!' thought he.

The good fellow had certainly taken care to eat as much as he possibly could before leaving the *Carnatic*, but after walking about all day he felt the pangs of hunger. He had observed that the flesh of sheep, goats and pigs was absolutely wanting in the butchers' stalls, and, knowing as he did that it is sacrilege to kill cattle, which are strictly reserved for the needs of agriculture, he came to the conclusion that meat was scarce in Japan, and he was right. But, in default of butcher's meat, he would have done quite well with the joints of wild boar or deer, the partridges or quails, the poultry or fish which, together with the produce of the paddy-fields, make up almost the whole culinary resources of the Japanese. However, he had to put a good face on the matter, and decided he would not look for food till the morrow.

Night came; Passepartout returned to the native quarter, and wandered about the streets lit by many-coloured lanterns, watching the troops of dancers going through their wonderful performances, and the astrologers in the open collecting the crowd around their tel-escopes. Then he saw the harbour again, spangled with the lights of fishermen, who were attracting the fish with the glow of blazing resin.

The streets were at last deserted, and instead of the crowd, the yakoonins appeared on their rounds. These officers in their splendid costumes, and surrounded by their retinue, looked like ambassadors. Whenever Passepartout came across one of these dazzling patrols, he observed humorously: 'Hallo! Here's another Japanese embassy on its way to Europe!'

CHAPTER XXIII

In which Passepartout's nose assumes inordinate length

ON THE MORROW Passepartout, tired out and famished, reflected that he must get something to eat, no matter how, and the sooner the better. If everything else failed he could of course sell his watch, but he would have starved before doing that. So, now or never, the good fellow must make use of the powerful, if not melodious voice, with which Nature had gifted him. He knew a few French and English catches, which he resolved to try on the Japanese, feeling sure they must be fond of music, since they did everything to the accompaniment of cymbals, tom-toms and drums.

They could not fail to appreciate the performance of a European virtuoso. As it was perhaps rather early in the morning for a concert, it was possible that the dilettanti, startled out of their slumbers, might pay the singer with other coin than that which bears the effigy of the Mikado. Passepartout therefore decided to wait a few hours. As he went along, he reflected that he would look too well dressed for a strolling artist, and it then occurred to him to change his garments for old clothes more suitable to his condition. Moreover, this exchange should leave a balance, by means of which he could at once satisfy his hunger.

This resolution once taken, the next thing was to carry it out. After a long search, Passepartout succeeded in discovering a native dealer in old clothes, to whom he explained what he wanted. The dealer liked the European costume, and Passepartout left his shop rigged out in an old Japanese robe and a kind of corded turban, faded with age. As an offset, a few small silver coins jingled in his pocket. 'That's all right,' he thought; 'I shall imagine it is carnival time.'

Passepartout's first care, after he was thus 'Japanesed,' was to find a tea-house of modest appearance, where he breakfasted on the remains of a fowl and a few handfuls of rice, like a man for whom dinner was as yet an unsolved problem.

'Now,' said he to himself, when he had eaten his fill, 'I must take good care not to make a fool of myself. I can't help myself by selling this old outfit for one still more Japanese. I must therefore see what I can do to get out of this Land of the Sun as soon as I possibly can; the memories I shall take away will be anything but pleasant.'

It then occurred to him to pay a visit to the boats about to leave for America. His idea was to offer his services as cook or servant in return for his passage and food. Once at San Francisco he would find some way of getting out of his difficulties. The thing that mattered was to cross the four thousand seven hundred miles that separate Japan from the New World.

Passepartout, who was not the man to dilly-dally with an idea, at once directed his steps towards the docks. But as he drew nearer to his destination, his project, which had seemed so simple when he first conceived it, appeared more and more impossible of realisation. Why should they require a cook or a servant on board an American liner? And what sort of confidence would he inspire in such a rig-out? What recommendations could he produce in support of his application? What references could he give? As these thoughts were passing through his mind, his eyes fell upon an immense placard carried by a sort of clown through the streets of Yokohama. This placard was in English and ran as follows:

HONOURABLE WILLIAM BATULCAR'S TROUPE
OF JAPANESE ACROBATS

LAST PERFORMANCES
Before their Departure for the United States
of the
LONG, LONG NOSES
Under the Special Patronage of the God Tingou

GREAT ATTRACTION!

He followed the poster-bearer, and was soon once more in the Japanese part of the city. A quarter of an hour later he stood before a large building at the top of which fluttered several clusters of streamers, and bearing on its outside walls, in crude garish colours but without perspective, the picture of a whole company of jugglers.

This was the Honourable Batulcar's establishment. The man was a sort of American Barnum, the manager of a troupe of buffoons, jugglers, clowns, acrobats, equilibrists and gymnasts, who, according to the placard, was giving his last performances before leaving the Empire of the Sun for the States of the Union. Passepartout stepped in under a peristyle leading into the building, and asked to see Mr Batulcar, who at once came forward in person.

'What do you want?' said he to Passepartout, whom he at first took for a native.

'Do you require a servant?' asked Passepartout. 'A servant!' exclaimed the Barnum, stroking the thick grey goatee that covered the nether part of his chin. 'I have two obedient and faithful servants, that have never left me, and serve me for nothing, on condition I feed them – here they are,' he added, showing him his two sturdy arms, lined with veins as large as the strings of a double-bass.

'So I can be of no use to you?' 'None.' 'It's deuced bad luck! It would have suited me so well to have gone away with you.'

'Look here,' said the Honourable Batulcar, 'you are no more a Japanese than I am a monkey! Why are you dressed in this fashion?'

'A man dresses as best he can.' 'That's true enough. You're a Frenchman, eh?' 'Yes, a Parisian of Paris.' 'Then you surely know how to make funny faces?' 'As to that,' replied Passepartout, somewhat nettled to see that his nationality had suggested such a question, 'we Frenchmen can certainly make funny faces, but no better than the Americans.'

'I guess that's right – well, if I can't take you as a servant, I can take you as a clown. You understand, my friend; in France they exhibit foreign buffoons, and in foreign countries French buffoons.' 'Is that so?'

'And you're a strong fellow, eh?' 'Yes, particularly when I have had a good feed.' 'Can you sing?' 'Yes,' replied Passepartout, who had once sung his part in a few street concerts. 'But can you sing with your head down, a spinning-top on the sole of your left foot, and a sword balanced on the sole of your right foot?' 'Why, of course I can!' answered Passepartout, recalling the first performances of his early years. 'You see, everything depends on that,' replied the Honourable Batulcar.

The engagement was concluded there and then. Passepartout had at last found employment. He was engaged as a Jack-of-all-work in the celebrated Japanese troupe. It was not a very gratifying position, but within a week he would be on his way to San Francisco.

The performance, so noisily announced by the Honourable Batulcar, was to commence at three o'clock, and soon the fearsome instruments of a Japanese orchestra, drums and tom-toms, were thundering at the door. Needless to say, Passepartout had had no time to prepare a part, but he was to lend the support of his broad and robust shoulders in the wonderful feat of the 'human cluster' accomplished by the Long Noses of the god Tingou. This great attraction was to close the performance.

Before three o'clock the large hall was invaded by the spectators. Europeans, Chinese, Japanese, men, women and children, made a rush for the narrow benches and the boxes facing the stage. The musicians had taken up their position inside, and the full orchestra of gongs, tom-toms, bones, flutes, tambourines and big drums was working frantically.

The performance was much the same as all acrobatic displays; but there is no denying that the Japanese are the finest equilibrists in the world. One man, with nothing more than his fan and bits of paper, performed that most graceful trick of the butterflies and the flowers. Another, with the odorous smoke of his pipe, rapidly traced in the air a series of bluish words, which made up a compliment to the audience. A third juggled with some lighted candles, which he extinguished one after the other as they passed before his lips, and relit one from the other without interrupting his fascinating jugglery for one moment. Yet another produced, by means of spinning-tops, the most extraordinary combinations; under his touch these humming things seemed to assume a life of their own in their endless gyration; they ran along pipe-stems and the edges of sabres, and along wires, that looked no thicker than hairs, stretched across the stage; they careered round the brims of large crystal vases, climbed up bamboo ladders, scattered about into all corners, and produced weird harmonic effects by combining their various pitches of tone. The jugglers tossed them up, and they went on spinning in the air; they hurled them like shuttlecocks with wooden battledores, and still they went on spinning; they thrust them into their pockets, and when they took them out they were spinning as before – until at a given moment the release of a spring made them spread out into gerbes.

There is no need to describe the astounding feats of the acrobats and gymnasts. The performances with the ladder, the pole, the ball, the barrels, etc., were executed with remarkable precision. But the chief attraction of the show was the exhibition of the Long Noses, astounding equilibrists, unknown as yet to Europe.

The Long Noses form a peculiar company under the special patron-age of the god Tingou. Attired like heroes of the Middle Ages, they sported a magnificent pair of wings at their shoulders. But their chief distinctive feature was the long nose which adorned the face, and even more the use to which it was put. These noses were actually bamboo canes, five, six, or even ten feet long: some straight, others curved, some smooth, others covered with little knots. It was on these appendages, firmly fastened, that all their balancing feats were performed. A dozen of these followers of the god Tingou lay flat upon their backs, and their fellow-actors settled on their noses, placed as straight as lightning-conductors, jumping and tumbling from one to the other, and performing the most amazing feats. As a grand finale, special mention had been made of the human pyramid, in which some fifty Long Noses were to represent the Car of Juggernaut.[20] But, instead of forming this pyramid by using their shoulders as the supports of the structure, the Honourable Batulcar's artistes were to use nothing but their noses. It so happened that one of those who formed the base of the Car had left the troupe, and, as all that was required was strength and skill, Passepartout had been selected to take his place. The good fellow felt truly sorry for himself when – sad reminiscence of his youth – he donned his garb of the Middle Ages, adorned with many-coloured wings, and a nose six feet long was adapted to his face, but, all said and done, this nose meant bread and cheese, so he cheered up, went upon the stage, and took his place beside those who were to represent the base of the Car of Juggernaut. They all lay down flat on their backs, their noses pointing skyward. A second set of equilibrists took up its position on these long appendages, then a third established itself on top, and then a fourth, and on these noses that met just at their tips, a human structure soon rose to the very borders of the theatre.

The applause was more frantic than ever, and the instruments of the orchestra had just broken out like so many claps of thunder, when the pyramid tottered, the balance being destroyed through the failure of one of the noses at the base, and the structure collapsed like a house of cards.

Passepartout was the man at fault, for, leaving his post, he had suddenly cleared the footlights unassisted by his wings, clambered up to the right-hand gallery, and fallen at the feet of one of the spectators, crying out, 'Ah, my master! My master!' 'What, you here?' 'Yes, I, and no mistake.' 'Well, then, my friend, come with us at once to the boat.'

Mr Fogg, Aouda, who was with him, and Passepartout hurried out through the lobbies, but outside they found the Honourable Batulcar, who was furious, and claimed damages for the 'breakage' of the pyramid. His wrath was soothed by Mr Fogg, who threw a handful of banknotes to him. At half-past six, just as the American boat was about to leave, Mr Fogg and Aouda stepped on board, followed by Passepartout, with his wings still on, and the six-feet-long nose, which he had not yet succeeded in removing from his face.

CHAPTER XXIV

The voyage across the Pacific Ocean

WHAT HAPPENED WHEN the *Tankadere* arrived in sight of Shanghai scarcely needs telling. The signals of distress had been seen from the Yokohama boat, and the captain, observing a flag at half-mast, had directed his course towards the little schooner. A few minutes later, Phileas Fogg, paying the sum agreed upon for his passage, handed to the skipper, John Bunsby, five hundred and fifty pounds. Then he, Aouda, and Fix got on board the steamer, which at once resumed her route for Nagasaki and Yokohama.

Phileas Fogg arrived at his destination on the morning of the 14th of November, at scheduled time, and, leaving Fix to attend to his business, went to the *Carnatic*, where he was told, to Aouda's great delight – and perhaps to his own, though he betrayed no sign of it – that the Frenchman, Passepartout, had actually arrived the day before.

Phileas Fogg, who was due to leave for San Francisco that very evening, set out at once in search of his servant. He applied without success to the French and English consuls, and, having wandered about the streets of Yokohama without coming across Passepartout, was beginning to despair of finding him, when chance, or possibly a kind of presentiment, led him into the Honourable Batulcar's theatre. Without a doubt, he would never have recognised his servant in that fantastic, heraldic garb; but the latter, lying with his face upwards, caught sight of his master in the gallery.

He made an involuntary movement, which brought his nose out of position, thereby upsetting the balance of the 'pyramid,' with the consequences that we know.

So much Passepartout learnt from Aouda herself, who then told him the details of the voyage from Hong-Kong to Yokohama on the *Tankadere*, with a man called Fix.

Passepartout heard the name Fix without wincing. He did not think the moment had come to let his master know what had passed between the detective and himself. So, when giving an account of his own adventures, he simply expressed keen regret for having been accidentally overcome by the intoxication of opium in a smoking-house at Hong-Kong. Mr Fogg, having heard this narrative coldly, answered not a word, but advanced his servant a sufficient sum to allow him to procure on board garments more becoming than those he wore. Within an hour the worthy fellow had cut off his nose and shed his wings, and had nothing about him that recalled the follower of the god Tingou.

The boat about to sail from Yokohama to San Francisco belonged to the Pacific Mail Steamship Company, and was called the *General Grant*. She was a very large paddle-wheel steamer of two thousand five hundred tons, well fitted up and very fast. A huge beam rose and fell regularly above the deck; a piston-rod was jointed to one of its extremities, and to the other that of a connecting-rod, which, converting the rectilinear into circular motion, acted directly on the paddle-shaft. The *General Grant* was rigged like a three-masted schooner, and had a large spread of canvas, which greatly assisted her steam-power. As her speed was twelve miles an hour, she would not take more than twenty-one days to cross the Pacific. Phileas Fogg had therefore good reason for thinking that he would reach San Francisco by the 2nd of December, New York by the 11th, and London by the 20th – anticipating thus by a few hours the fateful date of the 21st of December.

There was a very fair number of passengers on board, some Englishmen, many Americans, a whole crowd of coolies emigrating to America, and a certain number of officers of the Indian Army, who were spending their leave in making the tour of the world.

The voyage, from a sailor's point of view, was quite uneventful; the boat, supported on her large paddles, steadied by her great spread of sail, rolled but little. The Pacific Ocean about justified its name.

Mr Fogg was as calm and reserved as ever. His young companion felt more and more that the ties which bound her to her protector were other than those of mere gratitude. The silent, yet more generous nature of the man impressed her more than she thought, and almost unconsciously she was giving way to feelings to which her inscrutable companion seemed absolutely impervious. And apart from sentiment, Aouda took the keenest interest in Mr Fogg's plans, and worried over any mishaps that might endanger the success of the journey. She often chatted with Passepartout, who saw well enough what was going on in Aouda's heart, guarded though she was. The good fellow, whose attitude towards his master was now one of perfectly blind faith, could never speak highly enough of Phileas Fogg's uprightness, generosity and unselfishness. He likewise calmed Aouda's apprehensions concerning the termination of the journey, assuring her that the worst was over, telling her again and again that they had left behind them those fantastic lands of China and Japan, and were on their way back to civilised countries, and that a train from San Francisco to New York, with a transatlantic liner from New York to London, would, without a doubt, enable them to complete this impossible journey round the world within the stipulated time.

Nine days after leaving Yokohama, Phileas Fogg had traversed exactly one half of the terrestrial globe, for, on the 23rd of November, the *General Grant* crossed the hundred and eightieth meridian, in the southern hemisphere, and was therefore at the very antipodes of London. Mr Fogg, it is true, had taken up fifty-two out of eighty available days, and had only twenty-eight left. But, though he was only half-way by the difference of meridians, one must not forget that he had really travelled over more than two-thirds of the total distance to be accomplished; for consider what roundabout journeys he had been obliged to make, from London to Aden, from Aden to Bombay, from Calcutta to Singapore, and from Singapore to Yokohama.

Anyone following without deviation the fiftieth latitude, which is that of London, would not have travelled over more than twelve thousand miles, roughly speaking; whereas Phileas Fogg had been compelled by the unmethodical means of transport at his disposal to undertake a journey of twenty-six thousand, of which he had now, on the 23rd of November, accomplished about seventeen thousand five hundred. Now, however, the route was direct, and Fix was no longer there to multiply obstacles in his way!

It also happened, on this 23rd of November, that Passepartout was greatly elated. It will be remembered that the obstinate fellow had stubbornly refused to make any alteration in the London time of his precious family watch, holding that the time of all the countries he passed through was wrong. Now, on this day, although he had never put his watch on or back, it agreed exactly with the ship's chronometer. One can easily imagine Passepartout's exultation. With what pleasure he would have jeered at Fix, if he had been there! 'What buncombe that rascal told me about the meridians, the sun, the moon and what not!' repeated Passepartout. 'Eh, what! if people of that sort had their way, there would be some funny clocks and watches about! I knew well enough that, some day or other, the sun would settle to go by my watch!'

What Passepartout did not know was that, if the dial of his watch had been divided into twenty-four hours, like Italian clocks, he would have had no reason to exult, for at nine a.m. on board the ship the hands of his timepiece would have shown nine p.m., that is to say, the twenty-first hour after midnight, or a difference exactly equal to that between

London and the hundred and eightieth meridian. But, had Fix been able to explain this purely physical effect, Passepartout would undoubtedly have been unable to admit it, even if he had understood. And in any case, if, supposing the impossible to have happened, the detective had unexpectedly appeared on board at that moment, Passepartout, moved by just wrath, would very probably have discussed with him a totally different subject, and in an entirely different manner.

But where was Fix at that moment? He was actually on board the *General Grant*. On arriving at Yokohama, the detective, leaving Mr Fogg, whom he expected to meet again during the day, had gone straight to the British consulate. And there he at last found the warrant, which had followed him from Bombay, and was already forty days old. It had been dispatched from Hong-Kong by the *Carnatic*, the very boat on which he was supposed to be. The detective's disappointment may well be imagined. The warrant was now useless. The man Fogg, having left English soil, could only be arrested on an extradition order.

'Very well,' thought Fix, swallowing his wrath, 'my warrant is of no use here, but it will be good in England. There is every indication that the rogue intends to return home, in the belief that he has thrown the police off his track. Very well, I shall follow him all the way there. As for the money, Heaven grant there may be some left! But what with travelling, bribes, law-suits, fines, elephants, expenses of all sorts the fellow has already got through more than five thousand pounds. Anyhow, the Bank has plenty of money!'

Having made up his mind, he at once embarked on the *General Grant*, and was already on board when Mr Fogg and Aouda arrived. He was astounded at seeing Passepartout, for he recognised him in his heraldic attire. He forthwith hid himself in his cabin, to avoid an explanation which might spoil everything. Owing to the large number of passengers, he was confident of escaping his enemy's notice, when, on that very day, he found himself face to face with him on the foredeck. Without a word, Passepartout flew at him, seized him by the throat, and, to the great delight of certain Americans, who at once proceeded to bet on him, he administered to the wretched Fix a magnificent thrashing, thereby proving the great superiority of French over English boxing. When Passepartout had finished he felt relieved, as it were, and composed himself. Fix got up in a somewhat battered condition, and, looking at his adversary, said to him coldly, 'Have you done?' 'Yes, for the present.' 'Then come and have a word with me.' 'A word with you! You want me –' 'In your master's interest.'

As though subdued by the detective's coolness, Passepartout followed him, and they went and sat down right in the bow of the ship.

'You have given me a hiding,' said Fix. 'That's all right, I expected it. Now attend to what I say. So far I have been Mr Fogg's adversary; I am now playing on his side.' 'At last!' exclaimed Passepartout, 'you believe he is an honest man?' 'No,' replied Fix coldly, 'I believe he is a rogue. Hush! don't move, and let me speak. So long as Mr Fogg was on English soil, it was my interest to keep him back, until I should receive a warrant. I spared no effort to this end. I set the Bombay priests at him; I got you intoxicated at Hong-Kong; I separated you from your master; I made him miss the Yokohama boat – ' Passepartout heard all this with clenched fists. 'Now,' resumed Fix, 'Mr Fogg seems to be on his way back to England. Well, I shall follow him there. But henceforth I shall exert myself just as zealously to remove all difficulties from his path as I have hitherto done to multiply them. As you see, my game is no longer the same, and for the simple reason that my interest requires a change. I may add that your interest is the same as mine, for in England, and in England only, shall you know whether you are serving a criminal or an honest man.' Passepartout, who had listened to Fix with close attention, was convinced that he was perfectly honest in what he said.

'Are we going to be friends?' asked Fix. 'Friends, no,' replied Passepartout; 'allies, yes; but conditionally, for at the slightest sign of treachery I shall wring your neck for you.' 'That's agreed,' said the detective quietly.

Eleven days later, on the 3rd of December, the *General Grant* steamed into the Bay of the Golden Gate and reached San Francisco.

So far Mr Fogg had neither gained nor lost a single day.

CHAPTER XXV

Which contains a cursory view of San Francisco on the day of a political meeting

AT SEVEN IN THE MORNING Phileas Fogg, Aouda and Passepartout set foot on the American continent, if this name can properly be given to the floating quay on which they disembarked. These quays, rising and falling with the tide, facilitate the loading and unloading of ships. Clippers of all sizes, steamers of every nationality, and those steamboats with several decks, one over the other, which ply on the Sacramento and its tributaries, are moored alongside these floating quays. And there also are piled up the commodities produced by a commerce extending to Mexico, Peru, Chili, Brazil, Europe, Asia, and all the islands of the Pacific.

So overjoyed was Passepartout at having at last reached American soil, that he thought it right to land by means of a perfect somersault. But when he came down on the quay, the flooring of which was worm-eaten, he very nearly went right through. Much taken aback at the manner in which he had 'set foot' on the New World, the worthy fellow uttered a tremendous cry, which frightened away a multitude of cormorants and pelicans, the customary denizens of movable quays.

The moment Mr Fogg landed, he inquired at what time the first train for New York would start, and was told six o'clock in the evening. So Mr Fogg had a whole day to spend in the Californian capital. He ordered a carriage for Aouda and himself, and this conveyance, for which he paid three dollars, drove off to the International Hotel, with Passepartout on the box. From his commanding position, Passepartout observed the great American city with much curiosity. He saw wide streets, even rows of low houses, churches and chapels in Anglo-Saxon Gothic style, huge docks, warehouses like palaces, some made of wood, others built of brick; in the streets there were numbers of vehicles: omnibuses, 'cars,' tramways, and on the crowded pavements, not only Americans and Europeans, but Chinese and Indians; in fact enough people to make up a population of more than two hundred thousand inhabitants.

Passepartout was greatly surprised; he expected to see the legendary city of 1849,[21] the city of the bandits, incendiaries and assassins, who had rushed to the conquest of the gold-nuggets, the huge *omnium gatherum*[22] of all nondescripts, in which men gambled for gold-dust, with a revolver in one hand and a knife in the other. But those 'spacious days' had gone for ever. San Francisco now looked what it was, a great commercial city. The lofty tower of the town hall, where the watchers are on the look-out, commanded the whole network of streets and avenues, which intersected each other at right angles, and in the midst of which lay verdant squares, while beyond was a Chinese town, that seemed to have been imported from the Celestial Empire in a toy-box. No more sombreros, no more red shirts as worn by placer hunters, no more plumed Indians, but a number of silk hats and black coats, worn by gentlemen endowed with feverish activity. Certain streets, like Montgomery Street,[23] which corresponds to Regent Street in London, the Boulevard des Italiens in Paris, and Broadway in New York, were lined with magnificent shops, which displayed in their windows the products of the whole world.

When Passepartout reached the International Hotel, he felt just as if he had never left England. The ground-floor of the hotel was taken up by an immense 'bar,' a sort of refreshment-room open gratis to all passers-by. Dried meat, oyster soup, biscuit and cheese were distributed free to the consumer, who only paid for what he drank, whether ale, port or sherry. This Passepartout thought 'very American.'

The hotel restaurant was comfortable, and Mr Fogg and Aouda, taking their seats at a table, were copiously served in Lilliputian dishes by negroes of darkest hue.

After breakfast, Mr Fogg, accompanied by Aouda, proceeded to go to the English consulate to have his passport *visaed*. On coming out of the hotel he found his servant, who asked him if it would not be wise, before taking the train, to buy a few dozen Enfield rifles or Colt revolvers, as he had heard of Sioux and Pawnees holding up the trains just like ordinary Spanish brigands. Mr Fogg answered that it was an unnecessary precaution, but he left him free to do as he thought fit, and directed his steps towards the consul's office.

He had not walked two hundred yards when, 'by the merest chance,' he found himself face to face with Fix. The detective expressed the utmost surprise. What! had Mr Fogg and he crossed the Pacific together without meeting on board! Well, anyhow Fix felt it a great honour to meet once more the gentleman to whom he owed so much, and, as he must needs return to Europe for business reasons, he would be delighted to continue his journey in such pleasant company. Mr Fogg replied that the honour would be his, and Fix, who was most anxious not to lose sight of him, asked if he might see this curious city of San Francisco with him. The request was granted, and Aouda, Phileas Fogg and Fix were soon sauntering about the streets together. Before long, they found themselves in Montgomery Street, which was crowded with the lower orders. On the pavements, in the middle of the road, on the tramway rails, in spite of the incessant traffic of coaches and omnibuses, at the shop-doors, at all the windows, and even on the roofs, the people swarmed. Poster-bearers were going about through the crowd; flags and streamers fluttered in the wind, and shouts burst forth on every side:

'Hurrah for Kamerfield!'

'Hurrah for Mandiboy!'

It was a political meeting. This, at least, was Fix's opinion, which he imparted to Mr Fogg, saying: 'It might be well, sir, to keep out of this mob. There's nothing but blows to be got out of mixing with it.' 'Yes, indeed,' replied Mr Fogg, 'and blows, though political, are blows for all that.' Fix thought proper to smile at this remark, and, so as not to be caught in the crush, they all three took up a position at the top of a flight of steps leading to a terrace that overlooked Montgomery Street.

In front of them, on the other side of the street, between a coal wharf and a petroleum store, stood a large committee room in the open, towards which the various currents of the crowd seemed to converge.

Of the reason and object of this meeting Phileas Fogg had not the slightest idea. Was it to elect some high military or civil official, the governor of a State or a member of Congress? The extraordinary excitement and impassioned interest of the citizens justified the conjecture. At this moment there was a great commotion in the crowd. All hands were raised; some were firmly clenched and seemed to rise and fall swiftly in the midst of the cries – doubtless an energetic way of casting a vote. The throng swayed to and fro. The banners wavered, disappeared for a moment, then reappeared in tatters. The human waves came as far as the steps, and the mass of heads billowed on the surface like a sea suddenly stirred up by a squall. The number of black hats grew rapidly less, and most of them seemed below normal height.

'It is evidently a meeting,' suggested Fix, 'and the question at issue must be a most exciting one. I should not be surprised if it were still about the Alabama dispute, although it is settled.' 'Possibly,' replied Mr Fogg in his quiet way. 'At all events,' continued Fix, 'two champions are face to face – Mr Kamerfield and Mr Mandiboy.'

While Aouda, leaning on Phileas Fogg's arm, was gazing in astonishment at this tumultuous scene, and Fix inquired of one of his neighbours the cause of such popular excitement, the general commotion became more violent. There was a more frantic burst of hurrahs, seasoned with abuse; the staffs of the banners were converted into weapons; hands disappeared to make room for fists everywhere. From the tops of the carriages and omnibuses, now at a standstill, there was a liberal exchange of blows. Everything was good enough to hurl at an opponent. Boots and shoes described very low trajectories, and occasionally there was an impression that the revolver was adding its national bark to the bawling of the multitude. The seething mass drew nearer, and ebbed on to the lower steps. One of the parties had evidently been repulsed, but mere spectators could not tell whether Mandiboy or Kamerfield had the upper hand.

'I think it would be wise for us to retire,' suggested Fix, who did not want to see 'his man' knocked about or get into a scrape. 'If all this has anything to do with England, and we are recognised as Englishmen, we shall have a bad time in the scuffle.' 'An English subject – ' replied Phileas Fogg, but could not finish his sentence, for, behind him, from the terrace to which the steps led, broke out terrific shouts of 'Hurrah!

Hip, Hip, Hurrah for Mandiboy!' It was a party of electors coming to the rescue, and taking the supporters of Kamerfield in flank.

Mr Fogg, Aouda, and Fix found themselves between two fires; it was too late to escape. This torrent of men, armed with loaded sticks and clubs, was irresistible. Phileas Fogg and Fix were dreadfully hustled, in their endeavour to protect the young woman. Mr Fogg, as cool as ever, tried to make use of his fists, those natural means of defence of every Englishman, but in vain. A huge fellow with a red goatee, a ruddy complexion, and broad shoulders, who seemed to be the leader of the party, raised his dread fist over Mr Fogg, to whom he would have done serious harm had not Fix devoted himself and taken the blow in his stead. An enormous swelling at once appeared under the detective's silk hat, which assumed the shape of a muffin-cap.

'Yankee!' said Mr Fogg, glancing at his enemy with the utmost contempt. 'Englishman!' replied the other. 'We shall meet again!' 'When you please.' 'Your name?' 'Phileas Fogg. And yours?' 'Colonel Stamp Proctor.'

Thereupon the tide swept by; Fix was knocked down, but got up again without any serious hurt. His overcoat had been divided into two unequal parts, and his trousers were like those breeches of which it is the fashion among certain Indians to remove the seat before putting them on. Aouda was unharmed; Fix alone had suffered, and bore the mark of the American's fist. As soon as they were out of the crowd, Mr Fogg thanked the detective.

'Don't mention it,' replied Fix; 'but come along.' 'Where?' 'To a slop-shop.' Nor was this visit superfluous, for both Phileas Fogg and Fix were in rags. They might have been fighting on behalf of Messrs Kamerfield and Mandiboy.

An hour after, they returned to the International Hotel with respectable hats and clothes. Passepartout was there, waiting for his master, armed with half a dozen central-fire six-chambered revolvers, fitted with daggers. When he caught sight of Fix with Mr Fogg, his brow darkened; but he brightened up again when Aouda told him briefly what had occurred. It was obvious Fix was no longer an enemy; he was an ally, and was keeping his word.

Dinner over, a coach was procured to take the travellers and their luggage to the station. As he was getting in, Mr Fogg said to Fix, 'You have not seen this Colonel Proctor again, have you?' 'No,' answered Fix. 'I shall return to America to find him,' said Phileas Fogg calmly. 'It would not be proper for an Englishman to stand such treatment.'

The detective smiled, but said nothing. Mr Fogg, apparently, was one of those Englishmen who, while thoroughly opposed to duelling in their own country, are quite prepared to fight abroad in defence of their honour.

At a quarter to six the travellers were at the station and the train was ready to leave. As he was about to get in, Mr Fogg saw a porter, went up to him and said, 'Was there not a certain amount of rioting in San Francisco today?' 'It was a meeting, sir,' replied the porter. 'But I thought I observed a good deal of commotion in the streets.' 'It was only a meeting arranged for an election.' 'The election of a commander-in-chief, I suppose?' 'No, sir, a justice of the peace.'

Having received this reply, Phileas Fogg took his seat, and the train steamed out at full speed.

CHAPTER XXVI

In which Phileas Fogg and his companions travel by the Pacific Express

'FROM OCEAN TO OCEAN,' the Americans say; and these words ought to be the general designation of the grand trunk line which crosses the United States of America at their broadest part. As a matter of fact, however, the Pacific Railroad is really divided into two distinct lines: the Central Pacific, between San Francisco and Ogden, and the Union Pacific, between Ogden and Omaha. Five different lines converge upon Omaha, which is thus in frequent communication with New York.

Thus, at the present moment New York and San Francisco are joined together by an unbroken band of metal, which is not less than three thousand seven hundred and eighty-six miles long. Between Omaha and the Pacific, the railway crosses a vast tract which is still the haunt of Indians and wild beasts, and which the Mormons began to colonise about 1845, when they had been expelled from Illinois. In the most favourable circumstances, the journey from New York to San Francisco formerly took six months; it now takes seven days.

It was in 1862 that, in spite of the opposition of the Southern members of Congress, who wanted a more southerly route, it was settled that the railroad should lie between the forty-first and forty-second parallels. President Lincoln, so long remembered with affectionate regret, himself made Omaha, in the State of Nebraska, the terminus of the new network of railway lines.

The work was begun at once, and carried on with American energy, which eschews alike scribbling and red-tape; nor was the line to suffer in any way from the rapidity with which it was laid. The work progressed in the prairie at the rate of a mile and a half a day. An engine, running on the rails laid down the day before, brought the rails to be laid on the morrow, and advanced upon them as they were laid.

The Pacific Railroad is met by several branch lines – in Iowa, Kansas, Colorado and Oregon. On leaving Omaha, it runs along the left bank of the Plate River as far as the mouth of the northern branch, then follows the southern branch, crosses the Laramie territory and the Wahsatch Mountains, passes round the Great Salt Lake and reaches Salt Lake City, the capital of the Mormons, dives into the Tuilla Valley, skirts the American Desert, Mounts Cedar and Humboldt, Humboldt River, and the Sierra Nevada, and descends, via Sacramento, to the Pacific. The gradient never exceeds a hundred and twelve feet to the mile, even through the Rocky Mountains.

Such was the long artery which trains travel over in seven days, and which would enable Mr Phileas Fogg – at least, so he hoped – to leave New York for Liverpool on the 11th.

The carriage which he occupied was a sort of long omnibus resting upon two trains, each of which consisted of four wheels and whose mobility makes it possible to take sharp curves. The carriages were not divided into compartments; two rows of seats were arranged perpendicularly to the axis, and between these ran a passage leading to the dressing-rooms and lavatories, with which each carriage was provided. Throughout the whole length of the train, the carriages communicated with each other by means of platforms, so that the passengers could walk from one end of the train to the other. There were saloon-cars, balcony-cars, dining-cars, and refreshment-cars. The one thing lacking was theatre-cars, but even these will be supplied some day.

There was a constant stream of people selling books and papers, and of venders of drinkables, eatables and cigars, doing a good business.

When the travellers left Oakland station, at six o'clock, it was already night, a night cold and black; the heavens were overcast with clouds that threatened snow. The train was not going at a great pace; allowing for the stoppages, it was not doing more than twenty miles an hour; but that was speed enough to take it across the United States in accordance with the time-table.

There was but little talking in the carriage and the passengers soon became sleepy. Passepartout happened to be sitting next to the detective, but he did not speak to him. After what had lately happened, their relations had grown distinctly cold; there was no longer any sympathy or intimacy between them. Fix behaved in exactly the same manner, but Passepartout was extremely reserved, and prepared to strangle his former friend on the slightest suspicion of trickery. Snow began to fall an hour after they left the station, a fine snow, which fortunately could not impede the train's progress. Nothing could be seen through the windows but a boundless white sheet, which made the steam unravelling its coils over it look greyish.

At eight o'clock a steward entered the car and informed the passengers that it was bedtime. In a few minutes the carriage, which was a sleeping-car, was converted into a dormitory. The backs of the seats were lowered, neatly-packed couches were spread out by means of an ingenious device, berths were rapidly improvised, and each traveller soon had a comfortable bed at his service, in which he was screened from prying eyes by thick curtains. The sheets were spotless and the pillows soft. It only remained to go to bed and sleep. This everybody proceeded to do, just as if he had been in the comfortable cabin of a liner. Meanwhile the train was running at full speed across the State of California.

The country between San Francisco and Sacramento is mostly flat. This part of the line, the Central Pacific, first started from Sacramento and was produced eastward to meet the railroad from Omaha. From San Francisco to the capital of California the line ran in a direct north-easterly course, skirting American River, which empties itself into San Pablo Bay. The hundred and twenty miles that separate these two important cities were crossed in six hours, and towards midnight, while soundly asleep, the travellers passed through Sacramento. So they saw nothing of this important town, the seat of the Californian Government, nothing of its fine quays, wide streets, magnificent hotels, and squares and churches.

Having left Sacramento and advanced beyond the junctions of Rochin, Auburn, and Colfax, the train entered the mountain system of the Sierra Nevada. It was seven o'clock in the morning when it steamed through Cisco station. An hour later the dormitory resumed its ordinary appearance, and the travellers caught glimpses of the picturesque scenery of this mountainous region. The railway track followed the capricious exigencies of the Sierra, at one time clinging to the mountain side, at another hanging on the brink of a precipice, avoiding sharp angles by describing bold curves, plunging into narrow gorges with apparently no outlet. The engine, sparkling like a reliquary, with its great head-light throwing yellow beams, its silvery dome, and its cow-catcher protruding like a spur-ram, mingled its whistling and roaring with the noise of torrents and waterfalls, and sent its smoke writhing about the sombre boughs of pines.

There were few, if any, tunnels or bridges on the route. The railway did no violence to Nature by straight cuts in order to go the nearest way: it worked round the mountains.

The train entered the State of Nevada through the Carson Valley about nine o'clock; it was still running in a north-eastern direction. At twelve it left Reno, where the travellers had twenty minutes for breakfast.

From this point the railroad, skirting Humboldt River, struck north for some miles, following the course of the river. Then it turned eastward and kept close to the river until it reached the Humboldt Range, where the stream has its source, almost in the extreme east of Nevada.

After breakfast, Mr Fogg, Aouda and their companions resumed their comfortable seats in the carriage, and observed the varied scenery that passed before their eyes: vast prairies, mountains standing out on the horizon, and creeks with their seething, foaming waters. At times a great herd of buffaloes, massing in the distance, looked like a moving dam. These innumerable hosts of ruminants often oppose an insuperable barrier to the passage of trains. Thousands of these animals have been seen filing past across the rails, in serried ranks, for hours together. The engine is then forced to stop and wait until the road is clear again. And the very thing happened on this occasion. About three o'clock in the afternoon, a herd of ten or twelve thousand head of buffalo blocked the way. The engine, after slackening speed, tried to drive its spur-ram into the flank of the immense column, but the impenetrable mass brought it to a standstill.

These ruminants, improperly called buffaloes by the Americans, advanced with their tranquil step, at times bellowing loudly. They were larger than the bulls of Europe, short in the legs and tail, had prominent withers forming a muscular bump, horns wide apart at the base, head, neck and shoulders covered with long, flowing hairs.

To try and stop such a migration was out of the question. When bisons have settled on a line of march, nothing on earth can arrest or alter their course. It is a torrent of living flesh which no dam can keep back.

The travellers watched this curious sight from the platforms; but Phileas Fogg, to whom time must have been more precious than to anyone else, never left his seat, but waited philosophically until it should please the buffaloes to move out of the way. Passepartout was furious at the delay caused by this agglomeration of animals; it would have given him the greatest pleasure to have discharged his arsenal of revolvers upon them.

'What a country!' he exclaimed, 'where trains are stopped by mere cattle, that go along in a procession, and will no more hurry than if they were not interfering with the traffic! Egad! I should very much like to know if Mr Fogg has allowed for this mischance in his programme! And what of this engine-driver, who has not the pluck to send his engine at full speed through these obstructing beasts!'

The engine-driver had been very wise in not attempting to overthrow the obstacle. He would, no doubt, have crushed the first buffaloes struck by the spur-ram, but, no matter how powerful the engine might be, it would soon have been stopped, and the train would have infallibly been thrown off the metals and remained helpless. The best thing to do therefore was to wait patiently, and then make up for lost time by accelerating the train's speed. The march of the bisons lasted three full hours, and the line was not clear before nightfall, when the last ranks of the herd were crossing the rails, and the first were disappearing below the southern horizon.

It was eight o'clock when the train ran through the defiles of the Humboldt Range, and half-past nine when it entered the territory of Utah, the curious land of Great Salt Lake and the Mormons.

CHAPTER XXVII

In which Passepartout attends, at a speed of twenty miles an hour, a course of Mormon history

DURING THE NIGHT OF the fifth of December, the train ran in a south-easterly direction for about fifty miles; then, going up a like distance to the north-east, it drew near to Great Salt Lake.

About nine o'clock in the morning, Passepartout went out on the platform to take the air. The weather was cold, the sky grey, but it was snowing no longer. The sun's disc, magnified by the mist, looked like an enormous gold coin, and Passepartout was busy calculating its value in pounds sterling, when his attention was diverted from this useful occupation by the appearance of a somewhat strange personage.

This man, who had taken the train for Elko station, was tall, very dark, with black moustache, black stockings, a black silk hat, a black waistcoat, black trousers, a white tie and dog-skin gloves. He looked like a parson, and was going from one end of the train to the other, sticking, by means of wafers, on the door of each car a manuscript notice. Passepartout drew near and read one of these notices, which was to the effect that Elder William Hitch, Mormon missionary, taking advantage of his presence on train No. 48, would give a lecture on Mormonism in car No. 117, from eleven to twelve o'clock, and that he invited all gentlemen to hear him, who cared to learn about the mysteries of the religion of the 'Latter Day Saints.'

'I shall go without fail,' said Passepartout to himself, who knew practically nothing of Mormonism, except the polygamous habits on which the society rests. The news spread rapidly through the train, which was carrying some hundred passengers. At most thirty of them, drawn by the attraction of a lecture, were seated in car No. 117 by eleven o'clock.

Passepartout was in the front row of the faithful, but neither his master nor Fix took the trouble to go.

At the appointed hour Elder William Hitch rose, and, in a voice betraying anger, as if he had been contradicted in advance, exclaimed, 'I tell you that Joe Smith is a martyr, that his brother Hiram is a martyr, and that the persecutions of the prophets by the United States Government will also make a martyr of Brigham Young. Who would dare to assert the contrary?'

Nobody ventured to gainsay the missionary, whose fanaticism contrasted with his naturally calm facial expression. No doubt his wrath arose from the fact that Mormonism was at that moment subjected to severe trials. The United States Government had succeeded, with considerable trouble, in subduing these independent fanatics. It had made itself master of Utah, and compelled it to obey the laws of the Union, after imprisoning Brigham Young on a charge of rebellion and polygamy. Ever since, the disciples of the prophet redoubled their efforts and, while biding their time, opposed words to the claims of Congress. Apparently Elder William Hitch was proselytising on the very railway trains. Then, throwing impassioned force into his narrative by voice and gesture, he told the story of Mormonism from biblical times: how that, in Israel, a Mormon prophet of the tribe of Joseph published the records of the new religion and bequeathed them to his son Morom; how, centuries later, a translation of this precious book in Egyptian script was written by Joseph Smith, Junior, a Vermont farmer, who revealed himself as a mystical prophet in 1825; and how, finally, a heavenly messenger appeared to him in a luminous forest and gave unto him the records of the Lord.

Just then a few persons, not particularly interested in the missionary's retrospective account, left the carriage; but William Hitch, continuing his lecture, related how Smith, Junior, gathering together his father, his two brothers, and a few disciples, founded the religion of the 'Latter Day Saints' – a religion which has been accepted not only in America, but in England, Scandinavia and Germany, and numbers among its followers not only artisans, but many members of the liberal professions – how a temple was erected at a cost of two hundred thousand dollars and a town built at Kirkland; how Smith became a daring banker, and received from a humble mummy showman a papyrus containing a narrative written by Abraham, and others, famous Egyptians.

As Hitch's story was getting rather tedious, the ranks of his hearers were now thinned again, and the audience was reduced to some twenty persons. But the Elder, undeterred by this desertion, went on telling in detail how Joe Smith became bankrupt in 1837; how the ruined shareholders covered him with tar and rolled him in feathers; how he turned up again, more honourable and more honoured than ever, a few years later, at Independence, in Missouri, and the head of a flourishing community of at least three thousand disciples, when, pursued by the hatred of the gentiles, he fled into the far West.

There were now ten people in the audience, one of whom was honest Passepartout, who was listening intently. Thus he learnt that, after long persecutions, Smith reappeared in Illinois, and founded in 1839, on the banks of the Mississippi, the settlement of Nauvoo-la-Belle, which attained a population of twenty-five thousand souls, and of which he became mayor, chief justice, and commander-in-chief; that he was a candidate for the Presidency of the United States in 1843, and that finally he was lured into an ambush at Carthage, thrown into prison, and murdered by a gang of masked men.

By this time Passepartout was the only person left in the carriage, and the Elder, looking him straight in the face, fascinating him with his eloquence, reminded him that, two years after Smith's assassination, his successor, the inspired prophet, Brigham Young, left Nauvoo, and settled on the shores of Salt Lake, where in a beautiful and fertile country, on the route of emigrants crossing Utah on their way to California, the new colony, thanks to the principles of polygamy practised by the Mormons, had grown and flourished exceedingly.

'And,' added William Hitch, 'that is why the jealousy of Congress has worked against us! why the soldiers of the Union have trodden the soil of Utah! why our chief, the prophet Brigham Young, has been put in prison, in defiance of all justice! Shall we yield to brute force? Never! Driven out of Vermont, driven out of Illinois, driven out of Ohio, driven out of Missouri, driven out of Utah, we shall yet find some land

of freedom on which to pitch our tents. And you, my faithful one,'
added the Elder, fixing a wrathful stare upon his one and only hearer,
'shall you pitch yours under the shadow of our flag?' 'No,' answered
Passepartout bravely, and he too fled, leaving the fanatic to rant in the
desert.

During the lecture the train had made rapid progress, and, about
half-past twelve, it reached the north-west corner of Great Salt Lake.
Thence the passengers commanded an extensive view of this inland
sea, which is also called the Dead Sea, and into which flows an
American Jordan. It is a magnificent lake, framed in by grand, broad-
based crags, encrusted with white salt; a splendid expanse of water,
which once covered a greater area; its shores having gradually risen in
course of time, have thereby decreased its surface, while increasing its
depth.

Salt Lake, about seventy miles long and thirty-five wide, is three
thousand eight hundred feet above sea-level. Very different from
Asphaltic Lake, which lies twelve hundred feet below the sea, it
contains a considerable amount of salt, and its water holds a quarter of
its weight of solid matter in solution; its specific gravity, as compared
with distilled water, being as 1170 is to 1000. So fishes cannot live in it,
and those which are washed into the lake by the Jordan, the Weber and
other streams, soon perish. It is not a fact, however, that the density of
the water is such that a man cannot dive into it.

The country around the lake was very well cultivated, for the
Mormons are skilled agriculturists. Six months later, ranches and
corrals for domestic animals, fields of corn, maize, and sorghum,
luxuriant meadows, hedges of wild rose trees, clumps of acacias and
euphorbias, would have met the eye on all sides; but now the ground
was powdered over by a thin layer of snow.

The train arrived at Ogden at two o'clock, and the travellers
alighted, as they would not leave again before six. Mr Fogg, Aouda and
their two companions, having plenty of time, paid a visit to the City of
the Saints, connected with Ogden by a small branch line. Two hours
would be sufficient to see the town, American in every respect, and
therefore built on the pattern of all the towns in the Union, like great
chess-boards with long cheerless lines, and the 'sombre sadness of right
angles,' as Victor Hugo[24] expresses it. The founder of the City of the
Saints succumbed to that craving for symmetry which is a distinctive
characteristic of the Anglo-Saxons. In this strange land, where men are
undeniably not on a level with their institutions, everything is done
'squarely,' cities, houses, and follies.

By three o'clock the travellers were strolling in the streets of this town, which stands between one bank of the Jordan and the first heights, the Wahsatch Range. They noticed few, if any, churches; the only monuments were the prophet's habitation, the court-house and the arsenal; they saw houses built of bluish bricks, with verandas and galleries, surrounded with gardens and bordered with acacias, palms and carob trees. A clay and pebble wall, built in 1853, encompassed the town; and in the main street, where the market is held, there were a few hotels decked with flags, and among them was Salt Lake House.

To Mr Fogg and his companions the place did not appear to be very populous. The streets were nearly empty, except in the neighbourhood of the Temple, which they did not reach before they had passed through several quarters surrounded by palings. The women were fairly numerous, which is accounted for by the peculiar constitution of Mormon households. It would not be correct, however, to say that all Mormons are polygamous. Men are free to do as they please in that matter. But it should be said that the women of Utah are particularly anxious to become wives, because, according to the religion of Utah, female celibates are not admitted to the joys of the Mormon heaven. These poor creatures appeared to be neither well-off nor happy. A few, the wealthiest, doubtless, wore black silk jackets open at the waist, under a hood or very simple shawl. The others had nothing but print dresses.

Passepartout, who held decided views on the subject, could not see without a sort of dismay these Mormon women, two or more of whom were entrusted with the happiness of a single Mormon man. His common sense made him feel special pity for the man. It seemed to him a terrible thing to have to guide so many ladies at once through the vicissitudes of life, to have to lead them as a team up to the Mormon paradise, with the prospect of joining them there for eternity in the company of the glorious Smith, who no doubt was the shining light of that blissful abode. No, no, such a life did not appeal to him; and – he was possibly mistaken – it occurred to him that the ladies of Great Salt Lake City cast rather disquieting glances at his person.

Very fortunately his stay in the City of the Saints was not to be a long one. At a few minutes before four, the travellers were at the station again and went back to their places in the train.

The whistle sounded; but, just as the driving wheels of the engine, gliding on the rails, were beginning to impart a certain speed to the train, loud cries of 'Stop! Stop!' were heard. A train, once started, does not stop for passengers. The man who uttered these cries was evidently a belated Mormon. He rushed up breathless, and as, fortunately for him, the station had neither gates nor barriers, he was able to tear along the line, jump on the footboard of the last carriage, and drop panting on one of the seats.

Passepartout, who had watched these gymnastic incidents with considerable excitement, went up to have a look at this laggard, and was greatly interested when he heard that the headlong flight of this citizen of Utah was simply the outcome of a domestic quarrel. When the Mormon had recovered his breath, Passepartout ventured to ask him politely how many wives he had all to himself. This hurried Hegira had led him to suppose the man had a score at least.

'One, sir,' replied the Mormon, raising his arms to heaven; 'one, and that was enough!'

CHAPTER XXVIII

In which Passepartout was unable to make anyone listen to reason

ON LEAVING Ogden station and Great Salt Lake, the train ran on a northerly course for an hour, as far as Weber River, having travelled about nine hundred miles from San Francisco. From this point it struck east again across the bold Wahsatch Mountains. It was in the district included between these mountains and the Rocky Mountains, properly so called, that the American engineers had to contend against their most serious difficulties; and for this part of the railroad the Government's grant amounted to forty-eight thousand dollars per mile, whereas it was not more than sixteen thousand dollars for laying the line on the flat country. But the engineers, as we have pointed out before, did not hack their way through natural obstacles, so much as overcome them by skilfully turning them, so that, in order to reach the great basin, one single tunnel, fourteen hundred feet long, was pierced in the whole course of the railroad.

So far, the line had reached its highest elevation at the Great Salt Lake. From this point it described a very long curve, descending towards Bitter Creek Valley, and rose again up to the watershed between the Atlantic and the Pacific. There were many streams in this mountainous region; the Muddy, the Green, and others had to be crossed on culverts. Passepartout's impatience became greater and greater as he drew nearer to the goal. Fix, too, longed to be out of this country so full of obstacles. He feared delays, dreaded accidents, and was more anxious than Phileas Fogg himself to set foot on English soil.

The train stopped at Fort Bridger station at ten o'clock in the evening, and left again almost at once; twenty miles farther on it entered the State of Wyoming, formerly Dakota, following the whole length of Bitter Creek Valley, whence drain part of the waters which form the hydrographic system of Colorado. On the morrow, December 7, there was a quarter of an hour's stop at Green River station. During the night there had been a fairly heavy fall of snow, mixed with rain and half-melted, which could not impede the train's progress. But the bad weather worried Passepartout none the less, for the snow accumulating on the track would clog the wheels of the carriages, and would certainly be a possible cause of failure.

'Well, but what a mad idea it was to travel in winter!' he said to himself. 'Why on earth could not my master wait for the summer? It would have given him a better chance.'

At this very moment, when the worthy fellow was thinking of nothing but the state of the sky and the lower temperature, Aouda was a prey to worse anxiety, which had a totally different cause. A few travellers had got out of their carriage and were walking about on the platform of Green River station, awaiting the departure of the train, when she recognised one of them through the window as Colonel Stamp Proctor, the American who had treated Phileas Fogg with such gross rudeness at the San Francisco meeting. To avoid being seen, Aouda drew back instantly from the window.

The young woman was greatly alarmed by this incident. The man, who, dispassionate as his manner might be, gave her, day by day, proofs of the most absolute devotion, had become very dear to her.

Truly she did not quite realise how deep was the sentiment with which her deliverer inspired her, and to which she still gave the name of gratitude, but, though she knew it not, there was more than gratitude. So a pang shot through her heart when she recognised the unmannerly bully, from whom Mr Fogg intended sooner or later to demand satisfaction for his conduct. Of course, Colonel Proctor's presence in the train was a mere coincidence, but there he was, and everything must be done to prevent Phileas Fogg from getting sight of his adversary.

When the train had started, Aouda seized a moment when Mr Fogg was dozing to inform Fix and Passepartout of her discovery. 'What!' exclaimed Fix. 'This fellow Proctor is in the train! Well, you need not worry, madam; before settling accounts with that fellow – with Mr Fogg – he will have to deal with me! It seems to me that I was the most aggrieved party in that affair!'

'And, what is more,' added Passepartout, 'leave him to me, I'll tackle him, colonel as he is.'

'Mr Fix,' continued Aouda, 'Mr Fogg will never allow anyone to avenge him. He is quite capable of returning to America to find this bully. He has said so himself. If he sees Colonel Proctor, we shall not be able to prevent a duel, which might have deplorable consequences. He must not see him.' 'You are right, madam,' answered Fix; 'a duel might ruin everything. Victorious or not, Mr Fogg would be delayed, and –'

'And,' added Passepartout, 'that would be playing the game of the gentlemen of the Reform Club. In four days we shall be in New York. Well, if my master does not leave his car for four days, one may hope that chance will not bring him face to face with this cursed American; confound him! Surely we shall manage to prevent him –'

The conversation was interrupted. Mr Fogg had just woke up. and was looking at the landscape through the snow-flecked window. But some little time after, without being heard by his master or Aouda, Passepartout said to the detective: 'Do you mean to say you would really fight for him?' 'There is nothing I shall not do to bring him back alive to Europe,' replied Fix quietly, in a tone that denoted inflexible determination. Passepartout felt something like a shiver run through him, but his belief in his master remained unshaken.

Now was there any means whatever of keeping Mr Fogg in this compartment, so as to prevent all possibility of a meeting between him and the colonel? This should not present much difficulty, for Mr Fogg was neither restless nor curious. In any case the detective found this means, for a few minutes later he said to Mr Fogg, 'Time seems endless, travelling in a train, does it not, sir?' 'Yes,' replied Mr Fogg, 'but it passes all the same.' 'You used to play whist on board the liners?' 'Yes,' answered Phileas Fogg, 'but here it would not be an easy matter; I have neither cards nor people with whom to make a four.' 'As for cards, we could surely buy some. They sell everything on American trains. And if by chance this lady plays –' 'Of course I do, sir,' replied Aouda eagerly. 'I know whist; it is part of an English education.' 'I flatter myself I am a pretty good whist-player,' resumed Fix. 'So that with three of us and a dummy –' 'All right, sir,' replied Phileas Fogg, delighted to get back to his favourite game, even in a train.

Passepartout was dispatched to find the steward, and soon returned with two packs, scoring slips, counters, and a board covered with cloth. Everything was there; they began to play. Aouda had a very fair knowledge of the game; and Mr Fogg, severe critic as he was, paid her some compliments on her playing. As for the detective, he was simply a first-rate player, and quite a match for Mr Fogg. 'Now,' thought

Passepartout, 'we have got him. He won't stir.'

At eleven o'clock in the morning the train reached the dividing ridge of the watersheds of the two oceans, at a spot called Bridger Pass, seven thousand five hundred and twenty-four feet above sea-level, one of the highest points attained by the line as it crosses the Rocky Mountains. After a run of about two hundred miles, the travellers would at last reach the plains which sweep on and on to the Atlantic, and are so well adapted by Nature to the laying of a railway.

On the watershed of the Atlantic river-system the first streams, tributaries, direct or indirect, of the North Platte River, were already on their way. The whole northern and eastern horizon was shrouded by that immense semicircular curtain, the northern portion of the Rocky Mountains, the highest of which is Laramie Peak. Between this curved boundary of the mountains and the railway were far-spreading, well-watered plains. On the right rose one above the other the first slopes of the group of mountains which reach down southward to the sources of the River Arkansas, one of the great tributaries of the Missouri. At half-past twelve the travellers caught a glimpse of Fort Halleck, which commands the district. In a few more hours they would be across the Rocky Mountains. It was therefore reasonable to expect that no untoward event would mark the passage of the train through this difficult country. The snow had stopped, and dry cold was setting in. Big birds, scared by the engine, flew right away; no wild beast, whether bear or wolf, was to be seen on the plain, which presented the aspect of the desert in its boundless nakedness.

Mr Fogg and his partners had enjoyed a comfortable lunch, served in their carriage, and had just returned to their endless whist, when a violent whistling was heard, and the train stopped.

Passepartout put his head out of the window, but saw nothing to account for this stoppage; there was no station in sight.

Aouda and Fix feared for a moment that Mr Fogg might take it into his head to get down on the line, but all he did was to say to his servant: 'Just go and see what is the matter.'

Passepartout jumped down from the carriage; some forty passengers had already left their seats; among them was Colonel Stamp Proctor. The train was stopped before a red signal which blocked the way. The engine-driver and the guard had got down and were talking excitedly with a watchman, whom the station-master at Medicine Bow, the next station, had sent to meet the train. Some of the passengers had come up and were taking part in the discussion, one of them being Colonel Proctor, who was conspicuous for his loud tone of voice and hectoring manner.

Passepartout, on joining the group, heard the watchman saying, 'No! it is impossible to pass! The bridge at Medicine Bow is shaky, and would not bear the weight of the train.' The bridge in question was a suspension bridge over rapids a mile away from the spot where the train had stopped. According to the watchman, it was in a ruinous condition, several of the chains were broken, and it was impossible to venture across. The watchman's assertion that the train could not get over this bridge was therefore no exaggeration. Moreover, it is safe to say that, when Americans, so casual as a rule, show signs of caution, it would be the height of folly not to be cautious too. Passepartout, who did not dare to inform his master of what was happening, listened with clenched teeth, motionless as a statue.

'Look here!' cried Colonel Proctor. 'I suppose we are not going to be left here to take root in the snow?' 'Colonel,' replied the guard, 'we have telegraphed to Omaha for a train, but it is not likely that it will get to Medicine Bow in less than six hours.' 'Six hours!' cried Passepartout. 'Certainly,' replied the guard. 'In any case it will take us all that time to get to the station on foot.' 'But it is only a mile away from us,' observed one of the passengers. 'A mile, yes, but on the other side of the river.' 'How about getting across in a boat?' asked the colonel. 'That's impossible. The creek is swelled by the heavy rain. It is a rapid, and we shall have to walk ten miles to the north in a roundabout way to find a ford.' The colonel let fly a volley of oaths, finding fault with the Company and the guard, and Passepartout, who was furious, was very near joining him in his denunciations. Here was a material obstacle which all his master's banknotes would be powerless to surmount. Nor were Passepartout and the colonel the only people to give vent to their disappointment.

When the passengers realised that, apart from the loss of time, they would have to trudge fifteen miles over the snow-covered plain, there was such a hubbub, such exclamations and shouts, that Phileas Fogg's attention must have been drawn had he not been completely absorbed by his game. Passepartout now felt, however, that his master must be told, and, with hanging head, was proceeding towards the carriage, when the engine-driver, a typical Yankee, by name Forster, called out, 'Gentlemen, there might be a way of getting over.'

'Over the bridge?' asked a passenger. 'Yes, over the bridge.' 'With our train?' asked the colonel. 'With our train.' Passepartout stopped, and listened greedily to the engine-driver.

'But the bridge is in a ruinous condition!' rejoined the guard. 'No matter,' replied Forster. 'My idea is that, if we sent the train on at its highest speed, we should stand a chance of getting over.' 'The deuce!'

said Passepartout. But a certain number of the passengers were at once tempted by the proposal. Colonel Proctor in particular was delighted with it, and the crazy fellow thought the thing quite practicable. He even supported his belief by quoting the fact that engineers had thought of sending single-car trains over rivers, without bridges, by putting on full steam. In the end, all those who were interested in the matter fell in with the engine-driver's opinion. 'We have fifty chances out of a hundred of getting over,' said one. 'Sixty!' said another. 'Eighty! Ninety!'

Passepartout was astounded, and, though ready to attempt anything to get across Medicine Creek, he thought the proposed effort rather too American.

'And,' thought he, 'there's a much more simple way, and it has not even occurred to these people! Sir,' said he to one of them, 'the engine-driver's idea seems to me somewhat risky, but – ' 'Eighty chances!' replied the passenger, turning his back on him. 'Yes, I know,' answered Passepartout, addressing another, 'but on second thoughts – ' 'There's no need of second thoughts,' replied this American, with a shrug of his shoulders, 'since the engine-driver assures us that we shall get over!' 'Yes, of course,' returned Passepartout, 'we shall get over, but it might be more prudent – ' 'What's this? Prudent!' cried Colonel Proctor, who, on overhearing the word, became frantically excited. 'At full speed, don't you understand? At full speed, man!' 'I know – I see,' repeated Passepartout, who was never allowed to finish his sentence, 'but it would be – I won't say more prudent, since the word offends you, – more natural at any rate – ' 'What's all this? What does the chap mean by natural? What's the matter with him?' cried people all round him. The poor fellow could get nobody to listen to him. 'Are you afraid?' asked Colonel Proctor. 'Afraid, I!' cried Passepartout. 'All right, I shall just show these people that a Frenchman can be as American as they are!'

'Take your seats! Take your seats!' shouted the guard. 'Yes, yes, take your seats! Take your seats!' repeated Passepartout. 'We'll do it at once; but, all the same, they can't prevent my thinking that it would have been more natural to send us travellers first across the bridge on foot, and then the train.' But nobody heard this sensible reflection, nor would anyone have acknowledged its soundness.

The passengers returned to their places; Passepartout went back to his seat without saying anything about what had happened. The whist-players had no thought for anything but their game.

The engine whistled loud and long; the engine-driver, reversing, backed the train for nearly a mile, on the principle of the jumper, who takes a long run before leaping.

Then there was a second whistle, and the train moved forward again, faster and faster, and soon the speed was terrific. All that was heard was one continuous screech from the engine, whose pistons were doing twenty strokes per second; smoke came out of the axle-boxes. There was a sort of feeling that the train was flying bodily at a hundred miles an hour, and was no longer resting on the rails; gravity was almost cancelled by velocity.

And over they went, in a flash! Of the bridge they saw nothing; the train, it may fairly be said, leaped from one bank to the other, and shot five miles beyond the station before the engine could be brought to a standstill.

But hardly was the river crossed, when the bridge, now completely ruined, collapsed, and crashed into the rapids of Medicine Bow.

CHAPTER XXIX

In which is given an account of various incidents which happen only on the railroads of the union

THE TRAIN PURSUED its course that same evening, meeting with no mishap, passed Fort Saunders, crossed Cheyenne Pass and came to Evans Pass. The railroad here reached the highest point of the whole track, eight thousand and ninety-one feet above the level of the ocean. The travellers had now only to descend to the Atlantic over boundless plains, levelled by Nature.

At that spot on the Grand Trunk the branch line started for Denver, the chief town of Colorado, a country rich in gold and silver mines, where already more than fifty thousand people have settled.

Thirteen hundred and eighty-two miles had now been travelled over from San Francisco in three days and three nights. Four nights and four days, in all probability, would bring the travellers to New York. So Phileas Fogg was still within the prescribed time-limit.

During the night Walbach Camp was passed on the left. Pole Creek flowed parallel to the line and followed the rectilinear frontier between the States of Wyoming and Colorado. At eleven o'clock they entered Nebraska, then passed near Sedgwich and touched Julesburgh, situated on the southern branch of the Platte River. It was here that the inauguration of the Union Pacific Railroad took place on the 23rd of

October, 1869, the chief engineer being General J. M. Dodge. Two powerful engines brought nine wagons of invited guests, one of whom was Vice-President Thomas C. Durant. Ringing cheers enlivened the scene; and Sioux[25] and Pawnees treated the spectators to an Indian sham-fight, followed by a display of fireworks. There, too, was published on that great occasion, by means of a portable press, the first number of the *Railway Pioneer*. Thus was celebrated the inauguration of this great railway, an instrument of progress and civilisation, thrown across the desert and destined to link together towns and cities not yet in existence. The whistle of the locomotive, more potent than the lyre of Amphion, would soon bid them rise from America's soil.

Fort MacPherson was left behind at eight o'clock in the morning. A space of three hundred and fifty-seven miles separates this place from Omaha. The line running near the left bank of the southern branch of the Platte River followed the capricious windings of the stream. At nine o'clock the travellers arrived at the important town of North Platte, built between the two arms of the great river, which join again around it to form one artery, a large tributary whose waters mingle with those of the Missouri, a little above Omaha.

The one hundred and first meridian was passed. Mr Fogg and his partners were busy with the cards once more, and no one, not even the dummy, complained of the length of the journey. Fix had begun by winning a few guineas, which he was now in a fair way to lose, but he was just as keen as Mr Fogg. That morning luck was particularly kind to the latter. Trumps and honours rained down upon him. At one moment, having thought out a bold plan, he was about to play a spade, when a voice from behind his seat was heard saying, 'I would play a diamond.'

Mr Fogg, Aouda, and Fix looked up, and lo and behold, there was Colonel Proctor! Stamp Proctor and Phileas Fogg knew each other at once.

'Halloo, Britisher!' exclaimed the colonel; 'so you're the man who wants to play a spade!' 'And who plays it,' replied Phileas Fogg coolly, putting the ten of that suit on the table. 'Well, it is my pleasure that it should be a diamond,' returned Colonel Proctor in an angry tone of voice. He then made as if he would snatch the card that had been played, and added: 'You know nothing about this game.' 'There is another at which I may perhaps show greater skill,' said Phileas Fogg, rising from his seat. 'You can try your hand at that one whenever you please, son of John Bull,' replied the churlish fellow.

Aouda turned pale, and her heart stood still. She grasped Phileas Fogg's arm, but was gently forced back. As the American stared at his adversary in the most insulting manner Passepartout would have flung himself upon him, but Fix got up, went to Colonel Proctor and said, 'You forget, sir, that I am the man you must deal with, for I am the man you not only insulted but struck!'

'Mr Fix,' said Mr Fogg, 'pardon me, but this concerns me, and no one else. When the colonel maintained that I was wrong in playing a spade, he put a fresh insult upon me, and he shall give me satisfaction for it.'

'When you please, and where you please,' replied the American, 'and with whatever weapon you please.' Aouda made vain efforts to restrain Mr Fogg, and the detective tried in vain a second time to make the quarrel his. Passepartout was preparing to throw the colonel out of the window, but was checked by a sign from his master: Phileas Fogg left the carriage, and the American followed him on to the platform.

'Sir,' said Mr Fogg to his adversary, 'I am in a great hurry to return to Europe; the slightest delay would affect me very seriously.' 'Well, and what is that to me?' returned Colonel Proctor. 'Sir,' continued Mr Fogg very politely, 'after our encounter at San Francisco, I intended to come back and find you in America, as soon as I had settled the business which calls me to the old continent.' 'Really!' 'Will you arrange a meeting for six months hence?' 'Why not six years?' 'I say six months,' replied Mr Fogg, 'and I shall be there punctually.' 'All this is to put me off!' cried Stamp Proctor. 'It must be now or never.' 'Very good. You are going to New York, I suppose?' 'No.' 'To Chicago?' 'No.' 'To Omaha?' 'What difference does it make to you? Do you know Plum Creek?' 'No,' replied Mr Fogg. 'It is the next station. We shall be there in an hour. There will be a ten minutes' stop. Ten minutes is time enough to exchange a few revolver shots.' 'All right,' replied Mr Fogg. 'I will stop at Plum Creek.' 'I shouldn't wonder if you stayed there for good,' added the American with the utmost insolence. 'Who knows?' retorted Mr Fogg, returning to his carriage, as unruffled as ever.

The first thing he did was to reassure Aouda, telling her that blusterers were never to be feared. He then requested Fix to act as his second in the impending duel. Fix consented; he could hardly do otherwise; and Phileas Fogg calmly continued his interrupted game, playing a spade, as if nothing had happened.

At eleven o'clock the engine's whistle announced that Plum Creek station was near. Mr Fogg got up and went out on the platform, followed by Fix. Passepartout accompanied him, carrying a pair of revolvers. Aouda remained in the carriage, pale as death.

Another door opened at this moment, and Colonel Proctor likewise came forward on the platform, followed by his second, a Yankee of the same kidney. But just as the two opponents were about to step down to the line, the guard rushed up shouting, 'You can't get down, gentlemen!' 'Why not?' asked the colonel. 'We are twenty minutes late, so the train won't stop.' 'But I have to fight a duel with this gentleman.'

'I am sorry,' replied the guard, 'but we are off at once. There's the bell!' The bell was actually ringing, and the train started. 'I am really more than sorry, gentlemen,' said the guard, apologising again; 'in any other case it would have been in my power to oblige you. But, after all, since you have not had time to fight here, why shouldn't you fight on board the train?' 'This gentleman will possibly object,' sneered Colonel Proctor. 'I have not the slightest objection,' answered Phileas Fogg.

'Well, of one thing there can be no manner of doubt, this is America,' thought Passepartout, 'and the guard is quite the high-class gentleman!' And muttering thus to himself, he followed his master. The two principals with their seconds, preceded by the guard, passed through the carriages to the rear of the train. There were not more than nine or ten passengers in the last carriage, and the guard asked them to be so good as to leave it vacant for a few minutes, as two gentlemen wished to settle an affair of honour. This request seemed most natural to the passengers, who withdrew to the platforms, professing themselves only too happy to oblige.

The carriage, some fifty feet long, was very suitable for the purpose. The two combatants could advance against each other in the gangway between the seats, and shoot with perfect comfort. Never was a duel more easily arranged. Mr Fogg and Colonel Proctor, each equipped with two six-chambered revolvers, went into the carriage. Their seconds, who remained outside, shut them in. They were to open fire at the first whistle of the engine. After a space of two minutes, whatever remained of the two gentlemen would be removed from the carriage. What could be more simple? In fact it was all so simple that Fix and Passepartout felt their hearts beating as if they would burst.

They were thus waiting for the whistle, the signal agreed upon, when suddenly the air was rent with savage yells, accompanied by detonations, which did not come from the carriage reserved for the duellists, but extended all along the train, right up to the fore part. Cries of terror came from inside the carriages. Colonel Proctor and Mr Fogg came out at once, revolver in hand, and rushed to the fore part of the train, where shots and shrieks were loudest. They had at once understood that the train was being attacked by a band of Sioux. This was not the first attempt of these bold Indians; they had held up trains more than once. Some hundred of them had, as they always did, jumped on to the footboards, without waiting till the train should stop, and climbed into the carriages as a clown mounts a galloping horse.

These Sioux were armed with guns. Hence the reports, to which the passengers, who were almost all armed, replied with revolver-shots. The first thing the Indians did was to rush to the engine, where they half-killed the driver and stoker with blows of their tomahawks. A Sioux chief, wishing to stop the train, but not knowing how to work the handle of the regulator, opened wide the throttle-valve instead of closing it, and the engine bolted at a terrific speed.

Having at the same time swarmed up the carriages, the Sioux were running about like infuriated apes over the roofs, bursting the doors open and fighting hand to hand with the passengers. Out of the luggage-van, which had been broken into and plundered, the packages were flung upon the line. Cries and shots were incessant.

The travellers defended themselves bravely. Some of the carriages were barricaded and sustained a siege, just as if they had been real movable forts carried along at a hundred miles an hour.

Aouda showed great courage from the very beginning of the attack, defending herself heroically with a revolver, firing through the broken windows whenever a savage appeared before her. Some twenty Sioux fell mortally wounded to the track, and those who slipped from the platforms on to the rails were crushed like worms under the wheels of the carriages.

Several passengers, who had received serious hurt from the bullets or tomahawks, lay on the seats.

It was necessary to end the struggle, which had already lasted ten minutes and must result in a victory for the Indians, if the train could not be pulled up. Fort Kearney station was not two miles distant. But, if the train went beyond Fort Kearney, where there was an American garrison, it would be in the hands of the Indians before the next station could be reached.

The guard, who was fighting beside Mr Fogg, fell, struck by a bullet; whereupon he cried, 'Unless the train can be stopped within five minutes, we are lost!'

'Stopped it shall be,' said Phileas Fogg, who prepared to rush from the carriage. 'Stay, sir,' cried Passepartout, 'that is my job!'

The plucky fellow was too quick for Phileas Fogg, and, opening a door without being seen by the Indians, managed to slip under the carriage. Then, while the struggle went on, while the bullets crossed each other over his head, he made his way under the carriages with the agility and litheness of his old acrobatic days; clutching hold of the chains, helping himself along by means of the brakes and edges of the sashes, creeping from one carriage to the other with marvellous skill, he reached the front part of the train without being seen, for he was invisible. There, hanging by one hand between the luggage-van and the tender, he used the other to separate the safety-chains; but, owing to the force of traction, he would never have unscrewed the coupling-pin. Fortunately, a violent jolt of the engine snapped the pin, and the train, parted from the engine, was gradually left behind, while the engine itself raced ahead with increased velocity.

Carried on by the force it had acquired, the train did not stop for some minutes, but the brakes were applied inside the carriages and it came to a standstill less than a hundred yards from Kearney station. The soldiers of the fort, attracted by the firing, hurried up. The Sioux did not wait for them. The whole lot of them scampered away before the train had quite stopped.

But when the passengers were counted on the station platform, it was found that several were missing, one of whom was the brave Frenchman whose devotion had just saved them.

CHAPTER XXX

In which Phileas Fogg simply does his duty

THREE PASSENGERS, including Passepartout, had disappeared. As yet, it was impossible to say whether they had been killed during the conflict, or taken prisoners by the Sioux. The wounded were fairly numerous, but it was found that none were fatally hurt. One of the worst cases was Colonel Proctor, who had fought bravely and been struck down by a bullet in the groin. He was removed to the station with others whose condition required immediate attention.

Aouda was safe; and Phileas Fogg, who had been in the thick of the fight, had not a scratch. Fix had received a slight wound in the arm, but Passepartout was missing, and silent tears showed Aouda's grief. All the passengers had got out of the train.

The wheels of the carriages were stained with blood. From the naves and spokes hung mangled pieces of flesh. Long red trails could be seen as far as the eye could reach on the white plain. The last of the Indians were disappearing in the south, in the direction of Republican River.

Mr Fogg, with folded arms, stood motionless, debating in his mind the grave decision he had to take. Aouda, beside him, looked at him without uttering a word, but he understood. If his servant was a prisoner, ought he not to run any risk to get him out of the Indians' hands? 'I shall find him, dead or alive,' he said quietly to Aouda.

'Ah, Mr – Mr Fogg!' cried she, grasping his hands, which she covered with tears.

'Alive,' added Mr Fogg, 'if we do not lose a moment.' By this resolve, Phileas Fogg was making a complete sacrifice of himself. He had just decreed his own ruin. The delay of a single day would make him miss the boat from New York. His wager was lost irrevocably. But face to face with this thought, 'It is my duty,' he did not hesitate.

The captain in command of Fort Kearney was there. About a hundred of his men had taken up a defensive position, in case the Sioux should attempt a direct attack upon the railway station.

'Sir,' said Mr Fogg, addressing the captain, 'three passengers are missing.' 'Are they dead?' asked the captain. 'Dead or prisoners,' replied Phileas Fogg. 'That is the very thing that should not be left in doubt. Is it your intention to pursue the Sioux?' 'That is a very serious matter,' replied the officer. 'These Indians may continue their flight beyond the Arkansas. I cannot leave the fort committed to my charge without protection.' 'The lives of three men are at stake,' rejoined Phileas Fogg. 'Certainly, but can I risk the lives of fifty to save three?' 'I do not know whether you can, sir, but it is your duty.' 'Sir,' replied the captain, 'it is nobody's place here to teach me my duty.' 'Very well,' said Phileas Fogg coldly; 'I will go alone.' 'You, sir,' cried Fix, coming up, 'go alone in pursuit of the Indians!' 'Do you want me to leave this poor man to his fate, to whom everyone here owes it that he is still alive? I shall go.' 'No, then, you shall not go alone!' exclaimed the captain, conquered by his emotion. 'No! you're a gallant fellow! I want thirty volunteers!' he added, turning to his men. The whole company came forward in a body. All the captain had to do was to choose among these brave fellows.

Thirty soldiers were selected, and an old sergeant placed at their head. 'Thank you, captain,' said Mr Fogg. 'Will you allow me to accompany you?' asked Fix. 'Sir, you will do as you please,' replied Phileas Fogg. 'But, if you care to oblige me, you will stay behind with the lady. Should anything happen to me – '

A sudden pallor spread over the detective's face. Was he to part from the man whom he had followed so persistently, step by step, and let him thus venture out in this desert! Fix gazed searchingly at Mr Fogg, and then, in spite of himself, notwithstanding his suspicions and the struggle that was going on within him, his eyes fell before that calm, frank look.

'I shall stay,' he said.

A few minutes later, Mr Fogg pressed the young woman's hand, committed his precious travelling-bag to her keeping, and went away with the sergeant and his little band. But before starting, he said to the soldiers, 'My friends, there's a thousand pounds for you, if we save the prisoners.'

It was then a few minutes after twelve. Aouda withdrew to a room in the station and there waited by herself, thinking of Phileas Fogg, of his simple and large-hearted generosity and his serene courage. Mr Fogg, after sacrificing his fortune, was now exposing his life, and all this out of duty – no hesitation, no words. In her eyes Mr Fogg was a hero.

Very different were Fix' s thoughts, and his agitation was beyond control. He walked about the platform in a state of feverish excitement. He had allowed himself to be dominated by Fogg's personality for a moment, but was now his true self again, and now Fogg was gone, he fully realised what a blunder he had committed in letting him go. How could he consent to part from this man whom he had been following around the world! As his real nature prevailed again, he blamed and accused himself, and treated himself as though he had been the Chief of the Metropolitan Police reprimanding a police-officer guilty of a simpleton's blundering.

'I have behaved like a silly fool!' he thought. 'The other chap, of course, let him know who I was, and he has given me the slip! Where am I to lay hands on him again now? But how on earth could I be hoodwinked in this fashion – I, Fix, who have in my pocket an order for his arrest! Evidently, I am nothing but a fool!'

So argued the detective, while the hours passed all too slowly for him. He was at his wits' end. There were times when he felt inclined to tell Aouda everything; but he had a shrewd notion of the reception that awaited his revelations. Whatever should he do? He had a mind to set out in pursuit of Fogg over the great white plains. He thought it just possible he might overtake him. The footprints of the soldiers were still stamped upon the snow. But soon, under a fresh layer, every trace disappeared. Fix now grew thoroughly dejected, and felt an unconquerable temptation to give up the game. And lo, the opportunity of leaving Kearney station and continuing this journey, which had been so full of disappointments, now presented itself.

Towards two o'clock in the afternoon, during a heavy fall of snow, protracted whistling was heard from the east. A huge shadow, preceded by a lurid light, was approaching slowly, much magnified by the mist, which gave it a fantastic appearance.

No train was expected from the east at this hour; the help which had been telegraphed for could not arrive so soon, and the train from Omaha to San Francisco was not due before the morrow. The thing was soon explained.

This engine, which was approaching slowly, emitting loud and prolonged whistling, was that which had been detached from the train, and had pursued its course at such terrific speed, carrying off the stoker and the driver, both unconscious. It had run on for several miles, and then, the fire getting low for lack of fuel, the steam had lost its force, and, an hour later, the engine, slowing down gradually, had stopped at last, twenty miles beyond Kearney station.

Neither driver nor stoker was dead; after remaining insensible for some time, they had recovered consciousness. The engine was then standing still. When the engine-driver saw himself in the desert, with an engine that had no carriages behind it, he understood what had happened. He had no idea how the engine had got detached from the train, but he felt sure that the train which had remained behind was in distress. He at once decided what to do. Prudence counselled him to push on towards Omaha, for to return towards the train, which was still perhaps being pillaged by the Indians, was dangerous. Regardless of such peril, coal and wood were shovelled into the fire-box, the flames revived under the boiler, the steam-pressure rose anew, and about two o'clock in the afternoon, the engine returned, running backward, to Kearney station. The whistling in the mist came from this very engine.

The travellers were delighted to see the locomotive take its place at the head of the train. They would now be able to resume their journey, so unhappily interrupted.

When the engine came in, Aouda, leaving the station, went up to the guard and said, 'Are you going to start?' 'Immediately, madam.' 'But what about the prisoners – our unhappy fellow-travellers – ' 'I cannot stop the service,' replied the guard. 'We are three hours late as it is.'

'When will the next train pass here from San Francisco?' 'Tomorrow evening, madam.' 'Tomorrow evening! That will be too late! Really, you must wait – ' 'It is impossible,' replied the guard. 'If you wish to go, take your seat.' 'I shall not go,' was Aouda's answer.

Fix had heard this conversation. A few minutes before, when he saw no possible means of getting away, he was resolved on leaving Kearney, but now the train was standing there, ready to start, and all he had to do was to resume his seat in the carriage, a resistless force riveted him to the spot. To remain on the station platform was torture to him, yet he could not tear himself away. The struggle within him was starting all over again. The sense of failure maddened, stifled him. He wished to fight to the bitter end.

Meanwhile the passengers, a few of whom were wounded – Colonel Proctor's condition was serious – had taken their places in the train. The overheated boiler was buzzing away, and the steam escaping through the valves. The engine-driver whistled, and the train started, mingling its white smoke with the whirling masses of snow-flakes.

The detective had remained behind. Some hours passed. The weather was very rough, the cold intense. Fix, sitting on a bench in the station, never stirred. One might have thought he was asleep. In spite of the squall, Aouda kept coming out of the room which had been placed at her disposal; she walked to the end of the platform, peering through the blizzard, in her effort to see through the mist which narrowed the horizon around her, and to catch any sound that might be heard. But she saw nothing and heard nothing. Then she would come in again, chilled to the bone, to return a few moments after, and always in vain.

Evening came on, and the small detachment had not come back. Where were they at this moment? Had they been able to overtake the Indians? Had they fought, or were they lost and wandering about at random? The commander of Fort Kearney was very anxious, but tried to betray no sign of his fears. Night came, less snow fell, but the cold grew still more intense.

To look into this dark immensity would have appalled the most fearless. The plain was wrapped in perfect silence. Neither flight of bird nor tread of beast broke the infinite stillness.

Throughout the night Aouda, her mind full of dark forebodings, her heart athrob with anguish, wandered about on the edge of the prairie. Her imagination carried her far away and showed her dangers innumerable. What she suffered through the long hours of that night words cannot tell. Fix had not stirred, but he, too, was sleepless. Once a man approached and even spoke to him, but the detective shook his head in reply and sent him away.

The night passed in this manner. At dawn, the half-extinguished orb of the sun rose above a misty horizon; but it was now possible to see two miles away. Phileas Fogg and the detachment had gone south. In the south there was absolutely nothing to be seen, and it was now seven o'clock. The captain, who was extremely worried, could not make up his mind. Should he send a second detachment to the help of the first and sacrifice more men with so slight a chance of rescuing those who were already sacrificed? His hesitation was soon over. With one resolute gesture he called one of his lieutenants to him, and was in the act of ordering him to make a reconnaissance to the south, when gunshots rang out. Was it a signal? The soldiers rushed out of the fort, and saw half a mile off a small band of men returning in good order. Mr Fogg was marching at their head, and near him were Passepartout and the two other travellers, snatched from the hands of the Sioux.

There had been a fight ten miles south of Kearney. Just before the arrival of the detachment, Passepartout and his two companions were already at grips with their keepers, and the Frenchman had felled three with his fists, when his master and the soldiers rushed up to their assistance.

Rescuers and rescued were received with shouts of joy, and Phileas Fogg distributed the promised reward among the soldiers, while Passepartout was repeating to himself, with some show of reason, 'Upon my word, it cannot be denied that I cost my master a nice amount of money!'

Fix gazed at Mr Fogg without uttering a word; it would have been no easy matter to analyse the impressions that were warring within him. As for Aouda, she seized Mr Fogg's hand and pressed it between her own two hands, unable to speak a word.

Meanwhile Passepartout had no sooner arrived than he looked about for the train in the station. He expected to find it there, ready to proceed at full speed to Omaha, and he hoped it might yet make up the loss of time.

'The train! Where's the train?' he cried. 'Gone,' answered Fix. 'When will the next train come along?' asked Phileas Fogg. 'Not before this evening.' 'Is that so?' The impassive gentleman said nothing more.

CHAPTER XXXI

In which Detective Fix becomes a strong supporter of Phileas Fogg

PHILEAS FOGG was now twenty hours behind time; and Passepartout, the involuntary cause of this delay, was desperate. He had actually ruined his master!

At this moment the detective approached Mr Fogg and, looking him straight in the face, he said, 'Seriously, sir, are you in a great hurry?' 'I am, quite seriously, in a great hurry,' replied Phileas Fogg. 'Pardon me,' continued Fix, 'is it a matter of great importance to you that you should be in New York on the 11th, before nine o'clock in the evening, the time at which the boat leaves for Liverpool?'

'It is a matter of the utmost importance.'

'And if your journey had not been interrupted by this attack of the Indians, you would have reached New York no later than the morning of the 11th?'

'Yes, twelve hours before the departure of the boat.'

'Right; so you are twenty hours late. Between twenty and twelve, the difference is eight. You have eight hours to regain. Are you willing to try to do so?' 'On foot?' asked Mr Fogg. 'No; on a sledge,' replied Fix; 'on a sledge with sails. A man has suggested this means of conveyance to me.'

This was the man who had spoken to the detective in the night, and whose offer Fix had rejected. Phileas Fogg did not reply to Fix; but Fix having pointed out the man, who was walking about in front of the station, Mr Fogg went to him, and, an instant later, he and this American, whose name was Mudge, entered a hut standing below Fort Kearney.

There Mr Fogg inspected a somewhat strange vehicle. It was a kind of frame resting on two long beams, slightly curved upwards in front like the runners of a sledge, and on which five or six people could find room. At a third of the length of the frame, forward, rose a very high mast with rigging for a huge spanker. This mast, firmly secured by metallic shrouds, held out an iron stay for hoisting a very large jib. At the stern a sort of scull-like rudder served to steer the machine. As a matter of fact, it was simply a sledge rigged as a sloop. In winter, when the trains are stopped by the snow, these vehicles travel at very great speed over the frozen plains, from one station to another. They carry a prodigious spread of canvas, more than even a racing cutter can, as the latter is liable to capsize. With the wind behind them, they slip along on the surface of the prairies with a speed equal, if not superior, to that of express trains.

It took but a few minutes for Mr Fogg to come to terms with the skipper of this land-craft. The wind was favourable, blowing fresh from the west. The snow had hardened, and Mudge was quite confident of being able to convey Mr Fogg to Omaha station in a few hours. From that place there are frequent trains and numerous railroads to Chicago and New York. There was a possibility of making good the loss of time. There could be no hesitation about chancing it.

Not wishing to expose Aouda to the acute suffering of a journey in the open air, in such a cold atmosphere, which would be made still more intolerable by their speed, Mr Fogg proposed to her that she should remain at Kearney station in Passepartout's care. The trustworthy fellow would make it his duty to bring her to Europe by a better route and in more pleasant conditions.

Aouda refused to let Mr Fogg go without her, and Passepartout was only too delighted with this resolve, as nothing in the world would have induced him to leave his master in the company of the detective.

What Fix's thoughts were now, it would not be easy to say. Had Phileas Fogg's return shaken his conviction, or did he regard him as an exceedingly clever rascal, who, at the end of his journey round the world, would naturally think himself absolutely safe in England? Possibly Fix's opinion of Phileas Fogg was no longer the same; but he was none the less determined to do his duty, and was prepared to do his utmost to accelerate Fogg's return to England. No member of the party was now so impatient of delay as Fix.

At eight o'clock the sledge was ready to start. The travellers, one might almost say the passengers, took their places, and wrapped themselves up closely in their travelling-rugs. The two great sails were hoisted, and, impelled by the wind, the vehicle slid over the hardened snow at forty miles an hour.

The distance between Fort Kearney and Omaha, in a straight line, or, as the bee flies, to use the American expression, is at most two hundred miles. Should the wind hold, the distance could be traversed in five hours. If no accident occurred, the sledge would reach Omaha by one o'clock.

What a journey it was! The travellers, huddled together, could not even speak, for the cold, made more intense by the speed at which they were going, would have silenced them. The sledge glided over the surface of the plain as lightly as a boat on the surface of the water, and without waves to contend with. When the breeze came skimming along the ground, it felt as though the sledge were lifted up by its sails, as by wide-spreading wings. Mudge was at the helm, keeping a straight course, correcting by a shift of the stern-oar any sheering the machine showed signs of making. Every bit of canvas was taut, and the jib was now clear of the spanker. A topmast was swayed up, and another jib put out before the wind, adding its propelling force to that of the other sails. The speed at which the sledge was travelling could not be calculated mathematically, but it must have been quite forty miles an hour.

'If nothing snaps,' said Mudge, 'we shall get there in time!' It was Mudge's interest to get there within the time agreed on, for Mr Fogg, true to his method, had held out a handsome reward.

The prairie, which the sledge was traversing in a straight line, was flat as a sea. It looked like an immense frozen pond. The railway running through this district passed up from the south-west to the north-west, through Great Island, Columbus, an important town in Nebraska,

Schuyler, Fremont and Omaha. Throughout its course it followed the right bank of the Platte River. The sledge shortened this route by following the arc of the chord described by the railroad. Mudge had no fear of being stopped by the slight curve of the Platte River before Fremont, for its waters were frozen. The way was therefore quite clear, and Phileas Fogg had but two things to fear: an accident causing damage to the machine, or a change or lull of the wind.

But the breeze, far from falling, was blowing hard enough to bend the mast, strongly held in position by the iron shrouds. These iron ropes sounded like the strings of an instrument made to vibrate by the contact of a violin bow. The sledge flew along, accompanied by plaintive music of very peculiar intensity.

'These chords give the fifth and the octave,' said Mr Fogg. They were the only words he uttered during the whole journey. Aouda, carefully wrapped up in furs and travelling-rugs, was, as far as possible, protected against the biting cold. As for Passepartout, his face was as red as the sun's disc setting in the mist, and he sniffed up the keen air with positive delight. By nature incorrigibly sanguine, he was beginning to hope again. Instead of getting to New York in the morning, they would be there in the evening, but it was still possible this would be in time to catch the Liverpool boat. Passepartout even felt a strong inclination to shake hands heartily with his ally Fix. He remembered that it was none other than the detective who had procured the sailing sledge, the sole possible means of reaching Omaha in time. But some presentiment or other made him keep his usual reserve. There was one thing which Passepartout would never forget – that was the sacrifice which Mr Fogg had readily made to snatch him out of the hands of the Sioux. In doing so, Mr Fogg had staked his fortune and his life. No; never would his servant forget that!

While the travellers were pursuing such different thoughts, the sledge was flying over the boundless carpet of snow. It passed over creeks, the tributaries direct or indirect of Little Blue River, but no one noticed it. Fields and streams disappeared under one white shroud. The plain was perfectly desolate. Stretching between the Union Pacific railroad and the branch line which connects Kearney with Saint Joseph, it formed a vast uninhabited island. There was not a village, not a station, not even a fort. From time to time they saw fleeting by like a flash some distorted tree, whose white skeleton writhed in the blast. Now and again flocks of wild birds took wing all together, or packs of gaunt, ferocious prairie wolves, lashed by hunger, tore after the sledge, and Passepartout, revolver in hand, held himself in readiness to fire at the nearest. If the sledge had been stopped by some accident, the travellers would have been at once attacked by these fierce flesh-eaters, and their position would have been most critical. But the sledge held on bravely, and soon left the howling brutes behind.

At noon Mudge was aware, from certain facts, that he was crossing the frozen course of the Platte River. He said nothing, but now felt sure that he would reach Omaha station, twenty miles farther on. And before one o'clock, the skilful pilot, leaving the rudder, sprang forward, seized the halyards and lowered the sails, while the sledge, carried on by its enormous impulse, travelled half a mile more with furled sails. It stopped at last, and Mudge, pointing to a collection of roofs white with snow, said, 'Here we are.'

And, indeed, there they were at that station which is in daily communication with the east of the United States by numerous trains.

Passepartout and Fix jumped out, shook their benumbed limbs, and assisted Mr Fogg and the young woman to get down. Phileas Fogg paid Mudge liberally, and Passepartout gave him a friend's hand-grip. Then all hurried to Omaha station.

The Pacific Railway, properly so called, has its terminus at this important Nebraska city. The line connects the Mississippi basin with the great ocean. Omaha is connected with Chicago by the Chicago and Rock Island Railway, which runs due east and carries the traffic of fifty stations.

An express train was ready to start. Phileas Fogg and his party had only just time to get into a carriage. They had seen nothing of Omaha, but Passepartout confessed to himself that this was not a matter for regret, as they had a far more important object at heart than sight-seeing.

The train passed at very high speed across the State of Iowa, through Conneil Bluffs, Des Moines, and Iowa City. In the night it crossed the Mississippi at Davenport, and entered Illinois by Rock Island. On the morrow, which was the 10th, at four o'clock in the evening, it arrived at Chicago, already risen from its ruins, and standing more proudly than ever on the shores of its beautiful Lake Michigan.

Nine hundred miles separate Chicago from New York. There were plenty of trains at Chicago, and Mr Fogg was not kept waiting a moment. The fiery engine of the Pittsburg, Fort Wayne and Chicago Railroad left at full speed, as if conscious of the fact that the honourable gentleman had no time to spare. It ran through Indiana, Ohio, Pennsylvania, and New Jersey like a flash, passing through towns with antique names, a few of which had streets and tramways, but were as yet without houses. At last the Hudson came into view, and, on the 11th of December, at a quarter-past eleven in the evening, the train stopped in the station, on the right bank of the river, in front of the very pier of the Cunard Line, also called 'The British and North American Royal Mail Steam Packet Company.'

The *China*, bound for Liverpool, had sailed forty-five minutes before!

CHAPTER XXXII

In which Phileas Fogg comes to grips with mischance

PHILEAS FOGG'S last hope seemed to have gone with the *China*.

The boats of the French Transatlantic Company, of the White Star Line, of the Inman Company, of the Hamburg Line, and others plying between America and Europe, were all useless as far as Mr Fogg's projects were concerned.

The *Pereire*, of the French Transatlantic Company, whose admirable ships are equal in speed and superior in comfort to any of the other lines, without exception, would not sail before the 14th, that is two days later. Moreover, like the ships of the Hamburg Company, she did not go directly to Liverpool or London, but to Havre, and the extra passage from Havre to Southampton would have involved a delay fatal to his last efforts.

As for the Inman boats, one of which, the *City of Paris*, would sail on the next day, they were out of the question. Being specially used for the transport of emigrants, their engines are of low power; they run under canvas as much as under steam, and their speed is not great. They took more time crossing from New York to England than Mr Fogg had in which to win his wager.

This was all perfectly clear to Mr Fogg, who, by consulting his *Bradshaw*, was well informed of the sailings of the transatlantic liners.

Passepartout was in a state of prostration. The fact that they had missed the boat by forty-five minutes crushed him. And it was his fault: far from helping his master, he had done nothing but put obstacles in his path! When he reviewed all the incidents of the journey, when he reckoned up all the sums spent without any return, and purely on his own account, when he reflected that the enormous stake, together with the heavy expenses of this now useless tour, would completely ruin Mr Fogg, he called himself everything that bitter self-reproach could suggest. From Mr Fogg he heard not a word of blame. As he left the pier, all Mr Fogg said was, 'We shall see tomorrow what is the best thing to be done. Come.'

Mr Fogg, Aouda, Fix and Passepartout crossed the Hudson in the Jersey City ferry-boat and drove to St Nicholas Hotel, in Broadway. Rooms were given them, and the night passed, short for Phileas Fogg, who slept soundly, but very long for Aouda, Passepartout and Fix, who were too worried and excited to rest.

The next day was the 12th of December. From seven o'clock in the morning, of the 12th to a quarter to nine in the evening of the 21st there were left nine days, thirteen hours and forty-five minutes. If Phileas Fogg had left the day before in the *China*, one of the fastest boats of the Cunard Line, he would have reached Liverpool, and then London, within the required time.

Mr Fogg left the hotel alone, after giving his servant orders to wait for him, and to warn Aouda to he ready to start at any moment. He went to the banks of the Hudson, and, looking about among the vessels moored to the quay or anchored in the river, he took careful note of those about to put to sea. Several were flying the blue peter, and were making ready to sail out on the morning tide; for in this immense and admirable port of New York no day passes without a hundred ships leaving for every part of the world. But they were mostly sailing vessels and therefore unsuited to Phileas Fogg's purpose.

It looked as if he would fail in this, his last effort, when he saw, anchored before the Battery, a cable length away at most, a screw-steamer. She was a trading vessel of fine lines, and her funnel, emitting puffs of smoke, showed that she was making ready to leave port.

Phileas Fogg hailed a boat, got into it, and a few strokes of the oar brought him to the gangway-ladder of the *Henrietta*, an iron-hulled craft whose upper works were all of wood.

Phileas Fogg went up on deck and asked to see the captain, who was on board and came forward at once.

He was a man of fifty, a sort of sea-dog with a growl, who seemed anything but easy to tackle. He had large, bulging eyes, an oxidised copper complexion, red hair and a bull-like neck, and nothing of the man of the world.

'I wish to see the captain,' said Mr Fogg. 'I am the captain.' 'I am Phileas Fogg, of London.' 'And I am Andrew Speedy, of Cardiff.' 'Are you about to sail?' 'In an hour.' 'What is your destination?' 'Bordeaux.' 'And what cargo are you carrying?' 'Stones – no freight – going on ballast.' 'Have you any passengers?' 'No passengers. Never take passengers. They're cumbersome, grumbling goods.' 'Is your ship a fast sailer?' 'Between eleven and twelve knots. The *Henrietta*'s well known.' 'Are you willing to take me and three other persons to

Liverpool?' 'To Liverpool? Why not to China?' 'I said Liverpool.' 'No!' 'No?' 'No. I am about to sail for Bordeaux, and to Bordeaux I go.' 'No matter what money I offer?' 'No matter what money you offer.' The captain spoke in a tone which admitted of no reply. 'Possibly the owners of the *Henrietta* – ' continued Phileas Fogg. 'The owners – I am the owners,' answered the captain. 'The vessel belongs to me.' 'I will charter her.' 'No.' 'I will buy her.' 'No.' Phileas Fogg did not flinch, although the position was critical. New York was not Hong-Kong, nor was the captain of the *Henrietta* like the skipper of the *Tankadere*. Up till now money had overcome every difficulty. This time money failed. Yet it was absolutely necessary to find a way of crossing the Atlantic by boat – or by balloon, which would have been very venturesome, and, in any case, was not possible.

Phileas Fogg, however, seemed to think of something, for he said to the captain, 'Well, will you take me to Bordeaux?' 'No, not if you paid me two hundred dollars!' 'I offer you two thousand.' 'Per person?' 'Per person.' 'And there are four of you?' 'Four.' Captain Speedy began to scratch his forehead, as if he were trying to tear the skin off. Eight thousand dollars to be made without changing his route! It was worth his while to discard his strong objection to all passengers. And then passengers at two thousand dollars apiece are no longer passengers but valuable merchandise.

'I start at nine o'clock,' said Captain Speedy, simply; 'if you and your friends are ready to go on board – ' 'We shall be on board at nine,' replied Mr Fogg in the same manner.

It was then half-past eight. To go ashore from the *Henrietta*, jump into a cab, rush to St Nicholas Hotel, bring back Aouda, Passepartout, and even the inseparable Fix, to whom he graciously offered a passage, such was Mr Fogg's task, and he accomplished it with that serene self-possession of which no circumstance could ever deprive him.

They were all on board by the time the *Henrietta* was ready to weigh anchor. When Passepartout heard what the cost of this last voyage was going to be, he uttered a prolonged 'Oh!' that ran through the whole descending chromatic scale.

Detective Fix, for his part, came to the conclusion that the Bank of England would not come out of it without loss. For, as it was, in the event of their reaching England safely, and without Fogg throwing a few more handfuls of money into the sea, there would be a deficit of more than seven thousand pounds in the banknote bag.

CHAPTER XXXIII

In which Phileas Fogg shows himself equal to the occasion

AN HOUR AFTER, the *Henrietta* passed the lightship which marks the entrance of the Hudson, turned the point of Sandy Hook, and ran for the open sea. During the day she skirted Long Island, passed at some distance from the beacon on Fire Island, and made her way rapidly eastward.

On the morrow, December 13, at noon, a man went up on the bridge to take the ship's bearings. Of course, this man could be no other but Captain Speedy. Well, it was not. It was Phileas Fogg, Esquire. As for Captain Speedy, he was simply locked up in his cabin, roaring with pardonable rage; he was frantic.

What had happened was simple enough. Phileas Fogg wanted to go to Liverpool, and the captain would not take him there. Whereupon Phileas Fogg had agreed to go to Bordeaux, but, during the thirty hours he had been on board, he had handled banknotes with such skill and effect, that the whole crew, sailors and stokers, a somewhat scratch lot who were on pretty bad terms with the captain, were devoted to him. Thus it was that Phileas Fogg was in command instead of Captain Speedy; that the captain was locked up in his cabin, and that the *Henrietta* was heading for Liverpool. One thing was clear, however, from the way Mr Fogg handled the ship, Mr Fogg had been a sailor.

What the end of the adventure would be, the future alone could show. Aouda said nothing, but was none the less anxious. Fix was at first dumbfounded, while Passepartout thought it a simply splendid piece of work. Captain Speedy had said 'between eleven and twelve knots,' and, so far, that was the average speed of the vessel. If then – for there were still many ifs – the sea did not become too rough, if the wind did not shift round to the east, if the ship suffered no damage, and everything went well with the machinery, the *Henrietta* might cross the three thousand miles from New York to Liverpool in the nine days from the 12th to the 21st of December. It is true that, at the end of the voyage, the *Henrietta* affair, coming on top of the Bank affair, might land Mr Fogg in a worse mess than he might care for.

All went well with the ship during the first days. The sea was not too unkind; the wind seemed settled in the north-east; the sails were set, and, under her try-sails, the *Henrietta* forged ahead like a real transatlantic liner.

Passepartout was delighted. His master's last achievement, to the possible consequences of which he was wilfully blind, filled him with enthusiasm. Never had the crew seen a more cheery and nimble fellow. He was on the friendliest of terms with the sailors and astounded them by his acrobatic performances. He was profuse of the kindliest compliments and lavish of the most attractive drinks. In his opinion the sailors sailed the ship like gentlemen, and the stokers stoked like heroes. His genial good-humour was infectious. Forgetting the past, with its troubles and perils, he thought of nothing but the goal, now so nearly attained, and at times he boiled over with impatience, as if heated by the furnaces of the *Henrietta*. Often, too, the worthy fellow kept close to Fix, looking at him with eyes full of meaning; but he did not speak to him, for their intimacy was quite at an end.

As a matter of fact, Fix was now completely baffled. The *Henrietta* taken by force, the crew bribed, this fellow Fogg handling the boat with faultless seamanship: all this stunned the man. He no longer knew what to think. Yet, after all, a person who began by stealing fifty-five thousand pounds might well end by stealing a ship. So Fix was naturally led to believe that the *Henrietta*, under Fogg's direction, was not going to Liverpool at all, but to some place where the robber, now become pirate, would quietly seek safety. This supposition, it must be confessed, was a most plausible one, and the detective began to feel exceedingly sorry he had embarked in the affair.

As for Captain Speedy, he went on bawling in his cabin, and Passepartout, who had to see to his meals, performed this duty with the greatest caution, in spite of his own great strength. As far as Mr Fogg was concerned, the fact that there was a captain on board seemed to have passed out of his mind completely.

On the 13th they passed the end of the banks of Newfoundland – a dangerous spot this, especially in winter, when fogs are frequent and squalls dreadfully violent.

The barometer, which had fallen sharply since the day before, announced an approaching change in the atmosphere; and during the night there was a change in the temperature, the cold became sharper, and at the same time the wind shifted to the south-east.

This was a misfortune. Mr Fogg had to furl his sails and use more steam-power, so as not to get out of his course. Yet the vessel's speed slackened, owing to the state of the sea, the long waves of which broke against her stem. She pitched violently, and this delayed her progress. The breeze was gradually turning to a gale, and it became necessary to face the fact that the *Henrietta* might no longer be able to keep her head to the seas. But, should they have to run before the storm, they would be facing the unknown with all its possibilities of mishap.

Passepartout's face darkened with the sky; for two days the good fellow was in a state of cruel anxiety. But Phileas Fogg was a bold seaman; he knew how to fight the waves, and held on under full steam.

When the *Henrietta* could not rise to the wave, she went right through, swamping her deck, but undamaged. Sometimes her screw rose, lashing the air wildly with its blades, a mountainous sea having lifted the stern out of the water, but the ship still pressed on.

The wind, however, did not attain the force that might have been feared. It was not one of those hurricanes that sweep by at a velocity of ninety miles an hour. It never went beyond a gale, but, unfortunately, it remained persistently in the south-east, making it impossible to put up canvas. And we shall soon see how invaluable any aid to the steam-power would have been.

The 16th of December was the seventy-fifth day passed since the departure from London. After all, the *Henrietta* was not dangerously behind time. They were nearly half-way, and the worst parts of the sea were behind them. Had it been summer one could have answered for success. In winter there was always the weather to reckon with. Passepartout expressed no opinion, but was hopeful at heart. Should the wind fail them, he relied on the steam. Now on this very day the engineer came on deck, went up to Mr Fogg, and had an earnest talk with him. Without knowing why – it was doubtless some presentiment – Passepartout felt a vague uneasiness come over him. He would have given one of his ears to have been able to hear with the other the words that passed between them. He did catch something of what was said; he heard his master ask: 'Are you absolutely sure that what you state is correct?' 'Absolutely, sir,' replied the engineer. 'You must not forget that, since we started, we have been keeping all our furnaces going, and, while we had coal enough to go under easy steam from New York to Bordeaux, we have not enough to go with all steam from New York to Liverpool.'

'I will think it over,' replied Mr Fogg.

Passepartout understood, and was seized with mortal anxiety. The coal was running out! 'Ah, if my master can get over this,' thought he, 'he will indeed be a wonderful man!' Meeting Fix, he could not help telling him how matters stood.

'So,' replied the detective, with clenched teeth, 'you really believe that we are going to Liverpool!' 'Of course!' 'You fool!' returned the detective, shrugging his shoulders, as he drew off. Passepartout was on the point of showing sharp resentment of the epithet, though the real reason for Fix's offensive term necessarily escaped him; but he bethought himself how disappointed, how humiliated in his self-esteem the wretched detective must feel, after following a false scent so foolishly around the world, and he forgave him.

And now, what line of action was Phileas Fogg going to adopt? It was no easy matter even to imagine what he could do. Nevertheless he apparently did come to a decision in his own phlegmatic way, for, that very evening, he sent for the engineer and said to him, 'Go ahead with fully-stoked furnaces until your fuel is completely exhausted.'

A few moments later, the *Henrietta*'s funnel belched forth torrents of smoke.

The ship pressed on as before under full steam, but two days later, on the 18th, the engineer reported that the coal would run out during the day, as he had said it would.

'Do not let the fires down,' replied Mr Fogg. 'Far from that, let the valves be weighted for full pressure.'

About noon on that day, after ascertaining the ship's position, Phileas Fogg called Passepartout and ordered him to fetch Captain Speedy. The worthy fellow felt just as if he had been told to set loose a tiger, and he went down to the poop-deck muttering, 'He will be absolutely mad!' And in a few minutes, amid shouts and curses, a bomb tumbled on to the poop-deck. The bomb was Captain Speedy, and it was obvious that the bomb was going to explode. 'Where are we?' were the first words he uttered, choking with rage. Had the good man had the slightest tendency to apoplexy, he must have gone under. 'Where are we?' he repeated, purple in the face.

'Seven hundred and seventy miles from Liverpool,' answered Mr Fogg, absolutely unperturbed. 'You pirate!' cried Andrew Speedy. 'Sir, I sent for you – ' 'You sea-robber!' 'To ask you to sell me your ship.' 'No! By all the fiends in Hell. No!' 'The fact is, I shall be obliged to burn her.' 'To burn my ship?' 'Yes, her upper works at least, for we are running short of fuel.' 'Burn my ship!' cried Captain Speedy, who was now reduced to spluttering. 'A ship worth fifty thousand dollars!' 'Here are sixty thousand,' replied Phileas Fogg, offering the captain a bundle of banknotes. The effect on Andrew Speedy was prodigious. No American can remain quite unmoved at the sight of sixty thousand dollars. In one instant the captain forgot his wrath, his confinement, in fact every grievance he had against his passenger. His ship was twenty years old. There might be a fortune in this. The bomb was already non-explosive. Mr Fogg had taken the fuse out.

'And am I to keep the iron hull?' he asked in a peculiarly softened tone of voice.

'The iron hull and the machinery. Is that settled?' 'Done,' said Andrew Speedy, seizing the bundle of banknotes which he counted and slipped into his pocket.

While this scene was enacted Passepartout went white in the face, and Fix nearly had a stroke. After an expenditure of nearly twenty thousand pounds, there was this fellow Fogg giving up the hull and machinery, that is, about the total value of the ship. True, the sum stolen from the Bank amounted to fifty-five thousand pounds.

When Andrew Speedy had pocketed the money, Mr Fogg said to him, 'All this will cause you no surprise when I tell you that I stand to lose twenty thousand pounds, if I am not in London by the 21st of December, at eight forty-five in the evening. Now I missed the boat at New York, and you refused to take me to Liverpool – ' 'And, by the fifty thousand fiends in Hell, I did the right thing,' exclaimed Andrew Speedy. 'I made at least forty thousand dollars by that.'

Then he added more quietly, 'You know, Captain – ' 'Fogg.' 'Captain Fogg, there's something of the Yankee in you.' After paying his passenger what he considered a compliment, he was moving away, when Phileas Fogg said to him, 'The vessel now belongs to me?' 'Certainly, from the keel to the truck of the masts; that is, all the wood of her, of course.'

'Right; then have all the inside fittings pulled down, and use the pieces for fuel.' One can imagine what a quantity of this dry wood had to be consumed to keep the steam up to sufficient pressure. That day the poop-deck, deck-houses, cabins, bunks and spar-deck were all sacrificed.

On the morrow, the 19th of December, the masts, rafts and spars were burned. The masts were brought down and chopped up. The crew worked with amazing zeal, and Passepartout hewed, hacked and sawed away like ten men. There was a perfect frenzy of destruction.

On the 20th, the hammock-nettings, bulwarks, dead works and the greater part of the deck were given to the flames, and the *Henrietta* was now as flat as a hulk. But on that day they sighted the Irish coast and Fastnet Light.

At ten o'clock in the evening they were still only abreast of Queenstown, and Phileas Fogg had not more than twenty-four hours in which to reach London. It would take the *Henrietta* all that time to get to Liverpool, even under full steam; and our much-daring hero was at last on the point of having no steam left at all.

'Sir,' said Captain Speedy, who was now greatly interested in his project, 'I am truly sorry for you. Everything is against you. We are only off Queenstown.' 'Oh,' said Mr Fogg, 'are those the lights of Queenstown?' 'Yes.' 'Can we enter the harbour?' 'Not for three hours. Only at high tide.' 'We shall wait,' replied Phileas Fogg calmly; and his face showed not the slightest sign that a supreme inspiration was urging him to try and overcome once more the thwarting vagaries of fortune.

Queenstown is an Irish port at which the transatlantic liners from the United States drop their mail-bags. The letters are then carried off to Dublin by fast trains always in readiness. From Dublin they cross over to Liverpool in boats of great speed, thus gaining twelve hours on the fastest vessels.

Phileas Fogg meant to do like the American mail, and gain twelve hours also. Instead of arriving at Liverpool on the *Henrietta* in the evening of the next day, he would be there at noon, and so would have time to get to London before a quarter to nine in the evening.

The *Henrietta* entered Queenstown Harbour at high tide, about one o'clock in the morning, and Phileas Fogg left Captain Speedy on the levelled hulk of his ship, still worth half the money he had sold it for; the captain shaking him heartily by the hand at parting. The passengers landed at once. Fix, at that moment, was sorely tempted to arrest Fogg, but did not do so. Why? What conflict was going on within him? Had he changed his mind about Mr Fogg? Did he at last realise that he had made a mistake? Be that as it may, Fix did not leave Mr Fogg, but joining him, Aouda, and Passepartout, who was breathless with impatience, he got into the train at half-past one in the morning, arrived at Dublin at dawn, and embarked immediately on one of those steamers, regular spindle-shaped machines, all engine-power, which scorn to rise, and invariably go right through the surge.

On the 21st of December, at twenty minutes to twelve, Phileas Fogg at last landed on Liverpool Pier. He was now only six hours from London. At that very moment, Fix went up to him, laid his hand on his shoulder, and, showing him the warrant, said, 'There is no mistake, you are Phileas Fogg?'

'Yes, I am.'

'In the Queen's name, I arrest you!'

CHAPTER XXXIV

Which gives Passepartout the opportunity of making an
atrocious, but possibly new, pun

PHILEAS FOGG was in prison. He had been confined in the Custom
House lock-up, where he would spend the night; he would then be
transferred to London.

When his master was arrested, Passepartout would have fallen upon
the detective had he not been held back by policemen.

Aouda was horrified by the brutality of the proceeding and was quite
bewildered, for she knew nothing of the circumstances. Passepartout
enlightened her, telling her how the honest and courageous gentleman
to whom she owed her life was arrested as a thief. The young woman
protested against this monstrous allegation; her heart was filled with
indignation, and, when she saw she could do nothing, attempt nothing
to save the man who had saved her, she wept. As for Fix, he had
arrested the man, because it was his imperative duty to do so, guilty or
not guilty. The law-court would settle the matter.

It then occurred to Passepartout, and a terrible thought it was, that
he was the real cause of the whole trouble! Why had he concealed the
motive of Fix's journey from Mr Fogg? When Fix had revealed to him
his profession and his errand, why had he taken it upon himself to keep
his master ignorant of the fact? Had Mr Fogg been forewarned, he
would doubtless have given Fix proofs of his innocence, and convinced
him of his mistake. At all events, he would not have conveyed at his
heels, and at his own expense, this troublesome member of the police
force, who had made it his first business to arrest him the moment he
set foot on English soil. As he thought of his blunders and reckless
conduct, the poor fellow was wrung by remorse; he wept piteously, and
felt like dashing his head to pieces.

Aouda and he remained in the porch of the Custom House, in spite
of the cold. Neither of them would leave the spot, so anxious were they
to see Mr Fogg once more.

He was now a ruined man, and just as he was reaching the goal. This
arrest was quite fatal. Having arrived at Liverpool at twenty minutes to
twelve on the 21st of December, he had till a quarter to nine to put in
an appearance at the Reform Club; in other words, he had nine hours

and a quarter, and he only wanted six to reach London.

Anyone walking into the Custom House lock-up at this moment would have found Mr Fogg on a wooden bench, sitting perfectly still, without anger, impassive. Whether he was resigned or not, there was nothing to show, but this last blow had been powerless to produce any sign of emotion. Was there brewing within his breast one of those pent-up storms of wrath that are all the more terrible because they are repressed, and that burst at the very last moment with resistless force? None can say. But Phileas Fox was there, calmly waiting – waiting for what? Had he still some hope left? Did he still believe success possible, with this prison door between him and liberty?

What is certain is that Mr Fogg had carefully placed his watch on a table, and was observing the progress of the hands. Not a word passed his lips, but his gaze was strangely set. In any case, the situation was a terrible one; for any but the man who could have read in Mr Fogg's conscience, there was but one alternative: Mr Fogg was honest but ruined, or a rogue and caught.

That the thought of flight occurred to him, if there was a possible means of exit from the lock-up, seems credible, for, at one moment, he examined the room all round. But the door was safely locked, and the window secured with iron bars. So he went back to his seat and took out his journal from his pocket-book. On the line bearing the words, 'December 21st, Saturday, Liverpool,' he added, '80th day, 11.40 a.m.,' and waited.

The Custom House clock struck one. Mr Fogg observed that his watch was two minutes fast by this clock.

Two o'clock! If, at that moment, he could get into an express train, he might still be in London, and at the Reform Club, before a quarter to nine that evening. A slight wrinkle creased his brow. At thirty-three minutes after two there was a sudden din outside, as doors were noisily thrown open. Passepartout's voice and Fix's voice were heard.

Phileas Fogg's eyes brightened for one moment. The door of the lock-up opened and he saw Aouda, Passepartout and Fix rushing towards him. Fix, his hair all dishevelled, and so out of breath that he could not speak, mumbled, 'Sir, sir – forgive me – a most regrettable resemblance – thief arrested three days ago – you – are free!'

Phileas Fogg was free! He stepped up to the detective, looked him straight in the face, and, with the only quick motion he had ever made or would ever make, he drew back his arms and, with automatic precision, landed both his fists on the wretched detective.

'Well hit!' cried Passepartout, and, indulging in an atrocious pun, quite worthy of a Frenchman, he added, 'By Jove! this deserves to be called *Une belle application de poings d'Angleterre.*' *

Fix lay on the floor without saying a word. He had received nothing but his due. Mr Fogg, Aouda and Passepartout left the Custom House, jumped into a cab, and a few minutes brought them to Liverpool Station. Phileas Fogg asked if there was an express train about to leave for London.

The time was then forty minutes past two, and the express had gone thirty-five minutes before.

Phileas Fogg then ordered a special train. There were several fast engines with steam up, but, owing to traffic arrangements, the special train could not leave before three o'clock.

At three o'clock Phileas Fogg, after saying a few words to the engine-driver about a certain reward to be obtained, ran at high speed for London, with the young woman and his faithful servant.

He intended to accomplish the distance between Liverpool and London in five hours and a half, a perfectly possible achievement when the line is clear throughout. But forced delays occurred, and, when Mr Fogg reached the terminus, every clock in London informed him that it was ten minutes to nine.

After travelling all round the world, Mr Fogg was five minutes late. He had lost his wager.

CHAPTER XXXV

In which Passepartout does not need to be told twice what his master orders him to do

ON THE MORROW, the people in Savile Row would have been surprised had one assured them that Mr Fogg had returned home. Doors and windows were closed as usual. There was absolutely no change in the outward appearance of the house.

After leaving the station, Phileas Fogg directed Passepartout to buy some provisions, and went home.

He bore his trouble with his usual tranquillity. Here he was, ruined! And through the blundering of that detective! After treading that long road with a sure step, after overcoming a thousand obstacles, braving endless dangers, and finding time to do some good on the way, to be

* *Point d'Angleterre* means English lace.

wrecked in harbour by an act of brute force, which he could not foresee and against which he was unarmed, was truly terrible! Of the large sum he had taken with him he had very little left.

His fortune now consisted in the twenty thousand pounds deposited at Baring's, and these twenty thousand pounds were now due to his fellow-members of the Reform Club. The expenses had been so heavy that, had he won the bet, it would certainly not have enriched him; moreover, it is probable that he had not sought to enrich himself, for he was one of those who bet for honour's sake, but the loss of the wager spelt absolute ruin.

Howbeit, Mr Fogg's mind was made up; he knew what he had to do. A room in the house in Savile Row was set apart for Aouda, who was distracted with grief. Certain words of Mr Fogg had led her to conclude that he was revolving some fatal project or other.

Well aware that certain Englishmen, prone to monomania, some-times resort to the most lamentable of rash acts under the stress of a fixed idea, Passepartout kept an eye on his master without appearing to do so.

But the first thing the good fellow did on arriving was to go up to his room and turn off the gas, which had been burning for eighty days. Having found a bill from the gas company in the letter-box, he thought it was high time to put an end to this expense, for which he was responsible.

Mr Fogg went to bed; whether he slept or not is a matter for conjecture. Aouda had not a moment's rest; Passepartout watched outside his master's door, like a dog. So the night passed. On the morrow Mr Fogg called him, and in a few peremptory words bade him see to Aouda's breakfast. He himself wanted nothing more than a cup of tea and a piece of toast.

He hoped Aouda would excuse his absence from breakfast and dinner, as all his time would be devoted to putting his affairs in order. He would not come down, but begged Aouda to be good enough to give him a few minutes in the evening, as he had something to say to her. Passepartout, having received his instructions for the day, could only do what he was told. He gazed at his master, who gave no sign of what he felt, and could not make up his mind to leave the room. His heart was heavy, his conscience racked with remorse, for he blamed himself more than ever for the irreparable disaster. If only he had warned Mr Fogg and disclosed to him Fix's intentions, he would certainly not have taken the detective with him to Liverpool, and then –

Passepartout could hold out no longer. 'My master! Mr Fogg!' he cried. 'Curse me, for it was all my doing that – ' 'I blame no one,' replied Phileas Fogg in the calmest manner. 'Go!' Passepartout left him and went to Aouda, whom he informed of his master's wishes. 'Madam,' he added, 'personally, I am quite powerless! I have not the faintest influence over my master's mind. You might – ' 'What influence could I possibly have?' replied Aouda. 'Mr Fogg is proof against every influence! Has he ever understood that my gratitude is full to overflowing? Has he ever read in my heart? You must not leave him for a moment, my friend. You say he has expressed the wish to speak to me this evening?' 'Yes, madam; no doubt Mr Fogg is anxious to make arrangements for your stay in England.' 'Well, we can only wait and see,' said the young woman wistfully.

During the whole of that Sunday the house in Savile Row might have been empty, and for the first time since he had lived there, Phileas Fogg did not set out for his club when Big Ben struck half-past eleven.

Why should he go to the Reform Club? He was no longer expected there. Having failed to appear in the drawing-room of the Reform Club at forty-five minutes past eight in the evening, the day before, that fateful date of Saturday, December 21, Phileas Fogg had lost his wager. He was not even under the necessity of going to the Bank for the twenty thousand pounds, for his adversaries held a cheque signed by him, and all they had to do was to fill it in, endorse it, and pass it through Baring's, in order to have the amount placed to their credit.

There was therefore no reason why Mr Fogg should go out, and he stayed at home. He remained in his room and put his affairs in order.

Passepartout went up and down the stairs continually. Time stood still for the poor fellow, who kept listening at the door of his master's room without feeling in the least indiscreet. He even looked through the key-hole and thought himself perfectly justified, for he dreaded a catastrophe at any moment. Now and again he thought of Fix, but a complete change had come over his mind. He was no longer angry with the detective. Fix, like everybody else, had misjudged Phileas Fogg; in shadowing and arresting him he had only done his duty, whereas he, Passepartout – the thought crushed him; in his own eyes he was the lowest of low wretches. Whenever he could no longer bear his misery in solitude, he knocked at Aouda's door, went in, and sat down in a corner without saying one word, gazing at her sad, pensive face.

About half-past seven Mr Fogg sent word to Aouda asking whether she could see him, and a few moments later they were together alone in her room.

Phileas Fogg took a chair and sat down near the fire-place, opposite Aouda. His face expressed not the slightest emotion. Between the Fogg who had returned and the Fogg who had gone away there was not one tittle of difference. There was just the same impassive calm. He sat silent for five minutes, then, raising his eyes to Aouda, he said, 'Madam, can you forgive me for bringing you to England?' 'I, forgive you, Mr Fogg!' answered Aouda, trying to repress the throbbing of her heart. 'Please let me finish,' replied Mr Fogg. 'When I conceived the idea of taking you right away from that country which had become so full of danger for you, I was a rich man, and I intended to place part of my fortune at your disposal. Your life would have been one of happy freedom. Now I am ruined.' 'I know, Mr Fogg,' returned the young woman. 'I will ask you, in my turn, whether you can forgive me for following you, and – who knows – for having perhaps helped to ruin you by delaying your progress.'

'You could not remain in India; your safety could only be assured by removing you far enough to be out of reach of those fanatics.'

'So, Mr Fogg,' resumed Aouda, 'not content with snatching me from the jaws of a horrible death, you thought it your duty to secure my position abroad?' 'Yes, madam,' replied Mr Fogg, 'but I have been unfortunate. However, may I have your permission to dispose in your behalf of the little I still possess?' 'But, Mr Fogg, what is to become of you?' asked Aouda. 'Of me?' rejoined he coldly. 'I have need of nothing.' 'But how are you going to face the future that awaits you?' 'As it should be faced,' replied Mr Fogg. 'At all events,' continued Aouda, 'a man like you is beyond the reach of poverty, I suppose. Your friends – ' 'I have no friends.' 'Your relations, then – ' 'I have no relations left.' 'Then I am truly sorry for you, Mr Fogg, for loneliness is a sad thing. What! not one heart to share your troubles! Even poverty, they say, is bearable for two!' 'They say so, madam.' 'Mr Fogg,' said Aouda, standing up at this point of the conversation and stretching out her hand to him, 'would you have at once a relation and a friend? Will you have me for your wife?'

On hearing this, Mr Fogg stood up too. His eyes betrayed an unaccustomed light, his lips the semblance of a tremor. Aouda looked into his face. The sincerity, the candour, the firmness and sweetness of that glorious look of a noble woman, daring all to save the man to whom she owed all, first astonished and then thrilled him. He closed his eyes for a moment, as if to prevent this look from entering deeper still into his being. And when he opened them again, he said simply, 'I love you. Oh, yes, in the name of all that is most holy, I love you, and am yours heart and soul!' 'Oh!' cried Aouda, raising her hand to her heart.

Passepartout was summoned, and came forthwith, to see Mr Fogg still holding Aouda's hand in his. He understood, and his big, round face beamed like the tropical sun at its zenith.

Mr Fogg asked him whether it would not be too late to give due notice to the Reverend Samuel Wilson, of the parish of Marylebone.

Passepartout, with his best smile, replied, 'It's never too late for that.' It was then not more than five minutes past eight. 'You want it to take place tomorrow, Monday?' he added.

'Would tomorrow, Monday, do?' asked Mr Fogg, looking at Aouda.

'Yes, tomorrow, Monday,' she replied. And Passepartout hurried off as fast as he could go.

CHAPTER XXXVI

In which Phileas Fogg is again at a premium on 'Change

IT IS NOW TIME TO SAY what a great change took place in English public opinion when it was known that the real thief, one James Strand, had been arrested on December 17 at Edinburgh.

Three days before, Phileas Fogg was a criminal whom the police were making the most energetic efforts to capture; now he was a most honest gentleman, mathematically performing his eccentric voyage around the world.

The papers were full of it, and great was the excitement. All those who had made bets for or against him, and had already forgotten the case, came forward again as if by magic. All the old transactions became valid again, all engagements binding, and it should be said that the people's revived keenness resulted in many a new bet. Phileas Fogg's name was again at a premium on 'Change. His five fellow-members of the Reform Club passed those three days in a state of anxious suspense. Phileas Fogg, whom they had forgotten, now suddenly loomed before them! Where was he at this moment? On the 17th of December, the day of James Strand's arrest, Phileas Fogg had been gone seventy-six days and absolutely nothing had been heard of him. Was he dead? Had he given up the contest, or was he pursuing his journey along the settled route? And would he appear on Saturday, the 21st of December, at a quarter to nine in the evening, on the threshold of the Reform Club drawing-room, as the very god of punctuality?

The anxiety in which English society existed during those three days is beyond description. Telegrams were dispatched to America and Asia for news of Phileas Fogg. The house in Savile Row was kept under observation morning and evening. – Nothing. Even the police could not say what had become of Fix, who had so unfortunately followed up a false scent. But betting again took place on a larger scale than ever. Phileas Fogg, like a racehorse, was nearing the last turn in the course. The odds against him were no longer quoted at a hundred, but at twenty, at ten, and five, and paralytic old Lord Albemarle bet even in his favour.

Thus it was that, on the Saturday evening, a great crowd was assembled in Pall Mall and the adjoining streets. It looked like a dense mass of brokers permanently established around the Reform Club. The traffic was more or less blocked. People discussed and disputed, and quotations of 'Phileas Fogg Stock' were shouted, as with Government scrip. The police had great difficulty in controlling the crowd, and, as the hour at which Phileas Fogg was due approached, the excitement became prodigious.

In the evening of that day, his five fellow-members had been together in the large drawing-room of the Reform Club for nine hours. The two bankers, John Sullivan and Samuel Fallentin, the engineer Andrew Stuart, Gauthier Ralph, the director of the Bank of England, and Thomas Flanagan, the brewer, were all waiting anxiously. At the very moment when the clock in the drawing-room indicated twenty minutes past eight, Andrew Stuart got up and said, 'Gentlemen, in twenty minutes the time agreed between Mr Phileas Fogg and us will have expired.'

'At what time did the last train from Liverpool arrive?' asked Thomas Flanagan. 'At twenty-three minutes past seven,' replied Gauthier Ralph, 'and the next train will not come in before ten minutes past twelve.' 'Well, gentlemen,' continued Andrew Stuart, 'if Phileas Fogg had arrived by the 7.23 train, he would be here now. We can therefore look upon the bet as won.'

'We must wait; we must not decide yet,' rejoined Samuel Fallentin. 'You know that our friend is a thoroughly eccentric fellow. His precision in all things is well known. He never arrives too soon or too late, and I should not be altogether surprised to see him turn up at the last minute.'

'And I,' said Andrew Stuart, who was in his usual nervous state of mind, 'if I saw him appear, I should not believe my eyes.'

'Naturally,' resumed Thomas Flanagan, 'for Phileas Fogg's project was insane. No matter what his punctuality might be, he could not prevent delays that were bound to occur, and a delay of two or three days only was enough to make his enterprise next to impossible.'

'You will observe, too,' added John Sullivan, 'that we have received no communication from him, although there are telegraphs all along the route.'

'He has lost, gentlemen,' continued Andrew Stuart; 'he has lost a hundred times over! As you know, the *China*, which was the only liner he could come by soon enough from New York to Liverpool, arrived yesterday; and here is the list of her passengers, published by the *Shipping Gazette*; Phileas Fogg's name is not there. On the most favourable supposition, he has scarcely reached America! According to my reckoning, he will be twenty days late, and old Lord Albemarle will also be a loser, to the tune of five thousand pounds!' 'Of course,' replied Gauthier Ralph, 'and all we shall have to do tomorrow will be to present Mr Fogg's cheque at Baring's.'

At this moment the clock indicated 8.40. 'Five minutes more,' said Andrew Stuart. The five friends looked at each other.

One may surmise that their heart-beats were slightly accelerated, for, even for bold gamblers, the stake was a large one. But, wishing to appear perfectly calm, they took their places at a card-table, Samuel Fallentin having suggested a rubber.

'I would not give my four thousand pounds share of the wager, were I offered three thousand nine hundred and ninety-nine for it,' said Andrew Stuart as he sat down.

The hand at this moment pointed to 8.42.

The players took up their cards, but their eyes were constantly on the clock. One may safely say that, however secure they might feel, never had minutes seemed so long to them.

'8.43,' said Thomas Flanagan, as he cut the cards placed before him by Gauthier Ralph. There was a moment's pause, during which the spacious room was perfectly silent. Outside, however, the hubbub of the crowd could be heard, dominated at times by sharp cries. The clock's pendulum beat every second with mathematical regularity, and each player could count every sixtieth of a minute as it struck his ear.

'8.44!' said John Sullivan, in a voice that betrayed his emotion.

Only one minute more and the wager would be won. Andrew Stuart and his friends left off playing. They forgot the cards to count the seconds!

At the fortieth second, nothing. At the fiftieth, still nothing! At the fifty-fifth they heard a thunderous burst of noise outside, applause, hurrahs, and even curses, spreading far and wide in a continuous roll.

The players stood up.

At the fifty-seventh second the door of the drawing-room opened, and before the pendulum beat the sixtieth second, Phileas Fogg appeared, followed by a delirious crowd that had forced their way into the club, and in his calm voice, said, 'Here I am, gentlemen.'

CHAPTER XXXVII

*In which it is shown that Phileas Fogg gained nothing by
travelling round the world, unless it were happiness*

YES, Phileas Fogg himself.

The reader will remember that at five minutes past eight in the
evening – about five and twenty hours after the travellers arrived in
London – Passepartout was sent by his master to arrange with the
Reverend Samuel Wilson for a certain marriage ceremony which was
to take place on the very next day.

Passepartout set out on his errand highly delighted. He lost no time
in reaching the clergyman's house, but he had to wait, as the parson
was out. He waited a good twenty minutes. When he left, it was thirty-
five minutes past eight; and what a state he was in! dishevelled, hatless,
he ran along furiously, as never was man seen running before,
knocking down the passers-by, rushing over the pavements like a
waterspout.

He was back in Savile Row in three minutes, and staggered, out of
breath, into Mr Fogg's room.

He was unable to speak.

'What is the matter?' asked Mr Fogg.

'My master – ' stammered Passepartout, 'Marriage – impossible – '

'Impossible?' 'Impossible – for tomorrow.'

'Why?' 'Because tomorrow – is Sunday!'

'Monday,' replied Mr Fogg.

'No – today – Saturday.'

'Saturday? Impossible!'

'Yes, yes, yes, yes!' cried Passepartout. 'You made a mistake of a day!
We arrived twenty-four hours before the time – but there are only ten
minutes left!'

Passepartout had seized his master by the collar and was dragging
him away with irresistible force.

Phileas Fogg, thus rushed without having time to think, left his
room, then his house, jumped into a cab, promised the cab-man a
hundred pounds, and, having run over two dogs and collided with five
carriages, reached the Reform Club.

The clock indicated 8.45 when he appeared in the big drawing-room. Phileas Fogg had accomplished the journey round the world in eighty days!

Phileas Fogg had won his wager of twenty thousand pounds!

But how was it that a man, who was so precise and scrupulously careful, could possibly make this mistake of one day? How came he to think that the time at which he arrived in London was the evening of Saturday, December 21, whereas the real time was only Friday, December 20, not more than seventy-nine days after his departure?

His mistake is very easily explained. Without suspecting it, Phileas Fogg had gained one day on the journey, and for the sole reason that he had travelled ever eastward; he would, on the contrary, have lost a day had he travelled in the opposite direction, that is, westward. Going eastward, Phileas Fogg had advanced towards the sun, and, consequently, the days grew smaller for him by as many times four minutes as he crossed degrees of longitude in this direction. The earth's circumference contains three hundred and sixty degrees; these three hundred and sixty degrees, multiplied by four minutes, make exactly twenty-four hours – that is, the day he had gained without knowing it. In other words, as he advanced eastward, he saw the sun pass the meridian eighty times, whereas his friends of the Reform Club in London saw it pass seventy-nine times only. So it was that on that very day, which was Saturday, not Sunday, as Mr Fogg believed, they were waiting for him in the drawing-room of the Reform Club.

And the fact would have been recorded by Passepartout's precious watch, which had always kept London time, had it marked the days as well as the hours and minutes!

So Phileas Fogg had won the twenty thousand pounds, but, as he had spent something like nineteen thousand on the way, the proceeds were small.

As we have said before, however, the eccentric gentleman's object was sport, not money. The thousand pounds that remained he divided between the worthy Passepartout and the luckless Fix, to whom he could not find it in his heart to bear any grudge. But, as a matter of principle, and for the sake of regularity, he deducted from his servant's share the cost of the nineteen hundred and twenty hours of gas consumed through his fault.

That evening, Mr Fogg, as calm and phlegmatic as ever, said to Aouda, 'Is it still your pleasure to marry me?' 'Mr Fogg,' she said in reply, 'it is for me to ask you this question. You were ruined, you are now a rich man – '

'Pardon me, madam, my fortune is really yours. If the thought of this marriage had not occurred to you, my servant would not have gone to the Reverend Samuel Wilson's, I should not have been informed of my mistake, and – '

'Dear Mr Fogg!' said the young woman.

'Dear Aouda!' replied Phileas Fogg.

Needless to say, the marriage took place forty-eight hours later, and Passepartout, resplendent, simply dazzling, gave the bride away.

Had he not saved her? was not this honour his due?

Next day, however, as soon as it was light, Passepartout banged at his master's door. The door opened and Mr Fogg, without the least excitement, asked, 'What is it, Passepartout?' 'Why, sir, I have only just this moment heard – ' 'What have you heard?' 'That we might have gone round the world in only seventy-eight days.'

'Of course,' replied Mr Fogg, 'by not going through India. But if I had not gone through India, I should not have saved Aouda, she would not have been my wife, and – '

And Mr Fogg quietly closed the door.

So Mr Fogg had won his wager. He had made his journey around the world in eighty days! To this end, he had made use of every means of conveyance – liners, railways, carriages, yachts, trading vessels, sledges, elephants. The eccentric gentleman had displayed in this venture his marvellous qualities of coolness and precision. But what then? What had he gained out of all this travelling? What had he brought home?

Nothing, say you? Granted; nothing but a charming woman, who, unlikely as it may appear, made him the happiest of men!

And forsooth, who would not go round the world for less?

FIVE WEEKS IN A BALLOON

CHAPTER I

*The end of a much-applauded speech – Introduction of
Dr Samuel Fergusson – 'Excelsior!' – Full-length portrait of
the doctor – A convinced fatalist – Dinner at the
Travellers' Club – A long toast list*

THERE WAS a large audience at the meeting of the Royal Geographical Society of London,[26] 3 Waterloo Place, on the 14th of January, 1862. The President, Sir Francis M—, made an important announcement to his honourable colleagues in a speech frequently interrupted by applause. This rare piece of eloquence was at last brought to an end in a few sonorous sentences into which patriotism was poured with a lavish hand:

'England has always marched at the head of the nations' (for it is noticeable that the nations invariably march at each other's heads), 'through the intrepidity of her travellers in the sphere of geographical discovery. (*Hear, hear.*) Dr Samuel Fergusson, one of her famous sons, will not fail the land of his birth. (*Hear, hear, from all sides.*) This venture, if it succeeds (*It will succeed!*), will link together and complete the present scattered knowledge of African cartography, and – (*vehement applause*), and if it fails (*No! No!*) it will at least live as one of the most audacious conceptions of the human mind!' (*Frenzied cheers.*)

'Hurrah! hurrah!' shouted the assembly, electrified by these stirring words.

'Three cheers for brave Fergusson!' cried one of the more exuberant members of the audience, and there was an outburst of enthusiastic cheering. The name of Fergusson was on all lips, and we are justified in thinking that it gained considerably from its passage through English throats. The Session Hall was shaken with it.

Yet this was a gathering of bold explorers, aged and worn, whom their restless temperaments had dragged through the four quarters of the world. Physically or morally, they had practically all escaped from shipwreck, fire, the tomahawk of the Indian, the club of the savage, the torture-stake, and Polynesian stomachs! But nothing could restrain the leaping of their hearts during Sir Francis M—'s speech, and this was certainly the greatest oratorical success within the memory of the society.

In England, however, enthusiasm does not confine itself to mere words. It coins money faster than the engines of the Royal Mint. A sum of money voted on the spot for the encouragement of Dr Fergusson reached the figure of two thousand five hundred pounds. The importance of the sum was in proportion to the importance of the enterprise.

A member of the society questioned the President as to whether Dr Fergusson would not be officially presented.

'The doctor holds himself at the disposal of the meeting,' replied Sir Francis M—.

'Have him in!' they shouted. 'Have him in! We should like to see a man of such extraordinary audacity with our own eyes!'

'Perhaps this incredible scheme is only intended to hoax us,' said an apoplectic old commodore.

'What if Dr Fergusson didn't exist?' cried a malicious voice.

'He'd have to be invented,' replied a waggish member of this solemn society.

'Show Dr Fergusson in,' said Sir Francis simply.

And the doctor entered amid a thunder of applause, and without the least show of emotion. He was a man of about forty, of average height and build. His full-blooded temperament betrayed itself in the florid colouring of his face. His expression was cold, his features regular, with a prominent nose, the figure-head nose of the man predestined for discovery. His eyes, very gentle and intelligent rather than bold, gave great charm to his face. His arms were long, and he placed his feet on the ground in the confident manner of the great walker. The whole person of the doctor exhaled calm gravity, and it would never have occurred to anyone that he could be the instrument of the most innocent hoax.

And so the cheers and applause did not cease until the moment when the doctor, with a good-humoured gesture, called for silence. He made his way towards the chair prepared for his presentation, and then, upright, rigid, his eye radiating energy, he raised his right forefinger towards heaven, opened his mouth and uttered the single word: 'Excelsior!'

Never did an unexpected interpellation by Messrs Bright and Cobden, never a demand by Lord Palmerston for extraordinary funds for armouring the cliffs of England, meet with such a success. Sir Francis M—'s speech was thrown into the shade, and that easily. The doctor was at once sublime, great, self-controlled and restrained. He had struck the keynote of the situation: 'Excelsior!'[27]

The old commodore, completely won over to this strange man, called for the insertion, verbatim, of Dr Fergusson's speech in the *Proceedings of the Royal Geographical Society of London*.

What, then, was this doctor, and to what exploit was he about to devote himself?

Young Fergusson's father, a worthy captain of the British Navy, had from his son's earliest youth associated the latter with himself in the dangers and adventures of his profession. This estimable boy, who never appears to have known fear, quickly displayed a bright intelligence, an inquiring mind, a remarkable propensity for scientific work. In addition, he displayed unusual skill in getting out of difficulties. Nothing ever perplexed him, not even the handling of his first fork, with which children are not as a rule very successful.

Soon his imagination was kindled by the reading of bold enterprises and exploration by sea. He followed passionately the discoveries which signalised the early part of the nineteenth century. He dreamed of fame like that of Mungo Park,[28] Bruce, the Caillies, Levaillant, and even to some extent, I believe, that of Selkirk,[29] Robinson Crusoe, whom he placed on no less high a level. What absorbing hours he spent with him on his island of Juan Fernandez! The ideas of the solitary sailor frequently met with his approval, but at times he disputed his plans and schemes. He himself would have acted differently, perhaps better, certainly as well. But one thing is sure; he would never have left that joyous island, where he was as happy as a king without subjects, not even to become First Lord of the Admiralty.

I leave you to imagine how these tendencies developed during his adventurous youth, when he was tossed about between the four corners of the earth. His father, as an educated man, lost no opportunity of consolidating this alert mind by serious study of hydrography, physics and mechanics, with a dash of botany, medicine and astronomy.

After the death of the worthy captain, Samuel Fergusson, now twenty-two years of age, had already travelled round the world. He joined the Bengal Engineers and distinguished himself on several occasions. But a soldier's life did not suit him and, with little ambition to command, he was reluctant to obey. He resigned and, partly for purposes of hunting, partly botanising, he made his way towards the north of the Indian Peninsula, which he crossed from Calcutta to Surat: a mere jaunt.

From Surat we see him cross to Australia and take part, in 1845, in Captain Stuart's expedition to discover that Caspian Sea which was supposed to lie in the centre of New Holland.[30]

Samuel Fergusson returned to England about 1850 and, more than ever possessed by the demon of discovery, passed his time until 1853 accompanying Captain MacClure on the expedition which traversed the American continent from the Behring Straits to Cape Farewell.

In spite of every form of fatigue, and in every kind of climate, Fergusson's constitution stood the test wonderfully. He lived cheerfully amid the most complete privations. He was the type of the ideal traveller whose stomach contracts or distends at will, whose legs grow longer or shorter to match the improvised couch, can go to sleep at any hour of the day and wake at any hour of the night.

Nothing is less surprising than to find our indefatigable traveller from 1855 to 1857 exploring the whole of western Tibet, in the company of the Schlagintweit brothers,[31] and bringing back from this expedition curious ethnographical observations.

During these various journeys he was the most active and interesting correspondent of the *Daily Telegraph*, a penny paper whose circulation reaches 140,000 copies daily, which is hardly enough to satisfy several millions of readers. He was therefore well known, this doctor, in spite of the fact that he was not a member of any learned institution nor of any of the Royal Geographical Societies of London, Paris, Berlin, Vienna or St Petersburg, nor of the Travellers' Club,[32] nor even of the Royal Polytechnic Institution, where his friend Cockburn, the statistician, was supreme.

This learned man, in fact, with the idea of making himself agreeable, one day asked him to solve the following problem: Given the number of miles traversed by the doctor in going round the world, how many more would his head have covered than his feet as a result of the difference between the radii? Or, given the number of miles covered by the feet and head of the doctor, respectively, calculate his height to one place of decimals.

But Fergusson always held aloof from learned societies, as talking was not his strong point. He thought his time better employed in seeking subjects for discussion and discovery than in making speeches.

It is said that an Englishman one day went to Geneva with the idea of inspecting the lake. He was put into one of those old-fashioned carriages in which the passengers sit sideways to the horse, as in an omnibus. Now it happened that our Englishman was seated with his back to the lake. The carriage quietly completed its circular trip without its having occurred to him to turn round, and he went back to London delighted with the Lake of Geneva.

Dr Fergusson, however, was in the habit of turning round more than once during his travels, and to such good effect that he had seen much. In this, moreover, he was obeying his nature, and we have good reason to believe that he was a bit of a fatalist, though a very orthodox fatalist, relying on himself and even on Providence. He regarded himself as driven rather than drawn on in his travels, and traversed the world like a railway engine which does not guide itself but is steered by the track.

'I don't follow my path,' he would often say; 'it is my path that follows me.' There is therefore no cause for surprise in the coolness with which he received the applause of the Royal Society; he was above such trivialities, having no pride and still less vanity. The proposal he had made to the President, Sir Francis M—, seemed to him quite simple, and he was not even conscious of the tremendous effect it produced.

After the meeting the doctor was conducted to the Travellers' Club in Pall Mall, where a superb banquet had been prepared in his honour. The size of the dishes served was in keeping with the importance of the guest, and the sturgeon which figured in this sumptuous meal was not more than three inches shorter than Samuel Fergusson himself.

Numerous toasts were drunk, in French wines, to the celebrated travellers who had made themselves illustrious on the soil of Africa. Their healths or memories were toasted in alphabetical order, which is very English: Abbadie, Adams, Adamson, Anderson, Arnaud, Baikie, Baldwin, Barth, Batouda, Beke, Beltrame, du Berba, Bimbachi, Bolognesi, Bolwik, Bolzoni, Bonnemain, Brisson, Browne, Bruce, Brun-Rollet, Burchell, Burckhardt, Burton, Cailliaud, Caillie, Campbell, Chapman, Clapperton, Clot-bey, Colomien, Courval, Cumming, Cuny, Debono, Decken, Denham, Desavanchers, Dicksen, Dickson, Dochard, Duchaillu, Duncan, Durand, Duroule, Duveyrier, Erhardt, d'Escayrac de Lauture, Ferret, Fresnel, Galinier, Galton, Geoffrey, Golberry, Hahn, Halm, Harnier, Hecquart, Heuglin, Hornemann, Houghton, Imbert, Kaufmann, Knoblecher, Krapf, Kummer, Lafargue, Laing, Lajaille, Lambert, Lamiral, Lamprière, John Lander, Richard Lander, Lefebvre, Lejean, Levaillant, Livingstone, Maccarthie, Maggiar, Maizan, Malzac, Moffat, Mollien, Monteiro, Morrison, Mungo Park, Neimans, Overweg, Panet, Partarrieau, Pascal, Pearse, Peddie, Peney, Petherick, Pomcet, Prax, Raffenel, Rath, Rebmann, Richardson, Riley, Ritchie, Rochet d'Héricourt, Rongawi, Roscher, Roppel, Saugnier, Speke, Steidner, Thibaud, Thompson, Thornton, Toole, Tousny, Trotter, Tuckey, Tyrwhitt, Vaudey, Veyssière, Vincent, Vinco, Vogel, Wahlberg, Warrington, Washington, Werne, Wild, and finally, Dr Samuel Fergusson who, by his incredible exploit, was to link up the work of these travellers and complete the chain of African discovery.

CHAPTER II

An article from the Daily Telegraph *– A campaign by learned journals*

THE FOLLOWING DAY, in its issue of January 15, the *Daily Telegraph* published an article in the following terms:

> Africa is at last about to yield the secret of her vast solitudes. A modern Oedipus is to give us the key to this enigma which the scientists of sixty centuries have failed to solve. Of old the search for the sources of the Nile, *fontes Nili quærere*, was regarded as a mad project, an unrealisable chimera.
>
> Dr Barth, following as far as the Sudan the track traced by Denham and Clapperton; Dr Livingstone multiplying his daring investigations from the Cape of Good Hope to the shores of the Zambesi; and Captains Burton and Speke, by their discovery of the great lakes of the interior have opened three routes to modern civilisation. Their point of intersection which no traveller has yet succeeded in reaching is the very heart of Africa. It is upon this that all efforts should be concentrated.
>
> Now the work of these bold pioneers of Science is to be taken up again in the audacious scheme of Dr Samuel Fergusson, whose splendid explorations our readers have so often appreciated.
>
> This intrepid discoverer proposes to cross the whole of Africa, from east to west, in a balloon. If we are accurately informed the point of departure of this astonishing journey will be the Island of Zanzibar off the east coast. The point of destination is known only to Providence.
>
> This scheme of scientific exploration was yesterday officially announced to the Royal Geographical Society, and a sum of two thousand five hundred pounds was voted to meet the expenses of the enterprise. We shall keep our readers in touch with this venture which is without precedent in the annals of geography.

As will be imagined, this article caused a tremendous sensation. At first it roused a storm of incredulity. Dr Fergusson was taken to be a purely imaginary being invented by Mr Barnum, who, after having worked the United States, was preparing to 'do' the British Isles. A sarcastic reply appeared in Geneva, in the February number of the *Bulletins de la Société Géographique*, wittily making game of the Royal Geographical Society of London, the Travellers' Club and the prodigious sturgeon. But Herr Petermann, in his *Mitteilungen*, published in Gotha, reduced the Geneva journal to complete silence. Herr Petermann knew Dr Fergusson personally and vouched for the daring of his friend.

Moreover, further doubt soon became impossible. Preparations for the journey were being made in London. The Lyons factories had received an important order for silk for the construction of the balloon. Lastly, the British Government was putting the transport *Resolute*, Captain Pennet, at the doctor's disposal.

At once a thousand voices were raised in encouragement, thousands of congratulations were poured forth. The details of the enterprise were minutely reported in the bulletins of the Royal Geographical Society of Paris. A remarkable article was printed in the *Nouvelles annales des voyages de la géographie, de l'histoire et de l'archéologie* of M. V. A. Malte-Brun, and an exhaustive article published in the *Zeitschrift für allgemeine Erdkunde*, by Dr W. Koner, demonstrated irrefutably the possibility of the voyage, its chances of success, the nature of the obstacles, the immense advantages of air travel. It only condemned the point of departure and suggested for preference Massaua, a small Abyssinian port whence James Bruce had started out in 1768 in search of the sources of the Nile. For the rest it was unstinted in its admiration of Dr Fergusson's dauntless spirit and the heart of triple brass which could conceive and attempt such a journey. The *North American Review* could not see such glory reserved for England without displeasure. It turned the doctor's proposal into a jest and invited him to push forward as far as America while he was so far on the way. In short, among the journals of the entire world there was not a scientific periodical, from the *Journal of Evangelical Missions* to the *Algerian and Colonial Review*, from the *Annals of the Propagation of the Gospel* to the *Church Missionary Intelligence*, which did not describe the event in its every detail.

Considerable wagers were laid in London and throughout England; firstly as to the real or fictitious existence of Dr Fergusson; secondly as to the expedition itself, some holding that it would not be attempted at all, others that it would be carried through; thirdly, on the question of whether it would succeed or not; fourthly, on the probability or improbability of Dr Fergusson's return. Books were made involving enormous sums as though it had been the Derby.

Thus, the eyes of everyone, convinced or sceptical, ignorant or wise, were fixed upon the doctor, who became the lion of the day, though unconscious of his mane. He readily gave exact information about his expedition and was always approachable – the most natural man in the world. More than one bold adventurer presented himself and expressed a desire to share the glory and dangers of his venture, but he refused without giving his reasons. Many inventors of appliances adapted for balloons brought them before his notice. He rejected them all. Whenever he was asked if he had discovered anything in this respect, he invariably refused to commit himself and busied himself more strenuously than ever with the preparations for his journey.

CHAPTER III

*The doctor's friend – Origin of their friendship – Dick Kennedy
in London – An unexpected and not reassuring proposal –
A not very consoling proverb – A few words about African
martyrology – Advantages of a balloon – Dr Fergusson's secret*

DR FERGUSSON had a friend; not another self, not an *alter ego*, for friendship could hardly exist between two beings completely alike. But though they possessed distinct qualities, aptitudes and temperaments, in Dick Kennedy and Samuel Fergusson there beat but one heart, a fact which did not trouble them much – quite the contrary.

This Dick Kennedy was a Scotsman in the full significance of the word; open, resolute and dogged. He lived in the little town of Leith, near Edinburgh, a typical offshoot of 'Auld Reekie.' He was, on occasion, a fisherman, but always and everywhere a determined sportsman, which was entirely natural in a son of Caledonia, however little familiar he may have been with the mountains of the Highlands. He was said to be a wonderful shot. Not only could he split bullets on the blade of a knife, but he would cut them into two parts so equal that when they were weighed no appreciable difference could be detected.

Kennedy's face was very reminiscent of that of Halbert Glendinning[33] as he is painted by Walter Scott in *The Monastery*. He was over six feet, graceful and easy in his bearing, and appeared to be endowed with herculean strength. A face deeply tanned by the sun, quick black eyes, a very marked natural bravery; in fact, something good and solid in his whole personality made this Scotsman an attractive figure.

The two friends first met in India, where they both belonged to the same regiment. While Dick was hunting tigers and elephants Samuel was hunting plants and insects. Each could claim to be an expert in his own sphere, and more than one rare plant fell to the doctor which was as well worth winning as a pair of ivory tusks. The two young men never had a chance of saving each other's lives or of rendering each other any service; hence an unshakable friendship. Fate separated them at times, but sympathy always brought them together again.

Since their return to England they had been frequently separated by the doctor's distant expeditions, but whenever he returned he never failed to go and give a few weeks of his company to his Scottish friend. Dick would talk of the past, while Samuel made plans for the future. One looked forward, the other back; hence the restless spirit of Fergusson and the complete placidity of Kennedy.

After his journey to Tibet the doctor went for nearly two years without mentioning fresh explorations. Dick supposed that his traveller's instinct, his thirst for adventure, was dying down. He was delighted. It was bound to end badly one day or another, he thought. Whatever experience one may have of men, one cannot travel with impunity among cannibals and wild beasts. Kennedy therefore urged Samuel to give it up. Besides, he had done enough for science, too much for human gratitude. The doctor was content to meet this suggestion with silence. He remained thoughtful, and then plunged into secret calculations, spending his nights labouring over figures and even experimenting with strange apparatus of which no one could make head or tail. It was felt that some great idea was fermenting in his brain.

'What can he be worrying at now?' pondered Kennedy when his friend had left him in January to return to London. He found out one morning through the article in the *Daily Telegraph*.

'Heaven's mercy!' he cried. 'The fool! The madman! Cross Africa in a balloon! This is the last straw. So this is what he's been brooding over these last two years!'

In place of all these exclamation marks, imagine so many lusty punches on the head, and you will have an idea of the vigour with which the worthy Dick said this. When old Elspeth, the woman to whom he always opened his heart, tried to suggest that it might easily be a hoax, he replied: 'Hang it all! Don't I know the fellow? Isn't it him to the life? Travel through the air! Jealous of the eagles now! No, he won't. I'll put a spoke in his wheel! If there was no one to stop him he'd be off some fine day to the moon.'

The same evening, Kennedy, torn between anxiety and exasperation, took the train at the General Railway Station, and the following day arrived in London. Three-quarters of an hour later a cab set him down at the doctor's little house in Greek Street, Soho. He dashed up the steps and announced his presence by five heavy blows on the door.

Fergusson himself opened it.

'Dick?' he said, without betraying much surprise.

'Dick himself,' retorted Kennedy.

'What, you in London in the shooting season, Dick?'

'I'm in London.'

'And what are you here for?'

'To stop a piece of grotesque folly.'

'Folly?' said the doctor.

'Is what this paper says true?' asked Kennedy, holding out his copy of the *Daily Telegraph*.

'Oh, that's what you mean! These papers are very indiscreet. But sit down, Dick, old man.'

'I'm not going to sit down. You actually intend to undertake this journey?'

'I do. My preparations are well ahead, and I – '

'Where are they, these preparations? Let me get at them. Where are they? I'll smash them to pieces.' The worthy Scot was getting very seriously angry.

'Steady, old man,' went on the doctor. 'I can understand your irritation. You think I ought to have told you before about my new plans.'

'New plans, indeed!'

'I've been very busy,' Samuel continued, without heeding the interruption. 'I've had a lot to do. But you needn't worry; I shouldn't have started without writing to you – '

'Writing be hanged – '

'Because I'd thought of taking you with me.'

The Scotsman made a bound which would have done credit to a chamois.

'What!' he yelled. 'Do you want to get us both shut up in Bedlam?'[34]

'I was firmly relying on you, my dear Dick, and picked you out over the heads of many others.'

Kennedy stood thunderstruck.

'When you've listened for ten minutes to what I have to say,' the doctor continued calmly, 'you'll thank me.'

'You're talking seriously?'

'Absolutely.'

'And what if I refuse to go with you?'

'You won't refuse.'

'But what if I do?'

'I shall go alone.'

'Let's sit down,' said the sportsman, 'and talk quietly. Now I know you're not joking it's worth discussing.'

'We'll discuss it over lunch, if you've no objection, old man.'

The two friends sat facing one another over a little table on which was a pile of sandwiches and an enormous tea-pot.

'My dear Samuel,' said the sportsman, 'your plan is madness. It's impossible. It's unheard of, beyond all reason.'

'We'll see, when we've tried.'

'But that's just what we are not going to do; we're not going to try.'

'And why, if you please?'

'The danger, and the obstacles of every kind.'

'Obstacles,' Fergusson answered gravely, 'are created to be over-come, and as for dangers, who has the confidence to think he can avoid them? There's danger everywhere in life. It may be very dangerous to sit at this table or to put your hat on. Besides, what is to happen should be regarded as having happened already, and the future should be regarded like the present, for the future is only the present a little further away.'

'Bah!' said Kennedy, shrugging his shoulders. 'You're still a fatalist!'

'Yes, but in the best sense of the word. Well, don't let us bother our heads about what Fate has up her sleeve for us, and never forget our good old English proverb: "The man born to be hanged will never be drowned." ' This was unanswerable, but did not prevent Kennedy from producing a number of further arguments, easy to imagine but too long to reproduce here.

'But after all,' he said, after an hour's discussion, 'if you insist on crossing Africa, if you can't be happy unless you do, why not go the ordinary way?'

'Why?' answered the doctor, with spirit. 'Because up to now every attempt has failed. Because from Mungo Park's assassination on the Niger down to Vogel's disappearance in the Wadai; from Oudney's death at Murmur and Clapperton's at Sackatou down to the time when the Frenchman Maizan was cut to pieces; between the murder of Major Laing by the Tuaregs and the massacre of Roscher of Hamburg at the beginning of 1860, the names of many victims have been added to the records of African martyrology. Because to struggle against the elements, against hunger, thirst and fever, against savage animals, and still more savage people, is impossible. Because what can't be done in one way ought to be tried in another. Lastly, because where you can't go through you must go round or over.'

'Passing over would be all right,' Kennedy answered, 'but flying over – '

'Well, what is there to be frightened of ?' the doctor continued, completely unmoved. 'You'll admit that the precautions I have taken leave no fear of the balloon falling, so if I do come to grief, I'll be back on land in the same position as an ordinary explorer. But my balloon won't fail me; we needn't think of that.'

'We *must* think of it.'

'Not at all, Dick. I don't intend to leave it till I get to the West Coast of Africa. With it all is possible; without it I should be back among all the natural dangers and obstacles of such an expedition. With it there will be nothing to fear from either heat, torrents, storms, the simoon, unhealthy climate, wild animals or men. If I'm too hot, I go up; if I'm cold, I come down. If I come to a mountain, I fly over it; a precipice, I cross it; a river, I cross it; a storm, I rise above it; a torrent, I skim over it like a bird. I travel without fatigue and halt without need of rest. I soar over the new cities. I fly with the swiftness of the storm; sometimes near the limit of the air, sometimes a hundred feet above the ground, with the map of Africa unwinding below my eyes in the greatest atlas in the world.'

The excellent Kennedy began to feel excited, and yet the vision raised before his eyes made him dizzy. He regarded Samuel admiringly, but also in fear. He already felt as though he were hovering in space.

'Look here, Samuel. Hold on a bit. Do you mean to say you've found out a way of steering balloons?'

'Rather not, that's utopian – '

'But you're going – '

'Where Providence thinks fit, but in any case from east to west.'

'Why?'

'Because I'm going to rely on the trade winds whose direction is constant.'

'Oh, indeed, that's true,' mused Kennedy. 'Trade winds – yes – at a pinch one can – there's something in that – '

'Something, my good fellow! Why there's everything. The British Government has placed a transport at my disposal. They've also agreed for three or four ships to go and cruise off the West Coast about the time estimated for my arrival. In three months at the outside I'll be at Zanzibar, where I shall inflate my balloon and where we launch her – '

'*We?*' said Dick.

'Have you the shadow of an objection to raise now, Kennedy? Out with it.'

'Objection! I've a thousand. But to take one, tell me: if you intend seeing the country, and going up and coming down as you please, you can't do it without losing gas. So far there's been no way out of that, and that's what has always knocked on the head long journeys through the air.'

'My dear Dick, I'll merely tell you that I shan't lose an atom of gas, not a molecule.'

'And you'll come down when you please?'

'I shall come down when I please.'

'How?'

'That's my secret, old man. Rely on me, and let my motto be yours: *Excelsior!*'

'All right. *Excelsior!*' answered the sportsman, who didn't know a word of Latin.

But he was fully determined to oppose his friend's departure by every means in his power, so he feigned agreement and settled down to watch. As for Samuel, he went off to supervise his preparations.

CHAPTER IV

African Exploration

THE AERIAL COURSE which Dr Fergusson intended to follow had not been chosen at random; his point of departure had been very carefully studied, and it was not without reason that he decided to take off from the island of Zanzibar. This island, situated off the east coast of Africa, is in latitude 6° S., i.e. 430 geographical miles below the Equator. It was from this island that the last expedition, sent *via* the great lakes to discover the sources of the Nile, had recently set out.

But it will be well to indicate what explorations Dr Fergusson hoped to co-ordinate. They were two: that of Dr Barth[35] in 1849, and that of Lieutenants Burton and Speke in 1858. Dr Barth was a native of Hamburg, who obtained permission for his compatriot Overweg and himself to join Richardson's English expedition, Richardson being in charge of a mission into the Sudan. This vast country is situated between lat. 15° and 10° N., so that to reach it, it was necessary to advance over fifteen hundred miles into the interior of Africa. Hitherto this country was only known through the expedition of Denham, Clapperton and Oudney, 1822-24. Richardson, Barth and Overweg, eager to push their investigations still further, reached Tunis and Tripoli, like their predecessors, and got as far as Murzuk, the capital of Fezzan.

They then abandoned their direct line and made a deep detour westward towards Ghat, guided, not without difficulties, by the Tuaregs.

After incessant suffering from pillage, vexations and armed attack, their caravan arrived, in October, in the huge oasis of Asben. Here Dr Barth detached himself from his companions, made an excursion to the town of Agades and then rejoined the expedition, which resumed its march on the 12th of December. When it arrived in the province of Damerghu the three travellers separated, and Barth made for Kano, which he reached by dint of patience and the payment of considerable tribute.

In spite of severe fever he left this town on the 7th of March, accompanied by a single servant. The chief objective of his journey was to find Lake Tchad, from which he was still three hundred and fifty miles distant. He therefore turned east and reached the town of Zuricolo, in Bornu, the heart of the great Central Empire of Africa, where he learned of the death of Richardson, who had succumbed to fatigue and privation. He arrived in Kuka, the capital of Bornu, on the banks of the lake, and, three weeks later, on the 14th of April, twelve and a half months after leaving Tripoli, he at last reached the town of Ngourou.

We hear of him leaving again on the 29th of March, 1851, with Overweg, to explore the kingdom of Adamawa, to the south of the lake. He got as far as the town of Yola, a little south of lat. 9° N. This was the extreme southern limit attained by this bold explorer. He returned to Kuka in August, and from there traversed in succession Mandara, Baghirmi and Kanem, his eastern limit being the town of Masena, long. 17° 20' W.

On the 25th of November, 1852, after the death of Overweg, his last surviving companion, he plunged westward, visited Sokoto, crossed the Niger, and finally reached Timbuktu, where he had to cool his heels for eight long months, subjected by the sheik to persecution, ill-treatment and misery. But the presence of a Christian in the town could be no longer tolerated; the Fellanis threatened to besiege it. The doctor therefore left on the 17th of March, 1854, and fled to the frontier, where he remained thirty-three days in the most complete destitution, returned to Kano in November, and then back to Kuka, whence he rejoined Denham's route after four months' delay. He was back in Tripoli about the end of August 1855, and on the 6th of September returned to London alone. Such was Barth's daring expedition.

Dr Fergusson carefully noted that he had come to a stop in lat. 4° N., long. 17° W. Let us now observe what Lieutenants Burton and Speke accomplished in East Africa.

The various expeditions up the Nile never seemed to have been able to reach the mysterious sources of that river. According to the account

given by Doctor Ferdinand Werne, a German, the expedition organised, in 1840, under the auspices of Mehemet Ali, came to a halt at
Gondokoro, between lat. 4° and lat. 5° N.

In 1855 Brun-Rollet, a native of Savoy, who had been appointed
Sardinian consul in Eastern Sudan in succession to Vaudey, who had
just died, started from Khartum, and travelling as Yacoub, trading in
gum and ivory, reached Belenia, crossed the fourth parallel and,
overcome by illness, returned to Khartum, where he died in 1857.

Neither Dr Peney, head of the Egyptian Medical Service, who in a
small steamer reached one degree south of Gondokoro and returned to
die of exhaustion in Khartum, nor the Venetian Miani, who, doubling
the cataracts south of Gondokoro, reached lat. 2° N., nor the Maltese
merchant, Andrea De Bono, who pushed his expedition up the Nile
still farther, seemed able to cross this final limit.

In 1859 M. Guillaume Lejean, placed in charge of a mission by the
French Government, went to Khartum, through the Red Sea, and
embarked on the Nile with a crew of twenty-one men and twenty
soldiers; but he could get no farther than Gondokoro, and was exposed
to very serious danger among negroes in open revolt. The expedition
commanded by M. d'Escayrac de Lauture also attempted to reach the
famous sources. But the same fatal limit always brought the explorers
to a standstill. The envoys of Nero had of old reached lat. 9° N.; so that
in eighteen centuries there had only been an advance of from five to six
degrees, or from 300 to 360 geographical miles.

Several travellers had tried to reach the sources of the Nile from the
east coast of Africa. Between 1768 and 1772 the Scotchman Bruce,[36]
starting from Massaua, a port of Abyssinia, traversed Tigre, inspected
the ruins of Axum, saw the sources of the Nile where they did not exist,
and obtained no serious result. In 1844 Dr Krapf, an Anglican
missionary, founded a settlement at Mombasa, on the coast of Zanzibar, and, in the company of the Reverend Rebmann, discovered two
mountains three hundred miles from the coast. These were Kilimandjaro
and Kenia, which recently Messrs von Heuglin and Thornton have
partly climbed. In 1845 the Frenchman Maizan disembarked alone at
Bagamoyo, opposite Zanzibar, and reached Deje la Mbora, where the
chief had him put to death with cruel torture. In August 1859, the
young explorer Roscher, of Hamburg, setting out with a caravan of
Arab merchants, reached Lake Nyasa, where he was murdered in his
sleep. Lastly, in 1857, Lieutenants Burton and Speke, both officers of
the Indian Army, were sent by the Royal Geographical Society of
London to explore the great African lakes.

They left Zanzibar on the 17th of June and headed straight towards the west. After four months of unprecedented suffering, their baggage stolen and their porters beaten to death, they arrived at Kazeh, the rendezvous of traders and caravans, in the heart of the Moon country. There they obtained valuable information about the customs, government, religion, fauna and flora of the country, and afterwards set out for Tanganyika, the first of the great lakes, between lat. 3° and lat. 8° S. This they reached on the 14th of February, 1858, and visited the different tribes inhabiting its banks, for the most part cannibals.

Setting out again on the 22nd of May, they returned to Kazeh on the 20th of June. There Burton, who was in a state of exhaustion, lay ill for several months, during which time Speke made a detour of three hundred miles to the north as far as Lake Ukereue, which he saw on the 3rd of August, but only one end, in lat. 2° 30' S. He was back in Kazeh on the 25th of August and resumed with Burton the road to Zanzibar, which they reached again in March of the following year. The two intrepid explorers then returned to England and were awarded the annual prize of the Geographical Society of Paris.

Dr Fergusson carefully noted that they had not crossed either lat. 2° S. or long. 29° E.

Thus what remained to be done was to link up Burton and Speke's exploration with that of Dr Barth, which involved covering a distance of more than twelve degrees.

CHAPTER V

Kennedy's dreams – Plural personal pronouns – Dick's insinuations – A trip over the map of Africa – The difference between the two points of a pair of compasses – Expeditions actually in progress – Speke and Grant – Krapf, von Decken and von Heuglin

DR FERGUSSON was busily pressing forward the preparations for his departure and personally supervising the construction of his balloon, employing certain devices about which he preserved complete silence. For a long time he had been studying Arabic and various Mandingo dialects. Thanks to his gift for languages he was making rapid progress.

Meanwhile his friend the sportsman never left his elbow. He was doubtless afraid that the doctor would take to the air without saying anything about it. He was still using the utmost persuasion with regard to this subject, but without success, and giving vent to pathetic appeals which had little effect. Dick felt that the doctor was slipping through his fingers.

The poor Scot was indeed to be pitied. He could no longer think of the azure heavens without dark forebodings. In his sleep he felt himself dizzily swaying, and every night he fell from incalculable heights. It must be added that during these terrible nightmares he more than once fell out of bed. On these occasions his first thought was to show Fergusson the bruises on his head.

'A drop of only three feet,' he added good-naturedly; 'certainly not more, and a bruise like this. Just think it out!'

This doleful hint did not disturb the doctor.

'We shan't fall,' he said.

'But if we do?'

'We shan't.'

That was flat; and Kennedy had no reply to make.

What particularly exasperated Dick was that the doctor seemed completely to disregard Kennedy's own personality and to regard him as irrevocably destined to be his companion in the air. There could be no further doubt about this. Samuel abused in an intolerable way the word 'we.'

'*We* are making good headway . . . *We* shall be ready on the . . . *We* shall start on the . . .'

And also the word 'our': '*Our* balloon . . . *Our* car . . . *Our* expedition . . . *Our* preparations . . . Our discoveries . . . *Our* ascents . . .'

This made Dick shudder, determined as he was not to go. At the same time he did not want to vex his friend too much. It may even be admitted that without realising it he had quietly had sundry articles of clothing and his best sporting rifles sent from Edinburgh.

One day, realising that the chances of success were, with luck, one in a thousand, he pretended to give way to the doctor's wishes; but in order to postpone the voyage, launched upon a series of widely-varied evasions. He attacked the usefulness of the expedition and its opportuneness . . . Was this discovery of the sources of the Nile really necessary? . . . Would they really be working for the good of humanity? . . . After all, even if the African tribes were to be civilised, would they be any better off? . . . Was it certain, moreover, that there was not more civilisation there than in Europe? . . . Africa was certain to be crossed sometime or other, and in a less risky manner . . . In a month, six months, before the year was out, some explorer would undoubtedly succeed. These insinuations produced the contrary effect to what was intended, and the doctor quivered with irritation.

'Is this what you call friendship, you traitor? Do you want someone else to get all the glory? Am I to go back on my past? Am I to jib at paltry obstacles? Is this the way you want me to show my gratitude for what the British Government and the Royal Geographical Society have done for me?'

'But – ' went on Kennedy, with whom this conjunction was a habit.

'But,' said the doctor, 'don't you realise that my expedition has to compete with others which are already on the way? Don't you know that fresh explorers are making their way towards the centre of Africa?'

'Yet – '

'Now just listen to me, Dick. Have a look at this map.'

Dick did so with an air of resignation.

'Now make your way up the Nile.'

'Very well,' the Scot replied obediently.

'Go as far as Gondokoro.'

'I've got there.'

And Kennedy realised how easy such a journey is – on the map.

'Take this pair of dividers,' the doctor continued, 'and place one point on that town which the boldest travellers have not been able to get past to any extent worth mentioning.'

'All right, here it is.'

'Now find the Island of Zanzibar, near the coast, lat. 6° S.'

'I've got it.'

'Now follow this parallel until you get to Kazeh.'

'Here we are.'

'Follow the 33rd meridian as far as the end of Lake Ukereue, where Lieutenant Speke came to a stop.'

'I'm there. A little farther and I'll be falling into the lake.'

'Well, do you know what the information given by the natives along the banks justifies us in supposing?'

'I haven't the vaguest idea.'

'That this lake, whose lowest extremity is in lat. 2° 30' S., must also extend two degrees above the Equator.'

'Really!'

'Now from this northern extremity a water-course runs which cannot help but join the Nile, even if it is not the Nile itself.'

'That's odd.'

'Now place the other point of the dividers on this extremity of Lake Ukereue.'

'Done, my good Fergusson.'

'How many degrees are there between the two points?'

'Not quite two.'

'Do you know how far that is?'

'I don't in the least.'

'Less than one hundred and fifty miles. In fact, nothing at all.'

'Next to nothing, Samuel.'

'Now, do you know what is happening at this very moment?'

'No; I assure you I do not.'

'Well, this is what is happening. The Royal Geographical Society lays great importance on the exploration of this lake seen by Speke. Under its auspices Lieutenant, now Captain Speke, has been joined by Captain Grant of the Indian Army, and they have placed themselves at the head of a large and heavily subsidised expedition. Their object is to travel up the lake and return as far as Gondokoro. They've received a grant of over five thousand pounds and the Governor of the Cape has lent them native soldiers. They left Zanzibar at the end of October 1860. Meanwhile John Petherick, the British Consul at Khartum, has received from the Foreign Office about seven hundred pounds. He is to fit out a steamer at Khartum, go to Gondoroko, wait there for Speke's expedition and be ready to revictual it.'

'A good idea,' said Kennedy.

'So you see, there's no time to be lost if we intend to have a finger in these explorations. And that's not all. While these men are steadily advancing towards the sources of the Nile, other explorers are boldly pushing into the heart of Africa.'

'On foot?' Kennedy asked.

'On foot,' answered the doctor, disregarding the insinuation. 'Dr Krapf proposes to push west, following the Djob, a river below the Equator. Baron von Decken has identified Mount Kenia and Kilimandjaro, and is heading towards the centre.'

'On foot, too?'

'On foot, too, or else by mule.'

'It's exactly the same thing as far as I'm concerned,' Kennedy replied.

'Lastly,' the doctor went on, 'Herr von Heuglin, the Austrian Vice-Consul at Khartum, has just organised a very important expedition whose first objective is to search for Vogel, the explorer who was sent into the Sudan in 1853 to assist in Dr Barth's work. In 1856 he left Bornu and decided to explore the unknown country stretching between Lake Tchad and Darfur. He has never turned up again. Letters received at Alexandria in 1860 report that he was assassinated by order of the King of Wadai, but other letters sent by Dr Hartmann to the explorers also report that according to the story of a fellah of Bornu, Vogel appears to have been merely held prisoner at Wara, so that all hope is not yet lost. A committee has been formed under the presidency of the Duke Regent of Saxe-Coburg-Gotha. My friend Petermann is secretary, and a national subscription has been raised to defray the expenses of the expedition, to which many distinguished scientists have given their support. Herr von Heuglin left Massaua in June and, while looking for Vogel, he is at the same time to explore all the country between the Nile and Lake Tchad; that is to say, link up Captain Speke's operations with Dr Barth's. Africa will then have been crossed from East to West.'

'Well,' answered the Scot, 'as all this is working out so nicely, what do *we* want to go for?'

Dr Fergusson did not reply but merely shrugged his shoulders.

CHAPTER VI

An incredible manservant – He sees Jupiter's satellites – Dick and Joe at variance – Doubt and faith – Weighing in – Joe in the rôle of Wellington – Joe gets half-a-crown

DR FERGUSSON had a manservant who answered smartly to the name of Joe. He was an excellent fellow, who had devoted himself to his master's service with absolute competence and unlimited loyalty, even anticipating his orders and always carrying them out intelligently. He never grumbled and his temper was never ruffled. Had he been created purposely he could not have been better fitted for his job. Fergusson relied entirely on him for the details of his existence, and he was right. Rare and honest Joe! A servant who would order your dinner and whose tastes were yours; who would pack your trunk and forget neither socks nor shirt; who had possession of your keys and secrets and never abused his trust!

But on the other hand, what a master the doctor was for this estimable Joe! With what respect and confidence he received his decisions. When Fergusson had spoken, only a fool would have wanted to reply. All he thought was right, all he said wise, all he ordered practical, all he undertook possible, all he achieved admirable. You might have cut Joe in pieces, a job that no doubt would have caused you qualms, without making him change his opinion of his master. And so, when the doctor conceived the plan of crossing Africa by air, Joe regarded it as done; there could be no further obstacles. The moment

Dr Fergusson had decided to set out he had as good as arrived at his destination, together with his faithful servant; for the good fellow, without its ever being mentioned, knew well enough that he would be included in the journey. Moreover, he would be of the greatest usefulness by reason of his intelligence and wonderful agility. Had it been necessary to appoint a gymnastic instructor for the monkeys at the Zoological Gardens, themselves pretty nimble, Joe would certainly have had the situation. Jumping, climbing, flying, performing a thousand impossible tricks, were child's play to him.

If Fergusson was the brain of the expedition and Kennedy the arm, Joe would be the hand. He had already accompanied his master on several journeys, and had a smattering of science which he had picked up one way or another; but what specially distinguished him was his good-humoured philosophy and delightful optimism. To him everything seemed easy, logical and natural, and, in consequence, he felt no need to complain. Among other qualities he possessed an amazing power and range of vision. He shared with Moestlin, Kepler's tutor, the rare faculty of being able to distinguish with his naked eye the satellites of Jupiter and to count fourteen stars in the Pleiades, the smallest of which are of the ninth magnitude. This did not make him conceited; he bowed to you very correctly, and when occasion demanded, knew how to make good use of his eyes.

Given this confidence of Joe's in the doctor, it is not surprising that incessant discussions should arise between Kennedy and the worthy servant, all due deference being of course observed. The one was sceptical, the other convinced. One represented clear-sighted prudence, the other blind confidence. The doctor found himself placed between doubt and faith, and it may be said at once that he did not trouble his head about either.

'Well, Mr Kennedy?' Joe would say.

'Well, Joe?'

'The time's getting near. It seems we're setting out for the moon.'

'You mean the Country of the Moon, which isn't quite as far; but set your mind at rest, it's just as dangerous.'

'Dangerous! with a man like Dr Fergusson!'

'I don't want to destroy your illusions, my dear Joe; but what he proposes to do is nothing short of lunacy. He's not going.'

'Not going! So you haven't seen his balloon in Mitchells' workshops?'

'I'd see myself hanged first.'

'You're missing a fine sight, sir; such a beautiful thing, such a lovely car! We shall be very comfortable in it.'

'Are you seriously counting on going with your master?'

'Of course,' Joe replied with conviction. 'I shall go wherever he wants. That would be a nice thing, letting him go alone, after we've been all over the world together! Who'd cheer him up when he was tired? Who'd help him when he wanted to jump over a precipice? Who'd look after him if he was ill? No, sir, Joe will always be at his post by the doctor, or I should say, round the doctor.'

'Good laddie.'

'Besides, you're coming with us,' Joe went on.

'No doubt,' said Kennedy. 'I mean, I'm coming with you to try and stop Samuel, up to the last minute, from committing such a mad trick. I'll even follow him as far as Zanzibar so that there'll be a friend at hand to put a stop to his idiotic scheme.'

'You won't stop anything at all, sir, begging your pardon. My master's not a crazy fool. He thinks over what he's going to do for a long time, and once he's made up his mind, the devil himself wouldn't turn him.'

'We'll see.'

'Don't you pin any hope to that, sir. Besides, the main thing is that you should come. For a sportsman like you, Africa's a wonderful country; so however you look at it, you won't regret your trip.'

'No, I certainly shan't regret it, especially if this pig-headed fellow gives way to reason.'

'By the way, sir,' said Joe, 'you know that we weigh in today?'

'Weigh in, what do you mean?'

'We three, you and me and the master, will all have to get ourselves weighed, of course.'

'Like jockeys?'

'Yes, sir. But don't worry, sir; you won't have to waste if you are too heavy. They'll take you as you are.'

'I certainly have no intention of being weighed,' said the Scot firmly.

'But, sir, it seems we have to be, for the balloon.'

'Very well, his balloon will have to do without it.'

'Lord, sir! And supposing we couldn't go up because the weights weren't right?'

'By heaven, that's all I ask!'

'Come, Mr Kennedy, my master is coming to fetch us any minute.'

'I shan't go.'

'You wouldn't disappoint him like that.'

'Wouldn't I!'

'All right, sir,' said Joe, laughing; 'you talk like this because he isn't here, but when he says to your face, "Dick (begging your pardon, sir),

Dick, I must know your exact weight," you'll go, I'll answer for it.'

'I shall not.'

At this moment the doctor re-entered his study where this conversation was going on. He looked at Kennedy, who didn't feel too comfortable.

'Dick,' he said, 'come with Joe. I must know what you both weigh.'

'But –'

'You can keep your hat on. Come along.'

And Kennedy went.

They all three went to Mitchells' workshops, where a weighing-machine was ready. The doctor had to know the weights of his companions in order to arrange the equilibrium of his balloon. He made Dick get on to the machine, and Dick, without offering any resistance, muttered:

'All right, all right; that doesn't commit me to anything.'

'153 lbs,' said the doctor, writing down the figure in his note-book.

'Am I too heavy?'

'Oh no, sir,' Joe answered; 'besides, I'm light. I'll make up for you.'

So saying, Joe eagerly took Kennedy's place, nearly upsetting the machine in his excitement. He struck the attitude of Wellington trying to imitate Achilles at the entrance to Hyde Park, and was magnificent even without a shield.

'120 lbs,' muttered the doctor, writing it down.

'Ha! Ha!' laughed Joe, beaming with satisfaction. He could never have explained why he laughed.

'My turn,' said Fergusson, and he entered his own weight at 135 lbs.

'The three of us together,' he said, 'don't weigh much over 400 lbs.'

'But if it was necessary to your expedition, sir,' said Joe, 'I could easily get down twenty pounds by not eating.'

'There's no need, Joe,' the doctor answered; 'you can eat as much as you like, and here's half-a-crown to ballast yourself in any way you like.'

CHAPTER VII

*Geometrical details – Estimate of the balloon's capacity – The
double balloon – The envelope – The car – The mysterious
apparatus – The stores – Total weight*

DR FERGUSSON had long been busy with the details of his expedition.
It can be imagined that the balloon, that wonderful vehicle destined to
carry him through the air, was the object of his constant solicitude.

First of all, in order to avoid giving the balloon too big dimensions,
he decided to inflate it with hydrogen, which is fourteen and a half
times lighter than air. The gas is easy to produce, and has given the
best results in aerostatic experiments.

After very careful calculation, the doctor found that in order to have
with him all the things indispensable to his journey and apparatus, he
would have to carry a weight of 4000 lbs. He therefore had to find out
what would be the lifting force capable of raising this weight and
consequently what would be its volume.

A weight of 4000 lbs represents an air displacement of 44,847 cubic
feet, which means that 44,847 cubic feet of air weigh, approximately,
4000 lbs. By giving the balloon this capacity of 44,847 cubic feet and
filling it, not with air but with hydrogen, which is fourteen and a half
times lighter and weighs only 276 lbs, a change of equilibrium is
caused amounting to a difference of 3780 lbs. It is this difference
between the weight of the gas contained in the balloon and the weight
of the air surrounding it that constitutes the lifting force of the
balloon.

Yet if he put into the balloon the 44,847 cubic feet of gas we have
mentioned, it would be completely filled. Now this would not do, for
as the balloon rises into the less dense layers of the atmosphere, the gas
contained in it tends to expand, and would soon burst the envelope. It
is therefore usual only to fill the balloon up to two-thirds of its
capacity. The doctor, however, according to a certain plan known to
himself alone, decided to fill his balloon to only one-half of its capacity
and, since he had to carry 4447 cubic feet of hydrogen, to double,
approximately, the capacity of his balloon.

He designed it in that elongated form which is known to be the
best. Its horizontal diameter was fifty feet and the vertical diameter

seventy-five.* This gave him a spheroid with a capacity in round figures of 90,000 cubic feet.

Had Dr Fergusson been able to employ two balloons his chances of success would have been increased, for, had one happened to break down in the air, he could have thrown out ballast and kept up by means of the other. But it would have been very difficult to handle two balloons when it came to a question of keeping their lifting force equal.

After long reflection, Fergusson, by an ingenious device, obtained the advantages of two balloons without the inconvenience. He constructed two of unequal size and enclosed one within the other. His outer balloon, to which he gave the dimensions already stated, contained inside it a smaller one of the same shape, having a horizontal diameter of only forty-five feet and a vertical diameter of sixty-eight feet. The capacity of this inner balloon was therefore only 67,000 cubic feet. It was to float in the gas surrounding it. A tube connected one balloon with the other and, in case of need, allowed of connection between them.

This arrangement afforded the advantage that, should it be necessary to emit gas in order to come down, the gas of the outer balloon could be emitted first. Should it be necessary to deflate completely, the smaller one would remain intact. The outer envelope could then be removed as an unnecessary burden, and the second balloon, left free, would only offer to the wind the resistance of a half-deflated balloon.

Further, in case of an accident, such as a tear in the outer envelope, the second envelope would remain uninjured.

The two balloons were constructed of twilled taffeta from Lyons, treated with gutta-percha. This resinous substance has the advantage of being completely gas-tight. It is entirely proof against the action of acid or gas. The taffeta at the upper pole of the spheroid, where practically all the strain is concentrated, was of double thickness.

This envelope was capable of retaining the gas indefinitely. It weighed half a pound per nine square feet. Now the surface of the outer balloon having an area of about 11,600 square feet, the envelope weighed 650 lbs. The envelope of the second balloon, with a surface area of 9200 square feet, only weighed 510 lbs, making altogether 1160 lbs.

The net to support the car was made of hemp rope of great strength. The two tubes were the object of minute care, such as would be

* There is nothing extraordinary about these dimensions. In 1784, at Lyons, M. Montgolfier[37] built a balloon with a capacity of 340,000 cubic feet, or 20,000 cubic metres, and succeeded in carrying a weight of 20 tons or 20,000 kilos.

given to the steering gear of a ship. The car, circular in form and with a diameter of fifteen feet, was constructed of wicker-work strengthened by a light casing of iron and fitted below with shock-absorbing springs. Its weight, together with that of the net, did not exceed 280 lbs.

In addition, the doctor had four sheet-iron containers constructed of double thickness. They were connected together by pipes, to which taps were fitted. There was also a spiral tube two inches in diameter, ending in two straight pieces of unequal length, the longer measuring twenty-five feet and the other only fifteen. These containers could be packed into the car in such a way as to occupy the minimum of space. The spiral, which was not to be fitted until later, was packed separately, as was also a very powerful Bunsen electric battery. This apparatus was so cleverly contrived that it weighed no more than 700 lbs, even including twenty-five gallons of water in a special container.

The instruments selected for the journey consisted of two barometers, two thermometers, two compasses, a sextant, two chronometers, a theodolite, and an altazimuth for distant and inaccessible objects. The Greenwich Observatory had placed itself at the doctor's disposal. He did not, however, intend to make physical experiments, but merely wanted to determine his direction and the position of the principal rivers, mountains, and towns. He also furnished himself with three carefully tested iron anchors and a ladder of strong light silk, about fifty feet long.

He also calculated the precise weight of his stores, which consisted of tea, coffee, biscuits, salt meat, and pemmican, a preparation combining small volume with great nutritive properties. Apart from an adequate reserve of brandy, he provided two water containers, each having a capacity of twenty-two gallons. The consumption of these various stores would gradually diminish the weight carried by the balloon. For it must be realised that the equilibrium of a balloon in the air is extremely sensitive. The loss of an almost insignificant weight can produce a very appreciable displacement.

The doctor did not forget an awning to cover over a section of the car, nor the blankets which were to compose the sole bedding for the journey, nor the sporting guns, nor his supplies of powder and shot.

Here is a table giving his calculations:

	lbs
Fergusson	135
Kennedy	153
Joe	120
Outer balloon	650
Inner balloon	510

Car and net	280
Anchors, instruments, guns, blankets	190
Tent and sundry gear, meat, pemmican, biscuits, tea	386
Coffee, brandy, water	400
Apparatus	700
Weight of hydrogen	276
Ballast	200
Total	4000

Such were the details of the 4000 lbs which Dr Fergusson proposed to carry. They included only 200 lbs of ballast, 'for emergencies only,' he said, for, thanks to his special device, he was counting on not using it at all.

CHAPTER VIII

The importance of Joe – The captain of the Resolute *–*
Kennedy's arsenal – Allotment of space – The farewell dinner –
Departure on 21st February – The doctor's scientific lectures –
Duveyrier and Livingstone – Details of aerial travel – Kennedy
reduced to silence

TOWARDS THE END of February the preparations were nearly completed. The balloons, one inside the other, were quite ready and had been subjected to a strong pressure of air, which test provided convincing evidence of their strength and of the care taken over their construction.

Joe felt no exhilaration, but was continually running between Greek Street and Mitchells' workshops, always busy, but always beaming and ready to give details of the exploit to anyone who did not ask for them, and, above all, proud to be accompanying his master. I really believe that by showing the balloon, enlarging upon the doctor's ideas and plans, and pointing him out as he stood at the half-open window or walked through the streets, the worthy servant earned a number of half-crowns. One must not blame him, for he surely had the right to make a little out of the admiration and curiosity of his neighbours.

On the 16th of February the *Resolute* dropped anchor off Greenwich. She was a fast propeller-ship of 800 tons, and had undertaken the revictualling of Sir James Ross's last expedition to the Polar regions. Her commanding officer, Captain Pennet, was said to be a pleasant man. He took a special interest in the doctor's journey, which he had followed for a long time. He was rather a scientist than a naval officer, which did not prevent his ship from carrying four guns, but they had never harmed anyone and were only used to produce entirely pacific noises.

The *Resolute*'s hull had been adapted to hold the balloon, which was embarked with the utmost care on the 18th of February. It was stowed in the bottom of the ship in such a way as to preclude any accident. The car and its accessories, such as the anchors, ropes, stores, and water containers, which were to be filled on arrival, were all stowed under Fergusson's supervision.

Ten barrels of sulphuric acid and ten of old iron for the production of hydrogen were also taken aboard. This quantity was more than was required, but it was necessary to provide against possible loss. The apparatus for manufacturing the gas, consisting of thirty barrels, was stowed at the bottom of the hold.

These various preparations came to an end during the evening of the 18th of February. Two comfortably fitted cabins were ready for Dr Fergusson and his friend Kennedy. The latter, though still swearing that he was not going, went on board with a veritable sporting arsenal: two excellent double-barrelled breech-loading guns and a carbine that would stand any test, from the workshops of Purdey Moore and Dickson of Edinburgh. Armed with such a weapon, the sportsman would have found no difficulty in lodging a bullet in the eye of a chamois at a range of two thousand yards. He had, in addition, two six-chambered Colt revolvers for emergencies. His powder-bag and cartridge-case, his shot and bullets, of which he had a good supply, did not exceed the limit of weight prescribed by the doctor.

The three travellers went on board on the 18th of February, and were received with great deference by the captain and his officers. The doctor maintained most of his usual calm, and was entirely preoccupied with his expedition. Dick was excited but anxious not to show it, Joe exultant and venting his excitement in comic remarks. He at once became the wag of the boatswain's quarters where a place had been reserved for him.

On the 20th a grand farewell dinner was given in honour of Dr Fergusson and Kennedy by the Royal Geographical Society. Captain Pennet and his officers were also invited to this banquet, which was very lively and marked by many complimentary libations. Enough healths were drunk to assure to every guest the life of a centenarian. Sir Francis M— presided with restrained and dignified emotion. To his great confusion, Dick Kennedy had a share in the bacchic good wishes. After drinking to 'the intrepid Fergusson, the glory of England,' they went on to drink to 'the no less courageous Kennedy, his bold companion.' Dick blushed a good deal, and as this was taken for modesty, the applause redoubled. Dick blushed still more.

During dessert a message arrived from the Queen,[38] who presented her compliments to the two travellers and her good wishes for the success of the enterprise. This called forth fresh toasts 'to Her Gracious Majesty.' At midnight, after touching farewells and fervent handshakes, the guests separated.

The *Resolute*'s pinnaces were waiting at Westminster Bridge. The captain embarked with his passengers and officers, and the swift stream of the Thames bore them towards Greenwich. At one o'clock they were all asleep on board.

The next morning, the 21st of February, at 3 a.m., the furnaces began to roar. At 5 a.m. the anchor was weighed and the *Resolute*'s propeller drove her forward towards the estuary of the Thames. There is no need for us to say that conversation on board turned exclusively on Dr Fergusson's expedition. By his bearing and speech he inspired such confidence that soon, with the exception of the Scotsman, no one questioned the success of his enterprise. During the long unoccupied hours of the voyage the doctor gave a regular course of geography to the officers. These young men were full of enthusiasm for the discoveries made forty years before in Africa. Fergusson told them of the explorations of Barth, Speke, Burton and Grant. He described for them this mysterious country which was entirely given up to scientific investigation. In the north, young Duveyrier was exploring the Sahara, and taking back to Paris the Tuareg chiefs. Two expeditions, inspired by the French Government, were being prepared, which were to make their way from the North to the West, and cross one another at Timbuktu. In the South the indefatigable Livingstone was still going forward towards the Equator, and since March 1862 had been going up the River Rovuma, accompanied by Mackenzie. The nineteenth century would certainly not close before Africa had revealed the secrets that had lain hidden in her breast for six thousand years.

The interest of Fergusson's listeners was especially aroused when he explained to them in detail the preparations for his expedition. They wanted to verify his calculations. They argued, and the doctor entered whole-heartedly into the arguments. What caused general astonishment was the comparatively restricted quantity of provisions he was taking with him. One day, one of the officers questioned the doctor on this point.

'That surprises you?' said Fergusson.

'It certainly does.'

'But how long do you suppose my journey is going to last? Months? You are very much out of it. If it became prolonged we should be lost; we should never come through. You must realise, then, that it is not more than 3500 miles – call it 4000 – from Zanzibar to the Senegal coast. Now reckoning it at 240 miles every twelve hours, which is nothing like the speed of our railways, travelling day and night we should cross Africa in a week.'

'But in that case you'd see nothing; you'd collect no geographical information. You wouldn't even see the country.'

'And so,' the doctor replied, 'if I am master of my balloon and can rise and come down at will, I shall stop wherever I like, especially when the air currents are too strong and threaten to take me out of my course.'

'And you'll find they will,' said Captain Pennet. 'There are hurricanes blowing over two hundred and forty miles an hour.'

'You see,' answered the doctor, 'at a speed like that we should be across Africa in twelve hours. We'd get up at Zanzibar and go to bed at St Louis.'

'But,' went on one of the officers, 'could a balloon travel at such a speed?'

'It has happened,' Fergusson replied.

'And the balloon stood it?'

s'A balloon, yes, but what about a man?' Kennedy ventured to interpose.

'And a man, too. For a balloon is always motionless in relation to the surrounding air. It's not the balloon that travels but the air itself. You can light a candle in your car and the flame won't flicker. An aeronaut, if there had been one in Garnerin's balloon,[39] would not have suffered from the speed. Besides, I do not intend to experiment with such speeds, and if I can anchor during the night to some tree or declivity, I shall not fail to do so. After all, we are carrying stores for two months, and there will be nothing to prevent our adept sportsman from supplying us with plenty of game when we alight.'

'Ah, Mr Kennedy, you'll have the chances of a lifetime,' said a young midshipman, looking with envious eyes at the Scot.

'Not to mention the fact,' another went on, 'that your pleasure will bring you great glory in addition.'

'Gentlemen,' answered the sportsman, 'I much appreciate your – er – er – compliments, but – er – er – I have no right to them – '

'What!' came from all sides. 'You're not going?'

'I am not going.'

'You are not going with Dr Fergusson?'

'Not only am I not going with him, but my sole reason for being here is to stop him at the last minute.'

All eyes were turned upon the doctor.

'Don't listen to him,' he replied with his usual calm. 'It's a matter you mustn't discuss with him. At heart he knows perfectly well that he is going.'

'I swear by St Andrew – !' Kennedy cried.

'Don't swear anything, my dear Dick. You've been weighed and measured, and so have your powder, guns and ammunition, so we'll say no more about it.'

And indeed, from that day until the arrival at Zanzibar, Dick kept his mouth shut. He talked neither of that nor of anything else. He maintained complete silence.

CHAPTER IX

Doubling the Cape – The forecastle – Lectures on cosmography by Professor Joe – On the steering of balloons – On the study of atmospheric currents – Eureka!

THE *Resolute* was steaming rapidly towards the Cape of Good Hope. The weather continued fine though the sea was growing rougher. On the 30th of March, twenty-seven days after they left London, Table Mountain was seen silhouetted against the horizon. Cape Town, situated at the foot of an amphitheatre of hills, could be made out through marine glasses, and soon the *Resolute* dropped anchor in the harbour. But the captain was only stopping to coal. This was done in one day, and the ship proceeded south to double the southern extremity of Africa and enter the Mozambique Channel.

This was not Joe's first sea-voyage, and he had not taken long to make himself at home on board. His straightforwardness and good temper made him universally popular. A large share of his master's fame was reflected upon him. He was listened to like an oracle and made no more mistakes than anyone else might have done. And so, while the doctor was conducting his course of description in the officers' quarters, Joe held the forecastle and yarned in his own sweet way; a course, incidentally, that has been followed by the greatest historians of all time.

His subject was naturally aerial travel. Joe found difficulty in making some of the more sceptical spirits swallow the idea of the expedition, but once this was accepted, the imagination of the sailors, stimulated by Joe's account, began to regard nothing as impossible. The brilliant narrator convinced his audience that the expedition would be followed by many others; it was only the beginning of a long series of superhuman adventures.

'You see, you fellows, once a man has started this kind of travel, he can't get on without it; so, on our next expedition, instead of going sideways we'll go straight up higher and higher.'

'That's good,' said one astonished listener. 'Then you'll get to the moon.'

'The moon!' Joe retorted. 'Bless my soul, that's much too ordinary. Everybody goes to the moon. Besides, there's no water there and you'd have to take a big lot of stores, and even bottles of air if you wanted to breathe.'

'Is there any gin there?' asked a sailor who was very partial to that beverage.

'There's nothing else, mate. No, no moon for us. We're going to have a trip among those pretty stars, those jolly old planets my master's often told me about. We're going to start off with a trip to Saturn – '

'The one with the ring?' asked the quartermaster.

'Yes, a wedding ring. But they don't know what's happened to his wife.'

'What, you're going as high as that?' exclaimed a cabin-boy in amazement. 'Your master must be the devil himself.'

'The devil? He's too good for that.'

'And what next after Saturn?' asked one of the less patient of his audience.

'After Saturn? Oh, well, we'll have a look at Jupiter. That's a funny place, now, where a day is only nine and a half hours long. A good place for loafers, and the year lasts twelve years, which is nice for people who've only six months to live. It gives them a bit longer.'

'Twelve years?' the boy exclaimed.

'Yes, sonny. So in that country you'd still be drinking your mother's milk and that old fellow of fifty or so would still be a kid of four and a half.'

'Would you believe it!' cried the whole forecastle as one man.

'It's the absolute truth,' said Joe with conviction. 'But what can you expect? If you will persist in hanging on to this world you'll never learn anything; you'll stay a lot of ignorant sailors. Come and have a look at Jupiter and you'll see. And you've jolly well got to keep your weather eye open up there, some of those satellites are nasty customers!'

They laughed, but they half-believed him, and he talked to them about Neptune, where sailors are sure of a rousing reception, and Mars, where the soldiers monopolise the pavement, which after a bit becomes intolerable. As for Mercury, that was an ugly place, full of thieves and shopkeepers so alike, that it was difficult to distinguish one from another. And, lastly, he gave them a really charming picture of Venus.

'And when we get back from this expedition,' he went on, 'they'll give us the Southern Cross shining up there in God's buttonhole.'

'And you'll certainly deserve it!' the sailors replied.

And so the long evenings in the forecastle were spent in cheerful conversation, while the doctor's instructive talks pursued their course elsewhere. One day the conversation turned to the steering of balloons, and Fergusson was asked to give his views on this subject.

'I don't believe,' he said, 'that it will ever be possible to steer balloons. I know all the methods that have been tried or suggested. Not one has succeeded, not one is practicable. You will understand that I have had to study this question, which is, of course, of great interest to me, but I've failed to solve the problem with the data that the present state of mechanical science makes available. It would be necessary to invent a motor of extraordinary power and incredible lightness. And, in addition, it will be impossible to resist any considerable air current. Up to now effort has been most concentrated on steering the car rather than the balloon, which is a mistake.'

'But there's a close relationship between a balloon and a ship; and a ship can be steered,' someone replied.

'Oh no,' Dr Fergusson replied, 'the density of air is infinitely less than that of water; and besides, the ship is only half-immersed, while a balloon is completely enveloped in the atmosphere and does not move relatively to the surrounding air.'

'So you think aeronautics has spoken its last word?'

'No; indeed not! We shall have to find some other way, and if we can't steer a balloon we shall have to find out how to keep it in favourable atmospheric currents. As one gets up higher these become much more uniform and are constant in their direction. They're no longer influenced by the valleys and mountains which score the earth's surface, and, as you know, that is the principal cause of both the changes of the wind and the irregularity of its strength. Once these zones are determined, the balloon will merely have to enter the currents that suit it.'

'But in that case,' interposed Captain Pennet, 'in order to reach them you'd have to keep going up and down. There's the real difficulty, my dear doctor.'

'And why, captain?'

'Well, I grant you, the difficulty will only arise in the case of long journeys, not on short trips.'

'For what reason, may I ask?'

'Because you can only rise by throwing out ballast, and only come down by letting out gas, and if you go on doing that, your stores of gas and ballast will soon run out.'

'My dear Pennet, that's the whole point, the whole difficulty science has to overcome. The point is not to steer balloons but to move them up and down without losing gas, which is the life-force, the blood and the soul, so to speak, of a balloon.'

'You're right, my dear doctor, but this difficulty has not been overcome yet. This method has not yet been discovered.'

'I beg your pardon. It has.'

'By whom?'

'By me.'

'You!'

'You can rest assured that otherwise I should not have risked this voyage across Africa in a balloon. I should have run out of gas in twenty-four hours.'

'But you said nothing of this in England.'

'No; I didn't want to start a public argument. There seemed no point in that. I made my preliminary experiments in secret, and was entirely satisfied, so there was no need to make any more.'

'Indeed! And may one ask, my dear Fergusson, what your secret is?'

'It's this, gentlemen, and it's very simple.'

The attention of the audience was strained to the utmost, and the doctor quietly went on as follows.

CHAPTER X

Preliminary trials – The doctor's five containers – The gas

'MANY ATTEMPTS have been made, gentlemen, to rise and drop at will in a balloon without loss of gas or ballast. A French aeronaut, M. Meunier, proposed to achieve this object by means of compressed air. Dr van Hecke, a Belgian, using planes and paddles, developed a vertical force which in most cases would have been inadequate. The practical results obtained by these methods were negligible.

'I therefore made up my mind to approach the question more directly. To begin with, I do away entirely with ballast, except for emergencies, such as the breakdown of my apparatus or the need to rise instantly in order to avoid some unexpected obstacle.

'My method of rising and descending consists merely in expanding or contracting the gas contained in the envelope of the balloon by changing the temperature; and this is how I do it.

'You saw me bring on board with the car several containers the purpose of which was unknown to you. There are five of them. The first contains about twenty-five gallons of water, to which I add a few drops of sulphuric acid to increase its conductivity. I then decompose it by means of a powerful Bunsen battery. Water, as you know, is made up of two parts hydrogen and one part oxygen. Separated by the battery, the oxygen is collected from its positive pole in a second container, while a third, fitted above the second and of double its capacity, takes the hydrogen coming from the negative pole.

'These two containers are connected with a fourth by means of taps, the bore of one of which is double that of the other. This container is called the mixing chamber, for it is there that the two gases, separated by the decomposition of the water, mix. The capacity of this chamber is about forty-one cubic feet, and the upper part is fitted with a platinum tube to which a tap is fixed. You will realise, gentlemen, that the apparatus I am describing to you is purely and simply an oxy-hydrogen burner, the temperature of which is greater than that of a blacksmith's forge.

'That being clear, I will pass on to the second part of the apparatus. From the lower part of my balloon, which is hermetically closed, project two tubes a little distance apart. One begins in the middle of the upper layers of the hydrogen, the other among the lower. At intervals these two tubes are fitted with strong rubber joints which allow them to give to the swaying of the balloon. They both reach as far as the car where they enter a cylindrical chamber which is called the heating chamber, and is closed at its two extremities by strong discs. The pipe from the lower part of the balloon enters this cylinder through the lower disc, after which it becomes a spiral, the coil stretching to the full height of the cylinder. Before emerging again, this spiral passes through a small cone the convex base of which, shaped like a skull-cap, bulges downwards. To the apex of this cone is fitted the second pipe, which, as I have explained, connects with the lower part of the balloon.

'The convex base of the cone is of platinum to prevent its melting under the action of the heating chamber, which is situated at the bottom of the iron case, inside the spiral, so that the flame just touches the base of the cone.

'You know, gentlemen, the principle of a furnace for the central heating of a house. You know how it works. The air of the rooms is forced through the pipes and returned at a higher temperature. What I have just described to you is nothing more or less than a central heating furnace.

'Now, what actually happens? When the heating apparatus is lit, the hydrogen in the spiral and convex cone is heated and rises rapidly through the pipe leading to the upper part of the balloon. A vacuum is formed below which draws down the gas from the lower parts. This, in its turn, is heated and is constantly being replaced. In this way a very rapid flow of gas takes place through the pipes and spiral, the gas being continually drawn from the balloon and returning to it after being heated.

'Now gases expand by of their volume per degree of temperature. If, therefore, I increase the temperature by 18 degrees, the volume of the hydrogen in the balloon will be increased by or 1674 cubic feet. It will thus displace 1674 additional cubic feet of air, and this will increase its lifting force by 130 lbs. This, then, is tantamount to throwing out the same weight of ballast. If I increase the temperature by 180 degrees, the gas will increase in volume by , will displace 16,740 additional cubic feet, and the lifting force will increase by 1300 lbs.

'You see, gentlemen, I can easily obtain considerable variations in the conditions of equilibrium. The volume of the balloon has been so calculated that when it is half-inflated it will displace a weight of air exactly equal to that of the envelope, the hydrogen and the car together with all its passengers and accessories. Up to this point of inflation it is in exact equilibrium in the air, neither rising nor dropping.

'To rise, I raise the gas to a temperature higher than that of the surrounding air by means of my burner, obtaining a greater pressure and increasing the dilation of the balloon, which rises in proportion as I expand the hydrogen. Coming down is, of course, effected by diminishing the heat of the furnace and lowering the temperature. Rising, therefore, will generally be much more rapid than descending, but that is an advantage, as I shall never need to come down rapidly, whereas a quick ascent will be necessary to clear obstacles. The dangers are below, not above.

'Moreover, as I have already told you, I am taking a certain amount of ballast, which will allow me to rise even quicker still, should that prove necessary. My emission pipe, situated near the top of the balloon, becomes nothing more than a safety-valve. The balloon always retains its full charge of hydrogen, and the variations of temperature that I bring about in the enclosed gas are of themselves sufficient to allow me to rise or drop.

'There's just one thing, gentlemen, that I should like to add as a practical detail. The combustion of hydrogen and oxygen at the top of the furnace produces only steam. I have therefore fitted the lower part of the iron cylinder with an escape-valve functioning at less than two atmospheres' pressure. Consequently, as soon as the steam develops this pressure, it is automatically released.

'And now for some exact figures. 25 gallons of water decomposed into its constituent elements give 222 lbs of oxygen and 28 lbs of hydrogen. This represents, at atmospheric pressure, 2050 cubic feet of oxygen and 4100 cubic feet of hydrogen, making 6150 cubic feet of the mixture. The tap of my furnace when fully open can pass 27 cubic feet an hour, with a flame at least six times as strong as that of a large street lamp. On an average, then, to maintain an ordinary altitude, I shall not burn more than 9 cubic feet per hour. My 25 gallons of water therefore represent for me 683 hours of travel in the air, or rather more than 26 days. But, as I can come down when I like and replenish my supply of water on the way, my journey could be prolonged indefinitely.

'That is my secret, gentlemen. It is simple and, like all simple things, cannot fail to succeed. Expansion and contraction of the gas in the balloon; such is my method, and it involves no cumbersome planes or engines. A furnace to produce the changes of temperature, a chamber to heat the gas: these are neither cumbersome nor heavy. I think, then, that I have provided myself with all the essential conditions for success.'

With these words Dr Fergusson brought his discourse to a conclusion and was heartily applauded. There were no objections to his scheme. Everything had been foreseen and solved.

'All the same,' said the captain, 'it may be dangerous.'

'And what if it is?' the doctor answered quietly. 'So long as it's practicable.'

CHAPTER XI

*Arrival at Zanzibar – The British consul – Threatening
attitude of the inhabitants – The island of Koumbeni – The
rain-makers – Inflation of the balloon – Departure on the
8th April – Final farewells – The Victoria*

A CONSTANTLY FAVOURABLE wind had hastened the progress of the *Resolute* towards her destination. The navigation of the Mozambique Channel was performed in particularly calm conditions. The sea-journey augured well for the journey by air. Everyone was looking forward to the arrival and to giving the final touches to Dr Fergusson's preparations. At last the ship came in sight of the town of Zanzibar, which is situated on the island of the same name, and at 11 a.m. on the 15th of April she dropped anchor in the harbour.

The island of Zanzibar belongs to the Imam of Muscat, an ally of France and England, and is beyond doubt his finest colony. The harbour is used by a large number of ships from neighbouring countries. The island is separated from the African coast by a channel which is not more than thirty miles wide at its widest point. Zanzibar carries on a large trade in gum, ivory, and especially ebony, for the town is the great slave-market where all the booty captured in the wars in which the chiefs of the interior are constantly engaged is collected. This traffic also extends over the whole east coast as far north as the Nile, and Monsieur G. Lejean has seen the trade openly carried on under the French flag.

The moment the *Resolute* arrived, the British consul at Zanzibar came on board to place himself at the disposal of the doctor, of whose plans he had been informed through the European newspapers of the month before. Up to this time, however, he belonged to the large army of sceptics.

'I had doubts,' he said, as he shook hands with Samuel Fergusson, 'but now I'm convinced.'

He offered the hospitality of his own house to the doctor, Dick Kennedy, and, of course, the worthy Joe. Through him the doctor was able to acquaint himself with the letters received from Captain Speke. The latter and his companions had suffered terribly from hunger and bad weather before reaching Ugogo. They were only advancing with extreme difficulty and did not think that they would be able to send any more news through for some time.

'These are the dangers and trials we intend to avoid,' said the doctor.

The baggage of the three travellers was transferred to the consul's house and preparations were made for unshipping the balloon on to the beach of Zanzibar. There was a favourable site near the signalling mast, adjoining an enormous erection which would have protected it against the east wind. This great tower, shaped like a barrel standing on end, and beside which the Heidelberg tun[40] would have looked like a mere cask, was used as a fort, and on its platform Beloutchis, armed with lances, were lounging about like a collection of chattering loafers.

When it came to unshipping the balloon, however, the consul was warned that the population of the island would oppose this by force. There is nothing blinder than the rage of fanatics. The news of the arrival of a Christian who was to rise into the air was received with fury. The negroes, who were more excited than the Arabs, regarded the project as an attack on their religion. They imagined that it was an attempt against the sun and moon. These two astral bodies are objects of worship in Africa, so it was resolved to oppose such a sacrilegious expedition.

Hearing of this attitude, the consul discussed the situation with Dr Fergusson and Captain Pennet. The latter had no intention of giving way to threats, but his friend persuaded him to listen to reason.

'We shall, of course, get the better of them in the end,' he told him. 'The Imam's garrison would even come to our assistance at a pinch. But, my dear captain, an accident might easily happen. It would not require much to do an irreparable injury to my balloon, and then the trip would be hopelessly compromised. So we must act with great caution.'

'But what can we do? If we land on the African coast, we shall come up against the same difficulties. What are we to do about it?'

'Nothing could be simpler,' the consul replied. 'Look at those islands the other side of the harbour. Land your balloon on one of those, surround yourselves with a cordon of sailors, and you'll run no risks.'

'Splendid,' said the doctor, 'and we'll be able to get on with our preparations undisturbed.'

The captain gave in to this advice and the *Resolute* headed for the island of Koumbeni. During the morning of the 16th of April the balloon was safely placed in the middle of a clearing of the great woods that cover the island. Two masts eighty feet high were erected eighty feet apart. A combination of pulleys fitted to the ends of these enabled the balloon to be lifted by means of a cross-rope. It was completely deflated. The inner balloon was attached to the top of the outer so that it would be lifted at the same time. To the lower extremity of each balloon were fitted the two pipes for supplying the hydrogen.

The day of the 17th was spent in setting up the apparatus for producing the gas. This consisted of thirty casks in which the sulphuric acid, diluted with water, was decomposed by means of iron. The hydrogen, having been washed on the way, passed into a huge central cask and then through the pipes into the two balloons. In this way each balloon received the exact amount of gas required. The operation consumed 1,866 gallons of sulphuric acid, 16,050 lbs of iron and 966 gallons of water.

The work was begun during the following night, at about 3 a.m., and lasted about eight hours. In the morning the balloon, in its net, was swaying gracefully above the car, which was held down by a large number of sacks filled with earth. The expansion apparatus was mounted with great care, and the pipes projecting from the balloon were fixed to the cylinder. Anchors, ropes, instruments, rugs, tent, guns, all had to be stowed in their appointed places in the car. The supply of water was brought from Zanzibar. The 200 lbs of ballast were divided into fifty bags and placed in the bottom of the car, but within easy reach.

These preparations lasted until 5 p.m., and meanwhile sentries kept a constant look-out round the island, and the *Resolute*'s boats patrolled the channel. The negroes continued to give vent to their anger by means of yells, grimaces and contortions. The witch-doctors dashed about between the various groups, inflaming their excitement, and a few fanatics attempted to swim out to the island but were easily driven back. Then the witch-doctors, the 'rain-makers,' who claim to control the clouds, summoned the hurricanes and 'stone showers' (hail) to their aid. To do this they gathered leaves from all the different species of trees that grow in the country, boiled them over a slow fire, and meanwhile slaughtered a sheep by driving a long needle into its heart. But in spite of these rites the sky remained clear and the sheep and grimaces were wasted.

The negroes now abandoned themselves to frenzied orgies, making themselves drunk with 'tembo,' a potent liquor drawn from the coco-nut palm, or with a very strong beer called 'togwa.' Their singing, devoid of any distinguishable melody, but with a very regular rhythm, continued far into the night.

About six in the evening the travellers assembled at a farewell dinner given by the captain and his officers. Kennedy, whom they had given up questioning, was heard to mutter a few words, but no one caught what he said. He never took his eyes off the doctor. Altogether this was a gloomy meal. The imminence of the supreme moment filled the minds of all with anxious thoughts. What had fate in store for these bold venturers? Would they ever be restored to the circle of their friends? Would they ever again sit at their own firesides? If their means of transport happened to fail them, what would become of them among these savage races, in these unexplored regions, in the heart of these vast wastes? Such were the thoughts, hitherto only transient and little heeded, that invaded their over-excited imaginations. Dr Fergusson, still as cool and impassive as ever, chatted about one thing and another, but it was in vain that he tried to drive off this infectious depression: he met with no success.

As there was fear of some sort of demonstration against the persons of the doctor and his companions, they all three slept aboard the *Resolute*. At 6 a.m. they left their cabins and made for the island of Koumbeni. The balloon was gently swaying to the east wind. The sacks of earth which held it down were replaced by a score of sailors. Captain Pennet and his officers had come to watch the solemn departure. Just at this moment Kennedy went straight up to the doctor, took his hand and said:

'It's settled that I'm coming, Samuel?'

'Quite settled, old man.'

'I've done all in my power to stop this expedition?'

'Everything.'

'Then I have an easy conscience as far as that's concerned, and I'm coming with you.'

'I knew you would,' the doctor answered, an expression of emotion passing rapidly over his face.

The moment for the final farewells had arrived. The captain and his officers warmly shook hands with their intrepid friends, not forgetting the worthy Joe, who was full of pride and delight. All present were anxious to grip the doctor's hand.

At 9 a.m. the three men took their places in the car. The doctor lit his burner and forced the flame so as to produce heat rapidly. A few minutes later the balloon, which was hovering over the ground in perfect equilibrium, began to rise. The sailors had to pay out the ropes that were holding her. The car rose about twenty feet.

'My friends,' shouted the doctor, standing up between his two companions and raising his hat, 'let us christen our airship by a name that will bring her luck; let us call her the *Victoria*!'

A tremendous cheer went up: 'Long live the Queen! Hurrah for England!'

At this moment the lifting force of the balloon increased enormously. Fergusson, Kennedy and Joe called a last farewell to their friends.

'Let go!' cried the doctor. And the *Victoria* rose rapidly into the air, while the four guns of the *Resolute* thundered in her honour.

CHAPTER XII

Crossing the straits – Mrima – Kennedy's remarks and a suggestion from Joe – A recipe for coffee – Usaramo – The unhappy Maizan – Mount Duthumi – The doctor's maps – A night over a nopal

THE AIR WAS CLEAR, the wind moderate. The *Victoria* climbed almost vertically to a height of 1500 feet, indicated by a drop of not quite two inches in the column of the barometer. At this height a more decided current carried the balloon in a southwesterly direction. What a magnificent panorama unrolled itself below the eyes of the explorers! The island of Zanzibar was displayed in its entirety, its deeper colour causing it to stand out as though on a huge relief map; the fields looked like samples of various coloured stuffs, and the forests and jungle like small clumps of trees. The inhabitants of the island had the appearance of insects. The cheers and shouts gradually faded away and the gunfire of the ship alone shook the lower folds of the balloon.

'How beautiful it all is!' exclaimed Joe, breaking the silence for the first time. He received no reply. The doctor was busy watching the variations of the barometer and noting the different details of the ascent. Kennedy's eyes were inadequate to take in all he wanted to see. The rays of the sun came to the assistance of the furnace. The tension of the gas increased and the *Victoria* attained a height of 2500 feet. The *Resolute* now looked like a pinnace, and the African coast could be traced to westward by a long line of foam.

'You're very quiet,' said Joe.

'We're looking,' the doctor answered, pointing his glasses towards the continent.

'I can't help talking.'

'Go ahead, Joe. Talk as much as you like.'

Joe broke into a succession of onomatopœic sounds. A torrent of 'ohs,' 'ahs' and 'eehs' poured from his lips.

While they were passing over the sea the doctor thought it wise to maintain the height they had reached. It enabled him to command a wider view of the coast. The thermometer and barometer, hanging under the half-open tent, could be readily observed. A second barometer placed under cover was to be used for the night watches. In two hours the *Victoria*, now moving at rather more than eight miles an hour, was drawing near to the coast. The doctor decided to come down a little. He lowered the flame of the furnace and the balloon descended to 300 feet.

He found that they were above Mrima, as this part of the East African coast is called. It was edged by a thick border of mangroves, the thick roots of which, exposed to the waves of the Indian Ocean, were left exposed, for the tide was out. The dunes which had once formed the coast-line swelled up against the horizon, and Mount Nguru stood up sheer to the north-west.

The *Victoria* passed close to a village which the doctor recognised from the map as Faole. The whole population had turned out, and howled with rage and fear. Arrows were vainly shot at the monster of the air soaring majestically above all this impotent fury. The wind was blowing them south, but this did not worry the doctor, as it would enable him to follow the route taken by Captains Burton and Speke. Kennedy had by now become as talkative as Joe and the two exchanged ejaculations of admiration.

'A bit better than travelling by coach,' said one.

'Or steamer,' replied the other.

'I don't know that I think much of railways either,' went on Kennedy. 'I like to see where I'm going.'

'What price balloons!' said Joe. 'You don't feel as if you were moving and the scenery slides along under you to be looked at.'

'What a view! Splendid! Perfect! Like dreaming in a hammock.'

'What about some lunch, sir?' said Joe, whose appetite had been sharpened by the fresh air.

'Good idea, Joe.'

'It won't take long to cook; some biscuit and tinned meat.'

'And as much coffee as you like,' added the doctor. 'You can borrow a little heat from my furnace; there's plenty to spare and it might save the danger of a fire.'

'That would be pretty awful,' Kennedy answered. 'It's like hanging under a powder-magazine.'

'Not at all,' said Fergusson; 'and even if the gas did get on fire, it would burn gradually and we should come down, which would be a nuisance. But don't worry; our balloon is quite gas-tight.'

'Well, in that case, let's have something to eat,' said Kennedy.

'Here you are, gentlemen,' said Joe; 'and while I'm having mine I'll go and make you some coffee which I think you'll find extra special.'

'It's a fact,' said the doctor, 'that among his thousand virtues Joe has an extraordinary gift for preparing that delicious beverage. He uses a mixture of various ingredients which he has always kept a secret from me.'

'Well, sir. As we're in the open I can let you into the secret. It's only a mixture of equal parts of mocha, bourbon and rio-nunez.'

A few minutes later three steaming cups were served to crown a substantial lunch which was seasoned by the good-humour of the company, and afterwards each man returned to his post of observation. The landscape was remarkable for its extreme fertility. Narrow, winding paths were hidden under a vaulting of foliage. The balloon passed over fields of ripe tobacco, maize and barley. Here and there stretched vast fields of rice with its straight stems and purplish flowers. Sheep and goats could be seen penned in large enclosures raised on piles to protect them from the leopards. A luxuriant vegetation covered this rich soil. In many villages the sight of the balloon roused fresh clamour and bewilderment, and Dr Fergusson prudently kept out of range of arrows. The inhabitants, gathered round their groups of huts, continued for a long time to hurl their vain imprecations after the balloon.

At noon the doctor, consulting his map, reckoned that he was over the district of Usaramo. The balloon seemed to gambol over the masses of coco-nut palms, papaws and cotton-trees. Joe took this vegetation for granted the moment he knew he was in Africa. Kennedy saw hares and quails simply asking to be shot; but it would have been waste of powder in view of the impossibility of retrieving the game. Travelling at a rate of twelve miles per hour, the aeronauts soon found themselves in long. 38° 20' E., above the village of Tunda.

'That's the place,' said the doctor, 'where Burton and Speke were attacked by virulent fever and thought for a moment that it was all up with their expedition. Though they weren't far from the coast, fatigue and privations were already making themselves seriously felt.' In fact, a malaria hung perpetually over this country and even Dr Fergusson could only avoid it by lifting his balloon above the miasmas which the hot sun drew from the damp earth. Every now and again they caught sight of a caravan resting in a kraal, awaiting the cool of the evening to resume its march. These kraals are large plots of ground surrounded by hedges and jungle, affording shelter for travellers not only against wild beasts but also against the marauding tribes of the country. The natives could be seen running away in all directions at the sight of the balloon. Kennedy wanted to get a closer look at them, but Fergusson refused to listen to this suggestion.

'The chiefs are armed with muskets,' he said, 'and our balloon would offer too easy a target.'

'Would a bullet hole bring us down, sir?' asked Joe.

'Not immediately, but the hole would soon develop into a big rent through which all the gas would soon escape.'

'Well, let's keep away from the brutes. I wonder what they think of us flying through the air like this. I'm sure they'll want to worship us.'

'We'll let ourselves be worshipped then, but from a distance. That's always an advantage. Look, the country's changing. There aren't so many villages and no more mangroves. They don't grow in this latitude. The country is getting hilly and it looks as though we are coming near the mountains.'

'As a matter of fact, I think I can see some over there,' said Kennedy.

'To westward – those are the first chains of the Urizaras, probably Mount Duthumi, behind which I hope to spend the night. I'll turn up the flame, for we shall have to keep at a height of five or six hundred feet.'

'That's a great idea of yours, sir,' said Joe, 'it's so easy to work. Just turn a tap and the thing's done.'

'That's better,' said the Scotsman when the balloon had lifted. 'The glare of the sun on that red sand was getting unbearable.'

'What fine trees!' cried Joe. 'Of course they're what you'd expect, but they really are fine specimens. It would only take a dozen of them to make a forest.'

'Those are baobabs,' Dr Fergusson answered. 'Look! That one must have a girth of a hundred feet. It might have been at the foot of that very tree that Maizan, the Frenchman, died in 1845, for we're over the village of Deje la Mhora into which he ventured alone. He was captured by the chief of this country and tied to the trunk of a baobab, after which the bloodthirsty nigger cut his tendons one by one, while the tribe chanted their war-song. He then cut his throat a little way, stopped to sharpen his knife that had become rather blunted, and then tore off the wretched man's head before the neck had been cut through. The poor fellow was twenty-six years old.'

'And France has not demanded vengeance for the crime?' Kennedy asked.

'France put in a claim. The Sultan of Zanzibar did all he could to capture the murderer, but without success.'

'I vote we don't stop,' said Joe. 'We'll go up higher, sir, if you take my advice.'

'I'm quite ready to do so, Joe, especially as that's Mount Duthumi standing up ahead of us. If my reckoning is correct, we shall be over it before seven.'

'We're not going to travel by night, are we?' asked Kennedy.

'No more than we can help. If we take precautions and keep a good look-out we shall be able to without risk; but it's not enough just to cross Africa, we want to see it.'

'So far we've had nothing to complain of, sir. It's the best cultivated and most fertile country in the world instead of being a desert. Now we know how much good geography is.'

'Wait, Joe, wait. We'll see before long.'

About half-past six in the evening, the *Victoria* was directly in front of Mount Duthumi. To cross it, they would have to rise to over 3000 feet, to do which the doctor had only to raise the temperature by 18° Fahrenheit. Kennedy pointed out the obstacles that had to be cleared, and the *Victoria* sailed just over the mountain.

At 8 p.m. they were running down the opposite slope, which was less abrupt. The anchors were thrown out of the car and one, catching the branches of a huge nopal, established a firm hold. At once Joe slid down the rope and made it fast. The silk ladder was lowered and he climbed back again briskly. The balloon remained almost motionless in the lee of the mountain. The evening meal was prepared and the travellers, their appetites stimulated by their journey through the air, made a big hole in their stores.

'How far have we come today?' asked Kennedy.

The doctor took a reckoning on the moon and consulted the excellent map which served as his guide, and which was taken from the *Atlas der neuesten Entdeckungen in Afrika*, published at Gotha by his learned friend Petermann,[41] who had presented him with a copy. This atlas could be used for the whole of the doctor's journey, for it gave Burton and Speke's route to the Great Lakes, Dr Barth's discoveries in the Sudan, Lower Senegal according to Guillaume Lejean, and the Niger delta as surveyed by Dr Baikie.

Fergusson had also provided himself with a work which contained in one volume all the information that had been acquired about the Nile. This was called *The Sources of the Nile*, and was a general survey of the basin of that river and of its main stream, with the history of Nilotic discovery by Charles Beke,[42] D.D. He also possessed an excellent map published in *Bulletins of the London Royal Geographical Society*, so that no area already discovered was likely to baffle him.

Measuring on his map with his dividers, he found that their latitudinal route had covered two degrees or 120 miles in a westerly direction. Kennedy observed that the route was southerly, but the doctor did not mind this as he was anxious, as far as possible, to follow the tracks of his predecessors.

It was decided to divide the night into three watches so that each might take his turn in guarding the other two. The doctor was to take the watch beginning at nine, Kennedy that beginning at midnight, and he in his turn was to be relieved by Joe at 3 a.m. Kennedy and Joe therefore wrapped themselves up in their blankets, lay down under the awning and slept soundly while Dr Fergusson kept watch.

CHAPTER XIII

*Change in the weather – Kennedy attacked by fever – The
doctor's medicine – Travel by land – The Imenge basin – The
Rubeho Mountains – Six thousand feet up – A halt by day*

THE NIGHT WAS CALM, but when he woke up on Saturday morning Kennedy complained of lassitude and the shivering of fever. The weather was changing. The sky, covered with thick clouds, seemed to be gathering for rain. Zungomero is a dreary country, where it rains continually except, perhaps, for a fortnight in January. It was not long before heavy rain began to pour down upon the travellers. Below them the roads cut out by *nullahs*, a sort of intermittent torrent, became impassable, especially as they were also overgrown with thorny shrubs and gigantic creepers. The emanations of sulphuretted hydrogen mentioned by Captain Burton could be distinctly detected.

'According to Burton,' the doctor said, 'and he's right, it smells as though a corpse were concealed in every thicket.'

'Beastly country,' answered Joe, 'and I don't think it's done Mr Kennedy any good spending the night here.'

'As a matter of fact, I have a pretty bad touch of fever,' said the Scot.

'There's nothing surprising about that, old man. We're in one of the unhealthiest districts in Africa. But we're not going to stop long. Let's make a start.'

Joe skilfully freed the anchor and climbed back up the ladder into the car. The doctor quickly expanded the gas and the *Victoria* set off again before a stiffish breeze. Nothing was to be seen in the pestilent mist except a very occasional hut, but soon the appearance of the country changed. It often happens in Africa that an unhealthy area is of quite small dimensions and borders on districts which are perfectly salubrious. Kennedy was obviously very unwell, the fever sapping his natural energy.

'This is no place to be ill in,' he said, wrapping himself up in his blanket and lying down under the awning.

'Have a little patience, Dick, and you'll soon be well again,' Dr Fergusson replied.

'Look here, Samuel, if you've got anything in your medicine-chest that might put me right, give me some at once. I'll swallow it with my eyes shut.'

'I've something better than that, old man. I'm going to give you a cooling draught that will cost you nothing.'

'What is it?'

'It's quite simple. I'm just going to rise above those clouds which are swamping us and get away from this pestilent atmosphere. Give me ten minutes to expand the hydrogen.'

Before the ten minutes were up the travellers were above the rain zone.

'Wait a bit, Dick, and you'll feel the effects of the pure air and sunshine.'

'Well, that is a cure!' said Joe. 'It's wonderful!'

'No. It's quite natural.'

'Oh, yes, I suppose it's natural enough, sir.'

'I take Dick where the air is better, as they always do in Europe. Just as, if we were at Martinique, I should send him to the Piton Mountains to escape yellow fever.'

'Why, this balloon's a perfect paradise,' said Kennedy, already feeling more comfortable.

'At any rate, it takes us there, sir,' Joe answered solemnly.

It was strange to see masses of cloud now piled up under the car. They rolled over one another and formed a confused mass of light as they reflected the rays of the sun. The *Victoria* reached a height of four thousand feet. The thermometer registered an appreciable drop in the temperature. The earth was no longer visible. Some fifty miles to westward the Rubeho Mountains raised their glistening crests These mountains bound the country of Ugogo in long. 30°20'. The wind was blowing at twenty miles an hour, but the travellers had no sensation of their speed. They felt no swaying and were not even conscious that they were moving.

Three hours later the doctor's prediction was realised. Kennedy's fever had left him and he lunched with a good appetite.

'That beats sulphate of quinine hollow,' he said with relief.

'This is certainly the place I shall retire to in my old age,' said Joe.

About 10 a.m. the atmosphere cleared. A great hole appeared in the clouds and the earth once more came into view. The *Victoria* was dropping imperceptibly towards it as Dr Fergusson sought a current which might carry them more to the north-eastward. He found one six hundred feet above the ground. The country became broken, even mountainous. Zungomero faded away to the east together with the last coco-nut palms of that latitude. Soon the crests of mountains stood out more sharply. Peaks rose here and there. It was necessary to keep a constant look-out for the sharp cones which seemed to start up without warning.

'We're among the breakers,' said Kennedy.

'Don't worry, Dick, we shan't run aground.'

'It's a fine way of travelling, all the same!' Joe broke in.

The doctor was indeed handling his balloon with wonderful skill.

'If we had had to march over that waterlogged country,' he said, 'we should have had to plough through the foul mud. Since leaving Zanzibar half our pack animals would have died of fatigue. We should be looking like ghosts and feeling desperate We should have had constant struggles with our guides and porters, and no protection against their savagery. Damp, unbearable, crushing heat by day, and by night often intolerable cold; bitten by flies with mandibles that would go through the thickest canvas and drive men mad; not to mention the wild animals and savage tribes.'

'I'm in no hurry to try it,' Joe answered simply.

'I'm not exaggerating in the least,' Dr Fergusson continued, 'for travellers who have been daring enough to venture into these countries tell stories that would make your blood curdle.'

About eleven o'clock they crossed the Imenge basin. The tribes scattered over the hills vainly threatened the *Victoria* with their weapons. At length they reached the last undulations before the Rubehos which form the third and highest chain of the Usagara Mountains. The travellers took careful note of the geographical conformation of the country. The three ranges, of which the Duthumis form the first stage, are separated by immense longitudinal plains. These lofty ridges take the form of rounded cones between which the earth is strewn with stray boulders and rocks. The steepest declivity of these mountains faces the coast of Zanzibar, while the eastern slopes are merely tilted plateaus. The low-lying areas are covered with black rich soil, where vegetation is very vigorous. Various water-courses make their way eastward to join the Kingani, amid huge clumps of sycamores, tamarinds, calabash-trees and palmyras.

'Look,' said Dr Fergusson. 'We're getting near the Rubehos. In the native language the name means "passage of the wind." It will be wise to cross the sharp ridges at a good height. If my map is right we ought to go up to over five thousand feet.'

'Shall we often have to go as high as that?'

'No, only very seldom. The African mountains are not very high compared with the peaks of Europe and Asia. But in any case, the *Victoria* would have no difficulty in clearing them.'

The gas quickly expanded under the action of the heat, and the balloon lifted very considerably. The expansion of the hydrogen, moreover, presented no danger, as the enormous capacity of the balloon was only three-quarters filled. The barometer, by a drop of nearly eight inches, indicated a rise of six thousand feet.

'Is this going to last long, sir?' asked Joe.

'The atmosphere surrounding the earth extends to a height of six thousand fathoms,' replied the doctor. 'With a big balloon one might go far. MM. Brioschi and Gay-Lussac[43] did, but after a time they began to bleed at the mouth and ears. The air was not breathable. Some years ago two other bold Frenchmen, MM. Barral and Bixio, also ventured very high, but their balloon tore – '

'And they fell?' Kennedy asked sharply.

'Certainly. But as wise men fall, without hurting themselves.'

'Well, gentlemen,' said Joe, 'you may be able to fall like that, but I'm only an ignorant man and I'd rather stop at a reasonable height. It doesn't do to be ambitious.'

At six thousand feet the density of the air had already appreciably diminished. Sound carried badly, and it was more difficult for them to make themselves heard. Sight became blurred, and the eye could only distinguish large masses and that vaguely; men and animals became quite invisible; roads looked like strips of tape and lakes like ponds. The doctor and his companions felt that they were in abnormal conditions. An atmospheric current of tremendous velocity was sweeping them over arid mountains on whose summits great patches of snow startled the eye, and their convulsed appearance indicated some Neptunian labour of the world's first days. The sun shone in the zenith, pouring its rays vertically upon these barren crests. The doctor made a careful sketch of the mountains, which consist of four distinct ridges running almost in a straight line, the most northerly being the longest.

Soon the *Victoria* descended the opposite slope of the Rubehos, skirting a ridge covered with trees of very dark-coloured foliage. Then came the crests and ravines of the sort of wilderness which precedes the Ugogo district. Lower still stretched yellow plains burnt and cracked, and strewn here and there with saline plants and thorny shrubs. A few thickets which later gave place to forests adorned the horizon. The doctor came close to the ground and the anchors were dropped, one of them soon catching the branches of an enormous sycamore. Joe slid quickly down the tree and carefully made fast the anchor. The doctor kept his furnace going to give the balloon sufficient lift to hold her in the air. The wind had dropped almost instantly.

'Now,' said Fergusson, 'take a couple of guns, Dick, one for yourself and one for Joe, and see if between you you can't get us a few good slices of antelope for dinner.'

'Rather,' cried Kennedy. 'Come on, Joe.'

He climbed over the side of the car and went down. Joe had slid down from branch to branch and was stretching himself while he waited. The doctor, relieved of the weight of his companions, was now able to put out his furnace.

'Don't go and fly away, sir!' Joe cried.

'Don't worry, Joe; I'm firmly fixed. I'll get my notes up to date. Good hunting, and be careful. From up here I shall be able to overlook the country round about, and if I see anything the slightest bit suspicious, I'll fire a carbine. That will be the signal for return.'

'Right ho!' Kennedy replied.

CHAPTER XIV

The gum-tree forest – The blue antelope – The signal to return – An unexpected attack – Kanyemi – A night in the air – Mabunguru – Jihoue la Mkoa – Water-supplies – Arrival at Kazeh

THE COUNTRY, with its clayey soil, arid, parched and cracked by the heat, looked a wilderness. Here and there were to be seen the tracks of caravans, whitened bones of men and animals half gnawed away and scattered together in the dust. After walking for about half an hour, Dick and Joe, keeping a sharp look-out and their fingers held to the triggers of their guns, plunged into a forest of gum-trees. They did not know what they might meet with. Without being an expert shot, Joe knew how to handle a gun.

'It does you good to walk again, sir, and yet the going is none too good,' he said as he stumbled among the bits of quartz with which the ground was strewn.

Kennedy signed to his companion to be silent and to halt. They had to manage without a dog and, agile as Joe might be, he could not be expected to have the nose of a spaniel or greyhound. In the bed of a torrent where a few pools of water still stagnated a group of ten antelopes were drinking. The graceful animals seemed to scent danger and showed signs of uneasiness. After each drink they would raise their pretty heads quickly and, with their sensitive nostrils, sniff the air coming to them from their pursuers.

Kennedy skirted some trees while Joe stood motionless. When he came within range he fired. The antelopes vanished in the twinkling of an eye, but one stag fell, hit behind the shoulder, and Kennedy dashed towards his prey. It was a blaubok, a splendid animal of a pale bluish-grey, the belly and the inside of the legs pure white.

'That was a lucky shot,' cried Kennedy. 'This is a very rare species of antelope and I hope I'll be able to preserve his skin.'

'Why, sir, how could you?'

'Why not? Look what a splendid skin.'

'But Dr Fergusson will never allow the extra weight.'

'You're right, Joe. But it's annoying to have to leave such a splendid animal like this.'

'Like this? No, we won't do that, sir. We'll get all the nourishment out of it we can, and if you'll allow me, I'll deal with it as if I was the warden of the Honourable Company of Butchers in London.'

'Go ahead, Joe, but you know, as a hunter I'm as good at eating a bit of game as at shooting it.'

'I'm quite sure of that, sir, so perhaps you'd make an oven with three stones. There's lots of dead wood, and once you get them glowing I shall only be a few minutes.'

'I won't be a minute,' Kennedy replied, and at once set about building his fire, which a few minutes later was blazing.

Joe had cut a dozen cutlets from the antelope and the tenderest pieces from the fillet, which were soon transformed into a savoury grill.

'This will please Dr Fergusson,' said the Scotsman.

'Do you know what I'm thinking about, sir?'

'The job you're doing, I expect; your grill!'

'No, sir, I'm thinking what we should look like if we couldn't find the balloon again.'

'What an idea! Are you expecting the doctor to desert us?'

'No; but supposing his anchor broke away?'

'Impossible. Besides, the doctor could easily bring his balloon down again; he's pretty good at handling her.'

'Supposing the wind carried him off and he couldn't get back to us?'

'Oh, shut up, Joe; your suppositions aren't at all amusing.'

'Well, sir, everything that happens in this world is natural, and as anything may happen, we ought to be ready for anything –'

At this moment a shot rang out.

'What's that?' said Joe.

'My carbine. I recognised its report.'

'A signal!'

'We're in danger.'

'Perhaps he is,' cried Joe.

'Come on.'

The two men quickly picked up their bag and went back the way they had come, following their own footprints. The thickness of the foliage prevented them from seeing the *Victoria*, which could not be far away. Then came a second shot.

'He's in a hurry,' said Joe.

'Yes. There's another.'

'It sounds to me as though he was defending himself.'

'Come on!' and they ran as fast as their legs would carry them.

When they reached the end of the wood the first thing they saw was the *Victoria* still in position and the doctor in the car.

'What's wrong?' asked Kennedy.

'Good God!' cried Joe.

'What is it?'

'Over there. Niggers attacking the balloon.'

Indeed, in the distance there appeared a band of about thirty men hustling one another, gesticulating, shrieking and leaping about at the foot of the sycamore. A few had climbed into the tree and were already among the highest branches. The danger seemed immediate.

'It's all up with the master,' cried Joe.

'Come, Joe, keep calm and look out. We hold the lives of four of those blackguards in our hands. Come on.' When they had run about a mile a fresh gunshot sounded from the car. It hit a tall ruffian who was swarming up the anchor-rope. A lifeless body fell from branch to branch and remained hanging twenty feet from the ground, its arms and legs dangling in the air.

'Great Scott!' said Joe, stopping. 'What's holding the fellow up?'

'What's it matter?' replied Kennedy. 'Run, man, run!'

'Oh, I see, sir,' cried Joe, bursting into a guffaw of laughter. 'It's his tail. It must be a monkey. Why, they're only monkeys after all.'

'That's worse than men,' Kennedy replied as he dashed into the middle of the shrieking band. It was a troop of pretty fearsome baboons, ferocious, cruel and horrible to look at with their dog-like snouts, but a few shots were enough for them and the grimacing horde made off, leaving several victims on the ground. In an instant Kennedy seized the ladder. Joe climbed into the sycamore and freed the anchor. The car came down to him and he got in without difficulty. A few minutes later the *Victoria* was rising in the air and heading eastward before a moderate wind.

'What a battle!' said Joe.

'We thought you were being attacked by natives.'

'Luckily they were only monkeys,' the doctor replied.

'From the distance there's little difference, old man.'

'Nor near to, either,' Joe replied.

'In any case,' Fergusson went on, 'the attack might have been serious. If they'd shaken the anchor loose, who knows where I might have got to?'

'What did I tell you, Mr Kennedy?'

'You were right, Joe. But in addition to being right you were also at that moment cooking some antelope steaks, and it made me hungry to watch you.'

'It would,' the doctor replied; 'antelope's flesh is delicious.'

'You can judge for yourself, sir. Dinner is served.'

It was now four o'clock in the afternoon. The *Victoria* ran into a stronger air-current, the ground rose imperceptibly, and soon the barometer registered a height of 1500 feet above sea-level. The doctor was forced to buoy the balloon up by a considerable expansion of the gas and the burner was working continually. About seven o'clock the *Victoria* was soaring over the Kanyemi basin. The doctor immediately recognised this great stretch of cultivated land, stretching for ten miles, with its villages buried among baobab and calabash-trees. It contains the residence of one of the sultans of Ugogo, where civilisation is perhaps less primitive – the people do not sell the members of their own families quite so frequently, but animals and people all live together in the round, roofless huts that look like haystacks.

After Kanyemi the country became arid and rocky, but half an hour later, in a fertile valley not far from Mdaburu, the vegetation became as vigorous as ever again. As evening came on the wind dropped and the atmosphere seemed to fall asleep. The doctor vainly tried different levels in search of a breeze, and when he saw the whole of Nature at rest he decided to spend the night in the air and, as a precaution, rose about a thousand feet. The *Victoria* hung motionless. The night, splendid with stars, came down in silence.

Dick and Joe stretched themselves out on their peaceful couches and slept soundly during the doctor's watch. At midnight he was relieved by the Scotsman.

'If anything in the slightest degree unusual happens, wake me,' he said; 'and, above all, don't take your eyes off the barometer. It's our compass.'

The night was cold, the temperature being nearly 27 degrees lower than the previous day. The darkness awoke the nightly concert of the animals, driven from their lairs by hunger and thirst; the soprano of the frogs mingling with the howls of the jackals, while the sonorous bass of the lions provided a foundation to the harmonies of this living orchestra.

When he returned to his post in the morning, Doctor Fergusson consulted his compass and noticed that the wind had shifted during the night. The *Victoria* had drifted some thirty miles to the north-eastward during the last two hours or so. She was now passing over Mabunguru, a rocky district strewn with boulders of beautifully polished cyanite, and broken by rocks shaped like a camel's hump. Conical tors, like the rocks of Karnak, stood out of the ground like Druidical dolmens; many bones of elephants and buffaloes lay bleaching here and there. The trees were few, apart from some dense woods to eastward, which sheltered occasional villages.

About seven o'clock, a circular rock appeared, about two miles across, and shaped like an enormous turtle-shell.

'We're on the right track,' said the doctor; 'there's Jihoue la Mkoa, where we're going to halt for a few minutes. I want to get a fresh supply of water for my furnace. Let's look for somewhere to anchor.'

'There aren't many trees about,' Kennedy replied.

'Let's try, anyhow,' said Joe; 'over with the anchors.'

Gradually losing her lift, the balloon slowly neared the ground. The anchor-ropes ran out and one anchor caught a fissure in the rock, bringing the *Victoria* to a standstill. It must not be imagined that the doctor could completely extinguish his burner during a halt. The equilibrium of the balloon had been calculated at sea-level, but the country had been continually rising, and at a height of six or seven hundred feet the balloon would have had a tendency to drop to a lower level than that of the ground. It was therefore necessary to maintain a certain expansion of the gas. Only in an absolute calm would the doctor have allowed the car to rest on the ground, in which case the balloon, relieved of a considerable weight, would have kept in the air without the help of the burner.

The maps showed immense lakes on the western slopes of the Jihoue la Mkoa. Joe set off alone with a cask that would hold about ten gallons and had no difficulty in finding the place he wanted, not far from a little deserted village, where he filled his cask and was back again in less than three-quarters of an hour. He had seen nothing of special interest except, perhaps, the huge footprints of an elephant; he even nearly fell into one of these in which a half-eaten carcass was lying. But he brought back a kind of medlar which the monkeys were eating greedily. The doctor identified it as the fruit of the 'mhenbu,' a tree growing in great abundance in the eastern part of Jihoue la Mkoa. Fergusson was waiting for Joe with a certain amount of impatience, for even a short stay in these inhospitable regions always filled him with anxiety. The water was shipped without difficulty, for the car was almost on a level with the ground. Joe then loosed the anchor and climbed nimbly up to his master's side. The latter at once increased the flame and the *Victoria* resumed her voyage through the air.

She was at this time about a hundred miles from Kazeh, an important settlement in the African interior, which, thanks to a breeze from the south-east, the travellers had hopes of making in the course of the day. They were travelling at about fourteen miles per hour. The handling of the balloon became somewhat difficult. It was impossible to rise without a big expansion of the gas, for the level of the country was, on the average, about three thousand feet. As the doctor preferred, so far as was possible, not to force the expansion, he followed very skilfully the windings of a fairly rapid slope and skimmed over the villages of Thembo and Tura Wels. The latter forms part of Unyamwezi, a magnificent country where the trees attain enormous dimensions, especially the cactus which is gigantic.

About two o'clock, in splendid weather and under a burning sun which stifled the slightest breath of air, the *Victoria* was hovering over the town of Kazeh, about three hundred and fifty miles from the coast.

'We left Zanzibar at nine in the morning,' said the doctor, consulting his notes, 'and in two days our circuitous route has brought us nearly five hundred geographical miles. Burton and Speke took four and a half months to do the same distance.'

CHAPTER XV

Kazeh – The noisy market – The Victoria *sighted –*
The wagangas *– Sons of the Moon – The doctor's walk –*
Population – The royal tembe *– The sultan's wives – Royal*
dissipation – Joe worshipped – How they dance in the Country of
the Moon – Two moons in the sky

KAZEH, an important settlement in Central Africa, is not a town; there
is, in fact, no town in the interior. It is only a collection of six huge
excavations. Within these are enclosed dwellings and slave-huts with
little courts and carefully cultivated gardens. Onions, sweet potatoes,
aubergines, water-melons and delicious mushrooms grow there in
great abundance.

Unyamwezi is the Moon Country at its best, the fertile and luxuriant
park of Africa. In its centre is the district of Unyamyembe, a delightful
place where a few families of the Omani, of pure Arab origin, live in
idleness. They have long trafficked with Central Africa and Arabia in
gums, ivory, calico and slaves. Their caravans cross these equatorial
regions in every direction. They still go to the coast in search of articles
required for the life of luxury and pleasure led by the wealthy
merchants who, surrounded by women and servants, live in this
delightful country the most peaceful and placid life that can be
imagined. All day long they recline on couches, laughing, smoking and
sleeping.

Around these excavations are native dwellings, vast market-places
and fields of cannabis and datura, splendid trees and cool shade; such is
Kazeh. It is also the general rendezvous of caravans; those coming from
the south with their slaves and loads of ivory, and those from the west
carrying cotton and beads to the tribes of the Great Lakes. In the
markets, therefore, there is perpetual excitement, an indescribable
pandemonium made up of the shouts of the porters, the din of drums
and trumpets, the neighing of mules, the braying of donkeys, the
singing of women, the screaming of children, with the whip-cracks of
the jemadars (head-men of caravans) giving the beat for this pastoral
symphony. In attractive disorder are displayed brilliantly-coloured
stuffs, ivories, rhinoceros' horns, sharks' teeth, honey, tobacco and
cotton. The strangest bargains are conducted, in which the value of

each object depends solely on the desires it excites.

Suddenly all the excitement, movement and noise ceased. The *Victoria* had just been sighted in the sky, hovering majestically, and gradually dropping straight down. Men, women, children, slaves, merchants, Arabs and niggers all vanished, taking cover in the *tembes* and huts.

'My dear Samuel,' said Kennedy, 'if we go on producing an effect like this, we shan't find it easy to establish business relations with these people.'

'But there's one bit of business which would be easy enough,' said Joe, 'and that would be to go down quietly and pinch some of the more valuable goods, without bothering our heads about the merchants. It would be worth doing.'

'Steady,' answered the doctor. 'These natives were frightened at first, but superstition or curiosity will soon bring them back.'

'Do you think so, sir?'

'We'll see. But it will be just as well not to get too close. The *Victoria* is not armoured, so there's no protection against bullets or arrows.'

'Are you thinking, then, of trying to talk with these natives, Samuel?'

'Why not? If it can be done,' answered the doctor. 'In a place like Kazeh there must be Arab merchants a little more educated and less uncivilised than the rest. I remember Burton and Speke had nothing but praise for the hospitality of the inhabitants of the town, so we may as well try.'

The *Victoria* had been almost imperceptibly nearing the ground. They threw out one of the anchors, which caught the crest of a tree near the market-place. The whole population at this very moment emerged from their holes, sticking out their heads cautiously. Several *wagangas*, distinguishable by their ornaments of conical shells, came forward boldly. These were the local magicians. At their belts they carried little black gourds, smeared with fat, and various devices used in the practice of magic, all of typically medical dirtiness. Gradually a crowd collected round them, including women and children; the drums did their utmost to drown one another, hands were clapped together and arms stretched out towards the sky.

'That's their way of worshipping,' said Doctor Fergusson.

'Unless I'm mistaken, we're going to be called upon to play an important rôle.'

'All right, sir, get on with it.'

'It's quite likely, my dear Joe, that you are about to become a god.'

'Well, sir, that doesn't worry me, and I rather like the smell of incense.'

At this moment one of the magicians, a *myanga*, made a sign, and all the tumult died down into perfect silence. He addressed some words to the travellers but in an unknown language. Doctor Fergusson, who could not understand what was said, tried at random a few words of Arabic, and was at once answered in the same tongue. The orator burst out into a tremendous harangue in very ornate language, which was attentively listened to by the crowd. The doctor at once realised that the *Victoria* had been taken for the Moon herself who had graciously come down to the town with her three sons, an honour which would never be forgotten in this, her favourite land.

The doctor replied with great dignity that every thousand years the Moon toured her realm, as she liked to show herself more closely to her worshippers. He begged them, therefore, to put themselves at their ease and to use her divine presence as an opportunity for making known their needs and desires.

The wizard replied in his turn that the sultan, the *mwani*, who had been an invalid for many years, solicited the aid of heaven and invited the Sons of the Moon to visit him. The doctor communicated the invitation to his companions.

'And you really mean to visit this negro king?' Kennedy asked.

'Certainly. These people seem friendly and the weather is calm; there's not a breath of wind; so we have nothing to worry about as far as the *Victoria* is concerned.'

'But what will you do?'

'Set your mind at rest, old man. A little medicine will pull me through.' Then, addressing the crowd: 'The Moon, taking pity on the beloved sovereign of the children of Unyamwezi, has entrusted to us the charge of healing him. Let him prepare to receive us.'

The shouting, singing and demonstrations redoubled in vigour, and the vast swarm of black heads were once more set in motion.

'And now, my friends,' said Doctor Fergusson, 'we must be ready for anything. We may at any moment be forced to make a bolt for it. Dick, therefore, will remain in the car and keep the necessary lift with the furnace. The anchor is firmly fixed. There's nothing to be afraid of. I'm going down and Joe will come with me, but he will remain at the foot of the ladder.'

'What! you're going to see this cut-throat alone?' exclaimed Kennedy.

'What!' cried Joe, 'you're not going to let me come with you?'

'No! I'm going alone. These good people imagine that their great goddess the Moon has come to visit them. I'm protected by superstition, so don't worry, and each of you stay at the post I have assigned.'

'Since you insist – ' said the Scot.

'Keep an eye on the gas expansion.'

'Right ho!'

The shouts of the negroes grew louder still. They were energetically invoking celestial intervention.

'Just look,' said Joe. 'Surely they're taking rather a high line with their good moon and her mighty sons.'

Armed with his portable medicine chest, the doctor landed, preceded by Joe. The latter, solemn and dignified as the occasion demanded, sat down at the foot of the ladder with his legs crossed under him in the Arab fashion, and part of the crowd gathered round him in a respectful circle. Meanwhile Doctor Fergusson, accompanied by the blare of musical instruments and by religious dances, deliberately approached the royal *tembe*, which was situated some way outside the town. It was about three o'clock in the afternoon and the sun was shining brilliantly, which was the least it could do under the circumstances. The doctor walked with dignity, surrounded by the *wagangas*, who controlled the crowd. He was soon joined by the natural son of the sultan, quite a well-set-up young man who, in accordance with the custom of the country, was the sole heir to his father's possessions, to the exclusion of the legitimate children. He prostrated himself before the Son of the Moon, who raised him to his feet with a gracious gesture.

Three-quarters of an hour later the excited procession, following shady paths cut through the luxuriant vegetation, reached the sultan's palace, a square building called *Ititenya*, on the slope of a hill. A kind of veranda formed by the overhanging thatched roof surrounded the exterior, supported by wooden pillars upon which there had been some attempt at carving. The walls were ornamented with long lines of reddish clay, intended to portray the forms of men and serpents; the latter, of course, being the more successful. The roof of this dwelling did not rest immediately upon the walls, so that the air could circulate freely. For the rest, there were no windows and little in the way of doors.

Dr Fergusson was received with great ceremony by the guards and favourites, men of high birth called *wanyamwezis*, the purest breed of the Central African populations, strong and vigorous, well-built and of fine bearing. Their hair, divided into a large number of little plaits, fell on to their shoulders, and their cheeks were striped from forehead to mouth with black or blue scars. From their ears, which were horribly distended, hung wooden discs and resin ornaments. They were dressed in brilliantly-dyed stuffs. The soldiers were armed with assegais, bows with barbed arrows poisoned with the juice of the euphorbia, cutlasses, *simes* (a long sabre toothed like a saw), and small battle-axes.

The doctor entered the palace, where, in spite of the sultan's illness, the clamour, already terrific, redoubled as he entered. On the lintel of the door he noticed the tails of hares and the manes of zebras hanging as talismans. He was received by the whole troop of the sultan's wives to the harmonious music of the *upatu* (a kind of cymbal made from the bottom of a copper pot) and the crash of the *klindo* (a drum five feet high, hollowed out of a tree trunk), which two virtuosi were attacking with their fists.

Most of the women were very pretty. They laughed and smoked *thang* in great black pipes. Their well-formed figures were draped in long gracefully-hanging robes, and they wore kilts of calabash fibre fastened at the waist. Six of them, and these were not the least gay of the company, were set apart from the rest as they were under sentence of cruel torture. On the death of the sultan they were to be buried alive at his side to distract his eternal solitude.

Doctor Fergusson, who had taken all this in at a glance, approached the bedside of the sovereign. There he saw a man of about forty years of age, wrecked by debauchery of every kind, and with whom there was obviously nothing to be done. His malady, which had lasted for years, was nothing more than chronic drunkenness. The royal rake had practically lost consciousness, and all the ammoniac in the world could not have set him on his legs again.

During the doctor's solemn examination of the patient the favourites and women knelt in an attitude of reverence. With a few drops of strong cordial the doctor put a brief spark of life into the torpid body. The sultan moved, and this sign of life in what for some hours had seemed a corpse was received by a further redoubling of the shouting in the doctor's honour. The latter, who had had enough of it, waved aside his over-demonstrative admirers and left the palace. It was six o'clock in the evening.

During his absence Joe waited patiently at the foot of the ladder, the crowd meanwhile showing him the greatest respect. As a true Son of the Moon he resigned himself to this. For a divine being he looked a good fellow, showing himself approachable, even familiar towards the young African women, who never tired of gazing at him and kept up a friendly conversation.

'Worship away, ladies; keep it up,' he said. 'I'm not such a bad sort of cove, even though I am the son of a goddess.'

Propitiatory gifts were offered him, such as are usually deposited in the *mzimus* or fetish huts. These consisted of ears of barley and *pombe*. Joe felt called upon to taste this kind of strong beer, but his palate, though broken to wine and whisky, could not stand the potency of this beverage. He pulled a terrible face which the spectators took for a pleasant smile. Then, mingling their voices in a drawling melody, the girls executed a solemn dance around him.

'Dancing, are you? All right. I'm not going to be outdone. I'll show you one of our dances.' And he broke into a dizzy jig, twirling, leaping, dancing with his feet, knees and hands, throwing himself into amazing contortions and impossible postures and indulging in incredible grimaces, all of which gave the natives an extraordinary impression of the way gods dance in the moon. The Africans, however, who are as imitative as monkeys, soon began to mimic his extravagances. Not a single gesture or posture escaped them. It became a hustling, excited pandemonium, of which it would be impossible to convey even a slight idea. When the ball was at its height, Joe caught sight of the doctor hastily forcing his way through the shrieking, abandoned crowd.

This produced a strange reaction. Had the sultan been clumsy enough to die under the treatment of his celestial physician? Kennedy, from his look-out, saw the danger but did not realise its cause. The balloon, responding to a considerable expansion of the gas, was straining at her moorings, eager to take flight.

The doctor reached the foot of the ladder. A superstitious fear still held the crowd and prevented them from indulging in any violence. He quickly climbed up the rungs, followed nimbly by Joe.

'We haven't a minute to spare,' said the doctor. 'Don't bother to loose the anchor. We'll cut the rope. Follow me.'

'But what's the matter, sir?' asked Joe as he climbed into the car.

'What's up?' said Kennedy, carbine in hand.

'Look,' answered the doctor, pointing to the horizon.

'Well?' asked Kennedy.

'Well! The moon!'

Indeed, red and imposing against the azure background, the moon was rising like a globe of fire. There she was, and there, too, was the *Victoria*. Either there were two moons or these strangers were nothing but impostors, adventurers, false gods. Such had naturally been the reflections of the crowd; hence the reaction.

Joe could not restrain a great guffaw of laughter. The inhabitants of Kazeh, realising that their prey was slipping through their fingers, uttered long-drawn howls; bows and muskets were levelled against the balloon.

But, just then, one of the magicians made a sign and the weapons were lowered. Climbing into the tree he tried to seize the rope and bring the machine to the earth. Joe dashed forward, an axe in his hand.

'Shall I cut?' he asked.

'Wait,' replied the doctor.

'But this nigger – ?'

'We may be able to save our anchor, and I should like to. There'll still be time to cut.'

The magician, having climbed the tree, put in such good work that he managed, by breaking a few branches, to free the anchor which, answering to the strong pull of the balloon, caught the magician between the legs and, astride this unexpected hippogriff, he set off for the regions of the air. When they saw one of their *wagangas* flying through space, the amazement of the crowd was tremendous.

'Hurray!' shouted Joe, as the *Victoria*, impelled by her lifting force, leapt upwards at terrific speed.

'He's all right,' said Kennedy, 'a little trip won't do him any harm.'

'Shall we drop him off, sir?' Joe asked.

'Steady, Joe,' replied the doctor. 'We'll let him gently down, and I expect his trip will do a good deal to enhance his reputation as a magician among his contemporaries.'

'They're quite capable of making a god of him,' said Joe.

The *Victoria* had reached a height of about a thousand feet. The negro was frenziedly clinging to the rope in silence, his eyes starting out of his head with terror and astonishment. A light west wind was driving the balloon away from the town. Half an hour later the doctor, seeing that the country was now deserted, lowered the flame of the furnace and came down. When he was twenty feet from the ground the negro came to a rapid decision. Throwing himself off, he fell on his feet and made off towards Kazeh, while the balloon, suddenly relieved of his weight, rose once more in the air.

CHAPTER XVI

*Signs of a storm – The Country of the Moon – The future of
the African continent – The machine that will bring about
the end of the world – The landscape in the setting sun –
The fire zone – A night of stars*

'THAT'S WHAT COMES of pretending to be sons of the moon without her permission,' said Joe. 'She nearly got us into a nasty mess. I suppose, sir, you didn't do anything to damage her reputation with your medicine?'

'By the way,' asked Kennedy, 'what sort of a fellow was this sultan?'

'An old tippler on his last legs. He won't be much missed. But the moral is that glory is ephemeral, and it doesn't do to acquire too strong a taste for it.'

'Well, never mind,' Joe replied. 'I was getting on famously, being worshipped and playing the god in my own way. But it can't be helped. The moon came up, and all red, which shows she wasn't pleased with us.'

During the course of this conversation, in which Joe discussed the moon from an entirely novel point of view, the sky to the northward was becoming heavy with great clouds, lowering and sinister. A brisk wind, which they encountered three hundred feet from the ground, drove the *Victoria* north-north-east. The azure vault above them was clear but the atmosphere felt oppressive. About eight in the evening the travellers were in long. 32°40' E., lat. 4° 17' S. The atmospheric currents, under the influence of the approaching storm, were driving them along at a rate of thirty-five miles an hour. Below them, the undulating fertile plains of Mfuto swept past. It was a splendid sight, which the travellers watched with admiration.

'We're in the heart of the Moon Country,' said the doctor. 'It has kept the name given to it in antiquity, doubtless because the moon has always been worshipped here. It really is a wonderful country and it would be hard to find finer vegetation.'

'If it was near London it would be unnatural, but very nice,' said Joe. 'Why are all the beautiful things only to be found in such wild countries?'

'But how do we know that some day this country may not become the centre of civilisation?' the doctor answered. 'The nations of the future may come here when the land in Europe is no longer able to feed the inhabitants.'

'Do you really think that?' asked Kennedy.

'Certainly, old man. Think of the march of history, the successive migrations of the nations, and you'll come to the same conclusion. Asia was the cradle of the world, wasn't she? For about four thousand years she was continually bringing forth fruit, and then, when stones covered the ground that once yielded the golden crops we read of in Homer, her children left her exhausted, shrivelled lap. Next we see them pouring down upon Europe, then young and vigorous, and Europe has been suckling them for two thousand years. Already, however, her fertility is becoming exhausted, her productive faculties are diminishing every day. All these new diseases that are every year attacking the agricultural products, these ruined harvests, insufficient supplies, all this is a certain sign of flagging vitality and approaching exhaustion. Already the people are beginning to flock to the generous breasts of America as to a source, not inexhaustible, but as yet unexhausted. That continent will in her turn grow old, her virgin forests will fall under the axe of industry, her soil will weaken through trying to respond to the excessive demands made upon it. Where two harvests were gathered yearly, hardly one will force itself through the tired soil. When that time comes, Africa will offer to the new races the treasures accumulated in her breast for centuries. Irrigation and scientific agriculture will cleanse this climate, now fatal to foreigners. These scattered waters will unite in a single bed to form a navigable artery, and this world over which we are soaring, more fertile, richer, more virile than the rest, will become some great kingdom where discoveries will be made greater even than steam and electricity.'

'Really, sir, I'd like to see that,' said Joe.

'You've been born too early, Joe.'

'Besides,' said Kennedy, 'the time when industry gets a grip of everything and uses it to its own advantage may not be particularly amusing. If men go on inventing machinery they'll end by being swallowed up by their own machines. I've always thought that the last day will be brought about by some colossal boiler heated to three thousand atmospheres blowing up the world.'

'And I bet the Yankees will have had a hand in it,' said Joe.

'Quite likely,' the doctor replied. 'But don't let us get carried away by these discussions. Let us be content to admire this splendid Country of the Moon while we have the chance.'

The sun, glancing its last rays beneath the piled-up mass of cloud, was touching with a crest of gold everything that stood out in any way from the ground. Gigantic trees, tall shrubs, even the moss clinging to the soil, all caught this flood of light. The land, which was slightly undulating, swelled up here and there to form small conical hills, but there were no mountains in sight. Dense thickets, impenetrable hedges and thorny jungles divided the clearings in which numerous villages were to be seen, and which were surrounded by enormous euphorbias as by a natural wall in which the coralliform branches of the shrubs were tangled together.

Soon the Mlagarasi, the principal tributary of Lake Tanganyika, began to wind beneath these masses of foliage and absorb the many streams caused by the swelling of mountain torrents through the melting of the snows or by the overflowing of pools sunk in the clayey surface of the soil. From the air it gave the impression of a network of cascades pouring over the whole western part of the country.

Great humped animals were grazing in the lush meadows, being at times completely hidden by the tall grass. The forests from which fragrant scents arose had the appearance of vast bouquets, but in these bouquets lions, leopards, hyenas and tigers lurked, seeking shelter from the heat of the late afternoon. Now and again an elephant would sway the crests of the thickets, and the cracking of the trees before his ivory tusks could be heard.

'What a hunting country!' Kennedy exclaimed enthusiastically. 'You'd only have to let off a gun in any direction you liked and you'd be bound to hit something worth having. Couldn't we have a try?'

'No, old man. It's getting dark and we're in for a stormy night. In these parts the ground is like a huge electric battery and the storms are terrific.'

'You're right, sir,' said Joe. 'The heat is stifling and there's not a breath of wind. It makes you feel as if something is going to happen.'

'The whole atmosphere is charged with electricity,' replied the doctor. 'Every living creature reacts to this peculiar state of the air that comes before a storm, and I confess I never felt it as much as I do now.'

'Wouldn't it be a good idea to get down, then?' asked Kennedy.

'On the contrary, Dick, I'd much rather get up higher. The only thing I'm afraid of is that we might be swept out of our course in the cross-currents.'

'Don't you intend to hold on to the course we've been following since we left the coast?'

'If possible,' the doctor answered, 'I shall steer more directly north for seven or eight degrees. I want to get up towards the supposed latitude of the Nile sources. We might pick up some traces of Speke's expedition or even Heuglin's caravan. If my reckoning is correct, we are now in long. 32° 40', and I should like to make straight across the Equator.'

'Just look!' cried Kennedy. 'Look at those hippopotamus sneaking out of the water; and those are crocodile. You can hear them gasping for breath.'

'They're suffocating,' said Joe. 'There's a lot to be said for travelling like this. You can snap your fingers at all that nasty vermin. Look, sir; look, Mr Kennedy! Just look at those animals running, in packs. There must be a couple of hundred of them. They're wolves.'

'No, Joe, those are wild dogs. They're a tough breed and will even attack lions with impunity. They are the most terrible thing a traveller can meet with. He would be torn to pieces at once.'

'Well, you won't catch me trying to muzzle them,' the worthy fellow replied. 'After all, if they're made like that, I suppose we mustn't blame them.'

Little by little a hush came over the world under the influence of the oncoming storm. It was as though the air had lost its capacity to convey sound. Like a room muffled with hangings, the atmosphere had lost all resonance. The crested stork, red and blue jay, the mocking-bird and flycatchers, vanished into the great trees. All Nature revealed symptoms of an imminent cataclysm. At 9 p.m. the *Victoria* was hanging motionless over Msene, a large group of villages that could hardly be distinguished in the gloom. Now and again the glinting of a stray beam of light on the murky water showed the presence of a regular system of dykes, and in a final glow could be seen the dark and placid shape of palms, tamarisks, sycamores, and the gigantic euphorbias.

'I'm suffocating,' said the Scotsman, laboriously trying to fill his lungs with the rarefied air. 'We're not budging an inch. Let's go down.'

'But what about the storm?' asked the doctor with some anxiety.

'If you're afraid of being carried off by the wind it seems to me it's the only thing to do.'

'The storm may not burst tonight,' said Joe. 'The clouds are very high.'

'That's one of my reasons for not trying to rise above them. We should have to go very high. We should lose sight of the ground and shouldn't know whether we were making any way, or in which direction.'

'Make up your mind, Samuel. There's no time to lose.'

'It's a nuisance, the wind dropping,' said Joe. 'It might have blown us away from the storm.'

'It certainly is a pity, my friends,' replied the doctor, 'for the clouds are a danger for us. They contain cross-currents which may involve us in a tornado, and lightning that may set us on fire. On the other hand, if we made fast to a tree the force of the wind might dash us to the ground.'

'What's to be done, then?'

'We must keep the *Victoria* in an intermediary zone between the dangers of the earth and those of the sky. We've plenty of water for the furnace, and we've lost none of our ballast. If necessary I shall use it.'

'We'll keep watch with you,' said Kennedy.

'No, my friends. Stow away the stores and go to bed. I'll wake you if necessary.'

'But hadn't you better get some sleep yourself, sir, as there's no danger yet?'

'No, thanks, Joe. I'd rather keep a look-out. We're not moving, and unless something fresh happens we shall be in the same spot tomorrow morning.'

'Good-night, sir.'

'Good-night, if possible.'

Kennedy and Joe lay down under their rugs and the doctor was left alone in the immensity of space. Meanwhile the dome of clouds was lowering imperceptibly and the darkness became intense. The black vault of the night enveloped the earth as though to crush it. Suddenly a sharp, swift, stabbing flash of lightning striped the darkness. Before the rent had closed again a terrific peal of thunder shook the depths of the sky.

'Wake up!' shouted Fergusson; and the two sleepers, already roused by the tremendous din, were ready to carry out his orders.

'Let's drop,' said Kennedy.

'No. The balloon wouldn't stand it. We must rise before these clouds break and the wind gets up.' And he vigorously increased the flame of the burner in the spiral.

Tropical storms develop with a rapidity in keeping with their violence. A second flash tore the clouds and was immediately followed by a score of others. The sky was scored with electric flashes which hissed under great drops of rain.

'We're late,' said the doctor. 'Now we shall have to pass through a zone of fire with our balloon full of inflammable gas.'

'Get down to earth! Get down to earth!' Kennedy went on repeating.

'The risk of being struck would be about the same, and we should soon get torn to pieces in the branches of the trees.'

'We're rising, sir.'

'Quicker, quicker still!'

In this part of Africa, during the equatorial storms it is a common thing to count thirty or thirty-five flashes per minute. The sky is literally ablaze and there is no pause between the peals of thunder. The wind was unleashed with terrific violence in the torrid air. It twisted the incandescent clouds about like a bellows fanning the blaze. Dr Fergusson kept his burner going at full strength. The balloon dilated and rose. On his knees in the middle of the car, Kennedy was holding on to the ropes of the tent. The tossing of the balloon made him giddy. Great hollows were blown in the envelope of the balloon into which the wind drove with its full force, the silk cracking under the pressure. With a deafening roar a sort of hail battered down upon the *Victoria*, which however continued to rise, the lightning sparking off her surface in fiery tangents. She was in the heart of the storm.

'God help us!' said Fergusson. 'We're in His hands and He alone can save us. We must be ready for anything, even fire. We shan't drop too suddenly, perhaps.'

The doctor's voice scarcely reached his companions, but they could see his calm face in the light of the flashes. He was watching the play of the lightning on the net of the balloon. The *Victoria* was whirling and tossing but still rising. Quarter of an hour later she had passed above the lightning zone. The electric display could be seen below her like a vast cluster of fireworks hanging from the car. This was one of the finest spectacles that Nature has to offer. Below, the storm, and above, the starry sky, tranquil, silent and impassive, with the moon pouring her peaceful light upon the raging clouds. Dr Fergusson consulted his barometer and found it showed a height of twelve thousand feet. It was 11 p.m.

'By God's mercy we're safe,' he said. 'All we have to do now is to keep at this level.'

'That was awful,' Kennedy replied.

'At any rate, it gave a little variety to the trip,' said Joe, 'and I'm glad to have seen a thunderstorm from above. It was a fine sight.'

CHAPTER XVII

The Mountains of the Moon – An ocean of verdure

ABOUT SIX in the morning (Monday) the sun rose, the clouds scattered, and a pleasant breeze gave freshness to the early day. The fragrant earth reappeared to the eyes of the travellers. The balloon, twisting on her axis amid the cross-currents, had scarcely drifted from her former position. Allowing the gas to contract, the doctor came down in search of a wind that would carry him in a more northerly direction. For a long time he searched in vain; he was being carried to the westward, within sight of the celebrated Mountains of the Moon which enclose the extremity of Lake Tanganyika in a semicircle. Their almost unbroken outline stood out against the faint blue of the sky like a natural barrier to keep explorers out of the centre of Africa. A few isolated peaks bore traces of perpetual snows.

'We are now in unexplored country,' said the doctor. 'Captain Burton went very far west, but was unable to reach these famous mountains. He even denied their existence, which was affirmed by Speke, his companion. He makes out that Speke imagined them. In our case, at any rate, there can be no doubt about them.'

'Are we going to cross them?' Kennedy asked.

'No, if God is good. I hope to find a favourable wind that will take us towards the Equator. If necessary, I'll wait and anchor the balloon like a ship in a contrary wind.'

But what the doctor was hoping for was not long in coming. After trying different levels, the *Victoria* ran north-west at a moderate speed.

'Now we're on the right course,' he said, consulting his compass, 'and only two hundred feet up, so we shall be in a good position to view this new ground. When Speke was making for Lake Ukereue he took a course due north from Kazeh but farther to the east than ours.'

'Are we going on like this long?' asked Kennedy.

'Possibly. What we're trying to do is to veer towards the sources of the Nile, and we have more than six hundred miles to go before we come to the farthest point reached by the explorers from the north.'

'And we aren't going to land, not even to stretch our legs?' asked Joe.

'Oh, yes, we are. For one thing, we shall have to be careful with our stores, and you, Dick, will have to keep us supplied with fresh meat on the way.'

'You've only to say the word, Samuel.'

'We shall also have to renew our supply of water. For all we know, we may be carried off into districts where there is no water. We can't be too careful.'

At noon the *Victoria* was in long. 29° 15' E., lat. 3° 15' W. She passed the village of Uyofu, the northern extremity of Unyamwezi, with Lake Ukereue, as yet invisible, on her beam.

The tribes living near the Equator seem a little more civilised. They are governed by absolute monarchs with unlimited powers. Their most compact settlement constitutes the province of Karagwah. It was

decided among the three travellers that they would land at the first
favourable place they came to. They would make a considerable halt
and carefully overhaul the balloon. The flame of the burner was
lowered and the anchors, which had been dropped overboard, soon
began to brush the tall trees of a huge plain. From the height at which
they were, it appeared to be covered with smooth turf, but in reality the
grass was seven or eight feet tall. The *Victoria* skimmed over this
without touching it, like a gigantic butterfly. There was no obstacle in
sight. It was like an ocean of green without a breaker.

'We may go on like this for a long time,' said Kennedy. 'I see no
signs of a tree to which we could make fast. There doesn't seem much
chance of any shooting after all.'

'Wait a bit, old man, you couldn't go shooting in grass taller than
yourself. We'll find a place in time.'

The crossing of this green, almost transparent sea, undulating gently
in the breeze, made very pleasant travelling. The car cut its way
through the waves of tall grass, from which every now and again flocks
of brilliantly-coloured birds would burst out, uttering shrill cries of joy.
The anchors trailed through the lake of flowers, leaving a furrow which
closed up behind them like the wake of a ship. Suddenly a sharp shock
was felt. An anchor must have caught a rocky fissure hidden under the
long grass.

'She's got a hold,' said Joe.

'All right. Out with the ladder,' Kennedy answered.

Before these words were out of his mouth a trumpeting cry rent the
air, and the following remarks, punctuated with exclamations, came
from the travellers:

'What's that?' 'A curious noise!' 'Hello, we're off again!' 'The
anchor's broken loose!'

'No, it's still holding,' said Joe, who was pulling on the rope. 'It's the
rock that's moving!'

There was a tremendous commotion in the grass and soon a long,
sinuous shape emerged.

'A snake!' said Joe.

'A snake!' cried Kennedy, cocking his carbine.

'No,' said the doctor, 'it's an elephant's trunk.'

'Great Scott,' said Kennedy, bringing his gun to his shoulder.

'Half a minute, Dick. Wait.'

'He's towing us,' said Joe.

'Yes,' said the doctor, 'and in the right direction.'

The elephant was making good headway and soon reached a
clearing where his whole shape was revealed. From his enormous size

the doctor saw that he was a splendid male with two cream-coloured tusks, beautifully curved and probably eight feet long. Between these the anchor was firmly wedged. With his trunk the animal was making frantic efforts to rid himself of the rope by which he was attached to the car.

'Gee up! Get along!' shouted Joe, overjoyed and doing what he could to urge forward this strange steed. 'Here's a new way of travelling. No horses for us. An elephant, if you please!'

'But where's he taking us to?' asked Kennedy, waving his carbine, which he was itching to use.

'Where we want to go, my dear Dick. Have a little patience.'

Joe went on shouting and urging the animal forward. All at once it broke into a fast gallop, throwing its trunk from right to left, its heavy lurches shaking the car. Axe in hand, the doctor stood by to cut the rope should it become necessary, though he was anxious not to lose the anchor until the last possible moment. They travelled behind the elephant for about an hour and a half, the animal showing no signs of fatigue. These huge beasts can trot a long way and are found to cover long distances from day to day, like whales, which are similar in bulk and speed.

'It's like harpooning a whale,' said Joe. 'This is just what the whalers do.'

But a change in the conformation of the country forced the doctor to change his method of locomotion. A dense wood of camaldores came in sight about three miles to the northward. It became necessary to cut loose from their tug. Kennedy was therefore called upon to stop the elephant. He raised his carbine but was not in a favourable position for a sure shot. His first, aimed at the animal's head, flattened itself out as if it had struck a sheet of armour-plating. The animal seemed in no way disturbed. At the noise of the report it quickened its pace, and swept along like a horse in full gallop.

'The devil!' said Kennedy.

'There's a thick head for you!' said Joe.

'We'll try a few elongated bullets behind the shoulder,' replied Dick, carefully loading his rifle, and he fired. The animal emitted a terrible roar and went on faster than ever.

'Come, sir,' said Joe, 'I'll have to help or we shan't get the job over.' And two bullets pierced the animal's flank. It halted, threw up its trunk, and then dashed off again at full speed, making for the wood. Its huge head swayed from side to side and the blood began to flow freely from its wounds.

'Keep it up, sir!' said Joe.

'And fire as fast as you can,' added the doctor. 'We're only a few hundred yards from the wood.' Ten more shots followed. The elephant took a tremendous bound forward, the car and balloon cracking as though the whole thing were coming to pieces. The lurch caused the doctor to drop his axe, which fell to the ground.

The situation was now a terrible one. There was no hope of unlashing the rope under the present strain, and the travellers' pocket-knives were useless to cut it. The balloon was being dragged rapidly towards the wood, when the animal received a bullet in the eye as it was raising its head. It stopped and hesitated, then its knees gave way and its flank was exposed to the carbines.

'In the heart,' said Kennedy, firing for the last time. The elephant uttered a roar of distress and agony, stood erect again for a moment, waving its trunk, then fell with its full weight upon one of its tusks, which snapped. It was dead.

'He's broken his tusk!' cried Kennedy. 'The ivory would be worth forty guineas a hundredweight.'

'All that?' said Joe, dashing down the ladder.

'We can't help it, old man,' replied Doctor Fergusson. 'We're not ivory traders, and we haven't come here to make our fortunes.'

Joe examined the anchor, which was still firmly fixed in the undamaged tusk. Fergusson and Kennedy jumped to the ground and the half-deflated balloon hovered over the animal's body.

'What a splendid beast!' cried Kennedy. 'What a size! I've never seen an elephant this size in India!'

'That's very likely, Dick. The elephants of Central Africa are the finest in the world. Men like Anderson and Canning have hunted them so vigorously round the Cape that they are moving towards the Equator, where we'll see herds of them.'

'Meanwhile,' said Joe, 'I hope we shall get a taste of this one. I'll guarantee to serve you an appetising meal off it. Perhaps Mr Kennedy will go off shooting for an hour or two while Dr Fergusson has a look at the balloon and I get on with the cooking.'

'That's a good arrangement,' said the doctor. 'Do just what you like.'

'As far as I'm concerned,' said Kennedy, 'I shall take advantage of the two hours' leave Joe has been kind enough to allow me.'

'Yes, I should. But don't run any risks, and don't go far away.'

'You needn't worry,' Kennedy replied, as he shouldered his gun and plunged into the wood. Joe set to work. He first made a hole about two feet deep in the ground and filled it with the dry branches which covered the ground and which had been torn off by the passage of the elephant, whose track could be distinctly traced. When the hole was filled, he piled up the wood to a height of two feet and set fire to it. Then, turning to the elephant, which had fallen not fifty yards from the wood, he skilfully cut off the trunk, which was two feet thick at its upper extremity. From this he selected the tenderest part and added one of the spongy feet. These, indeed, are the tit-bits, like the hump of the bison, the paw of the bear, or the snout of the boar. When the bonfire had been completely consumed and the ashes cleared away, the hole in the ground was very hot. The flesh, encased in aromatic leaves, was placed at the bottom of this improvised oven and covered with the hot ashes. Joe then built a second bonfire over the top, and when the wood was burned away again the meat was cooked to a turn. Taking it out of the oven, Joe placed it on some fresh leaves and laid the meal in the centre of a splendid stretch of smooth turf. He next brought biscuits, brandy and coffee, and drew some fresh, clear water from a neighbouring stream. The feast thus arranged was pleasing to the eye, and Joe thought, without undue pride, that it would be even more pleasing to the palate.

'Travel without getting tired and without danger,' he repeated to himself, 'punctual meals, living in a hammock; what more could a man want? And to think Mr Kennedy didn't want to come!'

Dr Fergusson, for his part, undertook a minute examination of the balloon. It did not seem to have suffered any harm from the strain that had been put upon it. The silk and gutta-percha had stood it wonderfully. Measuring the present height of the balloon above the ground and calculating the lift, he was delighted to see that he had lost no hydrogen. So far the envelope was intact.

It was only five days since the travellers had left Zanzibar. The pemmican was still untouched, and the stores of biscuits and tinned meats were enough for a long journey. The water, then, was all that required replenishment. The pipes and spiral seemed in perfect order and, thanks to the rubber joints, had given to every oscillation of the balloon. When he had completed his examination of the balloon the doctor got his log up to date, and made a very successful drawing of the surrounding country, with the long plain stretching as far as the eye could reach, the forest of camaldore and the balloon hanging motionless over the body of the elephant.

When two hours had elapsed Kennedy returned with a string of fat partridges and a leg of oryx, a sort of gemsbok, one of the most agile species of antelope. Joe took charge of this addition to their provisions.

'Dinner is served,' he announced impressively, shortly afterwards. And the three travellers sat down simply on the green sward. The foot and trunk of the elephant were declared to be excellent. As always, they toasted England, and for the first time the aroma of choice Havanas lent its fragrance to the air of this delightful country. Kennedy ate, drank and talked enough for four. He was quite carried away and solemnly proposed to his friend that they should take up their abode in the forest, build a wigwam of branches and found a dynasty of African Robinson Crusoes. The proposal did not meet with approval, although Joe proposed himself for the position of Friday.

The country seemed so peaceful and deserted that the doctor decided to spend the night on land. Joe built a cordon of fires, an essential precaution against wild animals, for hyenas and jackals, attracted by the smell of elephant flesh, were prowling in the vicinity. Several times Kennedy had to fire his carbine at over-bold visitors, but in the end the night passed without any untoward incident.

CHAPTER XVIII

The Karagwahs – Lake Ukereue – A night on an island –
The Equator – Crossing the lake – The falls – View of the
country – The sources of the Nile – Benga Island –
Andrea Debono's signature – The British flag

AT FIVE O'CLOCK the following morning the preparations for the departure were begun. With the axe, which he had been lucky enough to recover, Joe cut the elephant's tusks, and the *Victoria*, free once more, carried the travellers north-west at a speed of eighteen miles an hour. The doctor had taken a careful reckoning of his position the previous evening by means of the stars. He was in lat. 2° 40', about 160 miles below the Equator. He passed over numerous villages without paying any attention to the outcry their appearance provoked, noting the conformation of these places by summary glances below. They crossed the Rubemhe range, the slopes of which are almost as sheer as the peaks of Usagara, and later, at Tenga, came to the first foothills of the Karagwahs, which, according to the doctor, originate in the Mountains of the Moon. Thus the ancient legend which held these mountains to be the cradle of the Nile was near the truth, for they border Lake Ukereue, which is supposed to be the reservoir of the great stream.

From Kafuro, the great merchant centre of the country, they at last caught sight, on the horizon, of the long-sought lake of which Speke had caught a glimpse on the 3rd of August, 1858. The doctor felt a thrill. He had almost attained one of the chief goals of his expedition and, his glass to his eye, he did not miss a wrinkle of this mysterious country, which he saw as follows:

Below him the land was, in general, sterile, only a few ravines showing signs of cultivation. Dotted with cone-shaped hills of moderate height, the ground flattened out as it neared the lake. The rice-fields gave place to fields of barley, and the plantain flourished from which the wine of the country is made, as also the *mwani*, a wild plant used for coffee. A collection of circular huts roofed with flowering thatch constituted the capital of Karagwah.

They could clearly distinguish the amazed faces of the inhabitants, a fairly handsome race of yellowish-brown complexion. Women of extraordinary bulk dragged themselves about the plantations, and the doctor caused his companions considerable surprise when he told them that this corpulence, which is greatly favoured, is obtained by a compulsory régime of curdled milk.

At noon the *Victoria* was in lat. 1° 45' S., and at one o'clock the wind drove her over the lake. This lake was named Victoria Nyanza (Nyanza means lake) by Captain Speke.[44] At this place its breadth might have been ninety miles. At its southern extremity the captain found a group of islands which he called the Bengal Archipelago. Pushing his survey as far as Muanza on the east bank, he was well received by the sultan. He made a survey of this part of the lake but was unable to obtain a boat to cross it or to visit the large island of Ukereue, a very populous island governed by three sultans and at low tide forming a peninsula.

The *Victoria* began to cross the lake farther north, to the great regret of the doctor, who would have liked to make a sketch of its lower contours. The banks, bristling with thorny shrubs and tangled creepers, were literally buried under myriads of mosquitoes of a light brown colour. The district must have been both uninhabitable and uninhabited. Herds of hippopotamus could be seen wallowing in the forests of reeds or diving beneath the whitish waters of the lake. Seen from above, the lake extended westward to such a distant horizon that it might have been a sea, the distance between the banks being so great that no communication was possible; moreover the storms are strong and frequent, for this elevated and exposed basin is at the mercy of the winds.

The doctor had some difficulty in holding his course and had fears of being carried eastward, but fortunately he found a current that bore him due north, and at 6 p.m. the *Victoria* made a small deserted island twenty miles from the bank, in lat. 0° 30' S., long. 32° 52' E. They managed to moor to a tree and, the wind dropping as night came on, they rode quietly at anchor. There could be no question of landing, for here, as on the banks of the lake, the ground was covered with a thick cloud of millions of mosquitoes. Joe even returned from the tree covered with bites, but was not perturbed as he found this behaviour very natural on the part of the mosquitoes. The doctor, however, less optimistic, paid out as much rope as possible, to get away from these merciless insects which had begun to rise with a disquieting hum. He confirmed Captain Speke's estimate of the height of the lake above sea-level: 3750 feet.

'Here we are, then, on an island,' said Joe, scratching himself desperately.

'It wouldn't take us long to explore it,' said Kennedy, 'and except for these friendly insects there's not a living creature to be seen.'

'The islands scattered over the lake,' said Dr Fergusson, 'are really nothing more than the summits of submerged hills, but we're lucky to have found a refuge here, for the shores of the lake are inhabited by fierce tribes; so get a good night's sleep, for we're going to have a calm night.'

'Aren't you going to sleep too, Samuel?'

'No. I shouldn't sleep a wink. I have too much to think about. Tomorrow, my friends, if the wind is favourable, we'll bear straight to northward and perhaps we may discover the sources of the Nile, the secret that has so far baffled everybody. I couldn't sleep while we are so near.'

Kennedy and Joe, who were less troubled by scientific preoccupations, soon fell into a deep sleep, while the doctor kept watch.

On Wednesday the 23rd of April, the *Victoria* got under way at four in the morning, under a grey sky. The darkness lingered over the waters of the lake, which were veiled in a dense fog, but soon a strong wind swept this away. For some minutes the *Victoria* drifted about in various directions and finally bore away due north. Dr Fergusson clapped his hands with delight.

'This is the way we want to go,' he cried. 'If we don't see the Nile today, we shall never see it. We are now crossing the Equator, entering our own hemisphere.'

'Oh!' cried Joe. 'Do you really think this is the Equator, sir?'

'In this very place, Joe.'

'In that case, begging your pardon, sir, oughtn't we to drink its health at once?'

'We might drink a glass of grog,' the doctor answered, laughing.

'Your methods of cosmography have their points.'

Accordingly they celebrated the *Victoria*'s crossing of the line. She was moving swiftly. To westward could be seen the low-lying coast, broken by a few hills, and beyond, the higher plateaus of Uganda and Usoga. The wind became very strong, nearly thirty miles an hour. The waters of the lake lashed themselves into foam like the waves of a sea; and from the movement of the water the doctor saw that the lake must be of great depth. One or two clumsy boats were all the craft they sighted during their rapid crossing.

'This lake,' said the doctor, 'is from its high situation obviously the natural reservoir of the rivers of East Africa. The rain replenishes it with the water evaporated from its tributaries. It seems to me certain that it is the source of the Nile.'

'We shall soon see,' replied Kennedy.

About nine o'clock the west bank closed in. It was thickly wooded and seemed deserted. The wind shifted a little towards the east, and they were able to catch a glimpse of the other shore. It curved in such a way as to form a very wide angle at the extremity of the lake (lat. 2° 40' N.). High mountains raised their barren peaks at this end of the lake, and between them a deep and winding gorge gave passage to a turbulent torrent. While attending to the handling of his balloon Dr Fergusson examined the country with an eager eye.

'Look, my friends!' he cried. 'The stories of the Arabs were correct. They spoke of a river by which Lake Ukereue poured its waters northward. That river exists and we are following it. It flows at about the same pace as we are travelling. This little stream gliding away below our feet will certainly merge into the waves of the Mediterranean. It's the Nile!'

'It's the Nile!' echoed Kennedy, who was becoming infected with the doctor's enthusiasm.

'Hurrah for the Nile!' cried Joe, who was always ready to cheer anything that pleased him.

In places huge rocks stemmed the course of this mysterious river. The water foamed, forming rapids and cataracts, which confirmed the doctor's prophecies. From the surrounding mountains many torrents poured down, foaming as they fell; there were hundreds of them. Scattered all over the ground thin threads of water trickled, joined one another and raced towards this nascent stream which, as it absorbed them, became a large river.

'That must be the Nile,' the doctor repeated with conviction. 'The origin of its name has been as eagerly sought by scholars as the origin of its waters. It has been traced to Greek, Coptic and Sanskrit; but, after all, it doesn't matter since it has at last been forced to reveal its sources.' *

'But,' said Kennedy, 'how are we to establish the identity of this river with that seen by the explorers from the north?'

'We shall have proofs certain, irrefutable and infallible,' replied Fergusson, 'if the wind keeps favourable for another hour.'

The mountains divided, giving place to numerous villages, fields of sesame, durra and sugar-cane. The tribes of this district seemed excited and hostile, more inclined to anger than worship, and regarded the travellers as foreigners, not as gods. They seemed to feel that by discovering the sources of the Nile the Europeans were robbing them of something. The *Victoria* had to be kept out of musket range.

'It will be difficult to make fast here,' said the Scotsman.

'Well, so much the worse for the niggers,' Joe answered. 'They won't get the benefit of our conversation.'

'I'll have to go down in any case,' the doctor answered, 'even if it's only for a quarter of an hour. Otherwise I shan't be able to confirm the results of our expedition.'

'Is it unavoidable, Samuel?'

'Yes, we shall have to go down, even if it means shooting.'

'I shan't mind that,' answered Kennedy, fondling his carbine .

'Whenever you like, sir,' said Joe, getting ready for the fray.

'It won't be the first time that science has been pursued weapon in hand,' answered the doctor. 'The same thing happened in the case of a French scientist in the mountains of Spain when he was measuring the earth's meridian.'

'Don't worry, Samuel. Trust your two guards.'

'Are we ready, sir?'

'Not yet. As a matter of fact, we're going to rise a bit first, to see the exact configuration of the country.'

The hydrogen was expanded and in less than ten minutes the *Victoria* was soaring at a height of 2500 feet. From this level they could distinguish a complicated tangle of rivers flowing into the bed of the main stream. Others flowed into it from the hills and fertile plains to the west.

'We're less than nineteen miles from Gondokoro,' said the doctor, pointing to his map, 'and less than five from the point reached by the explorers from the north. We must drop cautiously.'

The *Victoria* came down more than two thousand feet.

* A Byzantine scholar took Neilos[45] to be an arithmetical symbol, N representing 50, E 5, I 10, L 30, O 70, S 200, which gives the number of days in a year.

'Now, my friends, be ready for anything.'

'We're ready,' replied Dick and Joe.

'Good!'

The *Victoria* was soon following the bed of the river at a height of hardly a hundred feet. The Nile was three hundred feet wide at this place and the natives in the villages along both banks became tremendously excited. On reaching the second parallel the river forms a sheer cascade about ten feet high and consequently impassable.

'That's certainly the fall reported by Debono,' cried the doctor.

The river bed widened and became dotted with many islands, which Dr Fergusson eagerly scanned. He seemed to be looking for a landmark he had not yet seen. As some natives in a boat approached below the balloon, Kennedy greeted them with a shot which, though it did not hit them, forced them to turn back and make for the shore as fast as they could.

'A pleasant voyage,' Joe shouted to them. 'If I were in their place I shouldn't risk coming back. I'd be jolly frightened of a monster that spits out lightning whenever it likes.'

But suddenly Dr Fergusson seized his glass and trained it on an island lying in the middle of the stream.

'Four trees,' he cried. 'Look over there!' Indeed, four isolated trees rose from the end of the island.

'That's Benga. It must be,' he added.

'Well, what about it?' Dick asked.

'That's where we come down, if God is kind.'

'But it looks inhabited, sir.'

'Joe's right. Unless I'm mistaken I can see a score of natives collected there.'

'We'll soon make them run,' said Fergusson.

'Let's get at it,' replied Kennedy.

The sun was in the zenith. The *Victoria* drew near the island. The negroes, who were of the Makado tribe, uttered fierce cries, one waving his hat of bark. Kennedy took it as a target, fired, and the hat flew in pieces. There was a general rout, the natives plunging into the river and swimming across it. From both banks came a hail of bullets and arrows, but with no danger to the balloon, whose anchor had caught a rocky cleft. Joe slid to the ground.

'The ladder!' cried the doctor. 'Follow me, Kennedy.'

'What are you going to do?'

'Come along down. I want a witness.'

'I'm with you.'

'Keep a good look-out, Joe.'

'Don't worry, sir. I'll see to everything.'

'Come along, Dick,' said the doctor, jumping to the ground. He led his companion towards the group of rocks rising from the extremity of the island. There he searched for some time, hunting about amongst the thorns and scratching his hands till the blood ran. Suddenly he seized the Scotsman's arm.

'Look!' he said.

'Letters!' cried Kennedy.

Indeed, two letters appeared on the rock, clearly carved:

A. D.

'A. D.,' the doctor went on; 'Andrea Debono.[46] The initials of the traveller who got nearest to the sources of the Nile.'

'That's unanswerable, Samuel.'

'Are you convinced now?'

'It's the Nile. There can be no doubt about it.'

The doctor took a last look at these precious initials, and took a careful sketch of their shape and dimensions.

'Now,' he said, 'back to the balloon!'

'We'll have to be quick. There are some natives getting ready to cross back.'

'It doesn't matter now. If only the wind will take us north for a few hours we shall reach Gondokoro and shake hands with our countrymen.'

Ten minutes later the *Victoria* was majestically pursuing her course, while Dr Fergusson celebrated his success by unfurling the Union Jack.

CHAPTER XIX

The Nile – Trembling Mountain – Memories of home – Arab stories – The Nyam Nyam – Joe's reflections – The Victoria *severely tested – Balloon ascents – Madame Blanchard*

'WHAT COURSE are we following?' Kennedy asked, seeing his friend consult the compass.

'N.N.W.'

'Good Lord! but that's not north!'

'No, Dick, but I think we're going to have some difficulty in reaching Gondokoro. I'm sorry, but in any case we've linked up the eastern explorations with the northern, so we mustn't grumble.'

The *Victoria* was gradually leaving the Nile behind.

'One last look at this impassable latitude which has baffled the boldest travellers,' said the doctor. 'These will be the unruly tribes reported by Petherick, D'Arnaud, Miani and young Lejean, to whom we owe the best work on the Upper Nile.'

'Then do our discoveries agree with the prophecies of science?' asked Kennedy.

'Entirely. The sources of the White Klver, the Bahr-elAbiad, run into a lake as big as a sea, and it is this lake which gives birth to the river. No doubt poetry will suffer. Men liked to ascribe a celestial origin to this king of rivers. The ancients called it Ocean and almost believed that it flowed directly from the Sun. But one must give way from time to time before the teaching of Science. There may not always be scientists, but there will always be poets.'

'There are some more waterfalls,' said Joe.

'They are the Falls of Makedo, in the third parallel. Nothing could be more accurate. What a pity we couldn't have followed the course of the Nile for a few hours.'

'And over there, ahead of us,' said Kennedy, 'I can see the top of a mountain.'

'It is Logwek, the Trembling Mountain of the Arabs. All this country has been explored by Debono, who passed through it under the name of Latif Effendi. The tribes near the Nile are enemies and wage war to the death upon one another. You can imagine the dangers he had to face.'

The wind was now bearing the *Victoria* to the north-westward. To avoid Mount Logwek it was necessary to seek another current.

'My friends,' the doctor said to his two companions, 'we are now beginning to cross Africa in real earnest. Up to now we have been chiefly following the trail of our predecessors. Now we are about to launch into the unknown. Are we ready to face it?'

'Rather,' cried Dick and Joe together.

'Off we go, then, and Heaven prosper us.'

At 10 p.m., after crossing ravines, forests, and scattered villages, the travellers reached the side of Trembling Mountain and passed along its gentle slopes. On this memorable 23rd of April they had, after running for fifteen hours before a strong wind, covered a distance of over 315 miles. But this part of the journey had left upon them a melancholy impression. Complete silence reigned in the car. Was Dr Fergusson absorbed in his discoveries? Were his companions reflecting on this crossing of unknown regions? These thoughts were no doubt partly responsible, but with them were mingled poignant memories of England and distant friends. Joe alone maintained his good spirits, and thought it quite natural that the homeland should be no longer there the moment it was absent. However, he respected the silence of the other two.

At 11 p.m. the *Victoria* moored abreast of Trembling Mountain.* The travellers ate a substantial meal and fell asleep in turn, taking the watch in succession.

The following morning they wakened with brighter thoughts. The weather was beautiful and the wind blowing in their favour. Breakfast, much enlivened by Joe, put a final touch to their good humour. The district they were traversing was of vast dimensions, stretching from the Mountains of the Moon to those of Darfur, and so about the size of Europe.

'We are now crossing what is supposed to be the kingdom of Usoga,' said the doctor. 'Geographers have claimed that there used to exist in the centre of Africa a huge depression, a vast central lake. We'll see if there's any appearance of truth in this.'

'But how did they arrive at this idea?' asked Kennedy.

'Through the stories told by the Arabs. These people are great story-tellers, perhaps too much so. Travellers arriving at Kazeh or the Great Lakes saw slaves from the central districts, questioned them as to their country, put together a number of these stories and reduced them to a theory. Beneath it all there is always some grain of truth and, you see, they were not deceived as to the origin of the Nile.'

'Nothing could be more accurate,' replied Kennedy.

'It is upon these documents that the sketch-maps have been based. I intend to set our course by one of them and, if necessary, correct it.'

'Is all this region inhabited?' asked Joe.

'Without a doubt, and unpleasantly so.'

'I thought as much.'

'These scattered tribes are included in the general name of Nyam Nyams,[47] which is merely onomatopœic, and reproduces the sound of mastication.'

'That's good,' said Joe; 'nyam! nyam!'

'My dear Joe, if you were the immediate cause of this onomatopœia you wouldn't find it quite so good.'

'What do you mean, sir?'

'That these people are said to be cannibals.'

'Is that true?'

---

* Tradition says that it trembles whenever a Mussulman sets foot upon it.

'Quite true. It was also said that they possessed tails like animals, but it was soon discovered that these appendages belonged to the skins they wore.'

'Well, at any rate, a tail is a good thing for driving off mosquitoes, sir.'

'That may be, Joe, but this can be put down as a fable, like the dogs' heads attributed to certain tribes by the explorer, Brun-Rollet.'

'Dogs' heads? Useful for barking and not a bad thing for a cannibal.'

'One thing that has unfortunately been reported is the ferocity of these tribes and their avidity for human flesh, which they hunt down passionately.'

'I hope they won't show too much keenness for mine,' said Joe.

'Listen to that,' said Kennedy.

'It's this way, Mr Kennedy. If I've got to be eaten in case of need, I'd like it to be to your advantage or my master's. But as for providing food for these niggers, bless me, I'd rather die.'

'All right, Joe,' said Kennedy. 'That's understood. We shall rely on you when the time comes.'

'At your service, gentlemen.'

'Joe talks like this,' remarked the doctor, 'to make us pamper him and fatten him up.'

'Perhaps,' Joe answered. 'Men are selfish animals.'

During the afternoon the sky was hidden by a warm mist that rose from the ground. This made it almost impossible to distinguish anything on the earth, so at about five o'clock the doctor, afraid of running upon some unexpected mountain peak, gave the signal to halt. The night passed without any accident, but the intense darkness made it necessary to keep a doubly sharp look-out. Throughout the morning of the following day the monsoon blew with extreme violence. Wind drove into the lower cavities of the balloon, hurling to and fro the appendix through which the expansion pipes passed. These had to be made fast with ropes, a task which Joe carried out with great skill. At the same time he ascertained that the orifice of the balloon was still hermetically closed.

'That's doubly important for us,' said Dr Fergusson. 'In the first place, we avoid losing precious gas and, in addition, it prevents our leaving around us an inflammable trail which might end by setting us on fire.'

'That would be awkward,' said Joe.

'Should we be dashed to the ground?' asked Kennedy.

'No, not dashed; The gas would burn quietly and we should come down gradually. Such an accident did happen to a French aeronaut, Madame Blanchard. She set fire to her balloon by letting off fireworks, but she did not fall and would probably not have been killed if her car had not struck a chimney, from the top of which she was thrown to the ground.'

'It's to be hoped nothing of the sort will happen to us,' said Kennedy. 'Up to now our journey has not struck me as dangerous, and I see no reason why we should not reach our goal.'

'Nor I, old man. Besides, accidents have always been caused by the carelessness of the aeronaut or the faulty construction of the balloon. Moreover, out of several thousand ascents there have not been twenty fatal accidents. As a rule, landing and rising from the ground are the most dangerous parts of the business. But we can't afford to neglect any precautions.'

'It's lunch-time, sir,' said Joe. 'We'll have to be satisfied with tinned meat and coffee until Mr Kennedy can manage to get us a nice piece of venison.'

CHAPTER XX

The bottle out of the sky – Fig-palms – Mammoth trees –
The tree of war – Winged horses – A battle between
two tribes – A massacre – Divine intervention

THE WIND BECAME violent and irregular. The *Victoria* was blown about in all directions, now northward, now southward, and met with no regular current.

'We're moving very fast without making much headway,' said Kennedy, noting the oscillations of the compass needle.

'We're doing at least ninety miles an hour,' said Fergusson. 'Lean your head out and see how quickly the country is sliding away below us. Look at that forest dashing at us.'

'It's already a clearing,' replied Kennedy.

'And the clearing a village,' Joe put in a few moments later. 'Those niggers look pretty astonished.'

'And very natural,' answered the doctor. 'When they first saw balloons, the French peasants used to fire, taking them for monsters of the air, so it's permissible for a Sudan negro to open his eyes pretty wide.'

'Good Lord!' said Joe, while the *Victoria* was skimming over a village, a hundred feet from the ground. 'If I may, sir, I'll throw down an empty bottle. If it reaches them whole they'll worship it, and if it breaks they'll use the pieces as charms.'

So saying, he threw out a bottle, which was, of course, shattered into a thousand pieces. The natives dashed out of their round huts, shouting loudly. A little later Kennedy exclaimed: 'Just look at that strange tree. The top part is of a different species from the bottom.'

'Well,' said Joe. 'Here's a country where the trees grow on top of one another.'

'It's only a fig trunk on which a little vegetable loam has been spread,' replied the doctor. 'One fine day the wind blew a palm seed into it, and the palm has grown just as it would in a field.'

'A great idea,' said Joe. 'I'll try it in England. It would look well in the London parks, besides being a way of getting more fruit trees. You could have gardens one on top of the other. The people with small gardens would like it.'

At this moment the *Victoria* had to be lifted to clear a forest of trees over three hundred feet high, a kind of banyan, hundreds of years old.

'What splendid trees,' cried Kennedy. 'I know no finer sight than these ancient forests. Just look, Samuel.'

'These banyans are indeed of extraordinary height, Dick; and yet there would be nothing surprising about them in the American forests.'

'Do you mean to say there are trees taller than these?'

'What are called "mammoth trees" are certainly taller. In California they have found a tree measuring four hundred and fifty feet, higher than the tower of the Houses of Parliament or even the Great Pyramid in Egypt. At its base the trunk had a circumference of a hundred and twenty feet, and the concentric layers of wood showed that it was over four thousand years old.'

'Well, sir, in that case there's nothing to be surprised at. Anyone four thousand years old ought to be a good size.'

But during this conversation the forest had already given place to a large collection of huts, arranged in a circle round an open space in the centre of which a single tree stood. When he saw it Joe exclaimed:

'Well, if that tree has been producing flowers like those for four thousand years, it hasn't much to be proud of,' and he pointed to a gigantic sycamore, whose trunk was completely buried beneath a mass of human bones. The flowers Joe spoke of were freshly-cut heads, hanging from knives stuck into the bark.

'The war-tree of the cannibals,' said the doctor. 'The Indians remove the scalp, the Africans the entire head.'

'A matter of fashion, then,' said Joe.

But already the village with the bleeding heads was vanishing on the horizon. Another, farther on, afforded a spectacle no less repulsive. Corpses half-eaten away, skeletons crumbling into dust, and human limbs scattered over the ground, had been left for the hyenas and jackals to feed upon.

'Those are probably the bodies of criminals. It is the custom in Abyssinia to leave them to the mercy of the wild animals, which finish them off at their leisure after tearing their throats with their teeth.'

'After all, it's not much more cruel than the stake,' said the Scotsman. 'Messier, that's all.'

'In the southern parts of Africa,' the doctor went on, 'they merely shut the criminal up in his own hut, with all his livestock and perhaps his family, set fire to it and burn the lot together. That's what I call cruelty; but I agree with you, Kennedy, even if the gibbet is less cruel, it is just as barbarous.'

With his excellent sight, of which he made such good use, Joe reported some flocks of carnivorous birds soaring over the horizon.

'They're eagles,' exclaimed Kennedy, after looking at them through his glass, 'splendid birds, and they're flying as fast as we are.'

'Heaven preserve us from being attacked by them,' said the doctor. 'They're more dangerous to us than wild beasts or savage tribes.'

'Pooh!' retorted Kennedy; 'a few shots would soon scatter them.'

'I'd rather not have to rely on your skill, old man. The silk of our balloon wouldn't hold out against a peck from one of those. Luckily, I think the birds are more frightened by our balloon than attracted.'

'I've got an idea, sir,' said Joe. 'I'm full of ideas today. How would it be to harness some live eagles to our car and let them drag us through the air?'

'The idea has already been seriously considered,' the doctor replied, 'but I don't think it would be workable with such spirited birds.'

'They could be trained,' Joe said. 'Instead of bits they could be guided by eye-pieces to stop them from seeing. By covering one eye you could make them turn to right or left, and by covering both they could be stopped.'

'You must allow me to prefer a favourable wind to your harnessed eagles, Joe. It costs less for upkeep and is more reliable.'

'As you like, sir, but I stick to my idea.'

It was noon. For some time the *Victoria*'s pace had been more moderate. The country was still passing below them, but less rapidly. Suddenly shouts and the sharp whizz of arrows reached the travellers' ears. Leaning over, they saw upon the open plain a sight which might well stir them. Two tribes were engaged in a furious battle; clouds of arrows were flying through the air. The combatants, busy killing one another, did not notice the *Victoria*. About three hundred men were struggling in a tangled mass. Most of them, wallowing in the blood of the wounded, presented a hideous spectacle.

When they caught sight of the balloon there was a pause. Then the pandemonium redoubled and some arrows were loosed against the car, one flying so close that Joe caught it in his hand.

'Let's get up out of range,' cried Fergusson. 'No risks. We can't afford them.'

The mutual massacre continued with axe and assegai. As soon as an enemy fell to the ground his adversary would at once cut off his head. The women, mingling with the tumult, picked up these bleeding heads and piled them up at either end of the battlefield, often fighting among themselves for possession of the hideous trophy.

'What a ghastly scene!' exclaimed Kennedy in profound disgust.

'They're nasty fellows,' said Joe. 'If they were only in uniform they'd be just like other warriors the world over.'

'I feel a desperate itch to intervene in the fight,' continued the Scotsman, brandishing his carbine.

'No, no,' the doctor replied sharply. 'Let's mind our own business. Who are you to play the part of Providence, when you don't even know who's right and who's wrong! Let's get away from it as quickly as possible. If our great leaders could get a bird's-eye view like this of their exploits they might lose their taste for blood and conquest.'

The chief of one of these savage armies was distinguishable by his athletic build, combined with herculean strength. With one hand he would plunge his lance into the serried ranks of his enemies and with the other open up great gaps with his axe. Once he hurled away his blood-stained assegai, threw himself upon a wounded man, cut off his arm at a single blow, picked it up and, raising it to his mouth, bit into it with his teeth.

'Pah!' said Kennedy. 'The swine! I can't stand any more of this,' and the warrior fell backwards with a bullet in his forehead.

With his fall a deep stupor took possession of his men. This supernatural death struck terror into them, at the same time putting fresh life into their enemies, and in a second the battlefield was deserted by half the combatants.

'Let's get up and look for a breeze that will get us away,' said the doctor. 'This makes me feel sick.'

But he was not in time to avoid seeing the victorious tribe hurl themselves upon the dead and wounded and fight among themselves over the still warm flesh, which they devoured greedily.

'Pah!' said Joe. 'How disgusting!'

The *Victoria* rose as the gas expanded. The howling of the delirious horde followed them for a few moments, but at length, borne southward, they left the scene of carnage and cannibalism behind them. The ground then became broken with numerous watercourses flowing eastward and doubtless joining those tributaries of Lake Nu, or of the Gazelle River, about which M. Guillaume Lejean has furnished such curious details. With the fall of night the *Victoria* anchored, in long. 27° E., lat. 4° 20' N., after a journey of one hundred and fifty miles.

CHAPTER XXI

Strange noises – A night attack – Kennedy and Joe in a tree – Two shots – 'Help! Help!' – An answer in French – The plan of rescue

THE NIGHT GREW very dark. The doctor had been unable to recognise the country. He had moored to a strong, tall tree, whose vague bulk he could hardly distinguish in the darkness. As his habit was, he took the nine o'clock watch, and at midnight Kennedy came to relieve him.

'Keep a keen look-out, Dick.'

'Has anything happened?'

'No. But I thought I heard strange sounds below us. I'm none too sure where the wind has brought us, and a little extra caution can do no harm.'

'You must have heard the cries of the wild beasts.'

'No. This seems quite different. In any case, don't fail to wake us at the slightest alarm.'

'You needn't worry about that.'

After listening attentively once more, the doctor, hearing nothing, threw himself down on his blanket and was soon asleep. The sky was covered with thick clouds, but not a breath disturbed the air. The *Victoria*, held by a single anchor, made no movement. Kennedy, leaning his elbow on the side of the car so as to be in a position to keep an eye on the burner, gazed into the still darkness. He searched the horizon and as happens to uneasy or expectant minds, he thought from time to time that he could distinguish vague lights. Once, even, he thought he could clearly see one some two hundred yards away, but it was only a flash, after which he saw nothing further. Probably it was merely one of those imaginary flashes that appear to anyone who gazes into deep darkness. Kennedy reassured himself and was once more relapsing into his vague contemplation when a sharp hissing noise broke the silence.

Was it the cry of some animal or bird of the night? Was it from human lips? Kennedy, realising the full gravity of the situation, was on the point of awakening his companions, but he told himself that in any case the men or animals, whichever it was, were out of reach. He inspected his weapons and with his night-glass once more searched the space around him. Soon he thought he could make out vague forms gliding towards the tree below.

By the light of a moonbeam which filtered like a flicker of lightning between two clouds, he distinctly saw a group of individuals moving in the darkness. The adventure with the apes came back to his mind. He placed his hand on the doctor's shoulder. The latter awoke instantly.

'Hush!' said Kennedy. 'Whisper.'

'Has something happened?'

'Yes. Wake Joe.'

As soon as Joe had got up, Kennedy related what he had seen.

'Some more of those beastly monkeys?' said Joe.

'Possibly. We must take precautions.'

'Joe and I,' said Kennedy, 'will go down into the tree by the ladder.'

'And meanwhile,' the doctor put in, 'I'll fix things so that we can get away quickly.'

'Right, oh!'

'Come along, sir,' said Joe.

'Don't use your weapons except as a last resource,' said the doctor. 'We don't want to advertise our presence here.'

Dick and Joe replied with a nod. They lowered themselves noise-lessly towards the tree and took up their position on a fork of strong branches in which the anchor was fixed. For some minutes they remained silent and motionless among the foliage. Hearing a rustle against the bark, Joe seized Kennedy's arm.

'Do you hear?'

'Yes. It's getting nearer.'

'Suppose it's a snake? That hiss you heard – '

'No. There was something human about it.'

'I'd rather have savages,' Joe muttered to himself. 'These reptiles give me the creeps.'

'It's getting louder,' Kennedy said a few moments later.

'Yes. It's coming up, climbing.'

'Watch this side, I'll see to the other.'

'All right.'

They were sitting on a main branch which grew straight out of the centre of one of those huge trees called baobabs. The darkness, increased by the density of the foliage, was intense, but Joe, leaning towards Kennedy's ear and pointing to the lower part of the tree, said: 'Niggers!'

A few whispered words reached the two men. Joe raised his rifle.

'Wait,' said Kennedy.

Some savages had indeed climbed into the baobab. They were coming up from all sides, gliding along the branches like snakes, mounting slowly but surely. They could be distinguished by the smell of their bodies smeared with rancid fat. Soon two heads came into sight, on a level with the branch upon which Kennedy and Joe were sitting.

'Now!' said Kennedy. 'Fire!'

The double report rang out like thunder and died away amid cries of pain. In an instant the whole horde had vanished. But through the howls they had heard a strange, unexpected and impossible cry. A human voice had distinctly cried in French: 'Help! Help!'

Dumbfounded, Kennedy and Joe swung themselves up into the car with all speed.

'Did you hear?' the doctor asked them.

'We did. It's incredible. "Help! Help!" '

'A Frenchman in the hands of these ruffians!'

'A traveller.'

'A missionary, perhaps.'

'Poor devil,' cried Kennedy, 'they are murdering him, or torturing him.'

The doctor tried in vain to hide his emotion.

'There's no doubt about it,' he said. 'A wretched Frenchman has fallen into the hands of these beasts. We can't go without doing all we can to save him. When he heard our shots he must have realised that unhoped-for help was at hand, providential intervention. We won't destroy this last hope. Do you agree?'

'We do, Samuel, and we are at your orders.'

'Let's think it out, and as soon as it's light we'll try to rescue him.'

'But how are we going to get rid of these beastly niggers?' asked Kennedy.

'I feel sure, from the way they bolted,' said the doctor, 'that they don't know what firearms are, so we ought to make the most of their fright. But we can't act before it's light, and we shall have to make our plans according to the lie of the ground.'

'The poor wretch can't be far off,' said Joe. 'I – '

'Help! Help!' came the voice again, weaker this time.

'The swine!' cried Joe, shaking with indignation. 'But suppose they kill him in the night?'

'Do you hear, Sam?' Kennedy broke in, seizing the doctor's arm. 'Suppose they kill him in the night?'

'It's not likely. These savage races kill their prisoners in the daylight. They must have the sun.'

'How would it be,' said the Scot, 'if I took advantage of the dark to try and creep up to the poor fellow?'

'I'll come with you, sir.'

'Wait a minute! Wait a minute! The idea does you credit, but you'd be exposing us all and would only be doing still more harm to the man you're trying to save.'

'How?' asked Kennedy. 'These niggers are terrified, scattered. They won't come back.'

'Dick, I beg of you, do what I say. I'm acting for the safety of us all. If you happened to be taken by surprise it would be all up.'

'But this poor fellow waiting, hoping! No answer. No one coming to help him. He must be thinking his senses have deceived him, that he heard nothing – '

'We can reassure him,' said Dr Fergusson, and, standing up in the darkness and using his hands as a megaphone, he shouted loudly in French: 'You, there, whoever you are! Don't worry. There are three friends here looking after you.'

A terrible roar answered him, doubtless drowning the prisoner's reply.

'He's being murdered, or going to be,' cried Kennedy. 'All we've done is to hasten his death. We must act.'

'But how, Dick? What can we do in this darkness?'

'Oh, if only it was light!' sighed Joe.

'And supposing it were?' the doctor asked in a strange tone.

'Nothing simpler, Samuel,' replied the Scot. 'I'd go down and scatter the scum with a carbine.'

'And you, Joe?' asked Fergusson.

'I'd be more careful, sir. I'd give the prisoner a sign to escape in a special direction.'

'And how would you do that?'

'With this arrow I caught. I'd stick a note on it, or I could simply shout, for these niggers wouldn't understand.'

'None of these plans would work, my friends. The chief difficulty would be for the poor fellow to get away, even supposing he evaded his guards. As for your idea, Dick, old man, if you were very bold and took advantage of the fear our guns produced, your plan might succeed. But if it failed, it would be all over with you and we should have two to save instead of one. No, we must have all the chances on our side. We must try something else.'

'But we'll have to look sharp,' replied Kennedy.

'Perhaps,' Fergusson answered, emphasising the word.

'Do you know a way of breaking the darkness, sir?'

'Who knows, Joe?'

'Oh! If you could do that, I'd say you were the wisest man in the world.'

The doctor was silent for a few moments, lost in thought. His two companions watched him eagerly. The extraordinary situation had worked them up to a high pitch of excitement. Soon Fergusson went on: 'This is my plan. We have two hundred pounds of ballast left, for we haven't used any. We'll suppose this man, who is obviously exhausted by suffering, weighs the same as one of us. That would leave us about sixty pounds for a quick rise.'

'What are you getting at?' asked Kennedy.

'This, Dick. It's clear, if I reach the prisoner and throw out ballast equal to his weight, I shan't affect the equilibrium of the balloon; but then, if I want to rise quickly to get away from these negroes, I shall have to use something more drastic than the burner. Now, by throwing out this surplus of ballast at the given moment, I'm certain of rising very rapidly.'

'That's clear.'

'Yes, but there is one disadvantage; when I want to come down later I shall have to loose a quantity of gas in proportion to the excess of ballast I've dropped. But gas is precious. However, we can't grudge its loss when it's a question of a man's life.'

'You're right, Samuel. We must sacrifice anything to save him.'

'Come on, then, put those sacks round the edge of the car so that they can be thrown out by a single push.'

'But the darkness?'

'It will hide our preparations and we can deal with it when we're ready. Be careful to have all the guns ready to hand. We may need them. The carbine gives us one shot, the two guns four, the two revolvers twelve. That makes seventeen, which could be fired off in a quarter of a minute. But perhaps we shan't need to make all this din. Are you ready?'

'Aye, aye, sir!' Joe answered.

The sacks were set in position, the guns placed ready.

'Good,' said the doctor. 'Keep an eye on everything. Joe, you be ready to throw out the ballast, and you, Dick, to get hold of the prisoner; but don't do anything till I give the word. Now, Joe, you go down and loose the anchor and come back as quick as you can.'

Joe slid down the rope and was back a few seconds later. Set free, the *Victoria* floated almost motionless in the air. Meanwhile the doctor assured himself that there was enough gas in the mixing chamber to feed the burner if required, without having to use the Bunsen battery for a time. He removed the two conducting wires which were used to decompose the water, then, rummaging in his valise, took out two pieces of carbon, sharpened to a point, and fixed one to the end of each wire. His two companions watched him without understanding, but did not speak. When the doctor had finished his preparations he stood up in the middle of the car, took the pieces of carbon, one in each hand, and brought the two points together. With an intolerable glare, an intense and dazzling ray was produced between the two carbon points. A vast sheet of electric light literally tore through the blackness of the night.

'Oh! sir!' said Joe.

'Don't speak,' said the doctor.

CHAPTER XXII

The sheet of light – The missionary – He is picked up by the light from the balloon – A Lazarist priest – Little hope – Medical attention – A life of self-denial – Passing a volcano

FERGUSSON DIRECTED his powerful ray towards different points of space and brought it to a standstill over a place whence cries of terror could be heard. His two companions peered down eagerly. The baobab over which the *Victoria* hung almost motionless rose from the centre of a clearing. Among fields of sesame and sugar-cane they could see some fifty low, conical huts, round which a swarm of men were clustered. A hundred feet below the balloon stood a stake, at the foot of which lay a human creature, a young man of thirty at most, half-naked, with long black hair, emaciated, and covered with blood and wounds, his head hanging on his chest like Christ's on the Cross. His hair, cut close over the crown of his head, still showed where his tonsure had been.

'A missionary! A priest!' cried Joe.

'Poor wretch!' said Kennedy.

'We'll save him, Dick,' said the doctor. 'We'll save him.'

The crowd of negroes, seeing the balloon like a huge comet with a blazing tail, were seized with a terror that can easily be understood. Hearing their cries, the prisoner raised his head. A swift light of hope came into his eyes and, without too clear an idea of what was happening, he stretched his hands towards these unexpected helpers.

'He's alive!' cried Fergusson. 'Thank God. The brutes are scared out of their lives. We'll get him. Are you ready?'

'Yes, Samuel.'

'Joe, put out the burner.'

The doctor's order was carried out. A hardly perceptible breeze gently moved the *Victoria* over the prisoner and at the same time she gradually dropped as the gas contracted. For about ten minutes she remained floating in a sea of light. Fergusson directed his beams upon the crowd. The natives, panic-stricken, gradually vanished into the huts until the space round the stake was left empty. The doctor was right in relying on the fantastic apparition of the *Victoria* pouring rays of light into the intense darkness. The car drew near the ground, but meanwhile some of the bolder among the negroes, realising that their victim was about to escape them, returned, shouting. Kennedy picked up his gun, but the doctor told him not to fire.

The priest, on his knees and without the strength to stand, was not even tied to the stake, his weakness making this unnecessary. The moment the car was almost touching the ground, Kennedy threw aside his gun, seized the priest round the body and hauled him into the car. At the same moment Joe pushed out the two hundred pounds of ballast. The doctor was expecting to rise with extreme rapidity but, contrary to his expectation, the balloon, after rising three or four feet from the ground, hung motionless.

'What's holding us?' he cried in a tone of fear.

Some of the savages ran up, uttering fierce cries.

'Oh!' cried Joe, leaning over. 'One of these brutes is hanging to the bottom of the car.'

'Dick,' cried the doctor, 'the water container!'

Dick divined his friend's thought and, raising one of the water containers, which weighed over a hundred pounds, he threw it overboard. The *Victoria*, suddenly relieved of this weight, leapt three hundred feet into the air, amid the roars of the savages, who saw their prisoner escaping in a dazzling shaft of light.

'Hurrah!' cried the doctor's two companions.

Suddenly the balloon took another leap, which brought her to a height of a thousand feet.

'What's that?' asked Kennedy, who was almost thrown off his feet.

'Nothing. Only that blackguard letting go,' Fergusson replied calmly.

Joe, leaning over quickly, was in time to watch the savage twist through the air with outstretched arms and dash himself to pieces on the ground. The doctor then separated the two electric points and the darkness once more became profound. It was 1 a.m. The Frenchman, who had swooned, at last opened his eyes.

'You're safe,' the doctor told him.

'Safe,' he answered in English, with a sad smile. 'Saved from a cruel death. My brothers, I thank you. But my days are numbered, my hours even, and I have not long to live.' And the exhausted missionary again fell back, unconscious.

'He's dying!' cried Dick.

'No, no,' Fergusson answered, leaning over him, 'but he's very weak. Lay him under the tent.'

They gently stretched the poor emaciated body, covered with scars and still bleeding wounds which showed where iron and fire had done their cruel work. The doctor made some lint with his handkerchief and placed it on the wounds, after washing them. These attentions he carried out with the skill of an expert; then, taking a cordial from his medicine-chest, he poured a few drops on to the priest's lips. The man feebly closed his blistered mouth and with difficulty summoned strength to say: 'Thank you. Thank you.'

The doctor saw that he needed absolute rest. He closed the curtains of the tent and returned to take command of the balloon. Allowing for the weight of the new occupant, the *Victoria* had been lightened by nearly one hundred and eighty pounds, and so kept up without any help from the burner. With the first rays of daylight a current of air drove her gently west-north-west. Kennedy went to take a look at the sleeping priest.

'I hope we'll be able to save this man who has been sent to us. Do you think there's any chance?' he said.

'Yes, Dick, with care. This air is so pure.'

'How he must have gone through it!' said Joe with feeling. 'You know he had to be braver than us to go alone among these people.'

'That's quite true,' Kennedy answered.

Throughout the day the doctor would not allow the poor man's sleep to be disturbed. It lasted long, broken only by a few murmurs of pain, which made Fergusson feel anxious. Towards evening the *Victoria* came to a standstill in the darkness, and during the night, while Joe and Kennedy took turns by the sick man's side, Fergusson watched over the safety of them all The next morning the *Victoria* had drifted very little westward. The day dawned clear and splendid. The invalid was able to speak to his new friends more distinctly. The curtains of the awning were raised and he breathed the fresh morning air with satisfaction.

'How do you feel?' Fergusson asked.

'A bit better, I think,' he replied. 'But so far, my friends, I have only seen you in a dream. I can scarcely realise what has happened. Who are you, that you may not be forgotten in my last prayer?'

'We're English travellers,' the doctor replied. 'We're trying to cross Africa in a balloon, and on the way we've had the good luck to save you.'

'Science has its heroes,' said the missionary.

'But religion has its martyrs,' the Scotsman added.

'You're a missionary?' Fergusson asked.

'I'm a priest of the Lazarist Mission. Heaven has sent you to me. Heaven be praised. The sacrifice of my life was accomplished. But you come from Europe. Speak to me of Europe, of France. I have had no news for five years.'

'Five years alone among these savages!' exclaimed Kennedy.

'They are souls to be brought back,' said the young priest. 'Ignorant wild brothers whom religion alone can teach and civilise.'

Dr Fergusson, in response to the missionary's request, talked to him for a long time about France. The man listened, and tears poured from his eyes. He took the hands of the three men in turn in his own, which were burning with fever. The doctor made him several cups of tea, which he drank with enjoyment, and he then had sufficient strength to raise himself a little and smile at finding himself being carried through the clear air.

'You are brave travellers,' he said, 'and you will succeed in your audacious enterprise. You will see again your relations, your friends, your country – '

The young priest then grew so weak that he had to lie down again. A state of prostration lasting several hours kept him as though dead in Fergusson's arms, who could not restrain his emotion as he felt his life ebb away. Were they then so soon to lose this man they had snatched from death? He again dressed the dreadful wounds of the martyr, and had to sacrifice the greater part of his supply of water to cool his burning lips. He lavished upon him the tenderest and wisest care. In his arms the sick man gradually took a fresh hold on life and won back at least feeling. The doctor patched together his story from his halting words.

'Speak your own language,' he said. 'I understand it and it will be less tiring for you.'

The missionary was a poor young man from the village of Aradon, in the centre of Brittany. His earliest instincts had drawn him towards an ecclesiastical career. To this life of self-denial he desired to add the life of danger by entering the order of the mission founded by Saint Vincent de Paul. When he was twenty years old he left his country for the inhospitable shores of Africa whence, gradually overcoming obstacles and facing privations, marching forward and praying, he came among the tribes inhabiting the banks of the tributaries which flow into the Upper Nile. For two years his religion was rejected, his zeal misconstrued, his charity flouted. He remained a prisoner of one of the cruellest tribes of Nyambarra, the victim of persistent ill-treatment. But still he went on, teaching and praying. This tribe having been dispersed and himself left for dead after one of those battles so frequent between one tribe and another, instead of retracing his steps he pursued his evangelical pilgrimage. The most peaceful times he enjoyed were when he was taken for a madman. He had made himself familiar with the language of these districts, and he taught the Catechism. In short, for two more long years he traversed these barbarous regions, driven on by the superhuman strength that comes from God. For the last year he had been living with the Nyam Nyam tribe that is called Barafri, one of the most savage. When the chief died a few days before, the death was ascribed to the influence of the missionary, and it was decided to put him to death. His torture had lasted forty hours and, as the doctor had supposed, he was to die at noon. When he heard the shots, Nature carried the day. He shouted for help, and when a voice from the sky brought him words of encouragement, he thought he was dreaming.

'I don't regret this life which is leaving me. My life is God's,' he said.

'There's still hope,' the doctor replied. 'We are with you. We'll save you from death as we have saved you from torture.'

'I do not ask so much of Heaven,' replied the priest with resignation. 'Blessed be God, who has given me, before I die, the joy of pressing the hands of a friend and hearing the language of my country.'

The missionary weakened again. The day passed thus between hope and fear, Kennedy being deeply moved and Joe trying to keep his eyes averted. The *Victoria* made little headway, and the wind seemed to be sparing its precious burden.

Towards evening Joe sighted a great light in the west, which in more northern regions they would have taken to be the aurora borealis. The sky seemed on fire. The doctor examined the phenomenon attentively.

'It must be a volcano in eruption,' he said.

'But the wind is driving us directly on to it,' said Kennedy.

'Well, we shall clear it at a comfortable height.'

Three hours later the *Victoria* was over mountainous country. Her exact position was lat. 4°42' N., long. 24°15' E. Ahead of her a blazing crater was pouring out torrents of molten lava, and hurling great masses of rock to an enormous height. Streams of liquid fire poured down in dazzling cascades. It was a magnificent sight, but betokened danger, for the wind, remaining constant, was driving the balloon persistently towards this fiery atmosphere. As it was impossible to evade the obstacle, it would have to be cleared. The burner was heated to its utmost limit and the *Victoria* reached 6000 feet, leaving between the volcano and herself a distance of more than 1800 feet

From his bed of pain the dying priest could see this burning crater throwing out thousands of dazzling flames with a deafening roar.

'What a beautiful sight!' he said. 'How infinite is God's power – even in terrible manifestations!'

The stream of burning lava covered the sides of the mountain with a veritable carpet of flame. The lower slopes shone in the darkness; a torrid heat rose to the car and Dr Fergusson was anxious to escape with all speed from the dangerous situation.

About 10 p.m. the mountain had become merely a glowing point on the horizon and the *Victoria* was quietly pursuing her way on a lower level.

CHAPTER XXIII

Joe angry – Death of a good man – The vigil by the body – The burial – The blocks of quartz – Joe's hallucination – Precious ballast – Discovery of the auriferous mountains – Beginning of Joe's despair

A MAGNIFICENT NIGHT spread over the earth. The priest relapsed into a state of peaceful coma.

'He won't come round,' said Joe. 'Poor young fellow; not thirty!'

'He will die in our arms,' said the doctor in despair. 'His breathing is growing even weaker still, and I can do nothing to save him.'

'The blackguards!' exclaimed Joe, who was given to occasional sudden outbursts of temper. 'And to think that this good priest could still think of words to pity them, find excuses for them, forgive them!'

'Heaven has given him a splendid night, Joe; perhaps his last. He won't suffer much now, and his death will be like falling into a peaceful sleep.'

The dying man uttered a few halting words. The doctor drew close to him. The sick man's breathing became laboured. He was asking for air. The curtains were completely drawn back, and he drew in with enjoyment the light breath of this transparent night. The stars showered upon him their twinkling rays and the moon wrapped him in a shroud of white.

'My friends,' he said weakly, 'I'm going. May God, who rewards the righteous, bring you safe to port. May He pay for me my debt of gratitude.'

'Don't give in yet,' Kennedy answered. 'It's only a passing weakness. You're not going to die. Could anyone die on a beautiful summer night like this?'

'Death has come,' replied the missionary. 'I know it. Let me face it. Death, the beginning of eternal things, is only the end of earthly cares. Raise me to my knees, my brothers, I beg of you.'

Kennedy lifted him. It was pitiable to see his nerveless limbs give way beneath him.

'God, have pity upon me,' cried the dying missionary.

His face was radiant. Far above the earth, whose joys he had never known, in this night which shed upon him its gentlest radiance, on this road of Heaven towards which he was rising as in a miraculous ascension, he seemed already to have entered upon a new existence. His last gesture was a final benediction to his new friends. Then he fell back into the arms of Kennedy, whose face was bathed in tears.

'Dead!' said the doctor, bending over him. 'Dead!' and with a common impulse the three friends fell on their knees in silent prayer.

'Tomorrow morning,' Fergusson went on a little later, 'we'll bury him in this African soil upon which his blood has been shed.'

During the rest of the night the body was guarded in turn by the doctor, Kennedy and Joe, and not a word disturbed the religious silence. All were in tears.

The following day the wind was blowing from the south and the *Victoria* made her way rather slowly over a vast mountain plateau. Here could be seen extinct craters, there uncultivated ravines. Not a drop of water on any of these gnarled craters. Piles of rock, stray blocks of stone, grey marl-pits, everything indicated complete sterility.

About noon the doctor, in order to bury the body, decided to come down in a ravine amid gigantic rocks of primitive formation. The surrounding mountains would act as a shelter and allow him to bring his car to the ground, for there was no tree to which he could make fast. But as he had explained to Kennedy, owing to the loss of ballast at the time of the priest's rescue he could now only descend by losing a proportional quantity of gas. He therefore opened the valve of the outer balloon. The hydrogen escaped and the *Victoria* sank gently towards the ravine.

As soon as the car touched ground the doctor closed the valve. Joe leapt out, keeping one hand on the outer edge of the car while with the other he picked up a number of stones, which soon compensated for his own weight. He was then able to use both hands, and in a short time had piled over five hundred pounds of stone into the car. The doctor and Kennedy were then able to alight in their turn. The *Victoria* was in equilibrium, her lifting force counteracted.

Nor was it necessary to use a great quantity of stone, for the blocks picked up by Joe were extremely heavy, a fact which attracted Fergusson's attention. The ground was strewn with quartz and porphyritic rocks.

'What a strange thing!' the doctor mused.

Meanwhile Kennedy and Joe went off a few yards to select a site for the grave. It was intensely hot in this ravine, shut in as it was in a sort of furnace. The midday sun poured down vertically its burning rays. They first had to clear the ground of the fragments of rock which covered it, after which a grave was dug of sufficient depth to prevent the body being scratched up by wild animals. The corpse of the martyr was reverently laid in the grave. The grave was filled and large fragments of rock were arranged over it in the form of a tombstone.

Meanwhile the doctor remained motionless, deep in thought. He did not hear the call of his companions, and did not go with them to shelter from the heat of the day.

'What are you thinking of, Sam?' asked Kennedy.

'This strange contrast in Nature, this odd freak of chance. Do you know in what soil this self-denying man, this man, poor of heart, has been buried?'

'What do you mean, Sam?' his friend asked.

'This priest who had taken the vow of poverty is now resting in a gold mine.'

'A gold mine!' exclaimed the two others.

'A gold mine,' the doctor replied calmly. 'These blocks that you are trampling under foot like worthless stones are mineral of great purity.'

'It's impossible, impossible!' Joe repeated.

'You wouldn't have to search long in these fissures of schist before you found large nuggets.'

Joe hurled himself like a madman upon the scattered fragments, and

Kennedy was not long in following his example.

'Steady, Joe, my good fellow,' said his master.

'That's all very well, sir, but – '

'What! a philosopher like you.'

'Well, sir, no philosophy would hold out against this.'

'Come, think a little. What's the use of all this wealth to *us*? We can't take it away.'

'Not take it away?'

'It's a bit heavy for our car. I even hesitated to tell you about the discovery. I was afraid you'd be disappointed.'

'What!' said Joe. 'Leave all this treasure behind? It's a fortune for us. It's ours. Leave it behind!'

'Take care, my friend. Is the gold-fever taking hold of you? Didn't this dead man you've just buried teach you the vanity of human things?'

'That's all right, sir,' Joe answered; 'but, after all, gold! Mr Kennedy, aren't you going to help me to pick up a few millions?'

'What could we do with them?' said the Scot, who could not suppress a smile. 'We're not here to seek our fortunes, and we ought not to take it.'

'Your millions would be a bit heavy,' the doctor continued 'and they would hardly go into your pockets.'

'But, after all,' Joe replied, driven back to his last line of defence, 'can't we take the ore as ballast instead of sand?'

'All right. I'll agree to that,' said Fergusson. 'But you mustn't grumble when we have to throw a few thousands overboard.'

'A few thousands!' Joe exclaimed. 'Can all this be gold?'

'Yes, my friend. This is a storehouse into which Nature has been pouring her treasures for centuries. There's enough to enrich whole nations, an Australia and a Canada together in the heart of a desert.'

'And all no use!'

'Perhaps. In any case, I'll tell you what I'll do to console you.'

'It won't be easy, sir,' Joe replied, crestfallen.

'Listen. I'll make a note of the exact position of this place and give it to you, and when you get back to England you can tell your neighbours, if you think so much gold will bring them happiness.'

'Well, sir, I see you're right; so as there's nothing else to be done, let's fill the car and what's left at the end of the journey will still be so much to the good.'

Joe set to work eagerly, and had soon piled into the car nearly a thousand pounds of quartz fragments in which the gold was set like a hard vein. The doctor watched him with a smile, and while the work went on he took a reckoning and found the position of the missionary's tomb to be lat. 4° 55' N., long. 22° 23' E. Then, casting a last look at the mound under which the young Frenchman's body lay, he returned to the car. He would have liked to erect a rough and modest cross over this solitary tomb in the African desert, but there was not a tree in sight.

'God will remember where it is,' he said.

Another equally serious question was at the same time passing through Fergusson's mind. He would have given much to find a little water, for he wanted to replace that he had thrown overboard in the container when the negro was hanging to the car; but in this arid region it was impossible. This continued to cause him anxiety; obliged as he was continually to feed his burner, he had begun to run short for drinking purposes. He resolved, therefore, to neglect no opportunity for replenishing his supply.

When he reached the car he found it encumbered with the stones picked up by the avaricious Joe. He got in without a word. Kennedy took up his usual position and Joe followed them, not without throwing a covetous glance at the treasure in the ravine. The doctor lit his burner and the spiral grew hot. After a few minutes the hydrogen began to flow and the gas dilated, but the balloon did not budge. Joe watched uneasily and did not utter a word.

'Joe,' said the doctor.

No answer.

'Joe, do you hear?'

Joe made a sign that he had heard but would not understand.

'You'll be good enough,' Fergusson went on, 'to throw out some of this quartz.'

'But, sir, you said I could – '

'I said you could replace the ballast, that was all.'

'But – '

'Do you want us to stay in this desert for ever?'

Joe cast a despairing glance towards Kennedy, but the Scotsman assumed the air of a man who is helpless.

'Well, Joe?'

'Won't your burner work?' asked the stubborn fellow.

'The burner is lit, as you see. But the balloon won't rise until you've lightened her a bit.'

Joe scratched his head, picked up a bit of quartz, the smallest of all, weighed it in his hand repeatedly, throwing it up and catching it. It weighed three or four pounds. He then threw it overboard. The *Victoria* did not budge.

'Hello!' he said. 'We're not rising yet?'

'Not yet,' the doctor answered. 'Carry on.'

Kennedy was laughing. Joe threw out ten pounds or so. The balloon remained motionless. Joe turned pale.

'My poor fellow,' said Fergusson. 'We three, I believe, weigh about four hundred pounds. You'll have to throw out at least an equal weight, to compensate for us.'

'Throw out four hundred pounds!' cried Joe pitiably.

'And something extra to lift us. Come, hurry up.'

The worthy servant, sighing deeply, set to work to lighten the balloon. From time to time he would stop, saying, 'We're rising!'

'We're not,' was the invariable reply.

'She's moving,' he said at last.

'Carry on,' repeated Fergusson.

'She's rising. I'm sure she is.'

'Carry on,' replied Kennedy.

Then Joe picked up a last block and threw it desperately out of the car. The *Victoria* rose about a hundred feet, and with the help of the burner soon cleared the neighbouring peaks.

'Never mind, Joe,' said the doctor, 'you'll still have a useful fortune left if we manage to keep all this to the end of the trip, and you'll be a rich man for the rest of your days.'

Joe did not reply but stretched himself limply on his stony bed.

'You see, Dick, what gold can do with the best servant in the world. What passions, what greed and crime the secret of such a mine awakens. It's very depressing.'

By evening the *Victoria* had travelled ninety miles westward. She was now four hundred miles in a direct line from Zanzibar.

CHAPTER XXIV

The wind drops – The confines of the desert – Shortage of water – Equatorial nights – Fergusson's anxieties – The situation – Vehement replies from Kennedy and Joe – Another night

MOORED TO A SOLITARY withered tree, the *Victoria* passed the night in perfect calm. The travellers were able to enjoy a little of the sleep they so sorely needed, for the excitement of the last few days had left sad memories. Towards morning the sky resumed its brilliant clearness and heat. The balloon rose in the air and, after several fruitless attempts, fell in with a gentle current which bore them north-west.

'We're not making much headway,' said the doctor. 'Unless I'm mistaken, we've done half our journey in about ten days, but at the rate we're going now, it will take us a month to finish it. The worst of it is, we're threatened with a failure of the water supply.'

'But we'll find some,' Dick replied. 'We're bound to come across some river, some stream or pond in this great stretch of country.'

'I wish we could.'

'Mightn't it be Joe's cargo that's keeping us back?'

Kennedy said this by way of pulling Joe's leg, which he did all the more readily as he had himself for a moment shared Joe's illusions. But as he had not betrayed his feelings he could pose as a firm spirit, of course only in jest. Joe gave him a pitiful look. But the doctor did not reply. He was thinking, not without secret misgiving, of the vast solitudes of the Sahara, where caravans go for weeks without encountering a well to quench their thirst. He therefore scanned minutely the slightest depressions in the ground.

These precautions and recent events had done a good deal to damp the spirits of the three travellers. They talked less and buried themselves more in their own thoughts. Since his eyes had first lighted on that sea of gold, the worthy Joe was no longer the same man. He was taciturn and brooded greedily over the stones heaped up in the car, valueless today, tomorrow beyond price.

Moreover, the aspect of this part of Africa was disquieting. They were gradually entering the desert. Not a village or even a collection of huts to be seen. Vegetation was being left behind. At most there were a few stunted plants like the heather on the moors of Scotland, the beginning of white sands and bare stone, a few lentisks and thorny shrubs. In the middle of this sterility the rudimentary structure of the globe was revealed in sharp ridges of living rock. These symptoms of aridity gave Dr Fergusson food for thought. It looked as though no caravan had ever faced this deserted region. It would have left visible traces of camps, whitened bones of men or animals. But there was nothing. It felt as though soon an infinity of sand would overwhelm the desolate area. And yet there could be no going back, only forward, than which the doctor asked nothing better. He could have wished for a tempest to sweep him beyond this region, and there was not a cloud in the sky. By the end of the day the *Victoria* had made thirty miles.

If only the water had not failed! But there were only three gallons left. Fergusson set aside one gallon to slake their thirst, which a temperature of 90 degrees rendered intolerable. This left two gallons to feed the burner. At most, they could produce another 480 cubic feet of gas, and the burner used up about nine cubic feet an hour, so that they could only hold on for fifty-four hours. All this Fergusson carefully worked out.

'Fifty-four hours,' he said to his companions. 'Now, as I've made up my mind not to travel by night for fear of missing a stream or a well or pool, we have three and a half days' travel left during which we must find water at all costs. I thought I ought to warn you of this serious situation because I can only reserve one gallon for drinking, and we shall have to ration ourselves strictly.'

'Ration us, then,' Kennedy replied; 'but it's too soon to despair yet. You say we've three days before us?'

'Yes, old man.'

'Very well. It's no use worrying now. In three days it will be time to make up our minds what we're going to do. Meanwhile we must keep a sharper look-out than ever.'

At the evening meal the water was strictly measured out. The quantity of brandy in the grog was increased, but it was necessary to be sparing with this liquor, which is more of a thirst-producer than a thirst-quencher.

During the night the car rested on a great plateau which sank deeply towards its centre. The fact that it was not eight hundred feet above the level of the sea gave the doctor some hope, for he remembered the views of geographical experts as to the supposed existence of a vast stretch of water in the centre of Africa If this lake existed they must reach it, but, meanwhile, no signs of change appeared in the still sky.

The peaceful night, magnificently starred, was followed by a windless day with a burning sun. From early morning the temperature was torrid. At 5 a.m. the doctor gave the signal for departure, and for a considerable time the *Victoria* hung motionless in the leaden air. The doctor might have managed to escape from the intense heat by rising to a higher zone, but that would have required a lot of water, which was out of the question. He therefore contented himself with keeping the balloon a hundred feet above the ground where a faint breeze urged her westward. Lunch consisted of a little dried meat and pemmican. By noon the *Victoria* had only advanced a few miles.

'We can't go any quicker,' said the doctor. 'We can't command, only obey.'

'Yes, Samuel,' said Kennedy, 'this is one of those cases where a propeller would be useful.'

'No doubt, Dick, always supposing it didn't require water; otherwise the position would be precisely the same. Besides, so far, nothing practical has been invented. Balloons are still at the stage of development ships were in before the discovery of steam power. It took six thousand years to think of paddles and screws, so we've a long time to wait.'

'Curse this heat!' said Joe, wiping his dripping forehead.

'If we had some water the heat would be useful, for it expands the hydrogen in the balloon and saves the flame in the spiral. It's true, if we hadn't run short of water we shouldn't have to spare it. Damn that savage we wasted that precious container on!'

'You don't regret what you did, Samuel?'

'No, Dick, since we were able to save that poor fellow from a horrible death. But the hundred pounds of water we threw out would have been very useful. It would have meant twelve or thirteen days' travel, certain, which would have been quite enough to cross this desert.'

'We've done half the journey, at least?' Joe asked.

'In distance, yes; but as far as time is concerned, no, if the wind fails us. It's showing signs of dropping altogether.'

'Come, sir,' Joe went on. 'We mustn't complain. We've got on very well so far, and whatever I do, I can't give up hope. We'll find water, I tell you, sir.'

Meanwhile the land was sinking with every mile. The undulations of the gold mountains were dying away over the plain; sparse grass, the last efforts of exhausted Nature, replaced the fine trees of the east. A few clumps with wizened foliage still struggled against the invasion of the sand. Great rocks fallen from distant summits and smashed by their fall were scattered about in the form of sharp stones, which would soon form coarse sand and later become fine dust.

'This is Africa as you imagined it, Joe. I was right in telling you to be patient.'

'Well, sir,' Joe answered, 'it's very natural, all the same. Heat and sand. It would be absurd to look for anything else in such a country. You see,' he added, laughing, 'I hadn't much faith in your forests and plains. It didn't seem right. It's not worth while coming all this way only to find England over again. This is the first time I can really believe myself in Africa, and I'm not sorry to have a taste of the real thing.'

Towards evening the doctor found that the *Victoria* had not moved twenty miles during this burning day. As soon as the sun had disappeared behind a horizon drawn with the precision of a pencil line the hot night enveloped them.

The following day was the 1st of May, a Thursday, but day succeeded day with desperate monotony. Every morning was like the one before. Noon poured down the same relentless rays of heat, and night absorbed in its shadows the scattered heat that the following day was in its turn to bequeath to the night. The wind, now scarcely perceptible, became rather a sigh than a breeze, and the moment seemed at hand when this breath, too, would die away.

The doctor reacted to the gloom of the situation, and preserved the calm and sang-froid of tempered courage. Glass in hand, he searched every quarter of the horizon. He saw the last hills gradually fade, the last vegetation die out; in front of him stretched the whole immensity of the desert. The responsibility weighing upon him affected him much, but he showed no sign. He had dragged away these two men, who were both his friends, by the very force of friendship or duty. Had he acted rightly? Was it not venturing upon forbidden paths? Was he not in this expedition trying to pass the limits of the possible? Had not God reserved knowledge of this barren continent for later centuries?

As happens in hours of discouragement, these thoughts thronged his brain, and by an irresistible train of thought Samuel was carried away beyond logic and reason. After considering what he ought not to have done he fell to wondering what was to be done next. Would it be impossible to retrace his steps? Were there not higher currents which would bear him back towards less arid country? He knew the country they had passed but not that which lay ahead. And so, his conscience becoming insistent, he decided to have a frank talk with his two companions. He explained the situation clearly, showed them what had been done and what remained to do. At a pinch they could turn back, or at least try to. What did they think?

'I will follow my master,' Joe answered. 'I'll suffer what he suffers, and can stand it better than he can. I'll go where he goes.'

'And you, Kennedy?'

'I, my dear Sam, am not given to despair. No one realised better than I did the dangers of this venture. But I wanted to forget as soon as you were faced with them. I'm with you, body and soul. As things are, my view is we should go on to the end. Besides, it seems to me that there's just as much danger in going back. Forward, then. You can rely on us.'

'Thank you. You're good fellows,' the doctor replied with feeling. 'I knew I could rely on you, but I wanted to hear you say so. I'm very grateful.'

And the three men shook hands warmly.

'Listen to me,' Fergusson continued. 'According to my calculations we're not more than three hundred miles from the Gulf of Guinea. The desert can't go on for ever, for the coast is inhabited and the country is known for some distance inland. If necessary we'll make for the coast, and we're bound to come across some oasis or well where we can renew our supplies of water. But what we want is a wind, and without it we shall stay becalmed in the air.'

'We must make up our minds to wait,' said Kennedy.

But in vain each in turn scanned the horizon during this interminable day. Nothing appeared that could rouse the slightest hope. The last undulations of the ground vanished in the setting sun, whose horizontal rays stretched like long lines of fire over this vast expanse. It was the desert. The travellers had not covered fifteen miles and had used up, as on the previous day, one hundred and thirty-five feet of gas to feed the burner, while two pints of water out of eight had had to be sacrificed to slake their burning thirst. The night was calm, too calm. The doctor did not sleep a wink.

CHAPTER XXV

Another balloon – Traces of a caravan – A well

THE NEXT DAY brought the same clear sky, the same still air. The *Victoria* rose to four hundred feet but hardly made the slightest progress westward.

'We're in the heart of the desert,' said the doctor. 'Look at the stretch of sand. What a strange sight. What an odd whim of Nature. Why should there be all that luxuriant vegetation over there, and here this parched waste, and in the same degree of latitude, under the same sun?'

'The reason doesn't worry me,' Kennedy replied, 'as much as the fact. The important thing is that it is so.'

'We may as well philosophise a bit, old man. It can't do any harm.'

'Philosophise away, then, I'm quite agreeable. At least, we've plenty of time. We're hardly moving. The wind's afraid to blow. It's asleep.'

'It won't last,' said Joe. 'I think I see some strips of cloud in the east.'

'Joe's right,' the doctor said.

'Good,' said Kennedy. 'We could put up with a good cloud with rain and a fresh wind in our faces.'

'We'll see, Dick; we'll see.'

'But it's Friday, sir, and I'm suspicious of Fridays.'

'Well, I hope today will show the error of your forebodings.'

'I hope so, sir. Phew!' he said, wiping his face. 'I like warmth, and especially in summer, but it can be overdone.'

'Have you any fear of the effect of the heat on our balloon?'

Kennedy asked the doctor.

'No; the gutta-percha with which the silk is proofed can stand much higher temperatures. I've sometimes got a temperature of 158 degrees out of the coil and the envelope doesn't appear to have suffered.'

'A cloud! A real cloud!' Joe cried just at that moment, for his piercing eye scorned any kind of glass.

He was right. A thick bank of cloud was now rising slowly but distinctly above the horizon. It looked deep and swollen. It was made up of a heap of small clouds, each preserving its individual shape, from which the doctor concluded that there was no breeze affecting them. It was about eight in the morning when this compact mass appeared, and it was not until eleven that it reached the disc of the sun, which vanished completely behind the thick curtain. At the same moment the lower edge cleared the horizon, from which a brilliant light poured.

'It's a single cloud,' said the doctor. 'We mustn't count too much on it. Look, Dick! It's still the same shape as it was this morning.'

'Yes, Samuel, there's not going to be any rain or wind; not for us, at any rate.'

'I'm afraid not. It's keeping very high.'

'Well, suppose we go up to meet this cloud since it refuses to break on us?'

'I don't imagine that will help much,' replied the doctor. 'It will mean using up gas and also a good deal of water. But as things are, we must leave nothing undone. We must go up.'

The doctor turned up the flame of the burner inside the coil. A fierce heat was developed, and soon the balloon rose under the influence of the expanding hydrogen. When she reached about a hundred feet, she encountered the thick mass of the cloud and entered a dense fog, keeping the same elevation. But there was no breath of wind. The very fog seemed devoid of humidity, and objects exposed to its contact were scarcely damp. The *Victoria*, perhaps, moved forward more perceptibly in the mist, but that was all.

The doctor was disappointed at the poor result of his move, when he heard Joe exclaim in accents of keen surprise: 'Good Lord!'

'What is it, Joe?'

'Look, sir! Look, Mr Kennedy! that's strange!'

'What is it?'

'We're not alone here. It's a plot! They've pinched our idea.'

'Is the man going mad?' said Kennedy.

Joe looked like a statue of amazement. He stood transfixed

'Can the sun have affected the poor fellow's brain?' said the doctor, turning towards him.

'Are you going to tell me what's the matter?' he asked.

'But, just look, sir!' said Joe, pointing to a speck in space.

'Holy St Andrew!' cried Kennedy in his turn. 'It's impossible. Look, Sam! Look!'

'I see,' the doctor replied calmly.

'Another balloon with passengers like ourselves!'

Two hundred feet away, a balloon was floating in the air with car and passengers, following exactly the same route as the *Victoria*.

'Well, we've only to signal to it,' said the doctor. 'Get out the flag, Kennedy, and let's show our colours.'

Apparently the same idea occurred to the passengers of the second balloon at exactly the same moment, for the same flag repeated identically the same greeting from a hand waved in the same way.

'What does that mean?' Kennedy asked.

'They're a lot of monkeys,' Joe exclaimed. 'They're making fun of us.'

'It means,' replied Fergusson, laughing, 'that it's you who are making that signal, my dear Dick. It means that we ourselves are in that other car. That balloon is simply the *Victoria*.'

'Well, sir, begging your pardon, you'll never make me believe that.'

'Get up on to the side, Joe, and wave your arms, and then you'll see.'

Joe obeyed and saw his every gesture immediately repeated.

'It's only a mirage,' said the doctor. 'That's all. Merely an optical illusion. It's due to the unequal rarefication of the air strata.'

'It's wonderful,' said Joe who, reluctant to give in, continued his experiments with a wild waving of his arms.

'A strange sight,' said Kennedy. 'It's nice to see the good old *Victoria*. She looks well and behaves with dignity, you know.'

'However you explain it,' Joe replied, 'it's uncanny, all the same.'

But the mirage was gradually dimming. The clouds lifted to a very high level, leaving behind them the *Victoria*, who made no attempt to follow, and an hour later they had disappeared above her. The wind, which had been scarcely perceptible, now seemed to grow fainter still. The doctor, in despair, dropped towards the earth. The travellers, whom this incident had drawn out of their meditations, fell back upon their gloomy thoughts, overcome by the searing heat.

About four o'clock Joe reported an object standing out from the immense plateau of sand, and a little later saw two palm trees not far ahead.

'Palms!' said Fergusson. 'Then there must be a spring, a well!'

He took up his glass and assured himself that Joe's eyes had not deceived him.

'Water at last. Water! Water!' he repeated. 'We're saved; for though we're not moving fast, we are moving, and we'll get there in time.'

'Well, sir,' said Joe, 'what about a drink meanwhile? The air's stifling.'

'Yes, let's have a drink, Joe.'

No one waited to be asked. The whole pint vanished, reducing the supply to three pints and a half.

'Ah! that's good!' said Joe. 'That's jolly good! Beer never tasted like that!'

'That's one of the advantages of going without,' replied the doctor.

'Taking them altogether they're not great,' said Kennedy, 'and I'd gladly renounce water on condition I was never deprived of it.'

At six o'clock the *Victoria* was floating over two miserable withered palms, leafless ghosts of trees more dead than alive. Fergusson looked at them anxiously. At their foot could be seen the half-crumbled stones of a well which seemed to have been reduced to mere dust under the fierce heat of the sun. There was no sign of humidity. Samuel's heart contracted and he was about to impart his fears to his companions when their exclamations diverted his attention.

Westward, as far as the eye could see, stretched a long line of bleached bones. Fragments of skeletons surrounded the spring. A caravan must have struggled there, leaving this long trail of bones in its wake. The weakest had fallen one by one in the sand; the stronger, having reached the longed-for well, had met a horrible death at its edge. The travellers looked at one another and blenched.

'Don't let us go down,' said Kennedy; 'let's get away from this ghastly sight. We shan't find a drop of water.'

'No, Dick, we must have a clear conscience. We may just as well spend the night here as anywhere else. We'll search this well to the bottom. There has been a spring here; perhaps we shall find some trace of it.'

The *Victoria* touched ground. Joe and Kennedy put into the car a weight of sand equivalent to their own and disembarked. They ran to the well and climbed down inside it by steps which were crumbling to dust. The spring seemed to have been dried up for many years. They dug in the dry, fine sand; dry as a bone. Not a trace of damp did they find.

The doctor saw them emerge again, sweating, beaten, covered with fine dust, downcast, depressed and despairing. He realised that their search had been fruitless as he had expected. He said nothing but felt that henceforward he would require courage and strength for three.

Joe brought back the fragments of a shrivelled water-skin, which he threw away angrily among the bones which strewed the ground.

During supper the travellers did not exchange a single word and ate with effort. And yet so far they had not really experienced the torments of thirst. Their despair was for the future.

CHAPTER XXVI

113 degrees – The doctor's reflections – A desperate search –
The burner goes out – 122 degrees – Scanning the
desert – A walk through the night – Solitude – Exhaustion –
Joe's plans – He allows himself one day more

THE DISTANCE COVERED by the *Victoria* the previous day was not more than ten miles, and had cost them 162 cubic feet of gas. On Saturday morning the doctor gave the signal for departure.

'The burner can only hold out six hours more,' he said. 'If in the next six hours we don't find a well or spring, God only knows what will become of us.'

'There's not much wind this morning, sir,' said Joe. 'But perhaps it will get up,' he added, noticing Fergusson's ill-concealed distress.

Vain hope! They were in a dead calm; one of those relentless calms that grip ships in tropical seas. The heat became intolerable and the thermometer under the shade of the awning showed 113 degrees. Joe and Kennedy, stretched out side by side, tried to forget their situation in sleep, or at least torpor. The forced inactivity left them hours of painful leisure. The most pitiable of men are those without work or material occupation to distract their thoughts. But here there was nothing to attend to, no further effort to be made. The situation had to be submitted to; it could not be improved.

The agonies of thirst began to make themselves cruelly felt. The brandy, far from appeasing their compelling need, only increased it, justifying the name 'tiger's milk' given to it by the natives of Africa. They had rather less than two pints of liquid left, and that was hot. The eyes of all brooded covetously over the precious water and none dared touch it with his lips. Two pints of water in the heart of the desert!

Dr Fergusson, deep in thought, was asking himself whether he had acted prudently. Would it not have been better to preserve the water he had fruitlessly decomposed to hold them in the air? Certainly he had made a little headway, but was he any nearer his goal? What difference would it have made if he had been sixty miles farther back, since there was no water to be found? And again, if the wind did rise, would it not blow as strongly there as here, stronger even if it came from the east? But hope urged Samuel forward. And yet those two wasted gallons of water would have sufficed for a halt of nine days in this desert, and what changes might not come about in nine days! Perhaps, too, he should have kept this water, and risen by throwing out ballast, even if he had had to lose gas to come down again. But gas was the balloon's blood, her life.

A thousand such reflections jostled through his head, which he held in his hands without raising it for hours at a time.

'We must make one last effort,' he told himself about ten in the morning; 'one last attempt to find a breeze that will get us away. We must stake everything on a last throw.'

And while his companions were asleep he raised the hydrogen to a high temperature. The balloon swelled under the expansion of the gas and rose straight up through the vertical rays of the sun. The doctor searched the air from a hundred to a thousand feet but found no breath of wind. The place from which he started was still directly below him. An absolute calm seemed to extend to the last limits of breathable air. At last the water gave out and the burner died for want of gas. The Bunsen battery ceased to function and the *Victoria*, contracting, dropped gently to the sand on the very spot that still bore the imprint of the car. It was noon. A reckoning showed their position as lat. 6° 51' N., long. 19° 35' E., nearly five hundred miles from Lake Tchad and more than four hundred from the West Coast of Africa. As they touched, Dick and Joe woke from their heavy torpor.

'We're stopping?' said the Scotsman.

'We must,' Samuel replied gravely.

His companions understood. The ground here was at sea-level; indeed, of late it had been constantly sinking, so the balloon was maintained in perfect equilibrium, completely motionless.

As they disembarked, the travellers filled the car with a weight of sand equal to their own. Each was absorbed in his own thoughts and for several hours they did not speak. Joe prepared a supper of biscuit and pemmican which they hardly touched. A sip of hot water completed this dismal meal.

During the night no watch was kept, but no one slept. The heat was stifling. Next morning only half a pint of water remained, which the doctor set aside, resolving not to touch it save in the last extremity.

'I'm suffocating,' Joe gasped a little later. 'It's hotter than ever, and I'm not surprised,' he added after consulting the thermometer: '140 degrees!'

'The sand is scorching. It might be fresh from a furnace,' said Kennedy. 'And not a cloud in this grilling sky. It's enough to drive one mad!'

'Don't let us give in,' said the doctor. 'These fierce heats are always followed by storms in this latitude, and they come with the swiftness of lightning. In spite of the dreadful serenity of the sky great changes come about in less than an hour.'

'But, surely, there would be some sign,' said Kennedy.

'Well,' said the doctor, 'I rather think the barometer shows a slight tendency to drop.'

'Pray Heaven you're right, Sam. We're nailed down here like a winged bird.'

'With the difference, however, old man, that our wings are intact, and I sincerely hope we shall be able to use them yet.'

'Oh, for a wind!' cried Joe. 'Just enough to take us to a stream, and we shall be quite all right. We've got enough grub, and if only we could get some water, we could wait for months without taking any harm. But thirst is awful.'

Thirst, added to the unceasing glare of the desert, was eating into their souls. There was not the slightest break in the ground, not a sandhill, not a stone to distract their eyes. The flatness sickened them and produced the disorder known as desert sickness. The relentless stillness of the arid blue sky and the yellow immensity of sand eventually struck terror into them. In this burning atmosphere the heat seemed to quiver as over a red-hot furnace. Watching this calm, and seeing no reason why the situation should ever end, for immensity is a kind of eternity, filled their souls with despair. These unfortunate men, deprived of water in this fearful heat, began to experience symptoms of hallucination. Their eyes dilated, their sight became blurred.

When night had fallen the doctor resolved to fight this disquieting mood by means of a sharp walk. He intended to spend a few hours crossing this plain of sand, not with the idea of searching but simply for exercise.

'Come on,' he said to his companions. 'Believe me, it will do you good.'

'It can't be done,' replied Kennedy. 'I couldn't walk a step.'

'I'd much rather sleep,' said Joe.

'But sleep and rest are fatal. Try and rouse yourselves. Now then, come along!'

As the doctor could get no response, he set out alone through the starry clearness of the night. His first steps were painful, the steps of a man weakened and unused to walking; but he soon realised that the exercise would be beneficial. He went on several miles in a westerly direction and his mind was already feeling easier when he was suddenly seized with giddiness. It was as if he were leaning over an abyss. He felt his knees giving way. The vast solitude terrified him. He was as a mathematical point, the centre of an infinite circumference, of the void. The *Victoria* had disappeared completely in the darkness. An uncontrollable panic took possession of the doctor, the impassive, intrepid traveller. He tried to retrace his steps, but in vain. He called aloud, but not the slightest echo answered him, and his voice fell into space like a stone into a bottomless pit. He sank exhausted on the sand, alone amid the great silence of the desert.

At midnight he came round, to find himself in the arms of the faithful Joe, who, uneasy at his master's prolonged absence, had hastily followed his tracks, which were clearly printed in the sand. He had found him unconscious.

'What's happened, sir?' he asked.

'It's nothing, my dear fellow. A momentary weakness, that's all.'

'Nothing, indeed, sir! But get up; lean on me and we'll get back to the *Victoria*.'

Leaning on Joe's arm, the doctor returned the way he had come.

'It was unwise, sir. You shouldn't do these things. You might have been waylaid,' he added, laughing. 'Come, sir, let's be serious.'

'Go on. I'm listening.'

'We must really make up our minds. We can't go on like this for many days more, and if the wind doesn't come, it's all up with us.'

The doctor did not reply.

'Well, someone must sacrifice himself for the rest and it's only natural it should be me.'

'What do you mean? What's your idea?'

'It's quite simple. Take some food and walk straight ahead until I get somewhere. I'm bound to, sooner or later. Meantime, if Heaven sends you a favourable wind, you mustn't wait for me; you must start. As for me, if I come to a village I'll manage to get along with a few Arab words you can write out for me, and I'll bring back help or die in the attempt. What do you think of it, sir?

'It's mad, but does credit to your heart, Joe. It's out of the question. You're not going to leave us.'

'After all, sir, we must try something. It can't do any harm for, as I say, you won't wait for me, and at a pinch I may do some good.'

'No, no, Joe; we mustn't separate. It would only make it worse for the others. It was fated that this should be and it's probably arranged that it will be different later. So let us wait patiently.'

'All right, sir, but I'll tell you one thing. I'll give you another day, but I won't wait longer than that. Today is Sunday, or rather Monday, for it's one o'clock in the morning. If we don't get a move on by Monday, I'll risk it. I've quite made up my mind.'

The doctor did not reply. Soon afterwards he reached the car and took his place beside Kennedy, who was lying perfectly still; but that did not mean he was asleep.

CHAPTER XXVII

Terrific heat – Hallucinations – The last drops of water – A
night of despair – Attempted suicide – The simoon – The oasis –
A lion and lioness

IN THE MORNING the doctor's first thought was to consult the barometer. At most, there was the faintest drop.

'No good! No good!' he muttered to himself.

He left the car and took a look at the weather. The same heat, the same clear sky, the same implacable conditions.

'Must we give up hope?' he exclaimed.

Joe said nothing. He was wrapped up in his own thoughts, meditating his plan.

Kennedy got up feeling very ill, a prey to an alarming attack of nerves. He was suffering horribly from thirst. His blistered tongue and lips could hardly articulate a sound. There were a few drops of water left. They all knew it. The thoughts of each were drawn towards it as to a magnet, but no one dared go near it.

The three companions, the three friends, looked at one another with haggard eyes and with a feeling of brute greed which betrayed itself most in Kennedy, whose powerful frame succumbed more readily to this intolerable privation. Throughout the day he was in the grip of delirium. He walked up and down, uttering hoarse cries, gnawing his fists, on the point of opening his veins to drink the blood.

'Oh!' he muttered; 'they're right to call this the land of thirst, the land of despair!' Then he relapsed into a state of coma. Nothing was heard from him but the hissing of his breath between his parched lips.

Towards evening Joe began to show symptoms of mania. This vast sea of sand appeared to him as an immense pool of cool and limpid waters. More than once he threw himself down on the scorching sand to drink and got up again with his mouth full of dust.

'Damnation!' he cried angrily. 'It's salt-water!'

Then, while Fergusson and Kennedy lay stretched out motionless, he was seized with an overpowering temptation to drain the few drops of water that were being held in reserve. It grew too much for him. He dragged himself on his knees towards the car, fastened his eyes greedily upon the bottle containing the liquid, looked at it with a desperate glance, seized it, and raised it to his lips.

At this moment he heard the words: 'Water! Water!' in accents that tore the heart. It was Kennedy, dragging himself towards him. The poor fellow was a pitiable sight. He remained on his knees, the tears welling from his eyes. Joe, also in tears, offered him the bottle and, to the very last drop, Kennedy drained the contents. 'Thank you,' he gasped, but Joe did not hear him; he had fallen prone on the sand.

What happened during that dreadful night is known to no one, but on the Tuesday morning, under the douche of fire pouring from the sun, the wretched men felt their limbs gradually shrivelling When Joe tried to get up he found it impossible. He was unable to carry out his plan. He took a look round him. In the car the doctor lay prostrate, his arms folded over his chest, gazing at an imaginary point in space with imbecile fixity. Kennedy was a terrifying sight. His head swayed from side to side like that of a caged animal.

Suddenly the Scotsman's eye rested upon his carbine, the butt of which was projecting over the side of the car.

'Ah!' he cried, raising himself by a superhuman effort. He dashed at the weapon, desperate, insane, and placed the muzzle to his mouth.

'Sir! Mr Kennedy!' said Joe, throwing himself upon him.

'Leave me alone! Get away!' moaned the Scotsman, and the two struggled desperately.

'Clear out or I'll kill you,' Kennedy went on. But Joe clung to him fiercely. They fought together for nearly a minute, the doctor appearing not to notice them Then suddenly in the struggle the carbine went off. At the sound of the report the doctor got up, erect as a spectre. He looked around him. Then a sudden light came into his eye. He stretched his hand towards the horizon and, in a voice in which there was nothing human, rasped out: 'Look! Look over there!'

There was such energy in his gesture that Joe and Kennedy broke away and both looked. The plain was rising and falling like a sea lashed by a storm. Waves of sand broke one upon another, throwing up clouds of dust. From the south-east a huge, twisting column was approaching with incredible swiftness. The sun vanished behind a dense cloud whose gigantic shadow extended to the balloon. Grains of fine sand swept along with the quick flow of liquid and, little by little, the rising tide advanced.

A gleam of hope shone in Fergusson's eyes. 'The simoon!' he cried.

'The simoon!' Joe repeated, without much idea of what the word meant.

'Good!' muttered Kennedy, in the delirium of despair. 'All the better. We're going to die.'

'Yes, all the better!' replied the doctor. 'But we're going to live.' And he began rapidly to throw out the sand holding down the car. His companions, at last understanding, rejoined him and took their places at his side. 'And now, Joe,' said the doctor, 'throw out fifty pounds or so of your gold.'

Though he felt a swift pang of regret, Joe did not hesitate. The balloon rose.

'It was time,' said the doctor.

And indeed the simoon was sweeping towards them with the swiftness of lightning. A little longer and the *Victoria* would have been crushed to pieces – annihilated. The huge column was upon them. The *Victoria* was swept by a hail of sand.

'More ballast!' the doctor cried to Joe.

'Aye, aye, sir,' replied the latter, hurling out an enormous piece of quartz.

The *Victoria* rose rapidly above the column, but, caught in the great whirlpool of air, she was torn along at dizzy speed over this foaming sea of sand. Samuel, Dick and Joe did not speak but looked and hoped, refreshed by the whirlwind. By three o'clock the tumult had ceased. The sand fell again and formed a great quantity of little hills. The sky resumed its former calm. The *Victoria*, motionless again, was floating within sight of an oasis, an island of trees on the surface of the sandy ocean.

'Water! There's water there!' cried the doctor. And immediately, opening the upper valve, he let the hydrogen escape and came down gently, two hundred yards from the oasis. In four hours the travellers had covered two hundred and forty miles.

The moment the car came to a halt Kennedy jumped out, followed by Joe.

'Your gun!' cried the doctor. 'Take your guns, and look out.'

Dick seized his carbine and Joe one of the guns. They quickly approached the trees and plunged into the fresh foliage which promised abundant springs. They paid no heed to a number of large, broad footmarks freshly imprinted here and there on the humid earth. Suddenly, twenty yards away, a roar rang out.

'A lion!' said Joe.

'Good!' snapped the exasperated Kennedy. 'We'll fight him. We're strong enough when it's only a question of fighting.'

'Take care, sir. All our lives may depend on the life of one of us.'

But Kennedy was not listening. He strode forward, eyes blazing, carbine cocked, terrible in his audacity. Under a palm an enormous black-maned lion was crouching, ready to spring. Scarcely had he caught sight of Kennedy than he hurled himself through the air; but before he touched the ground a bullet struck him in the heart. He fell dead.

'Hurray!' cried Joe.

Kennedy dashed towards the well, slipping on the wet steps, and threw himself down by a fresh spring into which he greedily plunged his lips. Joe followed his example, and the silence was broken only by the lapping sound made by thirsty animals.

'Steady, sir,' said Joe, taking a long breath. 'We mustn't overdo it.' But Dick, without answering, went on drinking. He plunged his head and hands into the healing water. He was intoxicated.

'And what about Dr Fergusson?' said Joe. This brought Kennedy to his senses. Filling a bottle he had brought, he dashed up the steps. But what was his amazement when he found a huge opaque body blocking the entrance. Joe, who was following him, had to draw back too.

'We're shut in!'

'Impossible! what does this mean – ?'

Dick did not finish. A terrible roar made him realise with what new enemy he had to deal.

'Another lion!' cried Joe.

'No. A lioness. Damn the brute! Wait,' said the hunter, hastily reloading his carbine. An instant later he fired, but the animal had disappeared. 'Come on!' he cried.

'No, sir. You didn't kill her. The body would have rolled down here. She's waiting to spring on whichever of us comes out first, and it will be all up with him.'

'But what's to be done? We must get out. Dr Fergusson's waiting.'

'Let's draw her. You take my gun and pass me the carbine.'

'What's the idea?'

'You'll see.'

Taking off his canvas jacket, Joe stuck it on the end of the gun and held it out above the opening as a bait. The animal dashed at it in fury. Kennedy was ready, and with a shot broke its shoulder. The roaring animal rolled down the steps, knocking Joe over. Joe already imagined he could feel the animal's great claws piercing his flesh, when a second shot rang out, and the doctor appeared at the opening, his gun still smoking in his hand.

Joe got up hastily, climbed over the animal's body and passed the bottle of water to his master. To raise it to his lips and half-empty it was for Fergusson the work of a moment, and from the bottom of their hearts the three travellers thanked Providence, who had so miraculously saved them.

CHAPTER XXVIII

A delicious evening – Joe's cooking – Dissertation on raw meat – The story of James Bruce – The bivouac – Joe's dreams – The barometer drops – The barometer rises again – Preparations for departure – The hurricane

THE EVENING was a delightful one and, after a comforting meal, it was spent under the cool shade of the mimosas. The tea and grog were not spared. Kennedy had explored the oasis in all directions, and had beaten the undergrowth. The travellers were the only inhabitants of this earthly paradise. They stretched themselves out on their blankets and spent a peaceful night, which blotted out the memory of past discomforts. The next day, the 7th of May, the sun was shining with full brilliance, but its rays failed to penetrate the thick curtain of shade. As they had plenty of provisions, the doctor decided to wait in this place for a favourable wind. Joe had brought with him his portable kitchen and indulged in a great number of culinary experiments, using water lavishly.

'What a strange alternation of troubles and enjoyment!' Kennedy exclaimed. 'Abundance after want; luxury after misery! I jolly nearly went off my head.'

'My dear Dick,' the doctor said, 'without Joe you wouldn't be here to discourse on the instability of human things.'

'He's a good fellow,' said Dick, offering Joe his hand.

'Don't mention it, sir,' Joe replied. 'You'd do the same for me; but I hope there'll be no need.'

'What poor things we are to allow ourselves to despair for so little.'

'You mean for so little water, sir? It must be a very important thing.'

'It is, Joe. People hold out much longer without food than without drink.'

'I can quite believe that. Besides, at a pinch, a man can eat whatever turns up, even his fellow-men, though that must be hard to digest.'

'The savages seem to manage it all right,' said Kennedy.

'Yes; but they're savages and they're used to eating raw meat. That's a custom I could never get used to.'

'Yes, it is repulsive,' the doctor went on; 'so much so that no one would credit the stories of the first African travellers when they reported that several tribes fed on raw meat. In this connection a curious adventure happened to James Bruce.'

'Tell us about it, sir. We've plenty of time,' said Joe, stretching himself luxuriously on the cool grass.

'Certainly. James Bruce was a Scotsman from Stirling who between 1768 and 1772 explored the whole of Abyssinia as far as Lake Tyana in search of the Nile sources and then returned to England, where he did not publish the account of his travels until 1790. His story was received with extreme scepticism, as no doubt ours will be. The customs of the Abyssinians seemed so different from what people are used to in England that no one would believe him. Among other details James Bruce had stated that the people of East Africa ate raw meat. This roused the whole public against him. He could say what he liked; no one would listen. Bruce was a very brave man and very stubborn. This scepticism exasperated him. One day, when he was in an Edinburgh drawing-room, a Scotsman took up the subject, which had become a daily joke, and with regard to the point of raw meat declared flatly that the thing was neither possible nor true. Bruce went out and in a few moments returned with a raw steak, salted and peppered in the African manner. "Sir," he said to the Scotsman, "by doubting what I've told you, you have offered me a serious insult; in believing it impossible, you are entirely in the wrong, and to prove this to everyone, you're going to eat this raw steak now or give me satisfaction for what you have said." The Scotsman was frightened and obeyed, pulling dreadful faces. Then, with perfect coolness, James Bruce added: "Even admitting the statement isn't true, sir, you at least can't continue to maintain that it's impossible." '

'A good answer,' said Joe. 'If the Scotsman got indigestion it served him right, and if anyone doubts our story when we get back to England –'

'Well, Joe, what will you do?'

'I'll make them eat the remains of the *Victoria*, and without pepper or salt.'

They all laughed at Joe's remark. And so the day passed in cheerful conversation. With returning strength hope revived, and with hope, courage. The past faded away before the future with miraculous rapidity. Joe would have liked to stay for ever in this enchanted refuge, the kingdom of his dreams. He felt at home there. He made his master tell him its exact position, which he solemnly entered in his notebook: lat. 8° 32' N., long. 15° 48' E.

Kennedy had only one regret – that there was no shooting in this miniature forest. As he said, there weren't many wild animals.

'What about the lion and lioness, old man?' replied the doctor. 'You've soon forgotten them.'

'Oh, those creatures!' he said, with the true hunter's scorn for the killed quarry. 'But, as a matter of fact, their presence here at all gives good reason to suppose that we're not very far from more fertile country.'

'An uncertain proof, Dick. These animals often cover considerable distances when they're hard pressed by hunger and thirst. We shall do well to keep an extra keen look-out tonight, and light fires.'

'In this heat!' said Joe. 'Well, if we must, we will; but it seems a pity to burn this nice little wood which has been so useful to us.'

'We'll take special care not to set fire to it,' answered the doctor. 'Some day others may be glad to find shelter in the middle of the desert.'

'We'll see to that, sir. But do you think anyone knows about this oasis?'

'Of course. It's a halting-place for caravans crossing the centre of Africa. A visit from them might not be to your liking, Joe.'

'Are there any more of those beastly Nyam Nyams in these parts?'

'Without a doubt. It's the common name for all these people, and in the same climate the same races are bound to have similar habits.'

'Pah!' said Joe. 'Well, after all, it's only natural. If savages had the tastes of gentlemen, what difference would there be? At any rate, these good people wouldn't have needed any persuasion to swallow the Scotsman's steak, and the Scotsman into the bargain.'

After this very sensible remark Joe went off to prepare the fires for the night, making them as small as possible. Fortunately these precautions were unnecessary and, one after the other, all fell into a deep sleep.

The next day there was still no change in the weather, which remained obstinately fine. The balloon hung motionless, not the slightest oscillation indicating a breath of wind. The doctor began to grow anxious. If the expedition was going to drag out in this way they would run short of provisions. After almost dying for want of water were they to be reduced to death by starvation? But he was reassured at seeing the mercury of the barometer drop quite appreciably. There were obvious signs of an approaching change. He therefore resolved to get ready to leave so that he could take advantage of the first opportunity. The food and water containers were all filled to their full capacity.

Fergusson had then to re-establish the equilibrium of the balloon, and Joe was compelled to sacrifice a considerable part of his precious ore. With restored health, his ambitious ideas had returned, and he pulled several grimaces before obeying his master, but the latter convinced him that he could not lift such a weight. When he was offered his choice between water and gold Joe hesitated no longer, but threw a large quantity of his precious ore on to the sand.

'There's something for the next people who come along after us,' he said. 'They'll be very surprised to find a fortune in a place like this.'

'Suppose some scientific traveller should come across these samples – ?' said Kennedy.

'You needn't have any doubts about that, old man; you may be sure he'd be very surprised, and would publish his surprise in many volumes. Some day we shall hear of a wonderful vein of auriferous quartz in the middle of the African desert.'

'And Joe will be responsible for it.'

The chance of hoaxing a scientist cheered the worthy Joe and made him smile. During the rest of the day the doctor waited vainly for a change in the weather. The temperature rose, and without the shade of the oasis the heat would have been intolerable. The thermometer showed 149 degrees in the sun. A veritable rain of fire poured down through the air. It was the hottest weather they had yet encountered. In the evening Joe again prepared the bivouac for the night, and during Fergusson's and Kennedy's watches no incident occurred. About 3 a.m., however, during Joe's watch, the temperature suddenly dropped, the sky clouded over and the darkness increased.

'Wake up!' cried Joe, rousing his two companions. 'Wake up! Here's the wind!'

'At last,' said the doctor, scanning the sky. 'It's a storm. Back to the car.'

It was quite time. The *Victoria* was stooping under the force of the hurricane and dragging the car, which left a furrow in the sand. If any part of the ballast had happened to fall overboard the balloon would have gone and all hope of finding it again would have been lost for ever. But the fleet-footed Joe ran as fast as he could and held the car down, the balloon sinking to the sand, where it seemed likely to be torn. The doctor went to his usual post, lit his burner, and threw out the extra ballast. The travellers took a last look at the trees of the oasis, which were bending to the storm and, picking up the east wind two hundred feet from the ground, they soon vanished into the night.

CHAPTER XXIX

A French author's fantastic notion – Speke and Burton's exploration linked up with Barth's

FROM THE VERY MOMENT of their departure the travellers were dashed along at great speed. They were anxious to get away from this desert which had nearly proved so disastrous to them. About a quarter-past nine in the morning they caught sight of some signs of vegetation, grasses floating on the sea of sand and revealing to them, as to Christopher Columbus, the proximity of soil. Green blades pushed their way timidly between rocks which were themselves to become the shoals of this ocean. Hills, as yet of low elevation, undulated on the horizon, their outline, blurred by mist, being indistinctly defined. The country was growing less monotonous. The doctor greeted this change of scene with delight and, like a sailor keeping his watch, he felt inclined to shout: 'Land! Land!'

An hour later the continent stretched below their eyes, still wild, but less flat, less bare. A few trees stood out against the grey sky.

'We're in civilisation again!' said Kennedy.

'Civilisation, sir? That's one way of putting it. There's not a soul to be seen yet.'

'That won't last long at the rate we're travelling,' Fergusson answered.

'Are we still in negro country, sir?'

'Yes, Joe, until we get to that of the Arabs.'

'Arabs, sir, real Arabs, with camels?'

'No, without camels. Camels are rare, not to say unknown, in this region. They're not to be found until you come a few degrees farther north.'

'What a pity!'

'Why, Joe?'

'Because if the wind turned against us they might be useful.'

'How?'

'I've got an idea, sir. We could harness them to the car and make them tow us. What do you think, sir?'

'The idea has occurred to others before you, Joe, and it has been exploited in a novel by a witty French writer, M. Méry.[48] Some travellers have their balloons towed by camels. A lion eats the camels, swallows the tow-line and tows them in its turn, and so on. You see, it's all mere fancy and in no way connected with our method of locomotion.'

Joe, a little humiliated to find that his idea had already occurred to someone else, tried to think what animal could have eaten the lion, but as he could not think of one he returned to his contemplation of the scenery. A fair-sized lake stretched below him in an amphitheatre of high hills which could as yet hardly be called mountains. Among these wound fertile valleys with tangled thickets of many kinds of trees. These were dominated by the elæis, with leaves fifteen feet long and its stem covered with sharp thorns. The bombax threw the fine down of its seed to the passing wind. The strong perfume of the pendanus, the *kenda* of the Arabs, made the air fragrant even at the height at which the *Victoria* was travelling. The papaw, with its palmate leaves, the sterculier, which produces the Sudanese nut, the baobab and the banana-tree completed the luxuriant flora of these tropical regions.

'It's a splendid country,' said the doctor.

'There are some animals,' said Joe; 'the people won't be far off.'

'Oh, what fine elephants!' exclaimed Kennedy. 'Couldn't we manage a little hunting?'

'How are we to stop in this wind, Dick? No, you'll have to suffer a taste of the torture of Tantalus. You'll make up for it later on.'

There was indeed plenty to stir the imagination of a sportsman. Dick's heart beat hard and his fingers tightened on the butt of his Purdey. The fauna of the country was worthy of its flora. The wild ox wallowed in the thick grass which buried it completely. Grey, black and tawny elephants of enormous size passed like a tornado through the forests, smashing, tearing and wrecking, and leaving behind them a trail of ruin. Cascades and watercourses poured to the northward down the wooded slopes, and here hippopotamus splashed noisily, and manatees twelve feet long displayed their fish-like bodies on the banks, exposing their round udders, swollen with milk. There was a whole menagerie of rare animals in a wonderful setting where countless multi-coloured birds flitted among the trees and shrubs. This prodigality of Nature made it clear to the doctor that this was the splendid kingdom of Adamawa.

'We're getting into touch with modern discovery,' he said. 'I've picked up the broken trail of the explorers. We're in luck, my friends! We're going to connect the work of Burton and Speke with the explorations of Dr Barth. We've left the English to find a German, and we shall soon come to the farthest point reached by that brave discoverer.'

'Judging by the distance we've come, there seems to be a good stretch of country between the two,' said Kennedy.

'It's easy enough to calculate. Have a look at the map and see what is the longitude of the southern point of Lake Victoria reached by Speke.'

'About the 37th meridian.'

'And the town of Yola, where we ought to arrive tonight? Barth got there.'

'The 12th, about.'

'That makes 25 degrees, then; or, at sixty miles to the degree – fifteen hundred miles.'

'A nice little jaunt,' said Joe.

'It will be done, however. Livingstone and Moffat are still travelling towards the interior. Nyasa, which they discovered, is not very far from Lake Tanganyika, found by Burton. Before the end of the century all these great stretches of country will be explored without a doubt. But,' added the doctor, looking at the compass, 'it's a pity the wind is taking us due east. I wanted to go north.'

After twelve hours' travelling the *Victoria* found herself on the confines of Nigeria. The first inhabitants of this country, Choua Arabs, were nomads driving their flocks from one pasture to another. The huge crests of the Alantika Mountains projected over the horizon; mountains which no European foot had yet trodden and whose height is estimated at about eight thousand feet. Their western slope forms the watershed of all the rivers of this part of Africa; they are the Moon Mountains of this region.

At last the three men sighted a real river and from the huge ant-hills on its banks the doctor recognised the Benue, one of the chief tributaries of the Niger, which the natives call the 'Cradle of the Waters.'

'This river,' the doctor informed his companions, 'will one day become the natural line of communication with the interior of Nigeria. The steamboat *Pleiades* has already explored it as far as Yola. You see, we are now in known country.'

Numbers of slaves were at work in the fields, tending the sorghum, a kind of maize, which is their staple food. The appearance of the *Victoria*, flying like a meteor through the air, caused wide-eyed amazement. In the evening she hove to, forty miles from Yola. Ahead of her in the distance rose the two sharp peaks of Mount Mendif. The doctor had the anchors thrown out and moored to the crest of a high tree. But a sharp wind beat the *Victoria* down so that she lay almost horizontal, which at times made the position of the car extremely dangerous. Fergusson did not close his eyes once during the night. He was often on the point of cutting the cable to run before the wind. At last the storm died down and the oscillation of the balloon ceased to give cause for anxiety. The following day the wind moderated, but it carried the travellers away from Yola which, as it had recently been rebuilt by the Fellanis, had aroused Fergusson's curiosity. However, as there was no alternative, they had to resign themselves to travelling northwards, and even slightly east.

Kennedy suggested making a halt in this district where the hunting seemed good. Joe claimed that the need of fresh meat was beginning to make itself felt, but the wild nature of the country and the hostile attitude of the population, which was shown by the firing of guns at the *Victoria*, decided the doctor to hold his course. They were crossing country which is constantly the scene of massacre, fire, and war, where the sultans stake their kingdoms in bloody fighting. Many populous villages of elongated huts stretched between the wide pastures, where the thick grass was speckled with violet flowers. The huts, looking like huge hives, were protected by bristling palisades. The wild slopes of the hills, as Kennedy several times remarked, were reminiscent of the glens in the Scottish Highlands.

In spite of his efforts, the doctor was being carried due north-east, towards Mount Mendif, the summit of which was buried in the clouds. The high peaks of this range separate the Niger from the Lake Tchad basin.

Soon Bagele hove in sight with eighteen villages clinging to its sides, like a litter of young animals at their mother's breasts. Seen from above, where the whole effect was commanded, it was a magnificent spectacle. The ravines were covered with fields of rice and pea-nut.

At 3 p.m. the *Victoria* was face to face with Mount Mendif. As it had been impossible to avoid it, it would have to be cleared. By raising the temperature another 180 degrees, the doctor gave the balloon an additional lift of 1600 lbs and rose over eight thousand feet. This was the greatest elevation attained during the voyage and the temperature became so low that the doctor and his companions were obliged to resort to their rugs. Fergusson was anxious to come down again as soon as possible as the envelope of the balloon showed a tendency to crack. However, he had time to observe the volcanic origin of the mountain, the extinct craters of which were now merely deep abysses. Large accumulations of bird-droppings gave to the sides of the mountain the appearance of limestone. There was enough to fertilise the whole of the United Kingdom.

At five o'clock the *Victoria*, sheltered from the southern winds, was gently following the slopes of the mountain when she came to a stop in a large clearing far from any habitation. As soon as she touched land, precautions were taken to moor her firmly, and Kennedy, gun in hand, dashed down the slope. It was not long before he returned with half a dozen wild duck and a sort of snipe, which Joe dealt with in his best manner. After they had enjoyed a pleasant meal the night was spent in deep sleep.

CHAPTER XXX

*Mosfeia – The sheik – Denham, Clapperton and Oudney –
Vogel – The capital of Loggum – Toole – Becalmed
over Kernak – The governor and his court – The attack –
Incendiary pigeons*

ON THE FOLLOWING DAY, the 11th of May, the *Victoria* resumed her adventurous journey. The travellers had the confidence in her that a sailor has in his ship. In spite of the terrible hurricanes, tropical heat, hazardous risings, and even more dangerous descents, she had always and everywhere come out of her difficulties successfully. It might be said that Fergusson guided her with a wave of his hand. So, though ignorant of where he would eventually land, the doctor had no further fears as to the ultimate issue of the voyage. In this land of savages and fanatics, however, prudence forced him to take the strictest precautions; he therefore recommended his companions to keep their eyes open for anything that might happen at any moment.

The wind bore them on a slightly more northerly course, and about nine o'clock they caught sight of the large town of Mosfeia, built upon an eminence, itself shut in between two mountains. The situation was impregnable, a narrow way between a swamp and a wood providing the sole means of access.

Just at this moment a brilliantly-robed sheik was entering the town, escorted by men on horseback, and preceded by trumpeters and runners who pushed back the branches to make way for him. The doctor came down lower to examine these natives more closely, but as the balloon grew bigger, signs of utter panic showed upon their faces, and they at once made off at full speed. The sheik alone stood his ground. Picking up his long musket he cocked it and waited proudly. The doctor approached to within fifty yards of him and in his best manner greeted him in Arabic. At these words out of the sky the sheik alighted from his horse and prostrated himself in the dust of the road. The doctor was unable to distract him from his worship.

'These people can't help but take us for supernatural beings,' the doctor said. 'The first Europeans they saw they took for a superhuman race. When this sheik tells his story he is sure to embroider it with all the resources of an Arab's imagination. You can guess the sort of legend that will be woven around us.'

'That might be a nuisance,' replied Kennedy. 'In the interests of civilisation it would be better to be taken for ordinary men. It would give these niggers a different idea of European power.'

'I agree, Dick. But what can we do? At whatever length you explained to the local wise men the mechanism of a balloon, they would never understand you. They would cling to the idea of supernatural intervention.'

'You were talking about the first Europeans to explore this country, sir,' said Joe. 'Who were they, if I may ask?'

'My dear fellow, we are on the very road followed by Major Denham. It was at Mosfeia that he was received by the Sultan of Mandara. He had come from Bornu and was accompanying the sheik on an expedition against the Fellahs. He witnessed the attack on the town, which put up a brave resistance with their arrows against the muskets of the Arabs, and routed the sheik's troops. It was all merely a pretext for murder, pillage and raids. The major was robbed of all he had, even his clothing; and if he hadn't managed to slip under his horse's belly and escape from his conquerors at a desperate gallop, he would never have got back to Kuka, the capital of Bornu.'

'But who was this Major Denham?'

'A brave Englishman who between 1822 and 1824 commanded an expedition into Bornu, accompanied by Captain Clapperton and Dr Oudney. They left Tripoli in March, reached Murzuk, the capital of Fezzan, followed the road later taken by Dr Barth to return to Europe, and arrived in Kuka, near Lake Tchad, on the 16th of February, 1823. Denham explored Bornu, Mandara, and the east shore of the lake, while, on the 15th of December, 1823, Captain Clapperton and Dr Oudney penetrated the Sudan as far as Sakatu, Oudney dying of exhaustion in Murmur.'

'So this part of Africa has contributed a large number of victims to science?' observed Kennedy.

'Yes, it's a deadly district. We're making straight for the kingdom of

Baghirmi that Vogel crossed in 1836 on his way to Wadai, where he disappeared. The young fellow – he was only twenty-three – was sent to join Dr Barth. They met on the 1st of December, 1854, and Vogel then began his exploration of the country. In his last letters, about 1856, he announced his intention of surveying the kingdom of Wadai, where no European had then set foot. He appears to have got as far as Wara, the capital, where, according to some, he was taken prisoner, others saying he was put to death for attempting to climb a sacred mountain in the neighbourhood. But it doesn't do to be in a hurry to assume the death of an explorer, for that prevents a search being made. Dr Barth's death, for instance, was officially announced times without number, which often caused him justifiable irritation. So it is very possible that Vogel is still in the hands of the Sultan of Wadai, who would have hopes of getting a ransom for him. Baron Neimans was starting for Wadai when he died at Cairo, in 1855. We now know that von Heuglin, with the Leipzig expedition, is on Vogel's track, so we ought soon to have definite news about the fate of this interesting young traveller.' *

Mosfeia had long since vanished beyond the horizon. Mandara was displaying its amazing fertility, with its forests of acacia, red-blossomed locust and plantations of cotton and indigo. The Shari, which empties itself into Lake Tchad eighty miles away, swept on its impetuous course. The doctor traced it for his companions on Barth's maps.

'You see,' he said, 'the work of this able man is extremely accurate. We are heading straight for the Loggum district, and perhaps even for Kernak, the capital. That's where poor Toole died, hardly twenty-two. He was a young Englishman, a subaltern of the 80th Regiment who, a few weeks before, had joined Major Denham in Africa, where he so soon met his death. This great country may well be called the white man's grave.'

Canoes, about fifty feet long, were making their way down the Shari. At a height of a thousand feet the *Victoria* attracted little attention from the natives, but the wind, which hitherto had been blowing pretty strongly, showed a tendency to drop.

'Are we going to be becalmed again?' said the doctor.

'Never mind, sir. At any rate, we needn't be afraid of the desert, and we shan't run short of water.'

'No, but the people here are more formidable still.'

'Look,' said Joe. 'There's something that looks like a town.'

---

* Letters addressed from El Obeid written by Munzinger, the new chief of the expedition, after the doctor's departure, unfortunately leave no doubt about Vogel's death.

'It's Kernak. The wind will just manage to get us there and, if we like, we shall be able to make an exact plan of it.'

'Can't we get down nearer?' asked Kennedy.

'Nothing easier, Dick. We're right over the town. Let me lower the burner a little and we'll soon be down.'

Half an hour later the *Victoria* was hanging motionless two hundred feet from the ground.

'We are now nearer to Kernak than a man on the dome of St Paul's would be to London,' said the doctor, 'so we can view it at our ease.'

'What's that hammering noise all over the place?'

Joe looked carefully and saw that the noise was made by large numbers of weavers in the open air beating their cloth, which was stretched out on enormous tree trunks.

The capital of Loggum could now be seen in its entirety, as on an unfolded map. It was a real town, with rows of houses and fairly broad streets. In the middle of a large square a slave-market was in progress. Buyers were numerous, for the Mandarans, who have very small hands and feet, are much sought after and fetch high prices. When the *Victoria* was sighted, there was a recurrence of the effect she had already so often produced. It began with shouting, which gave place to dumb-founded amazement. Business was abandoned, work interrupted, and the place relapsed into silence. The travellers remained perfectly still and observed every detail of this populous city. They even came down within sixty feet of the ground, whereupon the ruler of Loggum emerged from his residence, accompanied by musicians blowing into harsh buffalo horns in a way that seemed certain to burst everything except their own lungs. He unfurled his green standard. The crowd gathered round him. Dr Fergusson tried to make himself heard, but in vain. These people, with their high foreheads, closely curling hair and almost aquiline noses, looked proud and intelligent, but the presence of the *Victoria* seemed to have a strangely disturbing effect upon them. Horsemen could be seen galloping in all directions, and it soon became evident that the chief's troops were being mustered to deal with this extraordinary enemy. It was no use for Joe to wave handkerchiefs of every conceivable colour; he produced no effect.

Meanwhile the sheik, surrounded by his court, called for silence and declaimed a speech of which the doctor could not understand a word. It was a mixture of Arabic and Baghirmi. From the universal language of gesture, however, he realised that it was a definite invitation to go away. He would have asked nothing better, but the absence of wind made it impossible. His standing still exasperated the sheik, and the courtiers began to scream to try and frighten the monster away.

These courtiers were odd-looking fellows, in their vividly-striped robes. They had enormous stomachs, some being quite pot-bellied. The doctor surprised his companions by telling them that this was a way of doing honour to the sultan. The rotundity of the stomach indicated the degree of ambition of its owner. These corpulent fellows gesticulated and shouted; especially one, who, if his dimensions had met with their just reward, must have been the prime minister. The negro crowd mingled their shrieks with those of the court and mimicked their gesticulations like monkeys, ten thousand arms waving as one.

These efforts at intimidation being apparently found inadequate, more drastic methods were adopted. Soldiers armed with bows and arrows ranged themselves in battle order. But the *Victoria* had already been dilated and quietly rose out of range. The governor seized a musket and levelled it at the balloon, but Kennedy was watching him, and a bullet from his carbine smashed the weapon in the sheik's hand. This unexpected coup produced a general rout. Every man bolted into his hut, and for the rest of the day the town remained completely deserted.

Night fell, but the wind still refused to blow. They had to reconcile themselves to hanging suspended three hundred feet above the ground. Not a light relieved the darkness. A silence reigned like that of death. The doctor redoubled his alertness; this calm might conceal a trap. He was right to keep on the lookout, for about midnight the whole town burst into a blaze of light. Hundreds of fiery lines intersected one another like rockets, forming a network of flame.

'That's odd!' said the doctor.

'But, God forgive me, it looks as though the fire was rising towards us,' said Kennedy.

It was true. Amid the din of dreadful shrieks and the crash of muskets this mass of fire was rising towards the *Victoria*. Joe got ready to throw out ballast, but Fergusson soon found the explanation of the phenomenon. Thousands of pigeons with some inflammable material fixed to their tails had been launched against the *Victoria*. In terror they flew upward, striping the air with zigzags of fire. Kennedy got ready to fire his whole armament into the middle of the mass, but what could he do against such a countless army? Already the pigeons were round the car and the balloon, whose envelope, reflecting the light, seemed to be caught in a mesh of fire.

Without hesitation the doctor threw out a lump of quartz and was soon out of reach of this dangerous attack. Two hours later the birds could be still seen flashing through the night, then gradually their numbers diminished, and finally they could be seen no more.

'Now we can sleep in peace,' said the doctor.

'Not a bad idea for savages,' Joe remarked.

'Yes; pigeons are often used to set fire to the thatch of villages, but this time the village flew higher even than those fiery messengers.'

'There's no doubt about it: a balloon has no enemies to fear,' said Kennedy.

'Oh, hasn't it!' the doctor answered.

'What, then?'

'The carelessness of its crew; so keep a good look-out, my friends, everywhere and always.'

CHAPTER XXXI

They set off in the dark – Still three – Kennedy's instincts –
Precautions – The course of the Shari – Lake Tchad – The
water – The hippopotamus – A wasted bullet

ABOUT THREE IN THE MORNING Joe, whose watch it was, at last saw the town moving away from below their feet. The *Victoria* was off again. Kennedy and the doctor woke up, and the latter, consulting his compass, was glad to see that the wind was bearing them north-north-east.

'We're in luck,' he said. 'Everything's going in our favour. We shall sight Lake Tchad before the day's out.'

'Is it a big lake?' Kennedy asked.

'It's a good size, Dick. At its longest and broadest it must measure a hundred and twenty miles.'

'It'll be a bit of a change to travel over water.'

'But I don't think we've anything to grumble at. We've had a good deal of change and the best possible conditions.'

'No doubt, Samuel; except for the trying time in the desert, we haven't met with any serious danger.'

'There's no doubt the good old *Victoria* has behaved wonderfully. Today is the 12th of May, and we left on the 18th of April. That makes twenty-five days. Another ten and we'll be there.'

'Where?'

'I've no idea. But what does it matter?'

'You're right, Sam. We can rely on Providence to guide us and keep us fit, as has been the case so far. We don't look as though we had crossed the most pestilent country in the world.'

'We could always rise, and that's what we've done.'

'Give me a balloon, every time!' cried Joe. 'Here we are after twenty-five days, healthy, well-fed and rested; perhaps over-rested, for my legs are beginning to get rusty, and I shouldn't be sorry to stretch them with a thirty-mile walk.'

'You'll be able to do that through the streets of London, Joe. But after all, we started out as three, like Denham, Clapperton and Overweg, and like Barth, Richardson and Vogel; but we've been luckier than they were, and there are still three of us. But it's very important we shouldn't separate. If the *Victoria* had to rise to escape some sudden danger while one of us was on the ground, it's quite likely we should never see each other again. I must tell you frankly, Kennedy, that I don't like you going off shooting.'

'But surely you don't want me to give it up, Samuel. There's no harm in replenishing our supplies and, besides, before we left you made me imagine a whole lot of splendid hunting and up to now I've done very little in that line.'

'You're forgetting your successes, Dick; or perhaps it's your modesty. If I remember right, not to mention small game, you already have an antelope, an elephant and two lions on your conscience.'

'Oh, yes. But what's that to an African sportsman who has to watch all the animals of creation wandering in front of his gun? Hello! Just look at that herd of giraffe!'

'Those, giraffes?' said Joe. 'They're no bigger than your fist.'

'That's because we're a thousand feet above them, but from close to, you'd see they are three times your height.'

'And what about that herd of gazelle?' Kennedy went on, 'and those ostriches legging it like the wind?'

'Ostriches!' said Joe. 'They're hens, just ordinary hens!'

'Come, Samuel, can't we get a bit closer?'

'We can, Dick, but we're not going to land. After all, what's the good of shooting them when they're no use to you? I could understand wanting to kill a lion, or a tiger-cat, or a hyena; that would always make one dangerous animal the less. But to shoot an antelope or a gazelle simply for the empty satisfaction of your hunting instincts really isn't worth while. After all, old man, we're going to keep at a hundred feet, and if you spot a fierce animal we shall be glad to watch you put a bullet in its heart.'

The *Victoria* was gradually dropping but still kept at a comfortable height. In this wild and thickly-populated country it was necessary to be on the look-out for unexpected dangers.

The travellers were now directly following the Shari, whose delightful banks were buried beneath leafy trees of many shades. Lianas and climbing plants wound in all directions, producing strange combinations of colour. Crocodiles disported themselves in the sunshine or dived under the water with the agility of lizards, landing again on the numerous green islands that broke the course of the river. Covered with this rich, luxuriant nature the surroundings of Mafate passed below them. About nine o'clock in the morning Dr Fergusson and his friends at last reached the southern shore of Lake Tchad. Here at last was this Caspian Sea of Africa whose existence had so long been relegated to the realms of fable; this inland sea touched only by the expeditions of Denham and Barth. The doctor attempted to establish its present configuration, which differed widely from that of 1847. In fact, it is impossible to make a chart of this lake. It is surrounded by spongy, almost impassable swamps in which Barth almost perished. From year to year these marshes, which are covered with reeds and papyrus fifteen feet high, merge into the lake itself. Often, even the very towns spread along its shores are submerged, as happened in 1856 to Ngornu. Where hippopotami and alligators now dive was once the site of Bornu dwellings.

The sun shone brilliantly on the tranquil water, which to northward stretched as far as the eye could see. The doctor was anxious to sample the water, which has long been thought to be salt. There was no danger in coming down to the surface of the lake, so the car skimmed over it like a bird at a height of five feet. Joe dipped a bottle in and brought it up again half full. It was tasted and found hardly drinkable, with a slight flavour of natron.

While the doctor was noting down the result of his experiment a shot rang out beside him. Kennedy had been unable to resist a desire to fire at an enormous hippopotamus. The animal, which was breathing peacefully on the surface, vanished at the noise of the report, and the sportsman's conical bullet did not seem to have had any other effect.

'We ought to have harpooned him, sir,' said Joe.

'And how?'

'With one of the anchors. It would have made the right sort of hook for an animal like that.'

'That's really rather a good idea of Joe's – ' said Kennedy.

'Which I'll ask you not to put into practice,' replied the doctor. 'The beast would soon have us away where we didn't want to go.'

'Especially now we've settled the quality of the Tchad water. Is that kind of fish eatable, Dr Fergusson?'

'That fish, as you call it, Joe, is a pachydermatous mammal. Its flesh is said to be excellent, and a good deal of trade is carried on in it between the tribes on the shores of the lake.'

'Well, in that case, I'm sorry Mr Kennedy didn't have better luck.'

'These animals are only vulnerable in the belly and between the thighs. Mr Kennedy's bullet won't have made the least impression. But if the landing looks good we'll halt at the northern end of the lake. You'll find a regular menagerie, Kennedy, and can blaze away as you like.'

'Good!' said Joe. 'I hope you'll have a try at the hippopotamus. I'd like to taste the meat. It certainly doesn't seem natural to cross the centre of Africa and live on woodcock and partridges, just as if you were in England.'

CHAPTER XXXII

The capital of Bornu – The Biddiomah Islands – Vultures –
The doctor's anxiety – His precautions – An attack in
mid-air – The envelope torn – The drop – Splendid devotion –
The northern shore of the lake

SINCE REACHING Lake Tchad the *Victoria* had fallen in with a breeze veering more to the west and a few clouds then tempered the heat of the day. Over the water the air had been fresh, but about one o'clock the balloon, having crossed this part of the lake diagonally, travelled for another seven or eight miles over land. The doctor was at first disappointed at this change of direction but forgot his grievance when he saw Kuka, the famous capital of Bornu. He had a momentary glimpse of the town girdled with its walls of white clay. A few crude mosques rose clumsily above the group of Arab houses which looked like a collection of dice. In the courtyards of the houses and in the public squares, palms and rubber-trees grew, crowned by a dome of foliage over a hundred feet wide. Joe pointed out that these huge parasols were appropriate to the intensity of the sun and drew conclusions flattering to Providence.

Kuka really consisted of two distinct towns separated by the 'Dendal,' a broad boulevard six hundred yards long, now thronged with pedestrians and horsemen. On one side the rich part of the town flaunts its lofty well-ventilated dwellings, while on the other is huddled the poor quarter, a dismal collection of low, conical huts, where a needy population vegetates, for Kuka is neither a commercial nor an industrial centre.

Kennedy thought it looked like Edinburgh situated in a plain, with its two perfectly defined towns. But the travellers were hardly able to obtain more than a fleeting glimpse, for, with the suddenness which is characteristic of the air-currents of this district, a contrary wind seized hold of them and brought them back some forty miles over Lake Tchad.

The view was now completely changed. They could count the many islands of the lake, which are inhabited by the Biddiomahs, blood-thirsty pirates who are as much feared in the district as the Tuaregs in the Sahara. These savages were getting ready to give the *Victoria* a formidable reception with arrows and stones, but she soon left the islands behind, flitting over them like a gigantic insect. Joe, who was watching the horizon, turned to Kennedy and said: 'My word, Mr Kennedy; you're always dreaming about shooting, there's something in your line.'

'What is it, Joe?'

'And this time my master won't interfere.'

'But what is it?'

'Don't you see that flock of big birds flying towards us?'

'Birds?' said the doctor, seizing his glass.

'I see them,' Kennedy replied. 'There's at least a dozen of them.'

'Fourteen, sir, begging your pardon,' Joe remarked.

'It's only to be hoped they're of a kind dangerous enough to prevent the humane Fergusson from interfering.'

'I shall have no objection,' replied Fergusson, 'but I'd rather they were not there.'

'You're not afraid of them, sir?' said Joe.

'They're bearded vultures, unusually big ones, and if they attack us – '

'Well, we'll put up a good fight, Samuel. We've a useful arsenal for their reception. I don't think they can be very formidable.'

'We'll see,' the doctor replied.

Ten minutes later the flock had come within range and the fourteen birds were making the air re-echo with their raucous cries. They swept towards the *Victoria*, more angry than frightened.

'What a din!' said Joe. 'I don't suppose they like us trespassing on their country and making bold to fly like they do.'

'They certainly look pretty fierce,' said Kennedy. 'They'd be nasty if they were armed with Purdey Moores!'

'They don't need them,' replied Fergusson, who had become very grave.

The vultures were circling through wide arcs which gradually narrowed round the *Victoria*. They drove through the sky at incredible speed, every now and again dashing straight at the balloon with the swiftness of a bullet. The doctor, filled with anxiety, decided to rise to escape from their dangerous proximity. He expanded the hydrogen and the balloon soon began to climb. But the vultures climbed with her, showing little inclination to leave her.

'They don't seem to like the look of us,' said Kennedy, cocking his carbine. The birds were indeed coming closer, and several, less than fifty feet away, seemed to be defying Kennedy's gun.

'I'm itching terribly to have a shot at them,' he said.

'No, no, Dick. Don't infuriate them if you can help it. You'd only make them attack us.'

'But I can easily deal with them.'

'You're wrong, Dick.'

'We've a bullet for each of them.'

'And suppose they made a dash at the upper part of the balloon, how should we get at them? Imagine yourself faced with a lot of lions on land or sharks in mid-ocean. The present position is just as dangerous for us.'

'Do you really mean that, Samuel?'

'I do, Dick.'

'In that case, let's wait.'

'Yes, wait. Get ready for an attack but don't fire unless I tell you.'

The birds were now massing quite a short distance away. Their naked throats, distended by the effort of their screams could be clearly seen, as well as their gristly crests, covered with purple spots and erect with anger. They were of the largest size, their bodies more than three feet long, and the inner side of their white wings shone in the sunlight. They looked alarmingly like a shoal of winged sharks.

'They're coming after us,' said the doctor, seeing them rise with the balloon. 'It's no good going up; they can fly higher than we can.'

'Well, what are we going to do?' Kennedy asked.

The doctor made no reply.

'Look here, Samuel,' the Scotsman went on, 'there are fourteen of these birds. We can put in seventeen shots if we fire all our guns. Shan't we manage to wipe them out or, at any rate, scatter them? I'll undertake to settle a certain number.'

'I'm not questioning your skill, Dick. I'm quite ready to regard all you aim at as dead; but I repeat, they've only to attack the upper half of the balloon and they'll be out of your sight. They'll tear the envelope which holds us up, and we've three thousand feet to fall.'

Just then one of the most savage of the birds darted straight at the *Victoria*, beak and claws open, ready to bite and tear.

'Shoot!' cried the doctor.

The word was hardly out of his mouth when the bird, struck dead, was hurtling downwards through space. Kennedy had seized one of the double-barrelled guns. Joe had the other at his shoulder. Frightened by the report, the vultures drew away for a moment, but almost at once returned to the charge with terrific fury. With his first shot Kennedy broke the neck of the nearest. Joe smashed the wing of the next.

'Only eleven more,' he said. But the birds now changed their tactics and with one accord rose above the *Victoria*. Kennedy looked at Fergusson. In spite of his courage and coolness the latter turned pale. There was a moment of awful silence. Then they heard the hiss of tearing silk and the car began to drop from below their feet.

'We're done!' cried Fergusson, casting a glance at the barometer, which was shooting up rapidly. Then he added: 'Ballast, throw out ballast!'

In a few seconds every lump of quartz had gone overboard. 'We're still dropping! . . . Empty the water cans! . . . Joe, do you hear? . . . We're dropping into the lake!'

Joe obeyed. The doctor leaned over. The lake seemed to be rushing towards him like a rising tide. Objects on the ground were growing perceptibly bigger. The car was only two hundred feet from the surface of Lake Tchad.

'The stores! The stores!' cried the doctor, and the box containing them was hurled into space. The fall became less rapid but they were still falling.

'Go on, throw out something else!' the doctor cried once more.

'There is nothing,' said Kennedy.

'Yes, there is,' Joe replied laconically, and with a rapid wave of his hand, he vanished over the side of the car.

'Joe! Joe!' yelled the doctor. But Joe was out of earshot. The *Victoria*, relieved of his weight, started upwards again and reached a height of a thousand feet, while the wind blowing into the deflated envelope bore her towards the northern shores of the lake.

'He's done for,' said Kennedy, with a gesture of despair.

'To save us,' Fergusson replied. And these strong men felt the tears running down their cheeks. They leaned over in an effort to see some sign of poor Joe, but they were already far away.

'What's to be done now?' asked Kennedy.

'Drop to the ground as soon as possible, Dick, and then wait.'

After travelling sixty miles the *Victoria* came down on a deserted shore at the north end of the lake. The anchors caught a low tree and Kennedy made them fast. Night came on, but neither Fergusson nor Kennedy could sleep for a moment.

CHAPTER XXXIII

Conjectures – Re-establishing the equilibrium of the
Victoria *– Fergusson's fresh calculations – Kennedy goes*
shooting – Complete exploration of Lake Tchad – Tangalia –
The return – Lari

THE NEXT DAY, the 13th of May, the travellers at once recognised the part of the shore in which they were. It was a sort of island of firm ground in the middle of a huge swamp. Around this patch of solid earth stood reeds as big as trees in Europe, stretching as far as the eye could see. These impassable swamps established the position of the *Victoria* beyond all doubt. It was only necessary to observe the shores of the lake; the great stretch of water broadened out continuously, especially in the east, and nothing appeared on the horizon, neither shore nor island. The two friends had not yet ventured to speak of their unfortunate companion. Kennedy was the first to give expression to his conjectures.

'Joe may not be lost,' he said. 'He's a clever fellow and can swim like a fish. He used to have no difficulty in swimming across the Firth of Forth at Edinburgh. He'll turn up again, though I don't know when or how. But we must leave no stone unturned to give him a chance to rejoin us.'

'Heaven grant you're right!' the doctor replied, much moved . 'We'll go round the world to find him. First let's see how we stand. The first thing is to rid the *Victoria* of this outer envelope, which is now useless. We shall be getting rid of a considerable weight, six hundred and fifty pounds, so it's worth the trouble.'

They got to work, but found themselves faced with serious difficulties. The tough silk had to be torn away strip by strip, and the strips had to be cut very small to get them through the meshes of the net. The rent made by the birds was several feet long.

This operation took quite four hours, but at last the inner balloon was completely freed and it appeared to have suffered no damage. The size of the *Victoria* was now reduced by a fifth, the difference being marked enough to surprise Kennedy

'Will it be big enough?' he asked Fergusson.

'You need have no anxiety on that score, Dick. I'll put the equilibrium right again and, if poor Joe returns, we'll manage to continue our route with him on board as well.'

'If I remember right, when we fell we weren't very far off an island.'

'Yes, I remember. But that island, like all the islands of Lake Tchad, is sure to be inhabited by a gang of pirates and cut-throats. They're sure to have seen our disaster, and if Joe falls into their hands, unless superstition comes to his rescue, what will happen to him?'

'As I said before, you can trust him to find a way out. I'll back his skill and brains.'

'I hope you're right. Now, Dick, you go and do a little shooting round about, but don't go far away. It has become very necessary for us to replenish our stores, for we've thrown away the greater part of them.'

'All right, Samuel. I'll not be long.'

Kennedy took a double-barrelled gun and plunged into the tall grass, making for a copse not far away. Frequent reports soon told the doctor that the sport was good. Meanwhile he was busy taking stock of the things still left in the car and establishing the equilibrium of the second balloon. There remained about thirty pounds of pemmican, a supply of tea and coffee, about a gallon and a half of brandy and an empty water container. All the dried meat had gone.

The doctor knew that, owing to the loss of the hydrogen in the other balloon, his lifting force was reduced by about 900 lbs. He had therefore to work on this difference in re-establishing his equilibrium. The new *Victoria* had a capacity of 67,000 cubic feet and contained 33,480 cubic feet of gas. The expanding gear seemed in good order. Neither the battery nor the spiral seemed to have been damaged. The lift of the new balloon was therefore about 3000 lbs. Adding together the weight of the apparatus, the passengers, the water, the car and its accessories, and allowing for a further addition of fifty gallons of water and a hundred pounds of fresh meat, the doctor arrived at a total of 2830 lbs. He could therefore carry seventy pounds of ballast for emergencies and the balloon would be in equilibrium with the surrounding air.

He made his plans accordingly, replacing Joe's weight by extra ballast. These various preparations occupied the whole day and were brought to an end as Kennedy returned. The sportsman had had a good day and brought back a regular load of geese, wild duck, woodcock, snipe, teal and plover. He set about dressing the game and smoking it. Each bird, spitted on a thin stick, was hung over a fire of green wood, and when they seemed ready to Kennedy, who incidentally knew what he was about, they were all stowed in the car. The following morning he finished off the provisioning.

Night found the pair still at work. Their supper consisted of pemmican, biscuits and tea. Fatigue, which had first given them appetite, now gave them sleep. During his watch, each searched the darkness and at times thought he heard Joe's voice. Unfortunately that voice they longed to hear was far away. At the first glimmer of daylight Fergusson woke Kennedy.

'I've been trying for a long time to think what is the best thing to do to find Joe,' he said.

'I'll fall in with whatever you've decided, Samuel. Tell me.'

'First and foremost, it's important that Joe should have news of us.'

'Of course. It would be awful if the good fellow thought we were deserting him!'

'Not he, he knows us too well. Such an idea would never cross his mind, but he must know where we are.'

'But how?'

'We'll get back into the car and go up.'

'What if the wind carries us away?'

'Luckily it won't. Look, Dick. The breeze will take us back over the lake, and if that was a nuisance yesterday it's in our favour today. All we shall have to try to do, then, is to keep over this big stretch of water all day. Joe can't fail to see us. He'll be looking out all the time. We may even manage to find out where he is.'

'Provided he's alone and free, he certainly will look out.'

'And if he's a prisoner,' the doctor replied, 'as these natives don't as a rule shut their prisoners up, he'll see us and realise what we're trying to do.'

'But after all,' Kennedy resumed, – 'for we must take everything into account, – what are we to do if we find no sign, if he's left no trace?'

'We shall have to try to get back to the north end of the lake, keeping in sight as far as possible. We'll wait there and explore the banks on that side, which Joe will certainly make for, and we won't leave before we've done all we can to find him.'

'Let's get away, then,' said Kennedy.

The doctor took the exact position of this strip of firm ground that they were leaving. From his map he estimated that it was north of Lake Tchad, between the town of Lari and the village of Ingemini, both of which had been visited by Major Denham. Meanwhile Kennedy completed his supplies of fresh meat. Although the surrounding marshes showed traces of rhinoceros, manatee and hippopotamus, he did not fall in with a single one of these huge animals.

At 7 a.m., and not without great difficulties, which Joe had managed to overcome so successfully in the past, the anchors were freed from the tree. The gas expanded and the new *Victoria* rose two hundred feet into the air. She hesitated at first, twisting on her own axis; but in the end, caught in a brisk current, she headed over the lake and was soon travelling at a speed of twenty miles an hour. The doctor continued to keep her at a level varying between two hundred and five hundred feet. Kennedy frequently fired his carbine. Above the islands they dropped perhaps incautiously close, their eyes searching the woods, thickets and undergrowth; everywhere where any shade or rocky cleft might have offered Joe a refuge. They came down also near some long canoes that were crossing the lake. On seeing them, the fishermen threw themselves into the water and swam back to their island in unconcealed terror.

'Two hours gone,' said Kennedy. 'Nothing so far.'

'We must wait, Dick, and keep our hearts up. We can't be far from where the accident took place.'

By one o'clock the *Victoria* had travelled ninety miles, when she encountered a fresh current almost at right angles, and this took her sixty miles to eastward. She was now over a very large and thickly populated island which the doctor took to be Farram, where the capital of the Biddiomahs was situated. They expected to see Joe emerge from every bush, running for his life and shouting to them. Had he been free, they could have got him away without difficulty, and even if he had been a prisoner, they could have repeated the manœuvre employed in the case of the missionary. But nothing appeared, nothing stirred. It seemed hopeless.

At 2.30 the *Victoria* came in sight of Tangalia, a village on the eastern shore of the lake which marked the extreme point reached by Denham's expedition. This persistent direction of the wind made the doctor anxious. He felt himself being driven back eastward, towards the centre of Africa, towards the boundless deserts.

'We must certainly halt,' he said, 'and even land. For Joe's sake especially, we must get back over the lake. But first of all, let's try to find a current in the opposite direction.'

For over an hour he tried various zones. The *Victoria* still drifted over terra firma. But at a thousand feet, fortunately, a very strong breeze took them back north-west.

It was impossible that Joe should be kept a prisoner on one of the islands of the lake. He would certainly have found some way of making his presence known. He might have been carried off overland. This was what the doctor thought when once more he came within sight of the northern shore. The idea of Joe's being drowned was inadmissible, but a horrible idea occurred to the two men: alligators abound in these parts! Neither of them, however, had the courage to voice this fear, which was obviously in the minds of both. At last the doctor said bluntly:

'Crocodiles are only to be met with on the shores of the islands or of the lake itself. Joe will be sharp enough to keep out of their way. In any case, they're not very dangerous. The Africans bathe as they like without fear of being attacked.'

Kennedy offered no reply. He preferred to remain silent rather than discuss this terrible possibility. About five o'clock in the evening the doctor pointed out the town of Lari. The inhabitants were working at the cotton harvest outside cabins built of plaited reed in the middle of clean and carefully kept enclosures. This collection of about fifty huts occupied a slight depression in a valley between low mountains. The strength of the wind carried them farther than the doctor wanted, but it shifted a second time and took them back to the exact point of their departure, the island of firm ground where they had spent the preceding night. The anchor, instead of finding the branches of a tree, took hold in some clumps of reed mixed with the thick mud of the marsh and of considerable resistance. The doctor had a good deal of difficulty in checking the balloon, but finally, with nightfall, the wind dropped and the two friends, reduced almost to despair, kept watch together.

CHAPTER XXXIV

*The hurricane – A forced departure – Loss of an anchor – Sad
reflections – A decision – The sandstorm – The buried
caravan – Contrary and favourable winds – Southward
again – Kennedy at his post*

AT THREE IN THE MORNING a gale sprang up, so violent that the *Victoria* could not remain near the ground without danger. The reeds rubbed against her envelope, threatening to tear it.

'We must get off, Dick,' said the doctor. 'We can't stay here.'

'But what about Joe?'

'I'm not going to desert him. I should think not. Even if the gale carries us a hundred miles north we'll come back. But by staying here we shall be risking the safety of all three.'

'I don't like the idea of starting without him,' said the Scotsman in accents of deep regret.

'Do you think it's less hard for me than for you?' Fergusson continued. 'But we can't help ourselves.'

'I'm with you,' Kennedy replied. 'Let's start.'

But starting presented great difficulties. The anchor, which was deeply buried, resisted all their efforts and the balloon, dragging in the opposite direction, made its hold firmer. Kennedy could not get it away. Further, in the existing circumstances, his position grew very dangerous for there was risk of the *Victoria*'s rising before he could rejoin her. The doctor, not wishing to run such a risk, told him to get back into the car and resigned himself to cutting the anchor rope. The *Victoria* leapt three hundred feet and headed due north. Fergusson had to let the storm have its way. He folded his arms and gave himself up to his sad reflections.

After a few moments of complete silence he turned to Kennedy, who was equally silent.

'We may have been tempting Providence,' he said. 'It's not for men to attempt such a voyage.' And he sighed deeply.

'It's only a few days since we were congratulating ourselves on having come through many dangers,' Kennedy replied. 'We all shook hands.'

'Poor Joe; he was a kind-hearted fellow, plucky and straightforward. After his wealth had dazzled him a moment he willingly sacrificed it. Now he's far away and the wind is rapidly taking us farther away still.'

'Come, Samuel, suppose he has found refuge among the lake tribes. Couldn't he do as the other travellers did, who have been there before us, like Denham and Barth? They got back.'

'But, my dear Dick, Joe doesn't know a word of the language. He's alone and helpless. The travellers you mention only got along by sending the chief lots of presents; besides, they were surrounded by an escort armed and equipped for such expeditions. And even then they couldn't avoid terrible suffering. What do you expect would happen to poor old Joe? It's awful to think of. I'm sorrier about it than I've ever been about anything.'

'But we'll come back, Samuel.'

'Yes, we'll come back, Dick; even if it means abandoning the *Victoria*, coming back to Lake Tchad on foot, and getting into communication with the Sultan of Bornu. The Arabs can't have unpleasant memories of their first European.'

'I'll go with you, Samuel,' Kennedy replied resolutely. 'You can rely on me. We'll give up the rest of the trip if necessary. Joe has sacrificed himself for us. We'll do as much for him.'

This resolve revived their courage somewhat. They felt themselves fortified by the same idea. Fergusson did all he could to find a contrary current that might take him back to the lake, but as yet without success, and besides it was impracticable to land in this denuded country in such a gale.

In this way the *Victoria* passed over the country of the Tibbus. She left behind her Belad el Djerid, a thorny wilderness forming the fringe of the Sudan, and penetrated the sandy desert scored by the long trails of caravans. The last line of vegetation was soon lost on the southern horizon, not far from the chief oasis of that part of Africa, whose fifty wells are shaded by magnificent trees. But it was impossible to stop. An Arab encampment, gaily-striped tents and a few camels stretching their snake-like heads over the sand, broke the solitude, but the *Victoria* passed over it like a shooting star, covering a distance of sixty miles in three hours, with Fergusson helpless to control her course.

'We can't stop,' he said. 'We can't go down. Not a tree. Not a break in the ground! Are we going to cross the whole Sahara like this? Heaven is obviously against us.'

As he uttered these words in impotent exasperation he saw the sands of the desert in the north rising in a dense cloud of dust and twisting under the force of the opposing winds. In the middle of the whirlwind a whole caravan, bruised, broken, and overthrown, was being buried under the avalanche of sand. The horses, thrown into panic, were uttering muffled but heart-rending moans. Shouts and shrieks came from the suffocating mist. From time to time a brightly-coloured garment would flash across the chaos, while the roaring of the wind dominated the whole scene of destruction.

Soon the sand gathered into compact masses and, where shortly before had stretched a smooth plain, there rose a still moving mound, the enormous tomb of the engulfed caravan. The doctor and Kennedy, with pale faces, watched this terrible drama. They had lost all control over their balloon, which was whirled about by the contrary currents and no longer responded to the expansion or contraction of the gas. Caught in the surging air, she twirled with dizzy speed, the car heaving about in all directions. The instruments hanging under the awning were dashed together and threatened to break. The pipes of the spiral bent and seemed ready to snap at any moment. The water containers were hurled crashing from their places. Though only two feet apart, the men could not make themselves heard, while with one hand clutching the rigging they strove to keep on their feet under the fury of the hurricane.

Kennedy, his hair blowing in the wind, looked on without a word.

The doctor's courage had revived in the face of danger, and no trace appeared on his face of the tumult of his feelings; not even when, after a final spin, the *Victoria* suddenly came to a standstill in an unexpected lull. The north wind had gained the upper hand and was driving her swiftly but smoothly back over the route travelled during the morning.

'Where are we off to now?' Kennedy shouted.

'Leave that to Providence, Dick. I was wrong to doubt; Providence knows better than we what is best for us, and here we are heading back again towards the places we had given up hope of seeing again.'

The surface of the ground, which had been so smooth as they came, was now broken as by waves after a storm. A succession of ridges, hardly yet settled into stillness, ruffled the surface of the desert. The wind was blowing strongly and the *Victoria* flew through space. The direction followed was somewhat different from that of the morning, so that about nine o'clock, instead of coming back to the shores of Lake Tchad, they saw the desert still stretching before them. Kennedy pointed this out.

'It doesn't matter much,' the doctor replied. 'The important thing is to be going south. We shall come across the towns of Bornu, Wuddie or Kuka, and I shall not hesitate to stop there.'

'So long as you're satisfied, I am,' Kennedy answered; 'but God grant we shan't be reduced to crossing the desert like those unfortunate Arabs! It was a horrible sight.'

'And it's quite a frequent one, Dick. Crossing the desert is more dangerous than crossing the ocean, for the desert has all the perils of the sea, including that of being swallowed up, and, in addition, intolerable fatigue and privation.'

'It seems to me,' said Kennedy, 'that the wind is showing a tendency to drop. The sand-dust is less dense, the waves of sand are smaller and the horizon is clearing.'

'All the better. We shall have to search it carefully with a glass and let no point escape us.'

'I'll see to that, Samuel, and as soon as the first tree appears I'll let you know.'

And Kennedy, glass in hand, took up a position in the forward part of the car.

CHAPTER XXXV

*Joe's story – The island of the Biddiomahs – Worship – The
engulfed island – The shores of the lake – Snakes in a
tree – The* Victoria *passes – The* Victoria *disappears –
Despair – The swamp – A last despairing cry*

WHAT HAD HAPPENED to Joe while his master was making this
fruitless search?

When he threw himself into the lake, Joe's first movement on
coming to the surface was to raise his eyes upwards. He saw the
Victoria, already high above the lake and mounting rapidly, gradually
dwindling. Soon she was caught in a swift air-current and disappeared
northwards. His master, his friends, were saved.

'It's lucky I thought of throwing myself out,' he told himself. 'Mr
Kennedy would have been sure to think of the same thing, and would
certainly have done what I did; for it's only natural for a man to
sacrifice himself to save two others. It's a matter of arithmetic.'
Reassured on this point, Joe began to think of himself. He was in the
middle of a huge lake, surrounded by unknown and probably fierce
tribes; an additional reason for summoning all his self-reliance to get
out of this nasty situation. He did not, however, feel any signs of fear.
Before the attack by the vultures, which he had found very natural, he
had noticed an island on the horizon. He now decided to make for this
and brought to bear all his skill in swimming, after first getting rid of
his heavier clothing. A swim of five or six miles was little to him, so
while he was in the middle of the lake his one thought was to swim
strong and straight. After an hour and a half the distance separating
him from the island was considerably diminished. But, as he approached land, a thought which had already passed fleetingly across his
mind began to take a firm hold. He knew that the banks of the lake
were haunted by enormous alligators of whose voracity he was fully
aware. Eager as he always was to find everything in this world natural,
the worthy fellow could not shake off a feeling of dismay. He was
afraid that white flesh might be particularly to the crocodiles' taste,
and therefore went forward with extreme caution, keeping a keen
look-out. Hardly was he within a hundred yards of a shady bank,
covered with green trees, when a puff of air heavy with the sickly smell

of musk reached his nostrils.

'There we are,' he said to himself. 'Just what I was afraid of. There's an alligator somewhere about.'

He dived swiftly, but not sufficiently so to avoid contact with a huge body whose scaly skin scraped against him as it passed. He gave himself up for lost and began to swim with desperate vigour. Reaching the surface, he took a long breath and dived again. Then followed a quarter of an hour of inexpressible anguish which all his philosophy failed to overcome, when he thought he heard behind him the sound of the great jaw ready to snap. He was swimming just below the surface, as quietly as possible, when he felt himself seized, first by the arm and then by the middle of his body.

Poor Joe! His last thought was for his master as he began a struggle of despair. Then he realised that he was being dragged, not towards the bottom of the lake, as is the habit of crocodiles before devouring their prey, but to the surface. Scarcely had he had time to take breath and open his eyes than he found himself between two niggers, black as ebony, who were holding him tightly and uttering strange cries.

'Hello!' Joe could not help exclaiming. 'They're niggers, not crocodiles! That's a jolly sight better! But how can these chaps dare to bathe in these places?'

Joe was unaware that the inhabitants of the islands of Lake Tchad, like many other negroes, dive with impunity into water infested with alligators, paying no heed to their presence. The amphibia of this lake especially have a justified reputation for being harmless.

But had he only fallen out of the frying-pan into the fire? This question he left the event to decide and, as there was no alternative, he allowed himself to be led to the bank without betraying any fear.

'These people must have seen the *Victoria* skimming over the lake like a flying monster,' he said to himself. 'They would see me fall, and they're bound to have some respect for a man who has fallen from Heaven. Let's see what they are going to do.'

He had just reached this point in his reflections when he arrived on land and found himself in the middle of a shrieking mob; men and women of every age but all of the same colour. They belonged to a tribe of Biddiomahs, who are as black as jet. Nor was there any need for him to blush at the scantiness of his costume. He found himself in the height of fashion. But before he had time to take stock of the situation, he saw that he was undoubtedly regarded as an object of worship. This naturally reassured him, in spite of his memory of what had happened at Kazeh.

'I see I'm going to be made a god again, a son of the moon or something! Well, it's as good a job as any when there's no other. The thing is to gain time. If the *Victoria* happens to come back this way I'll make the most of my new position to let my worshippers see a miracle.'

While these thoughts were passing through Joe's mind the crowd closed in on him, prostrated themselves, shouted, touched him and began to grow familiar. At least, however, they were thoughtful enough to offer him a splendid feast of sour milk and rice crushed in honey. The good fellow, making the best of the situation, then had one of the best meals of his life and gave his people an impressive idea of the way the gods eat on great occasions.

When evening came on, the sorcerers of the island took him respectfully by the hand and led him towards a hut surrounded with talismans. Before entering, Joe cast an uneasy glance at the bones that were heaped up round this sanctuary. Moreover, he had plenty of time to reflect on his situation when he was shut up in his cabin.

During the evening and part of the night he heard festive singing, the throbbing of a sort of drum, and the clang of metal, so sweet to African ears. Yelling in chorus, the natives were performing one of their interminable dances round the sacred cabin, with contortions and grimaces of every conceivable kind. Joe could hear the deafening din through the walls of his hut which were built of mud and reeds. No doubt under any other circumstances these strange ceremonies would have afforded him considerable interest, but his mind soon became racked by a very unpleasant idea. Though trying to look on the bright side of things, he found it dull and even depressing to be lost in this savage country in the middle of such people. Of the men who had ventured into these parts few had come home again. Moreover, could he rely on this worship of which he found himself the object? He had good reason to believe in the vanity of human greatness. He wondered whether in this country adoration might not be pushed to the point of eating the adored one. In spite of the outlook, after some hours of reflection fatigue got the better of his black thoughts and Joe fell into a fairly deep sleep, which no doubt would have lasted until daybreak had not an unexpected sensation of damp awakened the sleeper. The damp soon became water, and this water rose until he was immersed as far as the waist. 'What on earth's this?' he wondered. 'A flood; a cloud-burst; or a new torture invented by these niggers? I'm hanged if I'll wait till it gets up to my neck!' So saying, he burst through the wall with a blow from his shoulder and found himself in the middle of the lake. Of the island there was not a trace; it had been submerged during the night. In its place was the immensity of Lake Tchad. 'A nice country for land-owners!' Joe said to himself, beginning to swim vigorously.

The good fellow had been delivered by a phenomenon not infrequent on Lake Tchad. More than one island, apparently as solid as rock, had vanished in this way, the unfortunate survivors of these terrible catastrophes being frequently rescued by the dwellers on the shore. Joe did not know this custom, but he did not fail to take advantage of it. Catching sight of a stray canoe, he quickly swam to it. It was a trunk of a tree crudely hollowed out. Fortunately it contained a pair of paddles and Joe, making use of a fairly rapid current, let himself drift.

'Let's see where we are,' he mused. 'The North Star will help me. It's always ready to show the way north to anybody.'

He noted with satisfaction that the current was carrying him toward the north shore of the lake, and he let himself go. About two in the morning he set foot on a promontory covered with thorny reeds, which seemed unduly searching even to a philosopher. But he found a tree specially designed to offer him a bed in its branches. For greater safety Joe climbed it and, without sleeping much, awaited the dawn.

When morning broke, with the swiftness characteristic of equatorial regions, Joe cast a glance over the tree which had sheltered him during the night. A somewhat astonishing spectacle struck terror into his heart. The branches of this tree were literally swarming with snakes and chameleons. They completely hid the foliage. It was like some new species of tree bringing forth reptiles. The whole mass crawled and twisted in the first rays of the sun. Joe experienced a feeling of terror mingled with loathing and threw himself to the ground amidst the hissing of the creatures.

'Well, who'd have believed that!' he said.

He did not know that Dr Vogel's last letters had reported this peculiarity of the shores of the Tchad, where reptiles are more numerous than in any other country in the world. After what he had seen, Joe decided to be more circumspect in future and, taking his direction by the sun, set out north-east. He was very careful to avoid cabins and huts, or in fact anything that could serve as a receptacle for human beings.

His eyes were constantly fixed on the sky. He hoped to catch sight of the *Victoria*, and though he searched in vain during that day's march, his confidence in his master did not flag. He must have had great force of character to accept his situation so philosophically. Hunger began to join forces with fatigue, for a man cannot renew his strength on a diet of roots or the sap of such shrubs as the *mele* or the fruit of the doum palm, and meanwhile, according to his reckoning, he had travelled about thirty miles westward. Many parts of his body were scored by the thousands of thorns which bristle on the reeds of the lake, the acacia and mimosa, and his bleeding feet made walking extremely painful. But he managed to hold out against his sufferings, and when night came on he decided to spend it on the shores of the lake. There he had to suffer the maddening stings of myriads of insects, for flies, mosquitoes and ants half an inch long literally covered the ground. After two hours there was not a shred left of Joe's scanty clothing; the insects had devoured it completely. It was a terrible night which brought not an hour's sleep to the weary traveller. Meanwhile wild boars, buffaloes and ajoubs, a rather dangerous kind of sea-cow, plunged about in the bushes and beneath the waters of the lake, their fierce cries making the night hideous. Joe did not dare to stir, though his resignation and patience were hard put to it to cope with such a situation.

At last it was day again and Joe got up hurriedly. His disgust can be imagined when he saw what a loathsome creature had shared his bed – a toad five inches long, a monstrous, repulsive beast, was staring at him with its great round eyes. Joe felt sick and, his horror reviving some of his strength, he dashed off and plunged into the waters of the lake. This bath calmed somewhat the hunger that tortured him and, after chewing a few leaves, he set out again with a dogged stubbornness for which he found it difficult to account. He was no longer acting consciously, and yet he felt within himself a power that raised him above despair.

Meanwhile he was tortured by terrible hunger. His stomach, less resigned than himself, began to complain. He was forced to tie a creeper tightly round his body. Fortunately he could quench his thirst at any moment, and when he remembered his sufferings in the desert, he found comparative comfort in being spared the torture of this imperative need.

'Where can the *Victoria* be?' he asked himself. 'The wind's from the north. It should bring her back over the lake. Dr Fergusson is sure to have overhauled the balloon, but yesterday ought to have been enough for that. It's quite possible that today – but I'd better go on as though I was never going to see them again. After all, if I managed to get to one of the big towns of the lake, I'd be in the same position as the travellers my master told us about. Why shouldn't I get out of it all like they did? Hang it all, some of them got back! . . . Come on. We must buck up.'

Musing thus and going ahead all the time through the forest, brave Joe suddenly found himself in the middle of a group of savages. He stopped in time and was not seen. The negroes were busy poisoning their arrows with the juice of the euphorbia as the people of this region do; they make a kind of solemn ceremony of it.

Standing perfectly motionless and holding his breath, Joe lay hidden in the midst of a copse where, raising his eyes, he saw through a gap in the foliage the *Victoria* – the *Victoria* herself – making for the lake hardly a hundred feet above him. It was impossible to attract her attention. A tear came into his eye, not of despair, but of gratitude. His master was looking for him, was not deserting him! He had only to wait for the departure of the blacks and then he would be able to leave his retreat and run to the lake side.

But the *Victoria* was now lost in the distance. Joe resolved to wait for her. She would be sure to come back. She did so, in fact, farther westward. Joe ran, waved his arms and shouted – but all in vain. A violent wind was driving the balloon along at tremendous speed. For the first time, courage and hope failed the poor fellow. He gave himself up for lost. He thought his master was now gone for ever. He dared not think; he tried to keep the subject away from his mind.

Like a madman, feet bleeding, body bruised, he walked the whole day and part of the night, dragging himself along, at times on his hands and knees. He saw the time coming when his strength would fail him, and then it would be the end. Labouring along like this, he at last found himself facing a swamp, or rather what he knew to be a swamp, for it had been dark for several hours. Without warning he found himself involved in clinging mud. In spite of his efforts, in spite of his despairing struggles, he felt himself being dragged down little by little into the sticky ooze. A few minutes later it was up to his waist.

'This is death,' he thought; 'and what a death! . . .'

He struggled frenziedly, but his efforts only served to bury the poor fellow deeper in the grave he was making for himself. There was not the smallest bit of wood to stop himself with, not a reed to take hold of ! . . . He realised that the end had come . . . His eyes closed.

'Master! Sir! Help! . . . ' he cried. And this lonely cry of despair, already stifled, died away into the night.

CHAPTER XXXVI

*A crowd on the horizon – A band of Arabs – The pursuit –
'It's Joe' – The fall from a horse – The strangled Arab – A
bullet from Kennedy – Working the trick – A rescue in full
flight – Joe saved*

SINCE TAKING UP his post of observation in the front of the car,
Kennedy had not ceased to scan the horizon with close attention. After
some time he turned to the doctor and said: 'Unless I'm mistaken,
there's a band of men or animals moving over there. It's impossible to
make them out yet. But in any case they're moving quickly for they're
raising a cloud of dust.'

'Might it not be a contrary wind?' said Fergusson. 'A sand storm
coming to drive us back north?' And he got up to look.

'I don't think so, Samuel,' Kennedy replied. 'It's a herd of gazelle or
buffalo.'

'Perhaps, Dick; but they're at least nine or ten miles from us and I
can make nothing of them even with the glasses.'

'In any case I shan't lose sight of them. There's something curious
going on that puzzles me. At times it looks like cavalry manœuvring.
Ah! I was right; they're horsemen. Look!'

The doctor looked closely.

'I believe you're right,' he said. 'It's a detachment of Arabs or Tibbus.
They're travelling in the same direction as ourselves, but we are
travelling faster and gaining easily. In half an hour we shall be able to
see and decide what we ought to do.'

Kennedy had picked up his glass again and was watching attentively.
The mass of horsemen grew clearer. Some broke away from the rest.

'It must be a manœuvre or a hunt,' Kennedy continued. 'It looks as
though those fellows were chasing something. I'd very much like to
know what it's all about.'

'Patience, Dick. We'll soon catch them up and even pass them if they
keep to the same route. We're doing twenty miles an hour, and there
are no horses that can keep up that speed.'

Kennedy continued to watch and a few minutes later said: 'They're
Arabs, galloping hell for leather. I can see them distinctly. There's
about fifty of them. I can see their burnouses blowing in the wind. It's a

cavalry exercise. Their chief is a hundred yards ahead and they're galloping after him.'

'Whatever they are, Dick, we've nothing to be afraid of; and if necessary I'll rise.'

'Wait a bit, Samuel. Wait!'

'That's strange,' added Dick after another look. 'There's something I don't understand. Judging by their efforts and the irregularity of their line, they look more as though they were chasing something than following.'

'Are you sure, Dick?'

'Quite. There's no doubt about it. It's a hunt, but a manhunt. That's not the chief ahead, it's the quarry.'

'Quarry!' said Samuel with feeling.

'Yes.'

'Don't let's lose sight of him, and let's wait.'

They quickly gained three or four miles on the horsemen, who were sweeping forward at headlong speed.

'Samuel! Samuel!' cried Kennedy in a trembling voice.

'What is it, Dick?'

'Are my eyes deceiving me? Can it be possible?'

'What do you mean?'

'Wait.' And Kennedy quickly wiped the glass of his binoculars and began to watch again.

'Well?' said the doctor.

'It's he, Samuel!'

'He?' cried the doctor.

The word 'He' explained everything. There was no need to mention names.

'He's on horseback. Less than a hundred yards ahead. He's flying for his life!'

'Yes, it's Joe,' said the doctor, turning pale.

'He can't see us the way he's going.'

'He will,' Fergusson replied, lowering the flame of his burner.

'But how?'

'In five minutes we'll be fifty feet from the ground; in a quarter of an hour we'll be over him.'

'We must shout and let him know.'

'No, he can't turn; he's cut off.'

'What can we do, then?'

'Wait.'

'Wait! And the Arabs?'

'We'll catch them up and pass them. We're only two miles behind. If only Joe's horse holds out.'

'Good God!' exclaimed Kennedy.

'What's the matter?'

Kennedy had uttered a cry of despair on seeing Joe thrown to the ground. His horse, evidently played out, had collapsed.

'He's seen us,' cried the doctor. 'He's getting up and waving to us. But the Arabs will get him! What's he want? Ah! Good lad!'

'Hurray!' shouted the Scotsman, who could no longer control himself.

The instant he rose from his fall, and while one of the first horsemen was bearing down upon him, Joe leaped like a panther, swerved aside, threw himself on to the horse's croup, seized the Arab by the throat with his strong nervous fingers, strangled him, hurled him on to the sand and continued his terrific race. A great cry from the Arabs rose into the air, but, absorbed as they were in their pursuit, they had not seen the *Victoria*, five hundred yards behind them and less than thirty feet above the ground. They themselves were not twenty lengths behind Joe's horse.

One of them was perceptibly gaining and was about to stab Joe with his lance, when Kennedy, with steady eye and firm hand, stopped him short with a bullet and brought him to the ground. Joe did not even turn his head at the report. At the sight of the *Victoria* part of the troop pulled up and fell prostrate in the dust. The rest continued the chase.

'But what's Joe doing?' cried Kennedy. 'Why doesn't he stop?'

'He's doing better than that, Dick. I see! He's keeping our course, relying on our intelligence. Ah! Good lad! We'll snatch him from under their noses. Only two hundred yards more.'

'What are we going to do?'

'Put down your gun.'

'Right,' said Kennedy, obeying.

'Can you hold one hundred and fifty pounds of ballast in your arms?'

'Yes; more if you like.'

'No, that'll do.' And the doctor piled sacks of sand into Kennedy's arms.

'Keep at the back of the car and be ready to drop this out at one throw. But on your life don't do it till I tell you!'

'Don't worry.'

'If you do, we'll miss him; he'll be lost.'

'Leave it to me.'

The *Victoria* was now almost over the troop of horsemen who were riding neck or nothing behind Joe. The doctor, in the fore part of the car, held the ladder uncoiled, ready to throw it out when the moment came. Joe had kept his lead of about fifty feet. The *Victoria* overhauled them.

'Ready!' said Fergusson to Kennedy.

'Aye, aye!'

'Joe! Look out! – ' the doctor shouted with all his strength and dropped the ladder, the bottom rungs of which raised a cloud of dust.

At the doctor's shout Joe, without pulling in his horse, looked round. As the ladder swept past him he caught hold of it.

'Now!' the doctor cried to Kennedy.

'It's gone'; and the *Victoria*, relieved of a weight greater than Joe's, rose a hundred and fifty feet.

Joe clung stoutly to the ladder as it swung to and fro. Then with an indescribable gesture to the Arabs and climbing with the agility of a clown, he reached his companions, who received him in their arms. The Arabs uttered a cry of surprise and rage. The fugitive had been snatched from them at full speed and the *Victoria* was rapidly drawing away from them.

'Doctor! Mr Kennedy!' gasped Joe; and succumbing to emotion and fatigue, he fainted, while Kennedy, almost delirious with excitement, kept repeating: 'Saved! Saved!'

'Thank God!' said the doctor, who had resumed his usual impassivity.

Joe was almost naked. His bleeding arms and bruised body all testified to his sufferings. The doctor dressed his wounds and laid him under the tent. He soon recovered consciousness and asked for a glass of brandy, which the doctor had not the heart to refuse, as Joe was not to be treated as an ordinary man. After drinking, he shook hands with them both and declared himself ready to relate his story. This, however, he was not allowed to do, and the excellent fellow fell back into a deep sleep, of which he was obviously in great need.

The *Victoria* then headed diagonally towards the west. Driven by a strong wind they found themselves again over the fringe of the thorny wilderness, where the palms were bent and torn by the storm. That evening, after travelling two hundred miles since Joe's rescue, they passed the tenth meridian.

CHAPTER XXXVII

Westward – Joe's awakening – His obstinacy – The end of
Joe's story – Tagelel – Kennedy's anxiety – Northward –
A night near Agades

DURING THE NIGHT the wind rested from its efforts of the day before
and the *Victoria* hung peacefully over the crest of a great sycamore. The
doctor and Kennedy took turns to watch, and Joe spent the time in a
profound sleep which lasted twenty-four hours.

'That's the remedy he needs,' said Fergusson. 'Nature will put him
right.'

During the day the wind freshened again, but its direction was
capricious. It veered suddenly from north to south, but finally the
Victoria was carried westward. The doctor, map in hand, recognised the
kingdom of Damerghu, an undulating country of great fertility, its
villages formed of huts built with long reeds twisted with branches of
asclepia. The corn-stacks in the cultivated fields were raised on low
scaffolding to protect them from mice and white ants. Soon they
reached the town of Zinder, which could be recognised by its wide
square for executions. In the centre stands the tree of death with the
executioner watching at its foot, and whoever passes beneath its shade
is hanged on the spot. Consulting his compass, Kennedy could not
refrain from remarking: 'We're going north again.'

'What does it matter? Even if it leads us to Timbuktu we shan't
complain. It will be the finest expedition ever made – '

'And the healthiest,' Joe broke in, sticking his good-natured, beaming face through the curtains of the tent.

'Here's good old Joe,' cried Kennedy, 'the man who saved our lives.
How are you?'

'I'm all right, sir. It's only natural. I never felt better. Nothing could
make a man feel fitter than a little pleasure-trip after a bath in Lake
Tchad. What do you think, sir?'

'You're a fine fellow,' replied Fergusson, wringing his hand. 'You've
given us a very painful and anxious time.'

'But what about you, sir? Do you think I wasn't anxious about you?
You can be sure you gave me an awful fright.'

'We shall never agree, Joe, if you take things like that.'

'I see his fall hasn't changed him,' Kennedy added.

'Your sacrifice was wonderful, Joe, and saved our lives. The *Victoria* was falling into the lake, and once there nothing could have got her out.'

'But if my sacrifice, as you are good enough to call my somersault, saved you, it must have saved me too, for we're all three safe and sound now. So on that score you've nothing to blame yourselves for.'

'We'll never convince a fellow like Joe,' said Kennedy.

'The best way is to say no more about it,' Joe answered. 'What's done is done. Good or bad, it's over and finished with.'

'You're a pig-headed fellow,' said the doctor, laughing. 'At least, you'll be kind enough to tell us your story?'

'If you really want me to. But first I want to dress and cook this fat goose; for I see Mr Kennedy hasn't been wasting his time.'

'You're right, Joe.'

'Well, we must see how this African game suits a European stomach.'

The goose was soon cooked over the flame of the burner, and gradually vanished. Joe did his share like a man who has not eaten for several days. After some tea and grog he told his companions the story of his adventures. He spoke with a certain feeling, though regarding his adventures with his usual philosophy. The doctor could not refrain from gripping his hand several times when he saw his good servant more concerned with his master's safety than his own. When he came to tell of the submersion of the island of the Biddiomahs, the doctor explained to him the frequency of this phenomenon on Lake Tchad.

At last Joe came to the moment when, engulfed in the swamp, he uttered his last despairing cry.

'I thought it was all over with me, sir,' he said, 'and I thought of you. I began to struggle. I won't tell you how. I'd made up my mind I wouldn't let myself be swallowed up without arguing the point, when, two yards away, I saw – what do you think? A rope end, freshly cut. I made a last effort and somehow or other I got up to it. I caught hold and pulled and the rope held. I hauled away and in the end found myself on firm land. At the end of the rope I found an anchor. . . Oh, sir! It was a real anchor of refuge, if you'll let me say so. I knew it. It belonged to the *Victoria*. You'd landed in this very place. I followed the direction of the rope, which told me the way you'd gone, and after a bit of a struggle I got clear of the bog. I felt cheered up a lot, and stronger, as I walked on, part of the night, away from the lake. At last I came to the edge of a big forest. There, in an enclosure, I found some horses quietly feeding. Any man can ride a horse when it comes to a pinch, can't he? I didn't stop to think but jumped on to the back of one and off we dashed north at full gallop. I won't tell you about the towns I didn't see or the villages I kept away from. I dashed across sown fields, passed huts, climbed over palisades, rode my horse on, shouting and urging. I came to the end of the cultivated land. A desert was what I wanted. I could see better in front of me and farther. I was still hoping to see the *Victoria* waiting for me as I dashed along. But there was nothing. After three hours I came like an idiot into an Arab encampment. Then there was a chase! . . . You see, Mr Kennedy, a man who hunts doesn't know what hunting is unless he's been hunted himself; and I shouldn't advise him to try, if he can help it. My horse was done up and fell. They were pressing me hard. I jumped up behind one of the Arabs. I had no special grudge against him and I hope he won't bear me any ill-will for strangling him. But I'd seen you. . . You know the rest. The *Victoria* was following my tracks and you picked me up like a rider picking up a ring. I was right in counting on you, wasn't I? Well, sir, you see how easy it all was. Nothing more natural in the world. I'm quite ready to have it all over again, if it's any good to you. Besides, as I told you, sir, it isn't worth talking about.'

'Good old Joe!' the doctor said warmly. 'We were quite right in relying on your intelligence and skill.'

'Not at all, sir. A man has only to deal with things as they come and he'll get out of anything. The best way is to take things as they come.'

While Joe was telling his story, the balloon had rapidly crossed a broad stretch of country. Soon afterwards Kennedy pointed out on the horizon a collection of huts which looked like a town. The doctor consulted his map and found it to be Tagelel in Damerghu.

'Here we pick up Barth's route,' he said. 'This was where he separated from Richardson and Overweg. Richardson was to follow the Zinder route, and the other make for Maradi; and you'll remember that of these three Barth was the only one who got back to Europe.'

'So we're going due north,' said Kennedy, following the *Victoria*'s course on the map.

'Due north, Dick.'

'And you don't mind?'

'Why should I?'

'Well, this route takes us to Tripoli and over the great desert.'

'Oh we shan't go as far as that, old man; at least I hope not.'

'Well, where are you expecting to stop?'

'Wouldn't you like to see Timbuktu?'

'Timbuktu?'

'Of course,' said Joe. 'No one ought to come to Africa without seeing Timbuktu.'

'You'll be the fifth or sixth European to set foot in that mysterious town.'

'I'm for Timbuktu!'

'We will get between the 17th and 18th parallels and then we'll look for a favourable wind to take us west.'

'Right!' Kennedy replied. 'But have we to go much farther north?'

'A hundred and fifty miles at least.'

'Get some sleep, sir,' said Joe; 'and you too, Mr Kennedy. You'll need it, for I must have made you lose a lot.'

Kennedy lay down under the tent, but Fergusson, upon whom fatigue had little effect, remained at his post of observation. Three hours later the *Victoria* was flying at great speed over some stony country with ranges of high bare mountains with granite bases. Isolated peaks were as much as four thousand feet high. Giraffes, antelopes and ostriches were springing about with wonderful agility in the forests of acacia, mimosa and date-palms; for vegetation was establishing a hold again after the aridity of the desert. It was the country of the Kailuas, a tribe who veil their faces with strips of cotton like their dangerous neighbours, the Tuaregs.

At 10 p.m., after a splendid trip of two hundred and fifty miles, the *Victoria* came to a standstill over an important town. The moon lit up one part which was largely in ruins, and the domes of several mosques rising here and there caught the white light. The doctor took a reckoning from the stars and found that they were at Agades, once the centre of a far-reaching commerce, and already in ruins at the time of Dr Barth's visit.

The *Victoria*, unseen in the darkness, touched ground two miles above Agades in a large field of millet. The night was comparatively calm and day broke about five in the morning, when a light wind veered the balloon towards the west, with a slight tendency to south. Fergusson, at once seizing this opportunity, rose rapidly and made off away from the rising sun.

CHAPTER XXXVIII

*Rapid travelling – Prudent resolutions – Caravans – Continual
rain – Gao – The Niger – Golberry, Geoffrey and
Gray – Mungo Park – Laing – René Caillié – Clapperton –
John and Richard Lander*

THE 17TH OF MAY passed calmly and without incident. They were
on the confines of the desert, with a moderate wind bringing the
Victoria back south-west. She veered neither to right nor left, her
shadow drawing a perfectly straight line over the sand.

Before leaving, the doctor had prudently replenished his supplies of
water, as he was afraid of being unable to land in this country infested
by Awelimmidian Tuaregs. The plateau, which was eighteen hundred
feet above sea-level, fell away towards the south. Having cut across the
Agades-Murzuk road, much used by camels, the travellers reached lat.
16° N., long. 4° 55′ E., in the evening, after one hundred and eighty
miles of monotonous travel.

During the day Joe completed the preparation of the last of the
game, which had only been partially dressed before. At supper he
served a very appetising dish of snipe. The wind was good and the
doctor resolved to hold his course during the night, which was made
bright by an almost full moon. The *Victoria* rose to a height of five
hundred feet and during the night journey of about sixty miles her
motion would not have disturbed the light sleep of a child.

On Sunday morning there came a fresh change in the wind, which
veered to the south-east. A few crows were flying through the air, and
towards the horizon could be seen a flock of vultures, which fortunately
kept at a distance. The sight of these birds led Joe to congratulate his
master on his idea of a double balloon.

'Where should we be now if we'd only had one envelope?' he said.
'The second balloon is like a ship's pinnace; if you get shipwrecked you
always have it to fall back on.'

'You're right, my friend. But my pinnace is causing me some anxiety.
It doesn't come up to the ship herself.'

'What do you mean?' asked Kennedy.

'I mean that the new *Victoria* is not as good as the old. Whether the
silk has been too severely tried, or the gutta-percha has melted through

the heat of the coil, I don't know, but I notice a certain wastage of gas. So far it hasn't been much, but it is noticeable. We have a tendency to drop, and to keep up I'm forced to expand the hydrogen more than I used to.'

'Great Scott!' said Kennedy. 'I don't see any remedy for that.'

'There isn't one, Dick. That's why we shall do well to press on and avoid even halting at night.'

'Are we still a long way from the coast?' asked Joe.

'What coast, Joe? We don't know where fate will take us. All I can tell you is that Timbuktu is still four hundred miles to westward.'

'And how long will it take us to get there?'

'If the wind doesn't shift much I think we ought to strike it about Tuesday evening.'

'In that case,' said Joe, pointing to a long file of men and animals winding across the desert, 'we shall get there quicker than that caravan.'

Fergusson and Kennedy leaned out and saw a long string of creatures of every kind. There were over one hundred and fifty camels, of the kind which for twelve mutkals of gold (about five pounds) go from Timbuktu to Tafilet with a load of five hundred pounds. Each carried under its tail a small bag to receive its excrement, the only fuel that can be relied on in the desert. These Tuareg camels are among the finest that exist. They can remain from three to seven days without drinking and two without food. They are faster than horses and obey intelligently the voice of the khabir, the guide of the caravan. They are known in the country as *meharis*.

These details were given by the doctor while his companions watched the multitude of men, women and children labouring through the shifting sand, which was only held by a few thistles, clumps of dry grass and shrivelled bushes. The wind wiped out all trace of their footprints almost instantly. Joe asked how the Arabs managed to guide themselves in the desert and reach the wells that are thinly scattered over this vast solitude.

'The Arabs,' Fergusson replied, 'have been endowed by Nature with a wonderful instinct for finding their way. Where a European would be completely at sea, they never even hesitate. An insignificant stone, a pebble, a tuft of grass, the different shades of the sand, are sufficient to enable them to march with confidence. During the night they guide themselves by the Pole Star. Their average speed is not more than two miles an hour, and they rest during the midday heat; so you can imagine the time they take to cross the Sahara, a distance of more than nine hundred miles.'

But the *Victoria* had already vanished from the astonished eyes of the Arabs, who must have envied her her speed. In the evening they crossed long. 2° 20' E., and during the night they had travelled more than another degree. On Monday the weather changed completely. Rain began to fall with great violence and they had to force their way through this deluge, further handicapped by the increase of weight due to the water on the balloon and in the car. This continuous downpour explained the marshy swamps of which the surface of the country was entirely composed. Vegetation again made its appearance with mimosas, baobabs and tamarisks.

Such was Songhay with its villages capped by roofs turned down like Armenian bonnets. There were few mountains, and only just enough hills to produce ravines and reservoirs over which guinea-fowl and snipe skimmed. Occasionally an impetuous torrent broke the path. These the natives crossed by clinging to a creeper stretched from tree to tree. The forests then gave place to jungle alive with alligator, hippopotamus and rhinoceros.

'It won't be long before we sight the Niger,' said the doctor. 'Near great rivers the country changes. These moving roads originally brought vegetation with them, just as later they will bring civilisation. So in its course of two hundred and fifty miles the Niger has sown upon its banks the most important cities of Africa.'

'Oh,' said Joe, 'that reminds me of the fellow who thought it very wise of Providence to arrange that rivers should always run through big towns.'

At noon the *Victoria* passed over a small town, a collection of rather wretched huts. This was Gao, once a great capital.

'That's where Barth crossed the Niger on his way back from Timbuktu,' said the doctor. 'And here's the river. It was very famous in antiquity; the rival of the Nile to which superstition attributed a celestial origin. Like the Nile it has always been an object of interest to students of geography. And its exploration has claimed even more victims than the other river.'

The Niger flowed between widely-separated banks, its waters rolling strongly southwards; but the balloon was travelling so quickly that the three men only just had time to observe its curious windings.

'I wanted to tell you about this river,' Fergusson said, 'and it's far behind us already. It has had many names; the Dhïouleba, the Mayo, the Egghirrew, the Quorra, and others. It passes through a huge stretch of country and must almost rival the Nile in length. Its names simply mean "black river," according to the dialects of the different districts it flows through.'

'Did Dr Barth come this way?' asked Kennedy.

'No, Dick. After leaving Lake Tchad he passed through the chief towns of Bornu and crossed the Niger at Say, four degrees below Gao. He then plunged into the unexplored country contained within the bend of the Niger, and after eight months of continuous effort reached Timbuktu. With this wind we shall the there in less than three days.'

'Has anyone discovered the sources of the Niger?' asked Joe.

'A long time ago,' the doctor replied. 'The discovery of the Niger was the object of many expeditions. I can tell you the chief of these. Between 1749 and 1758 Adamson explored the river and visited Goree. Between 1785 and 1788 Golberry and Geoffrey crossed the deserts of Senegambia and got as far as the country of the Moors who murdered Saugnier, Brisson, Adam, Riley, Cochelet, and lots of others. Then came the famous Mungo Park, the friend of Walter Scott, and himself a Scotsman. He was sent out in 1795 by the London African Society, reached Bambarra, saw the Niger, travelled five hundred miles with a slave-dealer, found the river Gambia, and returned to England in 1797. On the 30th of January, 1805, he set out again with his brother-in-law Anderson, Scott the cartographer, and a band of workmen. He got to Goree, where he was reinforced by a detachment of thirty-five soldiers, and sighted the Niger again on the 19th of August. But by then, as the result of fatigue, privations, ill-treatment, bad weather and the unhealthiness of the country, there were only eleven left out of forty Europeans. Mungo Park's last letters reached his wife on the 16th of November, and a little later it was learned through a trader of the country that when he arrived at Bussa on the Niger on the 23rd of December, his boat was overturned by the cataracts and the poor fellow was murdered by the natives.'

'And that awful death didn't stop the explorations?'

'Quite the other way, Dick; for after that it was necessary not only to explore the river, but also to find Park's papers. In 1816 an expedition was fitted out in London with Major Gray in charge. It went to Senegal, entered Futa-Djallon, studied the Fullah and Mandingo populations, and returned to England without obtaining any other results. In 1822 Major Laing explored all the parts of Western Africa which border on English possessions, and it was he who first reached the sources of the Niger. According to his writings the source of this huge river was only two feet wide.'

'Easy to jump,' commented Joe.

'Easy enough,' replied the doctor, 'but according to tradition anyone trying to jump this spring is immediately engulfed. Anyone trying to draw water from it feels himself pushed back by an invisible hand.'

'And are we allowed to refuse to believe a word of it, sir?' asked Joe.

'If you like. Five years later Major Laing crossed the Sahara, reached Timbuktu, and was strangled a few miles above by the Oulad Shimans, who wanted to compel him to become a Mussulman.'

'Another victim,' said Kennedy.

'Then a brave young fellow with slender resources undertook and carried through the most astonishing expedition of modern times. I mean the Frenchman, René Caillié.[49] After several attempts in 1819 and 1824, he started off again on the 19th of April, 1827, from Rio Nuñez. On the 3rd of August he arrived at Time, so exhausted that he couldn't go on again until January 1828, six months later. He then joined a caravan, protected by his oriental dress, reached the Niger on the 10th of March, entered the town of Jenné, embarked on the river and went down it as far as Timbuktu, where he arrived on the 30th of April. In 1670 another Frenchman, Imbert, and in 1810 Robert Adams, an Englishman, were supposed to have seen this curious town; but René Caillié must have been the first European to bring back any exact information about it. On the 4th of May he left this queen of the desert and on the 9th found the very spot where Major Laing was murdered. On the 19th he came to El-Arauan, a commercial town, and braving a thousand dangers, crossed the vast solitudes that divide the Sudan from the northern regions of Africa. At length he reached Tangier, where he took ship on the 28th of September for Toulon. In nineteen months, including six spent in illness, he had crossed Africa from west to north. If only he'd been born in England, Caillié would have been acclaimed the boldest explorer of modern times, the equal of Mungo Park; but in France he is not appreciated at his real worth.'

'He must have been a brave fellow,' said Kennedy. 'What became of him?'

'He died at the age of thirty-nine, from overstrain. They thought they had recognised his services adequately by giving him the prize of the *Société de Géographie* in 1828. In England the greatest honours would have been showered upon him. As for the rest, while he was carrying out this wonderful expedition, the same idea occurred to an Englishman, who attempted it with equal courage, if with less luck. This was Captain Clapperton, Denham's partner. In 1829 he returned to Africa, landing in the Bight of Benin on the West Coast. He picked up the trail of Mungo Park and Laing, found in Bussa documents revealing the death of Mungo Park, reached Sakatu on the 29th of August, where he was kept a prisoner and died in the arms of his faithful servant, Richard Lander.'

'And what happened to Lander, sir?' Joe asked with great interest.

'He managed to get back to the coast and went back to London with the captain's papers and an exact account of his own journey. He then offered his services to the Government to complete the exploration of the Niger. His younger brother John – they were the sons of poor parents in Cornwall – joined him, and between 1829 and 1831 they travelled down the river from Bussa to its estuary, describing every village and every mile of the way.'

'So they escaped the usual fate?' Kennedy asked.

'Yes, at any rate as far as that expedition was concerned. But in 1833 Richard set out a third time for the Niger and was shot, it is not known by whom, near the river's mouth. So you see, my friends, this country we are passing over now has been the scene of splendid sacrifices, only too often rewarded by death.'

CHAPTER XXXIX

The country within the bend of the Niger – A fantastic view of the Hombori Kabra Mountains – Timbuktu – Dr Barth's plan

DURING THIS TEDIOUS Monday, Dr Fergusson devoted himself to recounting to his companions many details of the country they were crossing. The flat land presented no obstacle to their progress. The doctor's only anxiety was caused by the exasperating north-east wind, which blew furiously and carried them away from the latitude of Timbuktu. The Niger, after bending northwards as far as this town, curves back like a great jet of water to fall into the Atlantic Ocean in a wide spray. The country contained within this bend is very varied, sometimes of luxuriant fertility and sometimes of extreme aridity. Uncultivated plains follow upon fields of maize, which in turn give place to vast open spaces covered with broom. All kinds of aquatic birds, pelican, teal and kingfishers, live in great flocks on the banks of the torrents and *marigots*.

From time to time there would appear a camp of leather tents in which Tuaregs sheltered themselves, while the women sat in the open, milking their camels or smoking their pipes by the great fires. About eight in the evening, the *Victoria* had travelled over two hundred miles towards the west and the travellers witnessed a magnificent spectacle. Some rays of moonlight had cut a path through a cleft in the clouds and filtering their way through the streaming rain, fell on the Hombori mountain chain. Nothing could have been stranger than the appearance presented by these basalt crests. Their fantastic outline was silhouetted against the blackness of the sky like the legendary ruins of some great mediæval town or ice floes as they are seen on a dark night in Arctic seas.

'That would be a good setting for *The Mysteries of Udolpho*,' said the doctor. 'Ann Radcliffe[50] couldn't have cut those mountains into more fearsome shapes.'

'I'm blowed if I'd like to walk about alone in the dark in those weird parts,' said Joe. 'You know, sir, if it wasn't so heavy I'd like to cart that country to Scotland. It would look well on the banks of Loch Lomond, and the tourists would flock to see it.'

'I'm afraid the balloon would hardly hold it. But surely we are altering our course. Good! The local spirits are kind to us. They're sending us a little wind from the south-east, which is just what we want.'

Indeed the *Victoria* was returning to a more northerly course, and during the morning of the 20th she passed over a tangled network of channels, torrents, and rivers, the whole intricate system of the Niger tributaries. Several of these canals were covered with thick grass and looked like fat meadows. Here the doctor found Barth's route when he took to the river to make for Timbuktu. With a breadth of nearly five thousand feet the Niger here flowed between banks rich in cruciferæ and tamarisks. Herds of gazelle disported themselves there, their ringed horns blending with the tall grass in which alligators watched for them in silence. Long files of donkeys and camels carrying merchandise from Jenné plunged through the splendid forests, and soon an amphitheatre of low houses appeared at a bend of the river. On the terraces and roofs was heaped the forage gathered from the surrounding country.

'It's Kabra,' cried the doctor in delight. 'That's the port of Timbuktu. The town is only five miles away.'

'You're pleased, sir?' asked Joe.

'Delighted, Joe.'

At two o'clock the queen of the desert, mysterious Timbuktu, which, like Athens and Rome, once had her scholars and chairs of philosophy, was revealed to the explorers' eyes. Fergusson followed the slightest details on the plan made by Barth himself and confirmed the explorer's extreme accuracy. The town forms a huge triangle on a wide plain of white sand. Its apex lies to the north like a wedge driven into the desert, its surroundings are completely bare; at most a little grass, some dwarf mimosas and stunted bushes.

As for Timbuktu itself, the reader can imagine a heap of dice and marbles. That's what it looked like from the air. The somewhat narrow streets are fringed with houses of only one storey, built of sun-baked bricks and huts of reed and straw; some conical, some square. On the terraces a few inhabitants lounged carelessly, draped in brilliant robes, lance or musket in hand. Not a woman was to be seen at this hour of the day.

'But they are said to be beautiful,' the doctor added. 'You see the three towers of the three mosques which are all that are left of a large number. What a fall from the town's ancient splendour! At the apex of the triangle over there is the Mosque of Sankore with its rows of galleries supported by beautifully-designed arcades. That over there, farther on, near the Sane-Gungu, is the Sidi Yahia Mosque. Some of the houses near it have two storeys. It's no use looking for palaces or monuments. The sheik is simply a trader and his royal residence a shop.'

'I think I can see some broken-down ramparts,' said Kennedy.

'They were destroyed by the Fellanis in 1826. At that time the town was larger by a third, for since the eleventh century Timbuktu has been generally coveted and has belonged in turn to the Tuaregs, the Songhays, the Moors and the Fellanis, and this great centre of civilisation, where in the sixteenth century a scholar like Ahmed Bala possessed a library of sixteen hundred manuscripts, is now merely a warehouse for the commerce of Central Africa.'

The town certainly appeared to have been abandoned to a state of neglect and showed clear signs of the universal indifference of cities whose day is over. Great heaps of ruins stood in the outlying parts of the town and, with the hill on which the market stood, formed the sole break in the flatness of the site. When the *Victoria* passed, there was some movement and the drum was beaten; but it is doubtful whether the last remaining scholar of the place had time to observe this new phenomenon. Driven back by the desert wind, the travellers again followed the sinuous course of the river, and soon Timbuktu was no more than a fleeting memory of their journey.

'And now,' said the doctor, 'Heaven may take us where it will.'

'So long as it's west,' Kennedy replied.

'What does it matter?' said Joe. 'It wouldn't worry me if we had to go back to Zanzibar by the same way and across the ocean to America.'

'We should have to be capable of doing so first.'

'And what are we short of, sir?'

'Gas, Joe. The lift of the balloon is getting appreciably less, and it will take it all its time to get us to the coast. I shall have to throw out ballast. We're too heavy.'

'That's what comes of having nothing to do, sir. Loafing all day in a hammock makes a man soft. He's bound to put on weight. It's a lazy way of travelling, ours, and when we get back we shall find ourselves dreadfully fat.'

'Just the sort of thing Joe *would* think,' Kennedy replied. 'But wait till we get there. Who knows what fate has in store for us? We're a long way off the end yet. Where do you expect to strike the coast of Africa, Samuel?'

'I should find it very difficult to say. We are at the mercy of very variable winds. However, I should think myself lucky if we landed somewhere on the strip of country between Sierra Leone and Portendick. There we should find ourselves among friends.'

'And it would be good to shake their hands. But are we actually going the right way?'

'None too directly, Dick. Look at the compass needle. We are heading south, towards the sources of the river.'

'A fine chance to discover them,' said Joe, 'if someone else hadn't got there first. At a pinch, couldn't we find fresh ones?'

'No, Joe; but don't worry, I hope we shan't get as far as that.'

At nightfall the doctor threw out his last sacks of ballast and the *Victoria* rose. The burner, though working to its utmost capacity, could hardly keep her in the air. She was now sixty miles south of Timbuktu and the following morning found them on the banks of the Niger not far from Lake Debo.

CHAPTER XL

Dr Fergusson's uneasiness – Still south – A cloud of locusts – View of Jenné – View of Sego – The wind changes – Joe's disappointment

THE RIVER BED was now broken by large islands into narrow channels where the current was very rapid. On one stood some shepherds' huts, but it was impossible to take an exact bearing as the *Victoria*'s speed was continually increasing. Unfortunately she headed still more to southward and crossed Lake Debo in a few minutes. Fergusson, by forcing his expansion to the utmost, tried different elevations to find other atmospheric currents, but in vain. He soon gave up these attempts which increased the waste of gas by pressing it against the weakening walls of the balloon.

He said nothing, but grew very uneasy. This persistent course towards Southern Africa was upsetting his calculations. He no longer knew on what he could reckon. If he did not strike British or French territory, what would happen to them among the barbarians that infest the Guinea coast? The present direction of the wind was taking them towards the kingdom of Dahomey, which is among the most barbarous and at the mercy of a king who at public festivities was in the habit of sacrificing thousands of human victims. To fall into his hands would be fatal.

Besides, the balloon was visibly flagging and the doctor felt she was failing him. However, the weather clearing a little, he hoped that the end of the rain would bring a change in the atmospheric currents. He was soon brought back to an appreciation of the real situation by these words from Joe: 'Hello! Here's more rain; a regular deluge this time, judging from that cloud!'

'Another cloud!' said Fergusson.

'And a whopper!' Kennedy added.

'I've never seen one like that before,' Joe went on.

'It's nothing after all,' said the doctor, putting down his glass. 'It's not a rain-cloud.'

'Well, what is it, sir?' asked Joe.

'A cloud of locusts.'

'Those! Locusts?'

'Yes, thousands of them. They'll sweep over the country like a sandstorm and it will be a bad look-out, for if they come down the land will be devastated.'

'I'd like to see that.'

'Wait a bit, Joe. In ten minutes the cloud will have reached us and you'll be able to see with your own eyes.'

Fergusson was right. This dense opaque cloud, several miles in extent, advanced with a deafening roar, its shadow darkening the country as it passed. It was a countless legion of migrating locusts. A hundred yards from the *Victoria* they swept down on a verdant countryside. Quarter of an hour later the mass rose again into the air and the travellers could then see from afar the trees and hushes completely stripped and the meadows looking as though they had been mown. It was as if a winter had suddenly plunged the country into a state of complete sterility.

'Well, Joe?'

'Well, sir, that's very odd, but quite natural. What one locust would do on a small scale thousands do on a big one.'

'Like some appalling hailstorm,' said Kennedy, 'but much more destructive.'

'And there's no way of guarding against it,' said Fergusson. 'Sometimes the people have tried burning forests and even harvests to stop the flight of these insects. But those ahead dash into the flames and stifle them with their dense mass, and the rest pass over unchecked. Fortunately there is some sort of compensation for the havoc caused. The natives collect the insects in large numbers and eat them with relish.'

'Sort of air-shrimps,' said Joe, adding that he was sorry not to have been able to try them, 'by way of education.'

The country they passed over towards evening became more marshy, the forests giving place to isolated clumps of trees. On the banks of the river could be seen tobacco plantations and marshy land on which rich grass grew. On a large island they found the town of Jenné with the two towers of its mosque, which is built of earth, the air being laden with the noxious smell of the millions of swallows' nests which had accumulated on its walls. Tops of baobab trees, mimosas and date-palms projected between the houses. Even at night the town seemed very busy. It is, in fact, a considerable commercial centre and supplies all the needs of Timbuktu, to which place boats on the river and caravans on the shady road carry the various products of its industry.

'If it were not that it would prolong our trip,' said the doctor, 'I should be tempted to land in this town. There must be many Arabs here who have travelled in France or England and who will be acquainted with our method of travel; but it would be unwise.'

'Let's put off our visit until the next time,' laughed Joe.

'Besides, unless I'm mistaken, my friends, the wind shows a slight tendency to blow from the east, and it wouldn't do to miss such a chance.'

The doctor threw out a few articles which were now useless: empty bottles and a case of meat which had gone bad, and in this way managed to keep the *Victoria* in the favourable zone. At four in the morning the first rays of the sun shone on Sego, the capital of Bambarra, which was easily recognisable by the four distinct towns of which it is composed, its Moorish mosques and the incessant crossing backwards and forwards of the ferries carrying the inhabitants from one quarter to another. But the travellers passed over too quickly to see or be seen very much. The *Victoria* was speeding due north-west and the doctor's anxiety gradually vanished.

'Two days more in this direction and at this speed and we'll be at the Senegal River.'

'In a friendly country?' asked Kennedy.

'Not altogether. If the *Victoria* should happen to fail us, we could at a pinch find French settlements. But let's hope she'll hold out a few hundred miles more and we'll reach the West Coast without fatigue, alarm or danger.'

'And then it'll be all over,' said Joe. 'Well, it can't be helped. If it wasn't for the fun of telling the yarn I shouldn't mind if I never set foot on land again. Do you think they'll believe our story, sir?'

'Who knows, Joe? At any rate there will always be one indisputable fact. We must have had a thousand witnesses of our departure from one coast of Africa, and another thousand will see us arriving at the other.'

'In that case,' replied Kennedy, 'it would seem difficult to dispute the fact that we crossed.'

'I shan't find it easy to forget the loss of my gold!' said Joe with a deep sigh. 'That would have given a bit of weight to our story and made it more convincing. At the rate of one gramme of gold for everyone who listened, I'd collect a nice little crowd, and they might even think me a fine fellow.'

CHAPTER XLI

Nearing the Senegal – The Victoria *dropping lower and lower – Al Hadji, the marabout – Joe's feat*

ABOUT NINE IN THE MORNING of the 27th of May a change came over the country. The long ridges changed to hills which appeared to be the forerunners of mountains. The balloon would have to clear the chain separating the Niger basin from that of the Senegal, which divides the streams running into the Gulf of Guinea and Cape Verde Bay respectively. According to the stories of Fergusson's predecessors this part of Africa as far as the Senegal is dangerous. They had undergone many privations and run many dangers among the barbarous blacks who dwell there, and the deadly climate had accounted for the greater part of Mungo Park's companions. Fergusson was therefore more determined than ever not to set foot in this inhospitable country.

But he had not a moment's rest. The *Victoria* was drooping markedly. It became necessary to jettison further more or less superfluous objects, especially when it came to clearing a peak. And so it went on for more than a hundred and twenty miles, during which constant effort was required to keep the balloon in the air. This new stone of Sisyphus was constantly falling back. The outline of the inadequately inflated balloon already showed signs of leanness. It became elongated and the wind dug great hollows in its loose envelope. Kennedy could not refrain from pointing this out.

'Can she be leaking?' he asked.

'No,' the doctor replied; 'but the gutta-percha has evidently softened in the heat and the hydrogen is percolating through the silk.'

'How can we prevent it?'

'We can't. We must lighten her. It's the only way. Throw out everything we can spare.'

'But what?' asked Kennedy, looking round the already seriously dismantled car.

'Let's get rid of the tent; it's quite heavy.'

Joe, to whom this order was addressed, climbed outside the belt which held the net ropes together, and from there managed without difficulty to loose the thick curtains of the tent and throw them out.

'That will make a whole tribe of niggers happy,' he said; 'there's enough of it to dress a thousand natives, for they're pretty sparing with their material.'

The balloon rose a little, but it soon became clear that she was again beginning to drop.

'Let's get out,' said Kennedy, 'and see if we can't do something with the envelope.'

'I tell you, Dick, we've no means of repairing it.'

'Then what are we going to do?'

'We'll sacrifice everything that is not absolutely indispensable. At all costs I want to avoid a halt in this district. Those forests just below us are by no means safe.'

'Why not, sir; lions; hyenas?' said Joe scornfully.

'Worse than that, my good fellow; men, and the most bloodthirsty in all Africa.'

'How do you know, sir?'

'From the explorers who have been here before us, and then the French who occupy the colony of Senegal have, of course, had relations with the surrounding tribes. Under the governorship of Colonel Faidherbe, reconnaissances were made far into the country. Officers like Pascal, Vincent and Lambert have brought back valuable information from their expeditions. They explored these countries contained in the elbow of the Senegal and found that war and pillage have left them mere heaps of ruin.'

'How did that come about?'

'In 1854 a marabout called Al Hadji gave himself out as inspired by
Mahomet and drove the tribes into war against the infidels; meaning,
of course, the Europeans. He destroyed and laid waste all the country
between the Senegal and its tributary the Falémé. Three hordes of
savages led by him harried the country, sparing not a single village or
even hut; pillaging and massacring. They even pushed into the Niger
valley as far as the town of Sego, which they long threatened. In 1857
he headed north, and laid siege to the fort of Medina, which was built
by the French on the river bank. This settlement was defended by a
hero called Paul Holl, who held out for several months with no food,
little ammunition and few guns, until he was relieved by Colonel
Faidherbe. Al Hadji and his band then recrossed the Senegal and
returned to Kaarta to continue their rapine and massacre. So this is the
district to which he escaped with his hordes of bandits, and I assure you
it wouldn't be pleasant to fall into their hands.'

'We'll see we don't, sir,' said Joe; 'even if we have to throw out our
boots to lighten the balloon.'

'We aren't far from the river,' said the doctor; 'but I'm afraid our
balloon won't get us to the other side.'

'Well, at any rate, let's get to the bank,' Kennedy replied; 'that will
be so much to the good.'

'That's what we are trying to do,' said the doctor. 'But there's one
thing I'm anxious about.'

'What?'

'We have some mountains to get over and it won't be easy, for I can't
increase the lift even with the burner in full blast.'

'Let's wait and see,' said Kennedy.

'Poor old *Victoria*!' said Joe. 'I've got as fond of her as a sailor is of his
ship. It'll be hard to part with her. She's not quite what she was when
we started out, but it won't do to slight her. She's served us well and it
would be heartbreaking to desert her.'

'Don't worry, Joe. We won't desert her if we can help it. She'll go on
serving us as long as she can. I'm only asking her for another twenty-
four hours.'

'She's nearly done,' said Joe, contemplating the balloon. 'Look how
thin she's getting. She can't stick it much longer. Poor old *Victoria*!'

'Unless I'm mistaken,' said Kennedy, 'there are the mountains you
were talking about, Samuel, on the horizon.'

'Yes, those are the ones,' said the doctor, after examining them
through his glass. 'They look to me very high and we shall have our

work cut out to get over them.'

'Couldn't we go round them?'

'I don't think so, Dick. Look what a long way they stretch. They cover half the horizon.'

'They even seem to be closing round us on both sides,' said Joe.

'There's nothing for it but to go over.'

These dangerous obstacles seemed to be advancing towards them with great rapidity, or rather a very strong wind was rushing the balloon towards some sharp peaks. At all costs they would have to rise to avoid being dashed against them.

'Empty the water container,' said Fergusson. 'Keep only enough for one day.'

'There you are, sir,' said Joe.

'Is she rising?' asked Kennedy.

'A little; fifty feet perhaps,' replied the doctor, never taking his eyes off the barometer. 'But that's not enough.'

Indeed the lofty crests seemed to be dashing straight at the balloon, which was not nearly high enough to pass over them. She wanted over five hundred feet more. The supply of water for the furnace was also poured overboard, only a few pints being kept; but that again proved insufficient.

'But we've got to get over,' said the doctor.

'Let's throw out the containers as they're empty,' said Kennedy.

'Out with them.'

'Done, sir,' said Joe. 'It's hard to go overboard, bit by bit.'

'Now, Joe, no more of your sacrifices. Whatever happens, swear you won't leave us.'

'Don't worry, sir; we're not going to part.'

The *Victoria* had lifted about a hundred and twenty feet, but the mountain crest was still above her, a sheer ridge ending in a perpendicular wall of rock, still more than two hundred feet above the car.

'Another ten minutes,' the doctor mused, 'and the car will be smashed against the rocks, unless we manage to get over somehow.'

'What next, sir?' asked Joe.

'Keep only the pemmican; throw out all the rest of the meat.'

The balloon was relieved of another fifty pounds and rose distinctly, but it was of little use unless they could get above the level of the mountains. The situation was appalling. The *Victoria* was dashing forward and it seemed inevitable that she would be shattered in pieces. The shock would be terrific. The doctor looked round the car and found it almost empty.

'If necessary, Dick, you'll be ready to sacrifice your guns.'

'My guns!' exclaimed the Scotsman in agitation.

'I wouldn't ask you, old man, if it wasn't absolutely necessary.'

'Oh, look here, Samuel –'

'Your guns and powder and shot might cost us our lives.'

'We're on it!' cried Joe. 'Look out!'

They only required another sixty feet to clear the mountain. Joe seized the blankets and hurled them overboard, while Kennedy, without a word, did the same with several bags of powder and shot. As the balloon lifted above the dangerous crest, her upper part caught the sunlight; but the car was still slightly below some loose rocks, against which they were on the point of crashing.

'Kennedy!' shouted the doctor. 'Throw out your guns or we're lost!'

'Half a minute, Mr Kennedy,' Joe called. 'Wait!' And Kennedy, turning his head, saw him disappear over the side.

'Joe! Joe!' he yelled.

'He's gone!' said the doctor.

The crest of the mountain at this point was about twenty feet broad and the other side was less sheer. The car just reached the level of this fairly flat area. With a loud grinding noise it scraped over the sharp loose stones.

'She's going! She's going! She's over!' cried a voice which made Fergusson's heart bound.

The brave Joe was hanging by his hands to the lower edge of the car, running over the crest, and so relieving the balloon of his entire weight. He had even to hold her back vigorously to prevent her running away from him. When he reached the reverse slope and the abyss yawned before him, Joe heaved himself up and, clinging to the ropes, climbed back beside his companions.

'Quite easy, after all,' he said.

'That was splendid, Joe! You've saved us again,' cried the doctor enthusiastically.

'Oh, I didn't do it for you, sir,' Joe replied. 'It was to save Mr Kennedy's carbine. I certainly owed it that much after the business with the Arabs. I like paying my debts. And now we're quits,' he added, handing Kennedy his favourite weapon. 'I couldn't bear to see you parted from it.'

Kennedy wrung his hand, but was unable to utter a word. Now all that was required of the *Victoria* was to descend, which she found easy. She was soon back at two hundred feet above ground, where she was in equilibrium. The ground looked as though it had been the scene of some great upheaval and presented many projections which would be difficult to negotiate with the balloon out of hand. As night was rapidly coming on, the doctor, with great reluctance, had to make up his mind to halt until morning.

'We must look out for a likely spot,' he said.

'Oh, so you've made up your mind to it at last,' Kennedy remarked.

'Yes, for some time I've been thinking over a plan we'll try. It's only six o'clock, so we shall have time. Throw out the anchors, Joe.'

Joe obeyed, and the two anchors hung below the car.

'I can see some big forests,' said the doctor. 'We'll run over them and anchor to a tree. Nothing would persuade me to spend the night on the ground.'

'Shan't we be able to get out?' asked Kennedy.

'What would be the good? I repeat, it would be dangerous to separate. Besides, I want you to help me in a difficult job.'

The *Victoria*, which was skimming over an extensive forest, soon came to a sudden stop; her anchors had taken hold. The wind dropped as night came on, and she rested almost motionless over the vast area of green formed by the crests of the sycamores.

CHAPTER XLII

A battle of generosity – The final sacrifice – The expanding apparatus – Joe's skill – Midnight – Kennedy's watch – He falls asleep – The fire – The shouting – Out of range

THE FIRST THING Dr Fergusson did was to take a reckoning on the stars. He found he was hardly twenty-five miles from the Senegal.

'The most we can do is to cross the river,' he said, pointing to his map; 'but as there are no boats and no bridge, we must at all costs cross in the balloon, and to do this we must lighten her still more.'

'But I don't see how we're going to manage it,' Kennedy replied, fearing for his guns, 'unless one of us makes up his mind to sacrifice himself and remain behind. It's my turn and I claim the honour.'

'Certainly not, sir,' exclaimed Joe. 'I've got used to it – '

'It's not a question of jumping, Joe, but of getting to the coast on foot. I'm a good walker and a good shot – '

'I'll never agree to it,' Joe replied.

'Your battle of generosity is unnecessary, my friends,' said Fergusson. 'I hope we shan't be driven to anything of that kind. Besides, if necessary, rather than separate we'll tramp across the country together.'

'There's some sense in that, sir,' said Joe. 'A little walk won't do us any harm.'

'But first,' the doctor went on, 'we'll have a last try to lighten the *Victoria*.'

'How?' asked Kennedy. 'I'm very curious to know how you're going to do it.'

'We must get rid of the burner, the battery and the spiral. They give us a good nine hundred pounds to carry.'

'But how are you going to expand the gas, in that case, Samuel?'

'I shan't. We shall have to do without.'

'But after all – '

'Listen to me, my friends. I've calculated very exactly the lifting force we are left with. It's sufficient to carry the three of us with the few things we still have. We shan't weigh five hundred pounds, including the two anchors, which I intend to keep.'

'My dear Samuel,' Kennedy replied, 'you understand these things better than we do, and you're the only one in a position to judge the situation. Tell us what we've to do and we'll do it.'

'Hear, hear!'

'Well, as I said, however serious the step may be, we must sacrifice our apparatus.'

'Let's do it, then!' replied Kennedy.

'To work!' said Joe.

It was no small job, as it involved taking down the apparatus piece by piece. They began by taking out the mixing chamber, then that containing the burner, and finally, the chamber in which the water was decomposed. It required the united strength of the three men to wrench them from the bottom of the car, to which they had been stoutly fixed; but Kennedy was so strong, Joe so skilful, and the doctor so resourceful, that they succeeded in the end. The various sections were thrown over one by one, making great gaps in the foliage of the sycamores as they disappeared.

'The niggers will get a bit of a shock when they find these in the wood,' said Joe. 'They're quite capable of making idols of them.'

They next turned their attention to the tubes connecting the balloon with the coil. Joe managed to cut through the rubber joints, a few feet above the car, but the tubes were more difficult to deal with as they were held by their upper ends and fixed by brass wire to the safety-valve.

At this juncture Joe displayed wonderful skill. His feet bare to avoid tearing the envelope, he managed, in spite of the swaying of the balloon, to climb up the net to the top where, with great difficulty and hanging by one hand to the slippery surface, he removed the outer nuts holding the pipes. These then came away easily and were drawn out through the lower appendix, which was hermetically closed again by means of a strong ligature. The *Victoria*, relieved of this considerable weight, rose and pulled strongly on the anchor ropes.

This work was successfully finished by midnight after much labour. A hurried meal was taken of pemmican and cold grog, for the doctor had no more heat for Joe's use. Joe and Kennedy were dropping with fatigue.

'Lie down and sleep, my friends,' said Fergusson. 'I'll take the first watch. I'll wake Kennedy at two, and at four Kennedy will wake Joe. We'll start at six, and may Heaven continue to be kind to us during the last day!'

Without waiting for further persuasion the two men lay down in the bottom of the car and were soon in a deep sleep. The night was peaceful. A few clouds were crushing themselves against the last quarter of the moon, whose faint rays hardly relieved the darkness. Fergusson, his elbows on the side of the car, looked around him, scrutinising closely the dark curtain of foliage which stretched below his feet and hid the ground. He was suspicious of the slightest sound and tried to find an explanation even of the light rustle of the leaves.

He was in that state of mind, exaggerated by solitude, when vague terrors invade the mind. At the close of such a voyage, when so many obstacles have been surmounted and the end is in sight, anxiety increases, excitement grows stronger, and a successful termination seems to elude the imagination.

Moreover there was nothing reassuring about their present situation in the middle of a barbarous country and relying on means of transport which, after all, might fail them at any moment. The doctor could no longer place complete reliance on his balloon. The time was past when he could take risks in handling her because he was sure of her powers.

While these thoughts were passing through his mind the doctor from time to time thought he could hear vague noises in the great forest. He even imagined he could see flames flickering between the trees. After looking closely, he brought his night glass to bear upon the place, but nothing appeared and the silence seemed to have grown deeper still. Fergusson thought it must have been an hallucination, for he listened without hearing the slightest sound. As his watch was now over, he woke Kennedy, urged him to keep a very careful look-out, and then took his place beside Joe, who was sleeping like a log.

Kennedy quietly lit his pipe, rubbed his eyes, which he found it hard to keep open and, leaning his head on his elbow in a corner, began to smoke vigorously to keep sleep at bay. Absolute silence reigned around him, a light breeze stirred the crests of the trees, and the balloon swayed gently, lulling the Scotsman to sleep in spite of himself. He tried to fight against it; several times he opened his eyes and looked into the night without seeing and finally, succumbing to weariness, he fell asleep.

How long he had been unconscious he did not know, when suddenly he was awakened by a strange crackling noise. He rubbed his eyes and rose to his feet. He could feel an intense heat on his face. The forest was in flames.

'Fire! Fire!' he shouted, without too clear an idea of what had happened. His two companions woke up.

'What's the matter?' asked Fergusson.

'Fire!' cried Joe. . . 'But who can – '

At this moment a roar of yells broke from under the trees, which were brilliantly illuminated.

'Oh, it's the savages!' Joe cried. 'They've set fire to the forest to make sure of burning us.'

'It must be the Talibas, Al Hadji's marabouts!' said the doctor.

A circle of flames surrounded the *Victoria*. The cracking of the dead wood mingled with the hissing of the green branches. Creepers, leaves, the whole living tangle of vegetation, writhed in the destroying flames. The eye could see nothing but an ocean of fire, from which the great trees stood out black, their branches covered with glowing embers. The glow of the burning mass was reflected in the clouds and the travellers seemed to be imprisoned within a sphere of fire.

'Let's get away!' cried Kennedy. 'We must land. It's our only chance.'

But Fergusson laid a firm hand on his arm and, dashing to the anchor rope, severed it with one blow of the axe. The towering flames were already licking the envelope of the balloon, but, loosed from her bonds, the *Victoria* rose over a thousand feet at one bound. A terrible clamour, punctuated by the report of firearms, rose from the forest. The balloon, caught in a breeze which came with the dawn, headed away towards the west. It was 4 a.m.

CHAPTER XLIII

The Talibas – The pursuit – A country laid waste –
The wind moderates – The Victoria *droops – The last*
provisions – The Victoria's *bounds – Armed defence – The*
wind freshens – The Senegal River – The Guina Falls –
Hot air – Crossing the river

'IF WE HADN'T TAKEN the precaution of lightening the balloon last night,' said the doctor, 'we should have been lost.'

'That's the advantage of taking things in time,' Joe replied. 'You then get a chance to escape. Nothing more natural.'

'We're not out of the wood yet,' replied Fergusson.

'What are you afraid of?' asked Kennedy. 'The *Victoria* can't come down without your permission, and what if she did?'

'What if she did, Dick? Look!'

They had just crossed the edge of the forest and could see thirty horsemen, wearing broad trousers and floating burnouses. They were armed, some with lances, the rest with long muskets, and on their swift fiery steeds were following the *Victoria*, which was not travelling fast, at a short gallop.

When they saw the travellers, they uttered savage cries and brandished their weapons, their ugly fury showing plainly on their bronzed faces, the ferocity of which was increased by their scanty but bristling beards. They rode easily over the low plateau and gentle slopes which dropped towards the Senegal.

'Yes, those are the fellows,' said the doctor. 'The cruel Talibas, the fierce bandits of Al Hadji. I'd rather be surrounded by wild animals in the heart of the forest than fall into those bandits' hands.'

'They certainly don't look very friendly,' said Kennedy; 'and they're lusty-looking fellows!'

'Luckily those animals they're riding can't fly; that's always something,' Joe replied.

'Look at those ruined villages, those burnt huts,' said Fergusson. 'That's some of their work. They've devastated what used to be a broad stretch of cultivated land.'

'At any rate, they can't get at us,' Kennedy replied; 'and if we manage to get the river between ourselves and them, we'll be all right.'

'Yes, Dick; but we can't afford to drop,' the doctor replied, with a glance at the barometer.

'In any case, Joe,' Kennedy went on, 'it won't do any harm to have our guns ready.'

'No; we might as well do that, sir. It's lucky we didn't drop them out after all.'

'My carbine!' sighed Kennedy. 'I hope I shan't ever be parted from it.' And Kennedy loaded it with the greatest care. He had a fair quantity of powder and shot left.

'What's our height now?' he asked Fergusson.

'About a hundred and fifty feet. But we can't rise and fall, looking for favourable currents. We're in the *Victoria*'s hands.'

'That's awkward,' said Kennedy. 'It's not much of a wind, but if we had a gale like that of the last few days we should have left those fellows out of sight long ago.'

'They're keeping up with us easily,' said Joe. 'They're having a nice little ride.'

'If only we were within range it would be rather fun to knock them off their horses one by one,' said Kennedy.

'It would,' Fergusson replied. 'But we should be within range ourselves and the *Victoria* would offer too easy a target for those long muskets of theirs; and if they tore her, you can imagine the position we should be in.'

The Talibas continued to pursue them all through the morning. By eleven o'clock they had only covered fifteen miles to the westward. The doctor scanned the slightest cloud that appeared on the horizon, as his constant fear was a change in the weather. What would happen to them if they were to be driven back towards the Niger? Besides, he found that the balloon was showing a distinct tendency to droop. She had already dropped three hundred feet since they started and the Senegal was still a dozen miles away. At their present speed they must expect another three hours of travel.

Just at this moment his attention was attracted by a fresh outburst of shouting. The Talibas were urging forward their horses in great excitement. The doctor consulted the barometer and realised what was happening.

'We're dropping?' asked Kennedy.

'Yes,' Fergusson replied.

'The devil!' thought Joe.

Quarter of an hour later the car was less than a hundred and fifty feet from the ground, but the wind had freshened. The Talibas reined in their horses, and a volley rang out.

'Too far, you fools!' cried Joe. 'It's just as well to keep fellows like you at a distance.' And, taking aim at one of the foremost horsemen, he fired. The Taliba rolled to the ground. His companions halted and the *Victoria* drew away from them.

'They're a cautious lot,' said Kennedy.

'Because they think they're sure to get us,' the doctor replied; 'and they'll succeed if we drop any more. We must rise at all costs.'

'What is there to throw out?' asked Joe.

'All the rest of the pemmican. That will be thirty pounds less.'

'There you are, sir,' said Joe, obeying his master's orders; and the car, which was almost touching the ground, rose again amid fresh shouts from the Talibas. But a quarter of an hour later the *Victoria* was again dropping rapidly. The gas was escaping through the pores of the envelope. Shortly afterwards the car was just skimming the ground. Al Hadji's negroes dashed towards her; but, as happens in such cases, hardly had she touched ground than the *Victoria* leapt upwards, again to fall a mile farther on.

'So we're not going to get away,' said Kennedy in exasperation.

'Throw out our reserve of brandy, Joe,' cried the doctor; 'and the instruments, and anything that weighs anything at all; our last anchor too, since we must!'

Joe tore down barometers and thermometers, but all these weighed little and, after rising for a moment, the balloon fell back again at once towards the ground. The Talibas were in hot pursuit only two hundred yards behind.

'Throw out the two guns!' shouted the doctor.

'I'll fire them first at any rate,' Kennedy replied; and four shots struck the mass of horsemen. Four Talihas fell amid the frenzied cries of the troop. The *Victoria* rose again and leaped over the ground with huge bounds like a great rubber ball. These three men, escaping for their lives in these gigantic leaps and, like Antaeus,[51] seeming to gather fresh force each time they touched the ground, must have presented a strange sight. But there had to be an end to this state of affairs. It was nearly midday. The *Victoria* was becoming exhausted and empty, her shape lengthening, her envelope flabby and flapping in the breeze, the folds of distended silk rasping one against the other.

'Heaven is deserting us,' said Kennedy. 'We'll have to come down.'

Joe did not reply. He was watching his master.

'No,' the latter said. 'We've still a hundred and fifty pounds we can drop.'

'How?' exclaimed Kennedy, thinking his friend had gone mad.

'The car!' he answered. 'Hang on to the net. We can hold on there and get to the river. Hurry up!'

The brave men did not hesitate. They clung to the meshes of the net as the doctor had said, and Joe, hanging by one hand, cut the ropes of the car, which fell just as the balloon was finally collapsing.

'Hurrah! Hurrah!' he cried as the balloon rose three hundred feet. The Talibas, urging on their horses, were sweeping on at a desperate gallop, but the *Victoria*, finding a fresher breeze, gained on them and made rapidly towards a hill which hid the western horizon. This was lucky for the travellers, for they were able to clear it, whereas the pursuing horde were forced to turn northward to go round this final obstacle. The three friends hung on to the net, which they had to tie below them so that it formed a sort of floating pocket. Suddenly, as they cleared the hill, the doctor cried: 'The river! The river! The Senegal!'

Two miles away the river was rolling its broad mass of water. The opposite bank, low and fertile, offered them a safe refuge and a favourable landing.

'Quarter of an hour more and we're saved,' said Fergusson.

But this was not to be. The empty balloon was gradually dropping towards a stretch of completely bare country, consisting of long slopes and stony plains where a few bushes and some thick sun-dried grass were the only signs of vegetation. Several times the *Victoria* touched ground and rose again, but her bounds were weakening in height and length. At last the upper part of the net caught the high branches of a baobab, the only tree to be seen in the wilderness.

'This is the end,' said Kennedy.

'And only a hundred feet from the river,' said Joe.

The three unhappy men set foot to the ground and the doctor dragged his companions off towards the Senegal. At this place a prolonged roar could be heard rising from the stream, and when they reached the bank Fergusson recognised the Falls of Guina.[52] Not a boat on the bank; not a living creature.

Over a breadth of two thousand feet the Senegal was plunging with a deafening roar from a height of five hundred feet. The stream flowed from east to west and the line of rocks that barred its course ran north and south. Half-way down the fall some rocks projected in strange shapes like huge antediluvian animals petrified in the middle of the water. The impossibility of crossing this gulf was obvious. Kennedy could not repress a gesture of despair, but Dr Fergusson, in accents of dauntless courage, exclaimed:

'We're not done yet!'

'I knew it,' said Joe, with a confidence in his master that nothing could shake.

The sight of the dried grass had inspired the doctor with a bold idea. It was their one chance. Quickly he brought his companions back towards the envelope of the balloon.

'We've at least a quarter of an hour's start on those ruffians,' he said. 'There's no time to waste, my friends. Pick a lot of that dry grass; I shall want at least a hundredweight.'

'What for?' asked Kennedy.

'I've no gas left. Well, I'm going to cross the river on hot air!'

'Really, Samuel!' cried Kennedy. 'You're a great man!'

Joe and Kennedy set to work, and soon a great stack of grass was piled up near the baobab. Meanwhile the doctor had widened the orifice of the balloon by cutting away its lower part, taking care to get rid of any hydrogen that might be left through the valve. He then piled a quantity of dried grass under the envelope and set fire to it. It does not take long to fill a balloon with hot air. A heat of 180 degrees is sufficient to halve the weight of the enclosed air by expanding it. The *Victoria* therefore soon began to resume her rounded form. There was plenty of grass. The fire blazed brightly under the doctor's care, and the envelope swelled visibly. It was then a quarter to one.

At this moment the troop of Talibas came into sight two miles to the north; their shouts and the thunder of their galloping horses could be heard.

'They'll be on us in twenty minutes,' said Kennedy.

'Grass, Joe! Grass! We'll be up in ten minutes.'

'Here you are, sir.'

The *Victoria* was two-thirds filled.

'Catch hold of the net again.'

'Right away,' Kennedy answered.

Ten minutes later the jerking of the balloon showed that she was about to rise. The Talibas were coming on rapidly and were now hardly five hundred yards away.

'Hold tight!' cried Fergusson.

'All right, sir; all right.'

The doctor kicked a fresh heap of grass into the fire and the balloon, fully dilated by the increase of temperature, flew off, rustling the branches of the baobab.

'We're off!' cried Joe.

A volley answered him and a bullet ploughed through his shoulder; but Kennedy, leaning down and firing his carbine with one hand, brought one more of the enemy to the ground. Indescribable yells of rage hailed the escape of the *Victoria*, which rose to nearly eight hundred feet. A swift wind took hold of her and she swayed about alarmingly, while the brave doctor and his companions looked down into the depths of the falls that yawned below them. Ten minutes later, without having exchanged a single word, the three men were gradually dropping towards the other bank of the river.

Here stood a group of ten men wearing French uniform, amazed and terrified. Their astonishment when they saw the balloon rise from the right bank of the river can be imagined. They half thought it was some supernatural phenomenon. But their officers, a naval lieutenant and a midshipman, had heard through the European papers of Dr Fergusson's audacious adventure, and at once understood what was happening.

Gradually deflating, the balloon with the aeronauts clinging to her net was dropping, and it was doubtful whether she would reach land, so the Frenchmen dashed into the river and caught the three Englishmen in their arms just as the *Victoria* was finally collapsing, a few feet from the left bank.

'Dr Fergusson?' exclaimed the lieutenant.

'Yes,' the doctor replied quietly, 'and his two friends.'

The Frenchmen led the travellers away from the river while the half-deflated balloon, caught in the rapid current, plunged like a great bubble over the Guina Falls.

'Poor old *Victoria*!' said Joe.

The doctor could not hold back a tear.

CHAPTER XLIV

Conclusion

The inquiry – The French stations – The Basilic *– Saint Louis – The French frigate – The return to London*

THE EXPEDITION THEN on the banks of the river had been sent by the Governor of Senegal and consisted of two officers, Lieutenant Dufraisse of the Marine Infantry and Midshipman Rodamel, a sergeant, and seven men.

The last two days had been spent seeking the most suitable site upon which to establish a station at Guina, and they were still engaged in their search when they witnessed the arrival of Dr Fergusson. It is easy to imagine the congratulations with which the three travellers were received. The Frenchmen, who had themselves assisted at the conclusion of the audacious venture, naturally became Dr Fergusson's witnesses. The doctor therefore asked them at once to report officially his arrival at the Guina Falls.

'You won't mind signing the report?' he asked Lieutenant Dufraisse. 'I'm at your service,' the latter replied.

The Englishmen were taken to a temporary station on the banks of the river, where every attention and abundant food were lavished upon them, and here the report which today figures in the archives of the London Geographical Society was drawn up in the following terms:

GUINA FALLS *24th May, 1862.*

We, the undersigned, declare that today we witnessed the arrival of Dr Fergusson and his companions, Richard Kennedy and Joseph Wilson, clinging to the net of a balloon, which balloon fell a few yards from us into the river and, dragged away by the current, was swept over the Guina Falls. In confirmation of which, we sign the present report drawn up by the aforementioned gentlemen.

SAMUEL FERGUSSON, RICHARD KENNEDY, JOSEPH WILSON.

DUFRAISSE, *Lieutenant d'Infanterie de marine.*
RODAMEL, *enseigne de vaisseau.*
DUFAYS, *sergent.*
FLIPPEAU MAYOR, PELISSIER,
LORIS, RASCAGNET, GUILLON, LEBEL, *soldats.*

Thus was concluded the amazing voyage of Dr Fergusson and his brave companions, as confirmed by indisputable evidence. They were now among friends in the middle of tribes who were on friendly terms with the French establishments. They had reached the Senegal on Saturday, the 24th of May, and on the 27th they proceeded to the station of Medina, on the bank of the river a little farther to the north. Here the French officers received them with open arms and drew upon all the resources of their hospitality. The doctor and his companions were able to embark almost immediately on the small steamboat *Basilic*, which took them down the Senegal as far as its estuary.

A fortnight later, the 10th June, they arrived at Saint Louis, where they met with a magnificent reception from the Governor. They were now completely recovered from their excitement and fatigue. As Joe repeated to anyone who would listen to him: 'It was quite an ordinary trip, ours, after all, and I don't advise anyone to go and do the same thing who wants excitement. It was very dull at times towards the end, and if it hadn't been for the adventures at Lake Tchad and the Senegal I really think we should have been bored to death.'

An English frigate was about to sail and the three travellers boarded her. On the 25th June they reached Portsmouth, and were in London on the following day.

We will not describe the welcome they received from the Royal Geographical Society, nor the cordiality with which they were entertained. Kennedy at once set out for Edinburgh with his famous carbine, being in a hurry to reassure his old nurse. Fergusson and the faithful Joe remained as we have known them, but, unknown to themselves, a change had come about; they had become friends.

The whole European press could not say enough in praise of the audacious explorers, and the *Daily Telegraph* issued an edition of 977,000 copies the day it published its account of the journey.

At a public meeting of the Royal Geographical Society, Dr Fergusson gave a lecture on his aeronautical expedition, and he and his two companions received the gold medal awarded to the most noteworthy exploration work of the year 1862.

The chief result of Dr Fergusson's expedition was to confirm in the most precise manner the geographical facts and surveys reported by Barth, Burton, Speke and others. Thanks to the expeditions at present being undertaken by Speke and Grant, Heuglin and Munzinger, who are making for the sources of the Nile and Central Africa, we may before long be able to check in their turn the discoveries made by Dr Fergusson in that vast area lying between the 14th and 33rd meridians.

NOTES

1 (p. 3) *Sheridan* Richard Brinsley Sheridan (1751–1816), Irish-born dramatist best known for his play *The School for Scandal*

2 (p. 3) *said to be like Byron* Lord George Gordon Byron (1788–1824), English Romantic poet and satirist, whose career helped shape the nineteenth-century literary myth of the lethargic yet sporadically dynamic hero. Verne alludes to the fact that Byron had a club-foot.

3 (p. 3) *a member of the Reform Club* Situated at 104–105 Pall Mall in London, this exclusive gentlemen's club was founded in 1834 by the group of Liberal politicians who brought in the 1832 Reform Bill.

4 (p. 4) *Messrs Baring Brothers* a famous banking house, dating back to 1763, whose international influence prompted the French prime minister's comment in 1810 that Baring Brothers & Company was the sixth great European power. (In 1995, the company was bankrupted after unauthorised trading by a single reckless employee at its Singapore branch.)

5 (p. 6) *Jean Passepartout* The French noun *passe-partout* (literally, 'passes everywhere') can denote a master-key, a ready-made frame for mounting different photographs, or adhesive tape. Thus Passepartout's surname advertises his boundless versatility.

6 (p. 6) *Léotard* Jules Léotard (1830–70), French trapeze artist who, at the Cirque Napoléon in Paris in 1859, was the first to perform a somersault in mid-air without a safety net; his one-piece body-suit, designed to show his muscles to advantage, was the forerunner of today's leotard.

7 (p. 6) *Blondin* Charles Blondin (1824–97), French acrobat, renowned for his daring crossings of Niagara Falls on a tightrope

8 (p. 7) *Angelica Kaufmann* (1741–1807) Swiss-born portrait-painter and founder-member of the Royal Academy in London

9 (p. 16) *Continental Railway, Steam Transit and General Guide* Published from 1847 onwards by the mapmaker George Bradshaw (1801–53), this annual conspectus of continental timetables was considered the indispensable accompaniment to any journey outside Britain and is said to have hastened the adoption of a standard time throughout Europe.

10 (p. 19) *'Change* the Royal Exchange, Victorian London's stock-market

11 (p. 21) *M. de Lesseps* The French diplomat and engineer Ferdinand de Lesseps (1805–94) masterminded the building of the Suez Canal as a decisive trade link between the Mediterranean and the Red Sea. The Canal opened in 1869.

12 (p. 22) *Jack Sheppards of today* Jack Sheppard (1702–24) was an English thief famous for his repeated escapes from prison.

13 (p. 26) *Père Lachaise* the most famous cemetery in Paris

14 (p. 30) *Strabo, Arrian, Arthemidorus and Edrisi* ancient Greek geographers

15 (p. 31) *an enormous coffee-cup* The town of Mocha, at the mouth of the Red Sea, was renowned for its production of fine coffee.

16 (p. 38) *transire benefaciendo* Latin, literally 'to travel along while doing good', an adaptation of a comment by St Peter on the life of Christ

17 (p. 43) *Parsee* adept of the Zoroastrian faith, which originated in ancient Persia

18 (p. 55) *the Ramayana* Indian epic poem tracing the legendary exploits of King Rama

19 (p. 70) *Cochin China* the southern part of today's Vietnam

20 (p. 101) *the Car of Juggernaut* In Bengal, an annual procession took place in honour of the Hindu god Vishnu, whose image was placed on a massive cart or juggernaut so heavy that hundreds of worshippers were needed to shift it. The occasional accidental crushing of a participant gave rise to the myth of the juggernaut as an instrument of human sacrifice.

21 (p. 107) *the legendary city of 1849* In the year 1849, at the height of the Californian Gold Rush, the coastal settlement of San Francisco was invaded by a huge influx of fortune-seekers.

22 (p. 107) *omnium gatherum* a pseudo-Latin expression, meaning a miscellaneous gathering or medley

23 (p. 107) *Montgomery Street* main street in San Francisco, named for John Montgomer who, in 1846, claimed the hitherto Mexican territory for the United States

24 (p. 118) *Victor Hugo* Victor Hugo (1802–85), French poet and novelist, whose major collection *Les Contemplations* was published in 1856 by Jules Hetzel, later Verne's publisher

25 (p. 127) *a band of Sioux* Reputedly one of the fiercest native peoples of the North American Plains, the Sioux fought throughout the nineteenth century against the encroachment of white settlers, exploiting two European imports, the horse and the gun.

26 (p. 165) *Royal Geographical Society* Founded in 1830, this revered London institution is now located on Kensington Gore.

27 (p. 166) *Excelsior!* Ever higher! (Latin, literally 'more lofty')

28 (p. 167) *Mungo Park* Mungo Park (1771–1806?), Scottish explorer of the Niger and author of the bestselling *Travels in the Interior of Africa* (1799)

29 (p. 167) *Selkirk* Alexander Selkirk (1676–1721), having spent five years as a solitary castaway on an island off the coast of Chile, entered fiction as the hero of Daniel Defoe's novel *Robinson Crusoe* (1719).

30 (p. 167) *New Holland* Australia

31 (p. 168) *the Schlagintweit brothers* The three German brothers Schlagintweit – Hermann (1826–82), Adolph (1829–57) and Robert (1833–85) – undertook a magnetic survey of India and the Himalaya region in 1854–7, during which they climbed a peak in Tibet. Adolph was beheaded as a spy in Turkistan in 1857. Verne's suggestion that a Scotsman had accompanied the brothers is spurious, as is his later claim, in the novel *Robur the Conqueror* (1886), that the Schlagintweit brothers had traversed the pass of Ibi Ganim in a balloon.

32 (p. 168) *the Travellers' Club* Established in 1819, the Travellers' Club caters to globetrotters; it is situated at 106 Pall Mall, London, next to the Reform Club, where Phileas Fogg makes his momentous wager.

33 (p. 172) *Halbert Glendinning* hero of the historical romance *The Monastery* (1820) by Sir Walter Scott (1771–1832)

34 (p. 174) *Bedlam* popular name for the Bethlehem Royal Hospital for the insane in London

35 (p. 177) *Dr Barth*　Heinrich Barth (1821–65), German cartographer, linguist and African explorer, whose fame rests on his definitive mapping of the middle Niger; Verne would surely have consulted his *Travels and Discoveries in North and Central Africa* (1857–8).

36 (p. 179) *the Scotchman Bruce*　James Bruce (1730–94), early Scottish explorer and author of *Travels to Discover the Source of the Nile* (1790). In 1770, he found the source of the Blue Nile in Ethiopia (then Abyssinia), mistaking it for the source of the (White) Nile itself.

37 (p. 189n) *Montgolfier*　Modern ballooning dates back to the experiments of the Montgolfier brothers, Joseph (1740–1819) and Jacques (1745–99). Their heated-air balloon achieved the first manned free flight in 1783, crossing the skies above Paris and remaining aloft for twenty-five minutes.

38 (p. 193) *Queen*　Queen Victoria (1819–1901), after whom the largest lake in Africa, not to mention Fergusson's balloon, is named

39 (p. 194) *an aeronaut . . . Garnerin's balloon*　The balloonist André-Jacques Garnerin (1769–1823) is credited with the first parachute jump in 1797.

40 (p. 203) *the Heidelberg tun*　a gigantic (and empty) wine-barrel in the cellar of Heidelberg Castle, described by Mark Twain in *A Tramp Abroad* (1880)

41 (p. 210) *his learned friend Petermann*　Dr August Heinrich Petermann (1822–78), German geographer and an authority on Africa and the Arctic

42 (p. 210) *Charles Beke*　Charles Beke (1800–74), English explorer, mapmaker and linguist, who established the approximate course of the Blue Nile through Ethiopia in 1840–3

43 (p. 214) *Gay-Lussac*　Joseph Louis Gay-Lussac (1778–1850), French physicist whose balloon ascents of 1804 gave rise to important observations concerning terrestrial magnetism as well as air temperature and humidity at great heights

44 (p. 240) *Captain Speke*　In 1858, while on a Royal Geographical Society expedition led by Sir Richard Burton (1821–90), the English explorer John Hanning Speke (1827–64) discovered and named Lake Victoria, identifying it as the true source of the Nile. Though essentially valid, his claim was hotly disputed by Burton and others. On a second expedition in 1860–3, with James Grant, Speke ratified his findings, reaching Gondokoro in 1863. Verne

describes both expeditions (pp. 179–180 and 183). Speke's *Journal of the Discovery of the Source of the Nile* was published in 1863, some months after *Five Weeks*; meanwhile Verne had credited his fictional balloonists with the final act of confirmation (p. 242).

45 (p. 243n) *Neilos*   the Nile, the name of the river of ancient Egypt and also that of its god

46 (p. 245) *Andrea Debono*   Andrea De Bono (1821–71), a Maltese explorer and ivory trader, was the first European to journey to the upper reaches of the White Nile, where he noted its likely link to Lake Albert and beyond; in April 1853, he carved his initials on the island of Bonga near the cataracts above Gondokoro, at latitude 4 degrees north.

47 (p. 247) *the general name of Nyam Nyams*   The French locution *nyam nyam* is equivalent to the English *yum yum*, indicating pleasurable eating.

48 (p. 290) *M. Méry*   Joseph Méry (1798–1865), minor French novelist

49 (p. 331) *René Caillié*   René Auguste Caillié (1799–1838), French explorer and author of *Travels through Central Africa to Timbuctoo* (1830)

50 (p. 333) *Ann Radcliffe*   Ann Radcliffe (1764–1823), foremost exponent of the Gothic novel

51 (p. 349) *Antaeus*   giant of Greek myth, son of Neptune and the Earth, whom the hero Hercules conquers in battle by lifting him off the ground, thereby depriving him of his source of strength

52 (p. 350) *the Falls of Guina*   The Gouina Falls are situated on the Senegal River at a point well over four hundred miles above that river's delta on the Atlantic coast.